"DON'T YOU UNDERSTAND, TINK? YOU MEAN MORE TO ME THAN ANYTHING IN THIS WHOLE WORLD!"

PETER PAN TO TINKERBELL, *PETER PAN*

a boston love story

ONE GOOD REASON

USA TODAY bestselling author
julie johnson

Cover Design by ONE CLICK COVERS

Subscribe to Julie's newsletter: http://eepurl.com/bnWtHH

For the lonely girls
with big dreams
and broken hearts.

It gets better.

PROLOGUE

LET'S get something straight right off the bat — it's not called "Beantown" or "The Bean" or "The Town." (I'm looking at you, Ben Affleck.) It's sure as shit not called "The Hub" or the "City on the Hill." I don't know where those ass-backwards nick-names came from and, frankly, I don't want to know.

It's called *Boston*.

Sure, locals will pronounce this moniker with varying degrees of emphasis on the first vowel. (If you're from Southie, it's "Bah-ston," while if you're from the North Shore, it's a very proper, clearly annunciated "Bos-ton," which you say with one-pinky in the air as you sip your seven-dollar chai tea latte and wax poetic about that one time you saw Blue Man Group on your seventeenth birthday in the big bad city.) Accents aside, if you call my hometown anything else, these same locals will look at you with well-practiced New Englander scorn.

What can I say? We aren't the warmest bunch.

The second thing you should know — ninety percent of the people who claim they're from Boston actually aren't. They, in fact, live in affluent little suburbs with a median household income of a cool million, attend prosperous private schools, and grow up to be doctors and lawyers, just as their parents intended. (I see you, Newton.) If you're really from the city — and I mean born and bred with the Charles on your left and the Atlantic on your right — you're probably more like me.

A little rough around the edges. Quick to call bullshit when you see it. Borderline addicted to Dunkin Donuts coffee. And pretty fucking tired of people hating on Tom Brady just because he happens to be the best quarterback in the history of football.

You know that "Boston Strong" is more than a sticker on the back of a soccer mom's SUV — it's a 200-yard stretch of Boylston Street where terror filled the air one April afternoon. You understand that the Red Sox are, and always will be, better than the Yankees, no matter our batting averages. You realize there's a certain amount of pride that comes in shoveling your car out of a six-foot mound of snow only to have the plows cover it over again ten minutes later. And you're downright certain that no other place in the world will ever hold a candle to the beauty of our skyline when the sun streaks pink over the water.

This is my city.

I've lived here. I've grown here. I've bled and sweat and wept here.

I've walked its every winding, nonsensical avenue, from the sloping streets of Beacon Hill to the aromatic alleys of the North End. I've pushed past tourists crowding Quincy Market and weaved through shoppers on Newbury street. I've run the paths along the murky Charles River at sunset and stumbled home from the neon-lit bars outside Fenway Park at sunrise.

This city isn't just my home.

It's the heart beating in my chest. The blood thrumming through my veins.

I am Boston. Boston is me.

And, so help me god, I'm going to take it back from those who'd seek to poison it.

That's not a promise — it's a vow.

CHAPTER 1

THE CRIMINAL MASTERMIND

THEY KNOW ME ONLY AS "CLOVER."

Which, frankly, kind of sucks as code names go. I mean... you'd think they could've at least picked something badass.

Wonder Woman? That's a cool-as-shit nickname.

Elektra? Practically reeks of danger and mystery.

Black Widow? Come on, no one fucks with *that* girl.

Catwoman? ...Okay, well, to be honest I've always kind of thought Catwoman was just code for some crazy, perpetually-single girl with one too many felines and one too few men in her life.

But, kitties aside, you'd think the FBI could've come up with something a little better than *Clover* when they christened me last year.

Clovers are cute.

I take umbrage at being *cute*. I'm a god-damned criminal mastermind. Criminal masterminds are *not* cute.

Except Loki.

Shit, Loki is cute as hell.

Evidently, my name was inspired by the virus I developed

two years ago. Every hacker — correction, every *good* hacker — has a custom-built style of code. A brand. A trademark.

Like artists, we all have our own quirks and identifying characteristics. Things we leave behind after we're done creeping around inside a computer network.

Mine is a virus.

It's lethal once it's past the firewalls, embedding itself in the foundation and branching out in four directions, in the shape of... you guessed it... a four-leaf clover.

Hence the nickname.

It's probably a good thing — if they knew my real name I'd be in federal prison. Or worse: chained to a government cubicle somewhere, working some hack job at the NSA. *Thanks* but no thanks. I'm good right where I am — a fugitive, perhaps, but a happy one.

Well, mostly happy.

Fifty percent happy.

Fine. *Forty* percent.

Final offer: one quarter happy, three quarters miserable?

Okay. Whatever. I'm not happy at all.

So?

Thing is, I don't really believe in "happy." People who say they've found true happiness — a mythical, eternal state of bliss — are either delusional or drugged out of their minds on those bath salts that inspire cannibalism. Perpetual joy is about as real as the fairy unicorns I used to play with in my backyard at age four.

Life is one long series of punches to the gut. You either learn how to duck, or you figure out how to hit back. I've been hitting back so long, at this point I've got a mean left hook and more than my fair share of scars.

My fingers fly over the keyboard so fast I know they'd be nothing but a blur if I looked down, but my eyes are otherwise occupied — fixed firmly on the screen in front of me as I maneuver around a particularly difficult firewall, making sure to cloak my code so they can't detect a breach. Last time I did this, I was a bit careless — read: *cocky* — and tripped up some of their internal safeguards. Not my smartest move of all time.

Turns out, the Feds don't throw a piñata party when people hack their secure, top-secret servers. *Whoopsie.*

There are a few more security layers in place than last time, but as hacks go it's not a particularly difficult one. Not for me, anyway. Government agencies are freakishly easy to crack into, if you're fluent in Python and know how to find even a tiny fissure in their seemingly impenetrable networks.

Firewalls are like thick-stitched wool blankets, insulating a server from anyone outside. Code — even the encrypted, super secure code used by the FBI — is just like that woven fabric: over time, like any old blanket, tiny pulls and snags appear. Glitches. Inconsistencies. *Insecurities.*

Run your hands over the wool long enough, you'll find one eventually. A few tugs of a loose thread and the whole damn thing unravels to create a hole big enough for me to stroll inside, put my feet up on their metaphorical coffee table, and peruse their files at my leisure.

It's called a backdoor hack.

And it happens to be my specialty.

The goal is remarkably simple: get in, get what you need, and get out without leaving any traces. (That last part is often easier said than done.)

I reach out blindly to grab the can of Diet Coke on my left as my gaze scans the stream of content. A few more clacks of my fingers against the keys and I'm past the final firewall. I'm *in*. The unmistakable round seal glows bright from my monitor — blue and gold, bearing a logo of weighted scales and the words FIDELITY, BRAVERY, INTEGRITY. For a few seconds, I let the familiar rush of endorphins wash over me. There's nothing like it in the world — adrenaline mixed with danger, and just a hint of pride in my own skills.

My lips twitch.

Never let it be said that I don't enjoy a little backdoor action.

(I'm talking about computers. Get your mind out of the gutter.)

I click through from the desktop to the hard drive and begin my search, just as I've done every few months for the past three years, since the day I learned how to hack. Most of the files I've gained access to are encrypted or heavily redacted — with my system, which is in sore need of an upgrade, I'm lucky I was even able to crack into a lower-level consul in the federal building in Government Center. Hacking a top FBI official's computer would give me better security clearance in spades... but doing so would require a much bigger server than my four-year-old laptop possesses, along with something a bit more stable than my loft's occasionally spotty WiFi coverage.

One day, maybe I'll be able to afford an upgrade.

I type a familiar name into the search queue and hold my breath as the results fill the screen. Or, should I say, *result*.

One.

A single file — ninety percent redacted, one hundred percent useless to me.

Nothing new. Not since last time.

Not since all the times before last time either.

The breath slips from my lips, a gust of disappointment I can't contain. I should be used to it by now — this life without answers. But no matter how many times I do this, no matter how many times I'm let down by the dead ends in that file, I can't stomp out the tiny flare of inextinguishable hope that one day, I'll hack my way in here and find something new. A new lead. A new hope. A new answer.

It's almost certainly a lost cause. A sane person would give up.

I never said I was sane. And after twenty years of wondering, there's no way I'm going to quit now. Some day, I'll find out what happened that cold December night.

My eyes close as memories dance across my mind — faint and flickering, like a candle throwing shadows in a dark room.

My winter ballet recital. I'm dressed as a SugarPlum Fairy.

Mom kissing my cheek, handing me a bouquet of roses.

Dad scooping me up into his arms, tickling the breath out of me as we walk home on snowy streets.

Pain swamps me — I snap my eyes open, hoping it will drive back the memories, but it's no use. I can still feel the way their mittened hands engulfed mine as they swung me between them, how my boots skimmed across the thin layer of flurries coating the sidewalks.

Zoe, our little Sugar Plum! Can you believe Santa will be here in the morning?

We were laughing. Happy. Mouths open to the sky, snowflakes on our tongues. Christmas decorations on every corner. Roses cradled in the crook of an arm, cheeks red with cold and eyes bright with love.

It was the best day.

Until, quite suddenly, with no warning at all... the pure white snow was stained red with trampled rose petals and blood... and it became the worst day of my life.

My phone vibrates loudly on the table beside me, pulling me out of my most familiar nightmare. When I catch sight of the name flashing across the screen, I sigh deeply. I debate not answering, but I know he'll just keep calling.

There's no avoiding Luca. Persistent bastard.

"Hello?"

"Got a job for you." The gruff, familiar voice cracks over the line.

"I'm listening."

"Lancaster Consolidated." There's a pause. "You heard of it?"

I roll my eyes. Lancaster Consolidated controls almost all of the foreign oil and natural gas shipments coming in and out of New England, not to mention several dozen steel factories scattered across the continental United States. They build everything from airplanes to railroads. Everyone in the country's heard of Lancaster Consolidated.

"Give me a little credit, Luke."

"Don't get your panties in a twist. It's a valid question."

"I'm not wearing any panties," I throw back at him.

A laugh rumbles across the line — it's low and it sounds a little like he's trying to muffle it, but it's definitely a laugh. I feel my eyes widen slightly. Luca is not typically one to tip his hand when it comes to emotions. That's part of the reason we've managed to stay friends all these years.

No touchy-feely bullshit.

"Just stop being a priss for two seconds and listen to me," he says, abruptly back to his normal, caustic self. "Last week Lancaster Consolidated closed two of their biggest factories — the one in Lynn, plus another one out in the sticks of Western Mass somewhere — and put about ten thousand people out of jobs."

"I heard. It was all over the news." Frown lines crease my forehead. "Apparently it's cheaper to farm the work overseas than keep the production lines on American soil."

"Yeah, well, did you hear Lancaster is refusing to pay out pensions for ninety percent of those workers?"

"That's impossible." My frown lines deepen. "In fact, that's *illegal*."

"Well, illegal or not, apparently Robert Lancaster found some loophole in the contract. Says he's bankrupt and can't afford to pay — not even two weeks' severance. Even though everyone knows he's sitting on millions in a tax shelter somewhere."

"What a prick!"

"That's why I'm calling."

"I'd love to pin Lancaster to the wall as much as anyone, trust me." I sigh and rub my temple. "But I don't know what you think I can do about this, Luca. I've already tried to crack into the LC network remotely, remember? Last spring, when that oil rig went down in the Atlantic and all those crew members died, I wanted proof Lancaster gave the order for them to set out in a fucking hurricane to make his shipping quotas. I was going to show the world the asshole signed the death warrants of thirty good men." My fingers curl into fists, remembering. "But... *It. Didn't. Work.* Whatever software they're using was custom built from the inside-out, probably to cloak their shady financial shit from the IRS. There's a massive firewall. And, let me tell you, in this case — size matters."

"Babe." There's a hint of a laugh in his voice. "Pretty sure size *always* matters."

"Yeah, well, this code is complex. I'd be impressed by whoever built it if I weren't so fucking annoyed." I lean back in my chair and glare up at the ceiling. "Even if I wanted to help, there's nothing I can do and you know it."

There's a pause. "You could hack it on-site."

"Oh, sure, I'll just stroll right into the offices downtown and ask politely if I can use one of their computers, pretty please with sugar on top?" I snort. "Oh! Maybe if I wear a low-cut shirt and bat my eyelashes while pinky-swearing not to cause any trouble, they'll let me into their network."

"You — always there with the bitchy answers," Luca mutters, exasperated.

"And *you* — always there with the unreasonable requests," I counter, equally pissed.

Why does he always expect the impossible from me? Since the first day we met, two lost kids picking pockets and sleeping on street corners, he's pushed me to ask for *more* — from strangers with fat wallets, from the system, from the entire goddamned world.

Take more. Make more. Be more.

Asshat.

"Zoe."

I go still. Luca never uses my first name — it's always *priss* or *babe* or some equally mocking nickname I pretend to hate but secretly find charming. If he's using my real name, he's more serious about this than I thought.

I sigh. "What?"

"Some of those people worked there fifty, sixty years. They don't know how to do anything else. They won't find new jobs, won't get hired anywhere new. They were counting on those pensions to carry them for the rest of their lives — now they've got nothing. We don't help them... who will?"

My stomach clenches. Damn it. Damn *him*. Always trying to save the world.

I don't know why — it's not like the world has ever done jack shit for him.

"Zoe."

"Fine," I bite out. "I'll see what I can do. But I'm not making any promises!"

"Knew you'd cave, babe." His voice is smug. "You were always a sucker for lost causes."

"Guess that's why I'm your friend," I mutter. "If there was ever a lost cause, it's you."

"If that was supposed to be an insult, we gotta work on your sparring skills."

I roll my eyes. "After this, I'm done with your vigilante shit, Luca. I mean it."

"You always mean it, babe. Doesn't make it true." His voice is gruff again. "Let me know when you figure out how to pin Lancaster to that wall."

He clicks off before I can say anything else, leaving me with an insurmountable challenge and not a single, reasonable suggestion as to how I'll find a solution to it.

Typical Luca.

We met ten years ago, when we were fourteen, at a group home for homeless teens in Charlestown. The first few times we crossed paths, we eyed each other like two fighters in a cage-match — practiced wariness with a vague threat of violence, each poised to attack if the other got too close or made any sudden moves. We kept our distance for a few months, sleeping in lumpy, adjacent cots but never saying a word... until one rainy afternoon, when a group of drunk, older guys cornered me in an alleyway behind the youth center. I knew what they planned to do — I could see it in their eyes — just as I knew I wasn't remotely strong enough to stop them.

My shirt was in tatters by the time Luca appeared out of nowhere, melting from the shadows like the grim reaper himself to deliver an unequivocal serving of justice. When the vengeance finally faded from his eyes, there was blood on his hands — *not his* — and the men who'd intended to use me up and spit me out like a wad of chewing gum were limping away as fast as their battered limbs could carry them.

Cowards.

I'd stared at the boy with blood on his knuckles — watched

the rapid rise and fall of his chest, saw the hatred for the whole damn world burning bright in his eyes —and knew our days as careful strangers had come to an end.

Instead, he became my family.

It took time. I'd been burned in the past; so had he. On the streets, it's every man for himself, so friends aren't exactly easy to make. They're even harder to keep. Being part of Luca's life wasn't — *isn't* — easy. Tethering two wolves together on a single chain is always going to result in some scratches.

Somehow, we managed. Somehow, we stayed close. Somehow — *together* — we stayed alive, even when the odds were stacked so far out of our favor, I thought we'd wind up dead before we made it to twenty. So, when we sorted out our lives, when I taught myself how to code on the free computers at the Boson Public Library and he started fighting for money instead of survival... there was no way I could say no to anything he wanted.

Even when, what he wanted most of all, was to save the damn world from itself.

We share not a drop of blood, but he's my brother. We're a team. So, no matter how much shit I talk, no matter how many times he calls in the middle of the night asking for impossible favors, no matter how many international laws he asks me to break... I'll say yes. I'll find a way.

That's what family does.

A WEEK LATER, I'm seriously regretting that familial loyalty.

I tug hard on the hem of the boxy, white button-down dwarfing my frame and fight the urge to scratch at my scalp. It's all I can do not to toss the wig in the closest trash bin and hope no one notices the cater waiter with the pin straight black bob is suddenly sporting a thick blonde mane of waves halfway down her back.

Yeah. That'd be a great way to blow my cover.

With a deep sigh, I eye the tray of disgusting-looking finger foods resting on the stainless steel prep table. For the life of me, I'll never understand why rich people insist on eating this crap.

Foie gras?

Dude. You're eating duck liver. *Liver.* Aka the avian bile secretion center.

Escargot?

Why yes, that's a fucking *snail* in your mouth. A glorified slug with a shell.

Caviar?

Two words: Fish. Eggs.

I rest my case.

I'm not sure exactly which "delicacy" is on my newest tray — it looks like a slab of lukewarm tofu with some kind of shaved tartar on top. In short, it's about as appetizing as a turd on a communion wafer.

Amuse-bouche my ass.

"Cindy!" The sharp bark assaults my ears. "Cindy, are you listening?"

My eyes swing to Miriam, the catering coordinator for the event, and I find she's glaring at me with unveiled hostility.

"Sorry," I mutter, belatedly remembering that *I'm* Cindy — for tonight anyway. Cindy Smith. That's the name I gave when I filled out the application for this job last week. As far as Miriam knows, I'm a fresh-faced post-grad new to the city, in need of a job and in possession of several fabulous — fictional — references that easily scored me the position.

"Did you hear me?" she snaps, a *tsk* noise escaping her tight-pressed lips. Her severe frown lines wage war against the Botox straining to keep her face two decades younger than the rest of her body. She clutches her clipboard tighter against her prim black blazer and narrows her eyes at me. "Cindy, I know you're new, but I expect basic competence. If you ever expect to work another event with me, get your head out of the clouds and your ass out there before the tray gets cold. I'm not paying you to stand around daydreaming. Move it!"

I, in fact, am not planning to *ever* work another event for The Catered Affair for the rest of eternity so long as I can help it, but Miriam doesn't need to know that. Biting back the withering retort poised on my lips, I nod, swipe the tray off the prep table and hoist it into the air with a mocking flourish.

I'm almost to the doors that lead from the kitchen to the function room when they swing inward. Mara, one of the other girls working the event, bustles through in the same ugly uniform I was forced into — black slacks, androgynous button down and a truly terrible mini-vest that makes Hilary Clinton's famed pantsuits look downright sexy by comparison. There's an empty tray in her hands and a haggard look on her face.

"Vultures," she mutters. "Picked my tray clean in under five minutes." Her clear green eyes focus on my face as she scoots out of my path and holds the door open for me. "Word of advice?"

My eyebrows lift as I step into the hallway.

"Watch out for the guy in the gray pinstripe suit. He's handsy if you get too close."

"Fabulous," I mutter as the door swings closed at my back. Steadying my shoulders, I shake the wig out of my eyes and prepare to face a room full of seventy of Boston's most affluent businessmen and their arm-candy trophy wives. By the end of the night, one of them is going to wish he'd never crossed my path, considering what I've got in store for him. And I'm not just talking about the tofu tartar.

"HONEY GLAZED EDAMAME?" I offer bleakly, tray extended to the cluster of men by the bar. They don't even glance at me as they grab the appetizers and pop them in their mouths.

I fight a shudder as I watch the slimy green seeds go down the hatch.

I'm on my fourth and blessedly final circulation of the 40th floor ballroom where Lancaster Consolidated is hosting their annual pre-Christmas party. Once the cocktail hour is over, we get a twenty-minute break while the attendees find their seats in the adjacent parlor, before the dinner service starts. That's my window: twenty minutes. I hope it's enough.

It has to be enough.

It's the only window I'll ever get.

My eyes slide to the corner of the room where Robert Lancaster, CEO of Lancaster Consolidated and host of this exclusive soiree, is holding court. He's surrounded on all sides by brown-nosing associates hoping to get in good with Boston's premiere import-export kingpin.

Middle-aged and somewhat pudgy with thinning brown hair and a truly unfortunate hodgepodge of features, he's not exactly Johnny Depp. And yet he's quite popular with the ladies, if his string of high profile ex-wives and ex-mistresses — many of whose "acting" and "singing" careers he's bankrolled — are anything to go by.

I watch him laugh and snag a canapé off Mara's tray, shoving it into his mouth with gusto. Those hovering around watch avidly as he chews open-mouthed, waiting in suspense for his next words. To the casual observer, he's the epitome of a success: a beloved businessman basking in the glory of his financial empire.

I know better.

My eyes cut to the slim silver watch cuffing my wrist. Half past six. Dinner is scheduled to start at seven *sharp*, a point Miriam has belabored multiple times since I arrived. If my plan's going to work, I need to empty this tray ASAP and get a move on.

I head for the far side of the room with a smile pasted on my lips, unloading several glazed edamame balls on unsuspecting guests as I go. I'm circling toward the kitchen doors — and freedom — when a beefy hand lands on my ass.

"What do you have there, sweetheart?"

My spine snaps straight and my teeth clench. It takes every ounce of control I possess not to go claws-out alleycat mode as I slowly turn my head to face the man on my left.

Shoddy hair plugs. Dull brown eyes. *Gray pinstripe suit.*

God dammit, Mara wasn't joking. I'm tempted to make a scene and spit in his face, but the unwanted attention that will bring won't do me any favors. All it'll do is ensure I walk out of here without the intel I need.

He doesn't move his hand, even when I meet his eyes. *Pig.*

"Well?" he prompts, a challenge in his tone. His fingers flex ever so slightly and I try not to flinch. "What are they?"

"Honey glazed edamame balls," I grit out through my teeth. "Would you like one?"

His eyes scan my body and a chill slithers up my spine.

"I'm interested in whatever you're serving, honey."

I take a subtle step back as I offer the tray, trying to escape his grip. His hand drops away but he moves with me and, before I know it, I'm backed up against the wall between the bar and the exit doors. I'm just over five feet tall — the fugly black flats on my feet aren't doing me any favors — so while his girth is nearly wide enough to surpass his diminutive height, I still feel dwarfed by his presence. I hold the tray between us like a shield.

He takes a step closer. "What's a girl like you doing working at an event like this, sweetheart? You're much too pretty to be a waitress."

I swallow and try not to lose my shit. I've eaten men like him for breakfast. If I weren't determined to stay below the radar, he'd currently be on the ground cradling his family jewels.

"Dinner service is scheduled to start in just a few moments, sir." My voice is colder than ice. "If you'd like a final appetizer before—"

"You must be an actress." He cuts me off as his eyes scan me again from top to toe, like I'm wearing lingerie instead of one of the set costumes from the show *Party Down*. He leans a little closer. "Or a model, though you're a tiny little thing, aren't you? Too short for runways."

My fingers curl around the edge of the tray. Screw it. He takes one more step toward me and he'll find one of these luke-warm edamame balls shoved so far down his throat, he won't be able to eat solid foods for a week.

"Sir, if you'd like an edamame ball—"

His mouth twitches into a lewd half-smile. "Ah, don't be like that." He presses so close, I can feel his breath against my face — sour and smelling strongly of bourbon. "Come on, sweetheart, give me a smile—"

Before he can get the words out, a body slams into his with the force of a linebacker performing a tackle. My back presses tight to the wall and my eyes widen as I watch the blur of pinstripe jostle sideways and stumble off balance. I'm almost positive the creep is about to be sent sprawling on his ass but, at the last moment, a large hand clamps onto his shoulder and steadies him with what seems like very little effort.

"Whoa, there, Sanders." An amused male voice rumbles from my left. "Watch your step."

My eyes dart to the man who's just interrupted Pinstripe's lechery, and I feel the air constrict in my lungs as I take in his features.

It's an undeniably attractive face....

And, worse, one I recognize.

Parker West.

CHAPTER 2

THE MISSION

WE'VE NEVER MET in person, of course, but I'd know him anywhere. His picture appears several times a month in the society pages, always with some bimbo or another hanging on his arm like Spanish moss — decorative, but ultimately lacking in substance and purpose. Funnily enough, Parker doesn't seem to mind that his wafer-thin dates' weights are higher than their IQ points.

He's a notorious womanizer. Which should bother me.

I *know* it should bother me.

But...

Damn.

A bolt of electricity shoots straight between my legs as I take him in. He's sex and sin in a tanned, muscular package, and that's just the start of it.

He towers over me — at least six two, maybe taller. Again — *damn.* I've always had a thing for tall boys. His nose is straight, aristocratic, the type of feature that speaks to a long line of good genes. His light brown hair is sun-streaked with gold, as if he spends more time outside than in, and slightly tousled, as though running a comb through it for a formal dinner party was simply too much effort. I instantly want to slide my fingers into the thick waves, to messy it further.

Oh, boy.

His whole look — from his tailored Hugo Boss suit to his crisp black tie to his messy-on-purpose hair to his half-hooded bedroom eyes — works on an elemental level. Judging by the way he carries himself, he's fully aware of it, too.

Zoe, you hate pretty boys, I remind myself. *Remember?*

For some reason, it's hard to hold onto that thought as I look directly into his hazel-gold eyes, which are currently fixed on my face with an alarming amount of curiosity in their depths. He's staring at me like I'm a question he wants very much to answer.

I gulp.

His eyes crinkle.

Thankfully, the pinstripe groper — Sanders — chooses this moment to interrupt our little staring contest.

"Mr. West." He's breathing heavily and his face is getting red. "Watch where you're going, son, you almost plowed me over."

Parker's eyes lose a little of their heat as they slide away from me to focus on Pudgy Pinstripe.

"Yes, I'll have to be more careful," he says in a dangerously soft voice. "Just as I'm sure you'll be more careful about where you place your hands when selecting appetizers in the future. Isn't that your wife, over by the bar? I'd hate for her to hear about your..." His pause is lethal. "...*appetite*... for certain dishes."

The threat hangs there in the air for a moment and Sanders' face turns red as a tomato before he grumbles an excuse about needing the bathroom and storms away, no doubt to grope one of the other cater-waiters.

And then there were two.

I dare a glance at Parker and find he's staring at me again.

"What?" I ask sharply, gripping my tray tighter. "Are you waiting for a party in your honor? A cookie? A parade of some sort, complete with clowns and miniature horses?"

His grin widens. "I was hoping for a thank you. But, now that you mention it, I *am* a fan of miniature horses." His brow furrows. "I don't like clowns, though. Bad experience at my fifth birthday party. Never quite recovered."

"How tragic," I say dryly. "Now, if you'll excuse me—"

"I won't, actually," he says immediately, sidestepping to block me when I move to leave.

I crane my neck to glare up at him. "Won't what?

"Won't excuse you."

"It's an expression," I say incredulously. "Said while trying to be polite. It doesn't actually require the other person's permission."

"Then why say it at all?"

I scowl at him. "I know what you're doing."

"Standing here being charming and irresistible?"

"No. Playing dumb — or, rather, *dumber than you look* which is a feat in itself, so *bravo!* — to keep me here talking to you."

His lips twitch. "Has anyone ever told you that you're sassy?"

"Has anyone ever told you that you're annoying?"

"And that voice of yours." He leans in a fraction and I catch a waft of his aftershave. I feel my thighs press together of their own accord. "So husky. You should be a late-night radio host announcer. Or an audiobook narrator. Hell, you call up Apple and offer to voice the new Siri, I guarantee I'll never lose my iPhone again."

"You're sexually harassing me."

"Me? Harassing you?" He has the nerve to wink while acting outraged. "If I wanted to do that, I'd have suggested you become a sex line operator."

"So, to be clear, you saved me from sexual harassment only to sexually harass me yourself?" I lift my brows. "That's really what's happening here?"

"I'm not sexually harassing you," he insists. "In fact, you're sexually harassing me."

"How's that, exactly?"

"You just looked at my crotch."

Completely baffled by his accusation, I involuntarily drop my gaze to said nether region — *oh, boy, someone's a leftie* — and find my cheeks are suddenly on fire. "I most certainly did *not* look at your crotch!" I hiss, trying to get the uncharacteristic blush under control.

"You're looking at it right now," he points out.

"Only because you said—" I screech in frustration and tear my eyes away. "Ugh! You're more than annoying. You're a manipulative, self-entitled chauvinist."

"Would it shock you to know that's not the worst thing I've been called on a first date?" His eyes get warm. "We're doing pretty well, by comparison."

"D-date?" I splutter, staring at him like his head is about to explode. "I'm working. You're bothering me. This is *not* a date. This is the exact opposite of a date."

He adopts a thoughtful look as he glances around the room. "Ambient lighting. Dark corner. Intimate conversation. Discrete examination of my anatomy." He shoves his hands in his pockets and shrugs. "Sounds like a date to me."

"I pity the women forced to actually go out with you."

"Darling, I don't have to force them," he says, flashing a grin that makes me believe him. "Are you sure we haven't met before? You seem familiar."

We haven't met — not exactly. *And he couldn't possibly remember...*

Last spring, I helped his sister Phoebe out of a rather sticky situation. I called her phone once, to warn her of trouble... and her brother happened to be in the room at the time. But neither of them knows my name. He just heard my voice. And that was *months* ago.

"No," I say, shaking my head firmly. "We've definitely never met."

"Huh." His eyes scan my features curiously. "Strange. I feel like I know you."

"Well, you don't. Now, if you'll let me by..."

"I'm Parker, by the way." He grins again. "And you are?"

"Not interested," I return, wishing it were true as my heart pounds too fast inside my chest.

Because I'm angry, I tell myself. *Outraged. Incensed.*

That's the only explanation for the tightness in my stomach. The dizziness in my head. The sweatiness of my palms.

...The heat between my legs.

Damn.

"Listen, buddy," I snap, intensifying my glare for good measure. "If you're not going to take an edamame ball, you really have to let me by. I have work to do."

And, I remember alarmingly, a very narrow window of time to get my intel which, thanks to this little interlude, is now even shorter.

His eyes drop to my tray and his face screws up in a grimace. "Honestly, are those even edible?"

"Don't know, don't care. Now, move out of my way or I will *make you* move."

His eyes light up in anticipation, like a puppy offered a treat. "Promise?"

My only response is another withering glare.

"Fine, fine." He chuckles as he holds up his hands in surrender. "My ego has been bruised enough."

I step past him and this time he doesn't stop me. As I walk away, though, he calls out loud enough to draw the gazes of several surrounding party-goers.

"So, that's a no on the thank-you parade, then?"

I don't look back, but I can feel his eyes on me the whole way to the doors. I pretend not to notice the smile tugging at my lips and the swirl of unwanted butterflies in my stomach as I slip into the kitchens and out of sight.

"TWENTY MINUTES, people, then you need to be back here and ready to serve the main course." Miriam sounds like the green-scaled dinosaur lady from *Monster's Inc.* and, actually, bears a slight resemblance to her if you look close enough. "If you're going to smoke, you'll have to take the elevator up to the roof." She glances at the clock. "Time starts now."

The group of twelve cater-waiters disperses faster than high schoolers at a cop-busted kegger.

Mara looks at me, a box of cigarettes clasped tight in her hand. "You coming?"

I shake my head. "Don't smoke."

"I'm quitting. Just... not tonight." A sheepish grin lights up her whole face. "See you in a few."

I wait until everyone's cleared out, then hustle through the side door and beeline for the small women's bathroom at the end of the hall. The event is almost entirely male businessmen, so it's blessedly deserted — marking, perhaps, the only time in my life I've ever been thankful for that pesky glass ceiling the female CEOs smacked into when hoping for an invitation to this shindig. The handful of women actually in attendance are all using the fancy ballroom bathrooms, not trekking down the hall in their Manolos to this one. I should be totally under the radar, here.

Flipping the deadbolt behind me, I pull open the cabinets beneath the sink, push aside several bottles of cleaning products, and slide out the black backpack I stashed inside earlier. In less than a minute, I've shimmied out of the god-awful uniform and into a tight-fitting black ball gown with whisper-thin straps, a lace bodice, and a flared hem which falls just far enough to conceal my flats. Without letting myself consider the ramifications of this monumentally stupid plan, I shove the uniform into the backpack along with the itchy black wig, zip it closed, and stash it out of sight in the cabinet.

I hate wasting a few precious moments on my hair, but it can't be helped. There's a *lot* of it, and after being stuffed beneath the wig for two hours, it's flat and frizzy. I run my fingers under the tap for a moment, then work them the through the blonde mane to give it a little life. Scraping the pile into an up-do, I fasten it with a pretty tortoiseshell clip barely wide enough to contain the riot of waves. One swipe of lipstick is all I bother with for makeup. Staring at the blonde, blue eyed girl in the mirror, I pinch my cheeks for added color and examine my disguise. Not perfect, but good enough.

It has to be — there's no more time to waste.

I duck out of the bathroom a moment later looking entirely different from the pale, dark-haired waiter who entered. From a distance, no one will recognize me. And if I'm caught, chances are a security guard will be much more lenient with a pretty party guest than a rogue member of the wait staff. It's a hell of a lot easier to flirt your way out of a jam dressed in BCBG couture than a unisex button-down.

Moving on silent feet down the dimly lit hall, I scan door numbers as I pass.

4017

4020

4023

Copy room, storage room, conference room. All useless to me.

I keep going, growing more nervous the farther from the reception I get. Minutes tick by on my watch, taunting me like a child's hide-and-go-seek countdown.

Thirteen.

Twelve.

Eleven.

I finally spot what I'm looking for at the end of the hall. My pace increases as I hurry to it.

Ready or not, here I come.

I don't turn on the light as I crack open the door and step into the dark office. Moonlight shines through the wall of glass on my left, bright enough to illuminate the shape of a cubicle and — *finally!* — a computer console. My fingers tap impatiently against the shiny wood desk as I wait for it to power on.

Ten minutes.

When the home screen loads, I'm confronted with a password-protected login. I plunk myself into the leather swivel chair and punch in a quick series of commands to toggle the computer's terminal window. Green code text flows across the console as I type a few keystrokes to bypass the security system. For anyone who knows even the smallest amount of code, it's shockingly easy to access a "private" computer account.

Thanks for that, Microsoft. It makes my job a hell of a lot easier.

Once I'm in, I reach into my bra and fish out the flash drive that's been digging into my ribcage all night. It's still warm from my body as I pop it into the USB port and wait for the sluggish system to recognize the hardware. A glance at my watch makes my pulse skyrocket.

Seven minutes.

It takes only seconds for the virus I built to worm into the Lancaster Consolidated network, but that's only phase one of my plan.

Infect.

Retrieve.

Escape.

I don't have time to weed through mountains of computer data to find the financial files I need, so I copy the entire hard drive. The lightning-fast 512 GB storage stick cost more than my monthly rent payment, but at times like this it really comes in handy. Any self-respecting hacker needs one.

Well, that, and an endless supply of candy and caffeine.

My fingers tap nervous rhythms against the shitty particle-board as I wait. This office clearly doesn't belong to one of the executives. A lower-level manager, perhaps, or an accountant. That's fine, though — every computer in this building is on the same network, like Christmas lights on a string. Crack one fuse, you've cracked them all.

Easy.

So long as you don't get caught, that is.

If I end up in jail for this shit, I will personally kill Luca.

The file transfer takes a long time. Too long.

My gaze flips back and forth between the data percentage bar, inching closer to completion at a glacial place, and the face of my watch, where minutes dwindle from five to four to three. By the time the computer pings to signify the transfer is complete, I have less than two minutes to get back to the bathroom, whip off this dress, and change into my catering uniform.

Ejecting the thumb drive, I shove it back into my bra and power off the computer as fast as possible. I'm already reaching for my hair clip as I rush out of the office and hurry down the hallway, hoping like hell Miriam doesn't have a shit-fit when I'm a few seconds late, or beat me to death with that stick she's got shoved up her ass.

Doubtful.

I'm nearly back at the bathroom, so close to escape I can practically taste it, when a loud male voice rings out and stops me in my tracks.

"Hey! You! What are you doing out here? This area is off limits to attendees."

Fuck.

CHAPTER 3
THE SAVIOR

I PIVOT SLOWLY to face the two security guards striding toward me, their matching gray suits ill-fitting, their faces set in identical expressions of displeasure. I don't know where Lancaster drummed these guys up, but they could be Schwarzenegger stand-ins on the *Terminator* set. Their muscles have muscles; their necks seem to have disappeared entirely.

"Are you boys talking to me?" I ask, doing my best bimbo impression. My voice is so high and bubbly, I'm sure the dolphins at Boston Aquarium are on high alert. I force my dark blue eyes wide, channeling *I'm-just-an-innocent-piece-of-arm-candy* vibes.

I see the slight shift of their expressions as they take me in. Their gaits slow from angry strides to strolls as they come to a stop a few feet from me.

"Miss, this area is off-limits," the one on the right says, eyeing me skeptically.

"Oh." I make a pouty face. A sultry shake of my head sends tendrils of hair spilling over my bare shoulders in a gold curtain. I arch my back slightly, shamelessly using my B-cups to their best advantage as a *humph* sound escapes my pursed mouth. "Well, no one told *me* that. The party is just *so* boring, I thought I'd stretch my legs." I contort my face into mask of alarm and make my voice so breathy, Marilyn Monroe would be impressed. "I'm not... I'm not in *trouble*, am I?"

If only I had a stick of gum to chew, the Barbie illusion would be complete.

The men glance at each other and I see them silently dismiss me as a viable threat. Which is a good thing because, *seriously*, I have about twenty seconds before Miriam notices my absence and sounds the alarm.

"No, miss, you're not in trouble." The guard on the left, who's maybe ten years younger than his counterpart, smiles briefly at me. "Just make sure to stay in the ballroom for the rest of the night. We're not supposed to allow anyone back here."

"Oh, thank you, boys!" I exclaim, winking at them. "I promise I'll be a good girl from now on." My tone turns suggestive. "Well... I'll *try* to be good."

If I'm not mistaken, a blush creeps up the older guard's neck. The younger one is outright grinning at me.

Gotcha.

I tilt my head and bite my lip demurely. "You know, it's rare to meet honest-to-gosh gentlemen, nowadays. Thank you."

"No problem, miss."

"Y'all have a good night, now!"

"You too, miss," the younger guard says. "Enjoy the party."

"Oh, I won't," I say on a laugh, turning to go. It's hard to keep myself from taking off at a run, but I know they're still watching.

So, I'll be a few minutes late. Miriam will rant. At least I won't be cuffed in the back of a squad car.

Leaving the men behind, I'm flooded with so much relief I

don't notice the third guard coming around the corner until I've nearly bumped noses with her.

Yes, *her*.

Damn. Somehow, I doubt my bimbo routine will be equally effective on a woman.

"What's happening here?" she snaps in a no-nonsense voice at the male guards behind me. "Who is this and why is she back here?"

The men move to my either side — a Schwarzenegger sandwich.

"Well, uh," the younger guard hedges, glancing guiltily from me to the woman who is clearly his superior. "This young lady is with the party in the ballroom."

"And?" she barks again in that condescending tone.

Superior or no, she should rethink her management strategies.... and possibly her pantsuit. It really emphasizes her cankles.

"We were just about to escort her back," the older guard chimes in.

"Yes," I start. "I was—"

"Quiet!" she growls, dismissing me instantly. Her focus shifts back to her men. "Mr. Lancaster said no one was allowed back here. No exceptions. Anyone caught wandering was to be brought to his attention immediately."

"We know that, ma'am, but—"

"*No* exceptions," she repeats, eyes narrowing. "Have you even confirmed she's a guest?"

My mouth goes dry. I focus on the feeling of the USB in my bra and wonder if they'll strip search me here or down at the police station...

Don't panic, I tell myself. *What's the worst that can happen?*

Oh, you know. Just a felony charge for trespassing and

corporate espionage. Twenty years in federal prison. No big deal.

"You," she spits at the younger guard. "Go get Mr. Lancaster and Mr. Linus, the Head of Security." Her gaze swivels to pin the older guard in place. "If you think you can manage it, stay with her and make sure she doesn't move until we get—"

"Oh, *there* you are, snookums!" a familiar voice interrupts her tirade. "I've been looking for you everywhere."

My wide eyes fly past the female guard and catch sight of Parker West, who's striding down the hallway toward us with a determined look on his face. His gaze is locked on me as he pushes through the group and slides an arm around my shoulders, hauling me into his side with such familiarity, anyone watching would undoubtedly think we were something more than *just friends.*

"Where have you been?" Parker asks, peering down into my face. A warning squeeze of his fingers on the flesh of my upper arm tells me my vacant expression is blowing the whole act. The message in his eyes is clear: I'd better start playing along, pronto.

I don't know why he's helping me; right now, I don't care.

I need him and he knows it.

"Here I am," I say in bimbo-voice, turning into his chest and winding one arm between his shirt and his suit jacket. I can feel the muscled flesh beneath the fabric and instantly wonder what it would be like to run my hands down the bare planes of his back. My fingertips. My lips...

Zoe, focus! This is so not the time for sexual fantasies.

I try to banish the thought, but it's difficult to focus on anything with the heat of his skin still radiating against my palm.

"I missed you, snookums," Parker says, giving me another warning squeeze.

"I was on my way back, honey bear, I promise!" I bubble. His eyebrow twitches at the endearment. "These nice guards were just going to escort me."

Okay, so, *honey bear* might've been a little much. Whatever.

"Well, so long as you're back with me now, it doesn't matter." Parker steps forward, bringing me with him. "We must be getting back. Thank you all for looking out for my snookums, here."

If he calls me *snookums* one more time I'm going to murder him.

"Mr. West, sir, that's not exactly the case—" The female guard cuts in, trying to regain control of the situation. "She can't just leave, we have some questions—"

"Oh, my little love bug here is always going off to powder her nose and getting lost," he confides to the guards, who all look baffled and uncomfortable.

Pet names and PDA have that general effect, it seems.

Parker grins as he leads us down the hall, guards at our heels. "Terrible sense of direction, this one. Without me, she wouldn't be able to find the front door of our condo."

I grit my teeth in what I hope appears as a smile. "Thankfully, I have you to guide me, *honey bee*."

"Mr. West, to be clear... you're saying this woman is with you?" The female guard is frowning mightily as she trails behind us. "Because—"

"Of course she's with me," Parker says, coming to an abrupt stop. He pulls me closer until I'm practically fused to his side, my every curve plastered against the hard contours of his chest. I must admit, it's not an entirely unpleasant feeling. "She wanted to stay home and watch *The Real Housewives* marathon but I simply couldn't bear to be parted from my snookums for an entire night."

That's it. He's a dead man.

"But sir—"

Parker's demeanor shifts from playful to powerful so fast, it's like a switch has been flipped inside him. He straightens to full height, his muscles go tense, and his voice adopts a thread of steel that was absent before.

"If you have a problem with my date, you'll have a problem with me," he says lowly. "WestTech is one of Mr. Lancaster's most lucrative business partners, as I'm sure you're aware. But if we're going to be treated with suspicion and disrespect, maybe you *should* go get your boss." He pauses and stares into the female guard's eyes. "I have some of my own grievances I could air about his staff and their shortcomings."

"Oh, no, sir," the bitch backpedals quickly. "Of course not, sir. We meant no disrespect, you understand. Just doing our jobs." She swallows. "Please, have a pleasant evening."

"We will," Parker says, cheerful once again. I find it somewhat alarming how fast he can shift gears from intimidating to exuberant. For the first time, I wonder if there's something more to the playboy facade he puts on for paparazzi and the public.

I don't dwell on the thought, because we're suddenly moving again. This time, the guards don't follow as we make our way down the hallway toward the ballroom. His arm remains tight around my shoulders even after we've left their line of sight.

When we reach the bathroom where I changed earlier, I dig my heels in and draw to a stop. He glances at me curiously, mouth parting to ask a question I don't want to answer. Before he can say a word, I shove open the door, grab hold of his arm, and drag him in after me.

The door slams with finality, closing us together in the small space.

Breathe, Zoe.

I put as much distance between us as possible — which only amounts to about six feet, in the tiny bathroom. For a moment, we just stare at each other in silence.

With his hands shoved casually into his suit pockets and his tall frame leaning back against the door he looks totally relaxed, as if what just happened was no more interesting than the dinner party taking place thirty steps down the hall. His eyes though — they're totally alert and keenly intelligent as they hold mine. I get the sense they don't miss much.

"So," he says softly, shattering the quiet. I go tense, waiting for the inevitable questions. The threats. The demands.

Who are you? What were you doing?

Tell me, or I'll turn you in before you can say "twenty-five to life."

I'll keep your secret... if you make it worth my while...

I fight off a shudder and brace myself.

A tiny crease appears in the space between his eyes, like he's mulling something over.

"I'm thinking there should be one of those giant floating balloons, now," he murmurs. "Maybe a celebrity float. No one super famous, who'd overshadow me on my big day, obviously. Anthony Bourdain could work. I wonder if he's free for private events..." He shrugs his shoulders. "If not, we'll just go with two balloon floats."

The whole time he's talking, I feel my eyes getting wider.

He's insane, I realize bleakly. *Parker West is certifiably insane.*

"Excuse me?" I manage, when I've finally regained control over my vocal cords.

"Balloons." His head tilts and he looks at me like *I'm* the crazy one for not keeping up. "You know, like Macy's has every Thanksgiving."

I stare at him. "Are you having some kind of mental break, right now?"

"The parade. *My* parade. The one you promised me." He pushes off the wall and takes a step toward me, narrowing the number feet between us to five. This close, I suddenly recognize the humor lurking at the back of his eyes. "I'm thinking it's going to have to be pretty elaborate," he says quietly. "Considering I've saved your ass twice now, *snookums*."

"Don't call me that." I cross my arms over my chest, hoping it might muffle the sound of my heart slamming against my ribcage. "And, I will point out, I didn't ask you to save me. Either time."

"I didn't ask to be this good looking." He grins. "Things happen."

"Humble, aren't you?"

"Trouble, aren't you?" he counters, taking another step toward me.

Four feet left.

"No," I lie, heart still hammering.

His grin widens. He knows I'm full of shit.

"Too bad." His eyes flicker to my mouth. "I'm rather fond of trouble."

Gulp.

This whole night has been a clusterfuck of epic proportions. First the groper in the pinstripe suit, then the standoff with the guards, now the playboy billionaire with some weird tendency to channel his inner Lancelot like I'm a freaking damsel in distress... and, just so I have something to look forward to, later I'll have Miriam to deal with.

By this point there is a zero percent chance that she hasn't noticed my absence, which means I'll probably have to cut and run without finishing the job — *not* ideal, since if a breach is ever discovered in the LC network, they'll be much more likely to suspect responsibility lies with the cater-waiter who conveniently disappeared after the first half of her shift. To add insult to injury, I won't even get paid for the two hours I spent schlepping trays and fending off lewd advances.

"Listen, just tell me what you want so we can get this over with," I say, trying to sound like I'm in control and not about to defy national health statistics by having a heart attack at the ripe old age of twenty-four.

"What I want?" he asks in a precariously gentle tone.

"Yes." I take a breath that does nothing to steady me. "To keep quiet about this."

"Why would you assume I want something?"

"Everyone wants something."

"Maybe I don't."

"Well, what *I* want is to not be be indebted to you." I jerk my chin up. "I don't want to owe anyone anything. Ever."

There's a pause as he weighs my words and I get the sense he's trying to figure me out. I could save him the time — tell him I'm a puzzle with so many missing pieces he'd be better off throwing the whole damn thing in the trash — but I don't waste my breath.

"Have you considered the possibility..." he says after a while, his voice full of gravel. "...that I might want something you don't want to give me?"

"I..." I swallow. "I can give you money. Not upfront, but I could pay you in installments... or... something..." I finish weakly, watching him take another step toward me.

Three feet.

"I don't want your money."

"I could upgrade your computer system," I offer, shuffling backward until my spine hits the tile wall.

He shakes his head, amused.

"Walk your dog?"

His eyes spark with humor. "Don't have a dog, darling."

"Water your plants when you're out of town?"

"Do I look like the kind of guy who keeps a garden of delicate orchids?"

No. No, he does not.

He looks like the kind of guy who'd only ever see a flower if he decided to fuck you senseless in a field of wild daisies, just because he felt like it.

My mouth feels suddenly dry. When I speak, my words crack. "Then what do you want?"

His eyes flare with something dangerous. Something that makes my palms start to sweat and my legs press a little tighter together.

"I don't think you want to know," he whispers.

I agree. I definitely don't want to know.

We're silent for a long, heated moment, both waiting for the other to say something.

"Aren't you going to ask me?" I blurt, unable to stop myself. I clamp my lips shut as soon as the words are out, instantly regretting my lapse of control.

"Ask you what?" The humor in his stare has heated into something else entirely. "About your little Jane Bond act, with the costume change?"

I swallow my words when he takes another step closer and give a small nod of affirmation.

Two feet left.

"No," he murmurs. His eyes are fixed on my lips and suddenly my lungs feel too tight, like someone's sucked all the air out of them. "I'm not going to ask when I know you won't tell me."

I don't say anything, partly because he's right but mostly

because I don't think I'm capable of coherent words, at the moment.

"You don't know me. You don't trust me." He pauses and I see something in his eyes — the thrill of a challenge. I hear the echo of unspoken words humming in the air between us.

Not yet. But you will someday.

I push the strange thought away.

He takes that final step, until the space between us has all but disappeared. We're not touching, but our faces are so close if I rise onto my tiptoes we'll be kissing.

"What are you doing?" I breathe, pressing tight against the wall.

His eyes drag away from my mouth. Our stares clash like swords on a battlefield.

"I'm taking what I want."

Before I can blink, his mouth claims mine.

I make a sound of surprise, but it's lost as soon as our lips touch. He's everywhere, all over me — invading my senses, stealing my breath. His hands pull me close, cup my face, slide into my hair, touching me in all the places he can reach as if his desperate fingers can't decide where to linger. I'm stunned to find I'm just as ravenous – plastering my front to his, winding my arms around his neck, sliding my fingers through his thick, gorgeous, golden hair until it's messy, like I wanted to the first time I saw him.

Some distant part of my brain is screaming this is crazy, reminding me I don't even know this man, but I can't hear it over the rush of desire flooding my veins. I can't help myself.

Maybe I lived on the streets too long — learned the hard way that good things don't come easy. Ever. If someone hands you a dollar bill, you grab it and don't look back. You want something, you take it before it slips away.

And, for some inexplicable reason, what I want right now is

him. This infuriating, entitled, egotistical playboy whose easy jokes don't quite reach his eyes.

It's just sex. Just lust, I tell myself. *You want it.*

So... take it.

I pull him closer, my leg slipping out the slit in my dress to wind around the back of his thighs as my hands grip his shoulders to get better leverage. Feeling my response, he makes a rough sound as his tongue seeks entrance to my mouth. I open for him without hesitation. Our mouths collide with such heat I forget to breathe, to think, to do anything except press closer to him.

There's a terrifying edge of familiarity to this kiss — as though we've kissed a thousand times before, as though our mouths were made to fit together for only this purpose.

Not for speaking or eating or breathing.

Kissing.

I'm filled with need, a devouring, deep-rooted desire that surpasses the fact that we're strangers, that he doesn't even know my name, that I'm relatively sure we don't even like each other. Desire trumps it all, threading through me until I don't care about any of the reasons I shouldn't be making out with a stranger in a dingy bathroom.

The straps of my dress fall down my shoulders with a flick of his fingers. His hips pin me roughly against the wall, so hard I can't move, and I'm shocked to find I like it, shocked to find I want more.

More pressure, more weight, more *Parker*.

I've never liked to lose control. Never been the meek little girl in missionary position.

Oh, yes, let me lie here subdued while you fuck me.

Sex, like life, is about power. I don't relinquish mine in either the business world or the bedroom. My previous partners have learned quickly — try to domineer me and you'll find yourself blue-balled so hard, you'll look like an extra in *Avatar*.

But this is different. There's something about him that breaks every single one of my rules.

Maybe it's the knowledge that he doesn't know me, that he'll never see me after this moment... or maybe it's just *him*.

I don't care.

All I know is, he could have me any way he wanted and I'd like it. Up against a wall, flat on my back, driving in from behind. It's an addictive feeling. An adrenaline rush.

I pull him closer, until his frame dwarfs me completely, and abruptly find myself kissing empty air as he tears his lips from mine and moves them to my neck.

"I don't even know your name," he mutters against my skin as his hands move inside the bodice of my dress, beneath my bra.

Dear god, I'm going to come undone and he's barely touched me.

"Does it matter?" I ask, craning to give him better access.

Something about that question touches a nerve. He goes still and lifts his head so our eyes meet. I don't know him well enough to put a name on the emotion in their hazel depths. I feel dazed, my lips still tingling from his kisses as I stare up at him. His thumb moves to brush my bottom lip, as if he can't quite help himself.

"It matters," he says quietly. "I'm not fucking you for the first time in a bathroom stall. In fact, I'm not fucking you anywhere except my bed for the foreseeable future."

The way he says that — with such certainty, like there's no doubt in his mind we'll be doing this again — sends alarm bells ringing inside my head.

Common sense returns in a flash.

What the hell are you doing? my brain is screaming at me.

*You aren't the kind of girl who gets carried away because of...
what? Lust? The promise of a good fuck? You're here on a job.
Get your head out from between your legs and get the hell out of
here.*

"I have to go," I say, pushing against his chest and sliding past him before he has a chance to corner me again. By the time he's turned around, I've already crouched to retrieve my backpack and pulled it from the cabinet beneath the sink.

"Go?" His voice is full of disbelief. "I just had you pinned to a wall, with your hands in my hair and your tongue in my mouth. Darling, where exactly do you think you're going? If the answer isn't my place, you need to rethink it."

"Listen, this was..." I trail off, fighting a blush as I slide the strap of my backpack up over one shoulder and edge toward the exit door. "This was..."

"Hot as hell?" Parker supplies.

I shake my head.

"Not nearly enough?" he suggests.

Another head shake. God, I'm actually *blushing*. Like a virginal little schoolgirl.

What the hell is this guy doing to me?

I swallow. "I don't know what this was." I rise to full height, avoiding his eyes at all costs. "But I have to leave now. So... thanks for...for..."

"Saving you?" He's watching me carefully. "Or for the second part that happened just now, the part that's got you so turned on you can't even look at me?"

My defiant eyes fly to his. "I'm not turned on."

"Red cheeks? Swollen lips? Wild hair?" He smirks. "You look pretty turned on, darling."

"Well, I'm not," I snap.

He steps closer.

I step back.

"I'm leaving now."

"So you said," he murmurs, still watching me.

"Don't follow me."

"I wasn't planning to." He takes another step.

I hold out a hand to stop his advance. "And don't even think about kissing me again."

He grins. "Seems like you're the one thinking about it, *snookums*."

"Ugh!" I whirl around to the exit door and put my hand on the knob. Before I can turn it, he's there at my back, pressing into me — a wall of heat and need. Damn if it doesn't feel good.

"This isn't over," he whispers, his lips brushing the bare skin of my shoulder in the hint of a kiss, his hand tracing the sensitive skin of my spine. It takes all my strength not to lean back into his touch.

"You're right," I say, wishing my voice didn't sound so rough. "Something can't be over if it never even started."

Twisting hard on the knob, I yank open the door and slip out into the hallway.

This time, he doesn't follow me... but his voice carries softy at my back and I can't tune out his final words no matter how hard I try.

"I wouldn't count on that, darling."

CHAPTER 4

THE THREE STOOGES

MY UBER DRIVER shoots me a strange look as I clamor into his backseat and I can't exactly blame him— kiss-bitten lips, sex hair, and an ensemble featuring a white button down layered over an evening gown doesn't exactly scream *stable*. Thankfully, he chooses not to comment as he drives me across town to my loft in the Leather District. I wouldn't be able to keep up a conversation if he tried. My body's in the car but my mind is back in that bathroom — remembering the way Parker West's mouth felt against mine.

I've never been kissed like that in my life — kissed until I lost myself, kissed until I ceded control over my every autonomous instinct, kissed until I felt possessed, owned, kept like a bargain I didn't remember making. His mouth hit mine and suddenly I *belonged* to him. Worse, I *liked* it. His lips are the only shackles I've ever allowed to hold me; it's more than a little disquieting to realize I enjoyed the sensation of their weight against my skin.

My driver pulls up outside the towering brick warehouse.

The faded white paint that stretches across the side in bold letters is visible even in the dark.

EDISON PIANO FACTORY, EST. 1922

I punch in the building code, shuffle down the hallway, and shove my finger into the small illuminated panel to call the freight elevator. I hear it coming long before it arrives — rattling and groaning as it descends slowly down the shaft. The clanging, ancient brute of a machine is a relic from the original factory, built to haul thousand-pound pianos between floors. It refuses to fall apart no matter how many decades pass. With its iron bars and odd shape, it looks more like a birdcage than a viable mode of transportation. Hell, it almost makes the prospect of walking up six flights of stairs sound appealing.

Almost.

I've aged several years by the time it finally arrives. Sliding open the wooden hoistway gate, I wait for the inner metal doors to spring apart, step inside, insert my key into the panel, and breathe a sigh of relief as I feel the box jolt into motion.

I'm home.

Parker West will soon be a distant memory.

And, most importantly, I'm pretty sure I got the intel Luca needed.

A smile drifts across my face as the elevator rattles to a stop on the top floor and I step into my dark loft. Sure, the whole *Parker-saving-me* thing wasn't ideal, but that doesn't matter, now. *He* doesn't matter, now. All that matters is the Lancaster financial data, proving their CEO is a lying sack of dog shit.

My grin widens as I reach into my bodice, searching for the flash drive...

...and morphs into a grimace of shock when my fingers find nothing but flesh and fabric. I go completely still, panic overriding my every sense as I realize the USB is missing.

No.

No way in hell did I drop it. It was so tight against my skin, nothing save a full body search could've shaken it loose.

Then again, a quiet voice at the back of my mind whispers. *You do know someone who recently attempted a full search of your body... Someone with burnished blond hair and broad shoulders, who kissed like a vow and touched without hesitation... Someone who could've easily taken that flash drive from your cleavage without you noticing, so distracted by his touch you weren't even aware it was gone until now...*

My hands curl into fists as I realize exactly what happened to my flash drive. Or, should I say, exactly *who* happened to my flash drive. I hear a husky voice, still fresh in my memory, making me a promise.

This isn't over.

Parker. Fucking. West.

I admit, I'm shocked he found it while feeling me up. I'm even more stunned he was clever enough to pocket it. I underestimated him — dismissed him as nothing but a stacked wallet, high cheekbones, and unadulterated sex appeal. And yet, he's backed me neatly into a corner without my even realizing it.

Now, I'll be forced to seek him out. See him again.

Kiss him again.

No! No.

There will be no more kissing.

With a groan, I flip on an overhead chandelier, basking the industrial space in soft, feminine light. The loft is my sanctuary, my safe haven, though I'm probably the only person in a ten-mile radius who'd use those words to describe it. Even disregarding the ancient elevator, it's not in the greatest of neighborhoods. I don't participate in a weekly potluck with my neighbors or know their first names. It's frigidly cold in the winter months — the polished concrete floors are icy against my feet, the exposed brick walls essentially act as a meat locker. Most mornings, I can see my breath when I roll out of bed.

My little icebox.

But that's just it... it's *mine*.

When I turned eighteen, I finally gained access to the financial trust my parents left behind for me when they died. It's not much – certainly not enough to carry me forever – but it pays my meager rent each month and keeps me fully stocked in as many chocolate peanut butter cups as I can eat. So long as I take on a few freelance programming or graphic design jobs on the side every now and then, I'm able to live and work quite comfortably.

To soften its harsh industrial lines, I decorated in lush white fabrics and delicate glasswork. Colorful art prints span the interior walls; massive floor to ceiling windows look out over the city skyline to the north. A cluster of couches flank my black wood stove. A granite-topped breakfast bar divides the range from the rest of the space. My queen-sized platform bed dominates the far side, smothered in piles of down blankets and white faux-fur pillows. And in the corner, my most cherished possession — a bank of computer monitors on a massive black desk.

I peel off my flats, toss the backpack by the door, and shimmy out of my dress. Crossing to my dresser, I pull a loose-fitting white sweater from the bottom drawer and tug it on over my underwear. It drapes to mid-thigh, stretched out after a zillion washes. I shove the sleeves up above my elbows and feed a few fire-starters into the wood stove along with some kindling before I plop down in front of my computer.

I need that flash drive back, otherwise Luca will kill me and thousands of people will continue being screwed out of their hard-earned retirement accounts. Which means... Parker West just found his way onto my hit list.

Time to dig up some dirt.

As my fingers hover over the keys, I consider what I already know about the man, besides the fact that he kisses so well it should be illegal.

Not much.

My one and only interaction with the West family happened last spring, when Parker's younger sister Phoebe stumbled into trouble with Keegan MacDonough — head of Boston's most notorious Irish mob family. The MacDonoughs are a nasty lot, prone to brute force, bribery, and extortion. Taking Phoebe was just another one of their schemes to manipulate her sleazy father, Milo West, and tip the many, many millions controlled by the WestTech telecommunications company in their favor.

Twenty-five years ago, MacDonough bullied his way to the top the criminal food chain and never relinquished an ounce of his control, even with the DA breathing down his neck and the FBI searching his many properties for proof of illegal activities. He was a cancer, slowly eating away at everything that makes Boston beautiful. So, when I heard through the backchannels that he was holding the West heiress in a slum-house in Charlestown last April... Luca and I couldn't resist an opportunity to fuck with his carefully-constructed house of cards.

Now, I'm happy to report he's rotting in jail.

Plus, watching the Louboutin-wearing princess die at the hands of ugly thugs without lifting a finger to intervene isn't something that sits well on one's conscience — even a morally-hazy conscience like mine.

I may live in the gray area, but I'm not fond of watching innocents die.

And Phoebe is innocent. *Annoying*, but innocent — the girl talks a mile-a-minute, wears exclusively designer labels, and has never, not for a single moment in her privileged life, known what it feels like to go without food or heat or a safe place to lay her head.

We never spoke again, after that night. She doesn't even know my name — she never will.

Still, against my better judgment, I sort of... liked her, when we met.

Her brother is another story.

With their father facing prison-time for his collusion with MacDonough, Parker moved to the city a few months back and took over WestTech as interim CEO. I'm not sure what exactly makes a party-loving playboy qualified to run a Fortune 500 company, but no one asked my opinion on the matter.

My eyes narrow as his gorgeous face flashes in my mind. I still can't believe the jerk stole my flash drive. But, more so, I really can't believe he kissed me. I mean... the *nerve* of it all.

Who the hell does he think he is?

Only the most attractive man you've ever been pressed against, full-frontal...

I ignore the squirmy feeling in my stomach and focus on my anger. That's the only emotion I'm equipped to process, at the moment.

Cracking my knuckles, I turn my attention back to my computer screen and dive in.

BY MIDNIGHT, I've scoured the internet for all traces of Parker West... and, frustratingly, come up rather short. I sit back in my computer chair and exhale a heavy sigh. Besides the slew of Instagram pictures of him posing with half-naked Victoria's Secret models, there's really not a lot to go on. No criminal history, with the exception of a few teenage disorderly conduct charges his father's lawyers buried before they ever made it onto his permanent record. No marriage licenses; not even a trace of any long-term relationships, if his Facebook profile is anything to go by. No property listed in his name. In fact, I couldn't even find an address for him listed in the Registry of Deeds, which means he's either crashing with friends, staying with his sister, or booked at a hotel.

Or, more likely, he's shacking up with one of his many bimbos on the Eastern Seaboard.

Disquieted by the ridiculous thread of jealousy in my thoughts, I rise and head for the kitchen. I have to hop up onto the counter to reach the top cabinet where I keep my stash of candy — an intentional hurdle, since I figure if I have to climb to get my fix, there's a chance I'll eat less of it.

Fat chance. Emphasis on *fat*, because one of these days my metabolism is going to slow down and I'll actually have to work out to burn off the zillion calories contained in Reese's peanut butter cups.

...An eventuality I plan to ignore until the moment it happens.

I pop the chocolate into my mouth and let it melt on my tongue as my mind spins in indecisive circles. Since I can't track down where Parker's staying, I have no choice but to confront him somewhere I know he'll show up.

The WestTech offices.

I feel my lips tug up at one side as the beginnings of a plan take shape in my mind.

He told me this thing between us wasn't over — he was right.

It's just begun.

"DID you get the intel on Lancaster's finances?"

I squirm against the hard plastic subway seat and adjust my grip on the phone. "Yes. No. Kind of."

"What the hell does that mean, babe?" Luca sounds impatient. "You either got the intel or you didn't."

"I got it," I murmur, wincing. "And then... I kind of... lost it."

Silence blasts over the line. "Care to explain?"

"Listen, Luke, it's complicated."

"Uncomplicate it for me."

"I have the files on a flash drive."

"Okay, so what's the problem?"

"The flash drive may or may not be... misplaced at the moment." I wince again. "But I'm going to get it back. In fact, I'm on my way to get it back at this precise moment."

More silence.

"Don't freeze me out," I snap, making sure my voice is too low for the other passengers to overhear. "You should be thanking me for going on this crazy mission of yours at all. I almost got caught. Some..." I pause, searching for the right word to describe Parker. "...some stranger had to save my ass."

"Uh huh. Would this *stranger* have anything to do with your missing intel?"

My jaw clenches. He knows me too well.

"Guess the silent treatment is okay as long as you're the one using it, huh, babe?" he teases.

"Shut up."

"For real... you okay?" he asks, voice suddenly serious. "Don't like hearing you were almost caught. I shouldn't have asked you to put yourself at risk. I should've been there to help you."

"I'm fine." I sigh. "Parker — the guy who helped me — was there. He covered for me. I don't know why, but he did."

"I know why," Luca mutters. "I've seen that black dress."

I blink. "What?"

"Never mind." He clears his throat. "Just let me know how it goes."

"Aye, aye, captain."

He clicks off, leaving me listening to dead air.

I hate when he does that.

Ten minutes later I'm out of the dark subway tunnels, squinting as afternoon sunshine glares off the towering glass skyscrapers of the Financial District. This part of the city feels foreign to me — too new, too tall, to modern for Boston, a place steeped more strongly in history than the tea we once dumped into our harbors to piss off the British. These towers all look the same, totally devoid of charm and character. I head for the one with the WestTech logo on the side and step through the glass rotating doors, keeping my head held high and my strides confident.

The first rule of blending in anywhere: act like you belong and people will assume you do.

Luca's been saying it since we were kids. *Fake it till you make it, babe.*

The lobby is jammed with people returning from their lunch breaks, just as I'd hoped. Amid the chaos, I note the entire space is decked out in holiday decorations, complete with a fifteen foot Fraser fir and massive ornaments suspended from the ceiling, like model airplanes at a museum.

It takes effort not to physically recoil at the show of Christmas cheer.

In ten days, it'll be December 26th and all these painful reminders of the things you've lost will be packed back in their boxes for a whole year and shoved away in attics and basements, out of sight.

Ten days. 240 hours. 14,400 minutes.

You can make it, Zoe. You always make it.

I fall into step with a group of women on their way back from lunch. The uncomfortable heels I bought at PayLess for fifteen bucks on my way here are giving me blisters, but I don't pay them any attention. I trail behind the chatting women, trying to look like I'm part of their posse, and remind myself not to tug on the lapels of my navy blazer or white skirt.

Fidgeting is a dead giveaway.

I'm past the security desk and in line for the elevators before anyone has time to give me a second glance. When the doors open, I slip inside and stare down at my phone so no one has the urge to make small talk with me. The words are a blur on the screen — I can't focus on anything except the knowledge that in another twenty-seven — *ding!* Make that twenty-six — floors, I'll be face to face with a man I've been fantasizing about since last night.

The crowd thins as we slowly ascend, stopping to unload passengers every few floors. My pulse starts to skyrocket the higher we climb, as though my blood pressure is somehow linked to altitude.

Or proximity to Parker.

I swallow hard and tighten my grip the phone, trying to remind myself this is about business, nothing more. Plus, I'm not just going to walk into his office, wag a disapproving finger in his face, and say, "Return my flash drive, or else!"

Give me a little credit. I have a plan.

I get off on the twelfth floor, which — according to a quick internet search — houses the Tech Support Department, and push the chunky, cat-eye glasses further up the bridge of my nose as I make my way down the hall. The lenses are clear glass — just a prop — but they'll help me get the leverage I need.

Techie boys can't resist the allure of cute nerd girls. It's a scientific fact.

I follow a short hallway until I find their office and step

through the doorway. A trio of IT guys sit amidst a bank of computers. Satisfaction thrums though my veins when all three men look up and take notice, going still at their desks as their eyes sweep me from head to toe.

What did I tell you — cat-eye glasses and knee socks?

Nerd-boy kryptonite.

They're all in their mid to late twenties, pale from too much time in front of a computer screen and in serious need of some wardrobe advisement judging by their crumb-covered khakis and lopsided ties. I fight the urge to sigh. This is exactly why computer geeks never get the girl.

(At least, not until they make their first million.)

I linger in the doorway and watch as the three of them slide off their noise-cancelling headphones and pivot in their squeaky computer chairs to get a better look at me. The sound of fingers clacking against keys fades into silence and the air fills with hushed excitement. I can almost see the red alert messages flashing inside their brains.

GIRL. IN. OFFICE.

THIS IS NOT A DRILL.

"Can we help you?" the bespectacled man closest to me asks. The other two are leaning forward in their seats, looks of anticipation on their faces.

The Three Freaking Stooges, in the flesh. This is going to be almost *too* easy.

"I seriously hope so." I jut out a hip as I pull a laptop from my bag. "I'm Sandra — I work up in accounting. I spilled something on my keyboard this morning and I will be, like, eternally grateful if one of you can salvage it." I pause for effect. "The girls upstairs were like, 'Oh, you should take it to the geniuses at the Apple Store' but I was like 'Um, don't you know we have a whole department of geniuses right downstairs?'" I grin when I see Larry, Moe, and Curly are hanging on my every word.

"So..." I swivel my gaze around the office. "You think you guys could help me? If you're too busy... I guess I can go to the Apple store..."

"No!" All three of them practically yell at the same time.

My grin widens until I'm beaming. "Great!"

I step into the office and walk toward Moe, swinging my hips and stopping a fraction closer to him than I would a normal stranger.

It's safe to say he's affected by my nearness. The man can barely meet my eyes as he takes the junk laptop — another prop I keep handy for occasions such as this — from my hands. You wouldn't believe how many times this same routine has gotten me access into buildings I'm not supposed to be within a ten-block radius of.

Never underestimate the power of horny tech-support staffers.

(Spoiler alert: they're *always* horny.)

"We'll take a look and see what we can do," Moe tells me as Larry and Curly watch from the sidelines, no doubt envious they aren't the ones who'll be attempting to resuscitate a computer that's been dead since 2010, when a city-wide power outage fried my hard drive.

"Thanks so much!" I gush. "I owe you guys! And I'll be sure to tell the girls upstairs that they should stop walking all the way to the Apple Store every time they have an issue. This is much closer... and you guys are way cuter."

Moe's expression matches that of a child on Christmas.

Larry looks like he might start weeping tears of joy.

Curly looks a little nauseous.

God, I'm good.

"I suppose you guys won't mind if I hang out here for a bit, while you're fixing it?" I ask, batting my eyelashes. "I can just, like, play Solitaire or something on one of your extra computers."

"Of course not," Moe mutters quickly, looking slightly embarrassed as he examines the console beside his. The desktop is littered with empty Red Bull cans and old microwaveable burrito wrappers. "Let me just clear this off for you..."

"You can sit over here!" Larry calls.

"Or here!" Curly adds.

"No worries, boys." Holding Moe's gaze, I watch a blush creep up the side of his neck beneath his collar and try not to smirk as I backpedal toward a desk in the corner, where my screen won't be visible to them. "This one will be fine."

"Okay." Moe looks a little crestfallen, but turns his attention quickly back to the fried laptop in his hands. "This looks like it might take a while. Just hang tight and let us know if you need anything."

Oh, Moe, I think as I log onto their server and cue up the terminal window. *You've already given me everything I need.*

CHAPTER 5

THE MAGIC TRICK

AN HOUR LATER, I step off the elevators onto the penthouse floor with a spring in my step and a smile on my face.

"Do you have an appointment?" The pretty receptionist behind the desk tilts her head at me. Her hair is pinned up in a French-twist or some other elaborate, work-appropriate up-do that looks effortless but I'm sure took at least thirty minutes. Not a single shiny, brown lock is out of place.

Ugh. I can barely manage a freaking pony tail without compressing the nerves in my neck. Right now, I feel the weight of my curls straining against my clip. It's only a matter of time before it clatters to the marble floor — one more casualty in the war to tame my mane.

"No," I blurt when I realize she's staring at me, waiting for an answer. "I don't have an appointment."

"Well, I'm afraid Mr. West has no availability to see you today. Fridays are always busy — no time for walk-ins." She purses her lips as she gestures toward a prim stack of gray business cards to my left. "Feel free to take a card and call the office to make an appointment. Currently, we're booking into March."

I stare at her, not moving. "March. As in... three months from now?"

"Mr. West is a busy man."

"Oh, I'll bet he is."

Her eyes narrow at my thinly-veiled sarcasm. "If you'd like to leave a message with me, I'll make sure he gets it."

"Uh huh." It doesn't escape my notice that she makes no move to pick up her pen. I figure that means the chances of her passing on any messages are nil.

"So." She rises to her feet and I see the rest of her is as annoyingly put-together as her hair. I feel like an idiot in my thrift-store ensemble. "If you'll just make your way to the elevators..."

"Yeah, the thing is, March isn't going to work for me." I stare her down.

She goes still and her voice lowers. "Please leave and call back for an appointment."

"Nope, don't think so."

"Miss, I will not hesitate to call security."

"No need to waste their time." I shrug, turn, and cross to the white leather sofa across from her desk. "I'll just wait while you call Mr. West and tell him I'm here to solve his computer issues."

"But—" Steam is going to start leaking from her ears any second. "We aren't having any computer issues."

"Really?" I scrunch my nose at her as I settle back against the cushions. "You sure about that?"

"I...I..." Twin spots of red appear on her cheekbones. "I'm calling security."

"Go right ahead," I say, searching for a magazine on the end table beside me. They're all boring business crap — TIME, The

New Yorker, The Economist. I glance back at the receptionist briefly and find she's glaring at me.

I sigh. "You'll just have to track me down after security escorts me out. Because, as I said before... You're going to be having some computer problems very shortly, and I have a feeling Mr. West will want to chat with me about them."

Miss Perfect is practically quivering with outrage at my brazen disregard for her orders. "I'm calling security, now," she repeats in a haughty tone.

I smile blandly. "You do that. I'll just sit here and wait. And in precisely..." I glance at my watch. "*Two minutes*, without lifting a finger, I'm going to make your CEO appear right here in this lobby, like magic." I sweep my arms through the air like a magician preforming on stage in Las Vegas.

She huffs, pivots on her Louboutins, and struts back to her desk. I have to fight off laughter as I watch her snatch her phone from its cradle with righteous indignation.

Turning back to the magazines, I spy a flash of pink amidst all the black and blue bindings, and pull it from the bottom of the stack. The glossy cover proclaims LUSTER in magenta — one of those terrible girly rags full of articles like "ZUMBA YOUR WAY TO A BETTER BOD!" — and I wonder what it's doing amidst the snore-worthy business magazines.

My eyes move to the name in the address box.

PHOEBE WEST

I snort. I should've known.

I've barely flipped past the first page when the elevator doors chime open. Moe and Curly both barrel out, eyes wild and slightly paler than normal. When they catch sight of me on the couch, they slam to a halt and gape with a mixture of shock and fear.

"Hi, boys!" I call, waggling my fingers at them.

"You!" Moe hisses, staring at me. "What did you do to our system?"

"Little old moi?" I ask, batting my lashes. "Why, nothing, of course. I was busy playing Solitaire."

The receptionist is on her feet, gaze swiveling from me to Moe to Curly with varying levels of alarm. "What's going on?"

"We need to speak to Mr. West right away." Curly is wringing his hands and looks like he's about to revisit his breakfast. "There's an issue with our computer network. It's somehow been... crippled."

The receptionist's gaze slides to me. Her expression is not a friendly one.

"Ta-da!" I exclaim, making jazz-hands — as any good magician would, in this scenario. Rising to my feet, I drop my words to a whisper. "And now, for my next trick..."

"Patricia, why am I locked out of my computer?" a familiar voice carries from the wide hallway to the left of the reception area. All four of us turn to watch as the tall, golden-haired CEO strides into the room, his features set in a frown. "It won't recognize my password and—"

Parker's words dry up when he catches sight of his secretary on her feet. I see his face morph from frustrated to puzzled as he takes in Moe and Curly, who are practically falling over themselves in their haste to apologize.

"Mr. West, we take full responsibility—"

"We had no idea she was going to—"

By the time those hazel eyes finally lock on mine, my heart is pounding so hard inside my chest I'm sure it's audible twenty floors beneath us. I see a flash of recognition in his stare as he takes me in, from the top of my head all the way down to my cheap-ass heels.

"You," he says, cutting off Moe and Curly's rambles with a

single word. His voice is low with amusement and something else — something that makes my pulse quicken.

I clear my throat. "Me."

His mouth twitches. "I had a feeling you'd be showing up."

My eyes narrow. "You took something of mine. Didn't have much of a choice, did I?"

"Darling..." He shakes his head. "There's always a choice."

Not in the mood to deconstruct that comment, I tear my eyes away from him and glance over at Patricia, the receptionist, who is staring at me with open hostility.

"Like *magic*, right?" I stage-whisper just to piss her off. "Tickets are available at the box office. I'm here till next week."

"Mr. West." Moe takes a hesitant step toward Parker. "I can explain." He jabs a finger in my direction. "This woman is an imposter! A deceiver!"

"Moe, this isn't an episode of *Game of Thrones*." I shake my head and cross my arms over my chest. "You can just say *she tricked us into helping her*."

"We didn't help you!" Curly looks queasier than ever. "Sir, I promise you, we were in no way a part of her schemes—"

"Could you two be more dramatic?" I roll my eyes. "*Schemes*. As if flirting with you for two seconds until you folded like a lawn chair and gave me access to the secure network took any brain power at all."

"She— she— we didn't know..." Moe trails off uselessly.

"Oh, cheer up, Moe." I sigh and shake my head. "You're not the first one who's fallen for the damsel-in-distress shtick. You certainly won't be the last."

"My name is Marvin," he corrects coldly.

"Of course it is." My eyes swing back to Parker, who's watching this exchange unfold in silence. I can't read the expression on his face, though the twitching of his lips suggests he may be fighting off a smile.

"Listen, Curly and Moe are innocent bystanders," I inform him. "As is Larry. I think he's still downstairs."

Parker opens his mouth to respond, but the chime of the elevator arriving cuts him off. Two beefy security guards step into the fray, eyes scanning the room for potential threats.

"Sir." The larger of the two inclines his head to Parker. "Patricia called down and told us there was a woman causing a disturbance up here, who needed to be removed from the premises."

Parker glances at me. His lips tug up at one side. "You cause a lot of trouble for someone so small."

I shrug. "It's a talent."

"Sir?" The security guard edges closer to me. "Should we remove her?"

My eyes are locked on Parker's and I can't help but notice the green flecks in his irises, brought out by his emerald tie.

"That won't be necessary." He pauses. "She's with me."

She's with me.

His low decree sends everyone into motion — the guards back into the elevator with brisk nods, the receptionist back behind her desk with an annoyed huff, the tech boys back to the bank of couches, where they hover in awkward suspense. The only point of stillness in the room is me, frozen to the floor as Parker slowly closes the distance between us.

I don't move — I don't even breathe — as he comes to a stop less than a foot away. The air between us seems to hum with tension.

"My office." His eyes flicker down to my mouth for a brief moment. "*Now.*"

"That was pretty good, playboy. You almost sounded like an intimidating CEO." I tilt my head. "Almost."

His eyes narrow and he opens his mouth to respond, but Moe's shrill, nervous voice interjects.

"Sir, what would you like us to do about the computers? The entire network is frozen— no one can log in or access their work stations."

"Patricia," Parker says, never shifting his eyes away from mine. "Send everyone home."

"What?" I hear her gasp. "Sir... it's only just past lunchtime. We have more than one hundred employees on site—"

"Patricia." He turns his head just a fraction of an inch and shoots her such an intense look, I'm surprised she doesn't keel over. "*Send everyone home.*" His head moves again and he unleashes the look on Moe and Curly. "That includes you."

"But, sir, the network—"

"I'll fix it." Parker looks back at me and I see a muscle working in his jawline. "Or, I should say, I know who'll fix it. So, have a nice afternoon. Consider it paid vacation. I'll see you all on Monday."

Without another word, he takes hold of my arm, turns on the heel of one extremely expensive leather shoe, and drags me down the hall to his office with all the gentleness of a rugby player.

The opaque glass doors close soundlessly at our backs, entombing us inside the enormous space together. There's an incredible panoramic view of the entire downtown sprawl, but I don't bother looking. All my focus is used up by Parker.

As soon as we're inside, he releases his grip and puts a few feet of distance between us, crossing to lean against his desk with both arms folded across this chest. The sun beams shining through the wall of glass behind him surround his frame with a glowing halo, like he's some sort of angel.

I know the truth — he's no angel. He's a lion, ready to pounce.

King of the jungle.

And I'm a fucking gazelle.

His gaze is intent, almost intimate, as he stares at me in silence. I know I should say something to shatter it. In fact, I spent all morning carefully rehearsing exactly what I was going to say to him when I got him alone. And yet, staring at him now... all my words have fled.

The silence between us feels heavy, hard to swallow — like the summer runs I take along the Charles, when it's nearly impossible to haul humid breaths into my aching lungs. I stiffen my spine, telling myself he's not intimidating at all, leaning there like some Greek god sent down from Mt. Olympus to fuck with my head.

And possibly other parts of my anatomy.

He's watching me with that same look in his eye he had last night, the first moment we met — with razor-sharp curiosity, as though he's never seen anything quite like me before. The thought makes my throat start to close. I swiftly decide I'll happily lose our staring contest, if it means not being the subject of his study for another moment.

I drag my eyes from him and examine the office around me. I thought it would be soulless, colorless — the space of a corporate drone. Instead, I find myself surrounded on all sides by photographs. They line the walls in a kaleidoscope of color. Intrigued despite my better judgment, I wander a little closer to examine the ones on the nearest wall.

There's no discernible pattern or theme — every frame is a different size, a different subject. There are massive canvases that take up several feet of wall space alongside tiny frames no larger than a postcard. Some are portraits — young faces, wrinkled features, every age in between. Some are places — recognizable streets of Boston, entirely foreign lands I couldn't think to name.

Close-ups. Landscapes.

Unfocused. High-resolution.

They're all unique. In fact, they only have one thing in common.

They're all amazing.

Whoever took them knows their way around a camera lens, that's for damn sure. Some of these should be hanging in museums, not a CEO's office.

"Wow," I murmur, stopped in my tracks by a particularly vivid shot of a couple hand-in-hand on a cobbled street, surrounded by thousands of pigeons in flight with a blazing, orange sunset in the background.

"Piazza San Marco, in Venice." His response is quiet — I didn't realize he'd heard my hushed exclamation. "I was cutting through on my way to dinner and just happened to have my camera with me. Some shots you wait all day for — that one unfolded totally on its own. Right place, right time."

I glance at him. "You took this?"

He nods.

Spinning in a slow circle, I look around at the dozens of frames on his walls. "You took all of these," I marvel.

There's a beat of silence. "Did you come here to look at my pictures?"

The amused question draws my gaze back to him.

I suck in a breath. That half-smile of his is killer.

Focus! You're here to get your flash drive back, not make moony eyes at the man or compliment his dreamy photography skills.

I fold my arms over my chest to mirror his pose. Sadly, I doubt I'm equally intimidating.

"I don't care about your photos," I say, wishing my voice didn't sound so breathy. "That's not why I came."

"So, I'll just have to assume you were desperate to see me again." His grin is sinful. "Can't say I blame you."

I scoff.

He makes a *tsk* noise. "First you sexually harass me last night, then you track me down at my office... Do you have a crush on me, snookums?"

"I told you not to call me that."

"Fine." He chuckles. "How about boo-bear?"

"How about I shove my foot up your ass?"

"Okay, I'll take that as a *maybe*." His head tilts in thought. "Pumpkin?"

"Eat a dick."

"Cuddles?"

"Go die."

"Cookie? Sugar? Snickerdoodle?"

"Why are all of these food-themed?"

"I'm hungry." His grin widens. "Want to go grab lunch?"

"Are you seriously asking me out right now?"

"Of course not." He pauses. "Why, would you say yes if I did?"

"No."

"We'll get something light. Chinese food." His forehead creases. "I'm always starving thirty minutes after I gorge on Chinese. Why is that?"

I glare at him in lieu of a response.

"Okay, no egg rolls for you. Got it." He continues as though I'm fully engaged in the conversation. "Appetizers and drinks."

"Stop."

"Fine, fine. Just the drinks, then. You convinced me." He pushes off the desk and takes a step closer. His eyes gleam with good humor. "Unless you change your mind and want to grab dinner afterward, of course."

Shameless. The man is completely, totally, one hundred percent shameless.

I wonder why I find that so sexy.

"You're trying to distract me again," I say in an uppity tone.

"Is it working?"

"No." *Yes*.

"Most girls would love to have dinner with me."

"I can't imagine why."

He laughs and the sound pools in my stomach like a warm shot of whiskey. "You'll cave eventually. I don't know if you've noticed, but I'm extremely persistent when I find something I want." He takes another step in my direction. "Like the time I was in Thailand and I wanted a massive quarter-pounder with bacon and American cheese. It wasn't easy, I had to drive almost a hundred miles... but I found a burger place. And *damn* if it wasn't the best burger I ever had."

"Do you take anything seriously?" I ask, genuinely curious.

"Not if I can help it."

"So you aren't at all concerned about the fact that the entire WestTech server is down?"

He sighs. "You want to know what I'm concerned about?"

"Not really, no."

"Cronuts." He gestures at the plate of leftover baked goods on the sleek coffee table to his left. "I mean... is it a doughnut or is it a croissant? Who decides these things?" He shakes his head, as if deeply troubled. "What if someone put a gun to your head and made you separate all baked goods into categories? What then, huh? Where the hell would the cronuts wind up?"

I pause. "You think that's a likely scenario?"

"Highly probable."

I shake myself out of doughnut-related thoughts and contort my face back into my Ice Queen mask. "You're distracting me again."

"Am I?" he asks.

"You know why I'm here."

"Yes, we've discussed this already. You simply couldn't stay away." He takes another step toward me. "I mean... I've been told my kisses are irresistible, but this is taking things to a whole new level."

"Don't flatter yourself."

"Too late. I'm flattered." He takes another few steps. "How could I not be? You went through so much trouble to get my attention."

"Trouble?" I scoff. "Hacking your server took about as much brain power as chewing a stick of bubblegum."

"Speaking of bubblegum," he cuts in. "Funny story—"

"No!" I yell. "No more stories. No more tangents. No more charm or half-smiles or stupid little ploys to make me forget why I'm here."

"*Charm*, huh?" He winks. "Stop, you'll make me blush."

I glare. "You took my thumb drive."

"Did you say hump time?"

"Are you in seventh grade?"

"Sixth, actually, but I'm old for my year—"

"Shut up! God, how has no one strangled you yet? Are you always this annoying?"

"Would you believe, usually I'm even *more* annoying."

"My flash stick." I glare at him. "Portable hard drive. Fits in a USB slot."

"That was a lot of technical jargon for a dumb elementary schooler like myself. All I heard was something about me driving my stick into your slot."

"Cut the shit, okay? I know you have it and I want it back."

"How do you know I have it?"

"Because..." I feel my cheeks heat. "You're the only one who could've taken it."

"When?"

"When *what*?"

"When would I have taken it?"

God, he's going to make me say it. I grit my teeth. "Perhaps when you had your hands down my dress last night."

"Oh, right." His grin widens to epic proportions. "*Then*."

"Just admit you have it so I know I'm not wasting my time."

"I'll tell you whether or not I have it..." He pauses. "If you tell me your name."

"You can't blackmail me," I hiss. "I'm already blackmailing you!"

"How's that?"

I throw my hands up. "Oh, I don't know, maybe the blockade I created in your entire computer system?"

"Oh, right." His grin is unwavering. "That."

"Yes, *that*," I snap, slightly offended that my efforts at sabotage are being brushed off with such little concern.

"I'm sure my tech guys will figure it out. Eventually."

I snort. "Have you *met* your tech guys?"

"Unfortunately, yes." He stares at me and some of the humor bleeds out of his eyes. His voice goes low. "Tell me your name."

My heartbeat picks up speed. "No."

"Fine. Then I can't confirm or deny that your flash drive is in my possession."

"*Jesus Christ*." I look up to the heavens, seeking divine intervention. "This is torture."

"This? No. This is a conversation between... friends."

"We aren't friends."

"You're right." He shakes his head. "We're so much more, snookums. Our connection... it's deeper than words."

"I loathe you."

"You love me."

I snort. "The day I love *you* will be the day the Red Sox and Yankees have a giant group hug on the mound at Fenway. Never gonna happen."

"Come on. Tell me your name. I'm dying over here."

"In that case, I'll just wait for you to keel over, step around your corpse, and ransack your office until I find my flash drive."

"Stone cold." He shakes his head. "I bet you don't want to tell me because it's something hideous. Like *Minerva*. Or *Beatrice*. Or *Millicent*."

"My name is not Millicent."

"Whatever you say, Millie."

I roll my eyes. "I'll take Millie over your other nicknames."

"Come on. You know *my* name," he points out. "It's only fair."

"Since when is anything in life fair?"

"Touché, snookums, touché."

"Call me that again and I'll kill you."

"Tell me your real name and I won't call you that anymore," he counters. "Well, I won't call you that *as much*. I don't want to make sweeping generalizations about my potential future pet name use—"

"Oh my fucking god! My name is Zoe. *ZOE!*" I shout, just to shut him up. "Are you happy?"

He takes another step in my direction and I suddenly — scarily — realize he's rather close. So close, in fact, that I can see those green flecks in his eyes up close and personal when they crinkle in a victorious smile and he murmurs, "Yes. I'm happy, Zoe."

Hearing my name from his lips causes a visceral reaction within me. My throat goes dry. My stomach somersaults. My nipples harden beneath my bra.

Shit.

He stares at me. "*Zoe.* Such a tiny name for such a big personality. It suits you."

I haul in a breath, hoping he doesn't notice that my thighs are suddenly clenched together.

God, what is it about this man? I want to strangle the life out of him... and fuck his brains out. All at the same time.

I've never experienced anything like it before.

"Can I have my flash drive now?" My voice is breathy.

"Must be something pretty important on it, if you're going to this much effort to get it back." His gaze flashes down to my mouth for a nanosecond. "I should probably ask you what's on it."

I pause. "Why don't you?"

"You aren't ready to tell me your secrets yet." His voice is steady. "One day you will be."

"I wouldn't hold my breath," I murmur.

"I can actually hold my breath for a pretty long time. Once, I swam a hundred meters underwater from—"

Before he can launch into another ridiculous stalling tactic, I reach up and flick him right between the eyes.

"Ow!" Flinching back, he rubs at his forehead. "What was that for?"

I raise my eyebrows.

He grins. "Right. No more tangents. You didn't have to resort to violence."

I plant my hands on my hips and crane my neck to glare directly into his eyes.

"Okay, okay. You win." He holds his hands up in surrender. "Fix the computers and I'll give you your damn flash drive."

"How do I know you're telling the truth?"

His eyes narrow fractionally. "I suppose you'll just have to trust me."

I press my lips together, displeased by that notion. "That's assuring, considering you're the one who stole it from me in the first place."

"How about we shake on it?" he asks, extending his hand into the space between us. When I make no move to return the handshake, he waggles his fingers wildly. "Oh, come on. Humor me."

I sigh and, without letting myself think too deeply about what I'm doing, grudgingly reach up to slide my palm against his. The feeling of his callused skin against the soft pads of my fingertips jolts through me like static shock. It takes all my self-control not to react as he squeezes my hand and pumps it slowly up and down, his eyes locked on mine.

After a few seconds of torture, I yank my hand from his warm grip and spin away. I practically sprint over to the computer sitting on his desk. I feel him following close at my heels and do my best to ignore his presence.

Just fix the computers, get your flash drive, and get out of here before you do something you regret. Like jump his bones.

To my great annoyance, when we reach the desk he pulls out the computer chair for me to sit. He may be an ass, but he's a gentlemanly ass.

"Milady," he says with a mocking bow.

I flip him off and drop into the leather seat, wiggling the mouse to activate the screen.

"What did you change my password to?" he asks, watching my fingers key in the phrase.

I smirk. "*Parker West Wets His Pants*. One word. All lowercase."

"And you accuse *me* of being immature?"

"You are immature."

"Just fix the damn network."

I ignore him and get to work. It only takes a few minutes — blasting a dam apart is a lot easier than building one from scratch — and when I tap out the final sequence of code, I look up to find Parker staring at me incredulously.

"What?"

"Who *are* you?" he mutters, something like awe in his tone.

"CIA? NSA? FBI? Some other three-lettered agency whose name is too classified for public consumption?"

I shrug, push back the chair, and rise to my feet. "I'm the girl who'll kick your ass if you don't fork over her flash drive."

He grimaces. "Here's the thing..."

I go still.

"...I don't exactly have it," he finishes.

"What?" The word cracks out like a whip. "We had a deal! Don't fuck with me, playboy, or so help me, I will hack into the FBI database, steal your fingerprints, frame you for murder, and send you to rot in prison for the rest of your days."

"That's rather elaborate," he says, chuckling. "You've really given my demise some thought."

"Would you like a cellmate named Diablo or Hulk?" I tilt my head. "Then again, it probably doesn't matter. I'm sure either of them will be happy to make you their new bitch."

"Chill, Piper Chapman. You didn't let me finish. I don't have the flash drive *with me*." He grins, totally unaffected by my death threats, and reaches out to grab my hand. I'm so stunned by the casual action, I don't even move to pull away until it's too late.

"Where is it?" I ask as he starts walking, tugging me behind him. His fingers are fully intertwined with mine — I feel the soothing stroke of his thumb against the back of my hand when I try to squirm loose.

"Patience, grasshopper." He holds the door to his office open for me to step through. "You'll see."

"You expect me to just go along with you without asking any questions?" I stare hard at the spot between his shoulder blades as he leads us down the hallway. "I'm not one of your stupid bimbos. I don't even know you!"

He slams to a halt so suddenly, I almost run straight into

him. When he turns his head to catch my gaze, there's something simmering at the back of his eyes. It looks like a challenge.

"You're afraid."

"Of *you*? Hate to break it to you, but no." My denial is swift. "I could kick your ass."

"Doubtful," he mutters. "But that's not what I was talking about."

I raise my eyebrows.

"You're afraid to be alone with me."

I snort. "Oh, *please*."

"You're afraid you won't be able to control yourself in my proximity."

"Get over yourself."

"You're afraid, my sweet snookums, that one more minute in my presence will make you fall head over heels—"

"If you stop talking right now and don't say another word until we get the flash drive, I'll go with you."

His lips slam shut and his eyes crinkle in an undeniable smile. He's clearly pleased with himself.

"Great." I try to tug my hand from his grip, but he's still holding tight. With a sigh of resignation, I give up and use our linked arms to gesture at the elevator. "Lead the way, manchild."

He squeezes my hand before we start walking.

CHAPTER 6

THE TIPPING POINT

I SHOULD'VE KNOWN Parker wouldn't be able to stay quiet for more than twenty-five seconds. We're barely inside the elevator when he starts up again.

"So, I know we're going to get the flash drive, but what are your thoughts about stopping for thai food on the way?"

My jaw clenches and I glare over at him. "Do you know the definition of *silence*? Also known as *quiet*? Noiseless? Mute?"

"Would you believe it — none of those sound familiar."

"I don't believe anything that comes out of your mouth."

He gasps dramatically and drops his voice low. "You wound me!"

"Fatally?" I ask hopefully.

"I'll recover." He grins and swings our interlocked hands in the space between us. "You know, you should be nicer to me."

"I don't do things that make me want to stab my eyes out." I bury a laugh beneath a bitchy tone. "As a general rule."

"You didn't want to stab my eyes out last night."

He moves closer.

I shuffle away as far as his arm will allow.

How many more floors until we reach the fucking ground and I can put some much-needed distance between us?

Parker's voice goes husky. "Last night... You wanted to do something entirely different with me."

I swallow and ignore the burst of warmth in my stomach. "Push you off a cliff?"

"No, not that." He takes a stride into my space.

I side-step until my hip presses against the elevator wall, refusing to look at him. "Run you down with my car?"

"Nope." He leans closer and his palm tightens against mine.

"Set your clothes on fire?"

"Well, maybe, but only because you want to see what I look like naked underneath them."

I whip my head around to snap something snarky at him and practically butt noses with the man. He's close — dangerously close — and his eyes are locked on my mouth. Whatever I was about to say evaporates in an instant.

"No snappy retort?" he murmurs.

I try to summon words, but nothing comes out. He's invaded all my senses like some kind of plague and completely disabled my ability to speak.

His face tilts closer. "No sassy comeback?"

I tell myself to move out of his path.

My feet don't seem to cooperate.

He leans in so close I know he's about to kiss me... And, god help me, I'm about to let him. I'm a statue, waiting for that last shred of distance to disintegrate, waiting to be consumed once more by the passion that filled my veins last night, the desire that still laces my blood like a deadly neurotoxin...

"No witty insult?" he whispers, his mouth practically on mine.

I lick my lips.

And then the elevator jolts to a stop.

There's a chime and a metallic hum as the doors slide open, snapping me out of my daze. I pull away from Parker so fast he loses his grip on my hand and is left clutching only air as I practically race from the elevator, whirling around to glare at him as soon as there's some distance between us.

"You!" I bark. "Stop doing that."

"Doing what?" he asks innocently, a heated look in his eyes.

"You know what." I'm breathing hard; it takes effort to get my pulse under control.

"I really don't," he says, following me into the lobby.

It's odd to see such a busy office hub totally empty — I guess he wasn't kidding about sending everyone home early. I have a hard time reconciling the fact that the joking, adorable — shit, I mean *obnoxious, annoying* — playboy is actually in charge of so many people. The idea of him as a *boss* is totally at odds with the Parker I've encountered thus far. He's so charming and lighthearted — fuck, I mean *infuriating* and *tiresome* — it's tough to keep in mind that he's one of the most influential businessmen in the city.

"I mean it." I point at him menacingly as he advances on me. "No more."

"No more what?" His grin widens as I backpedal through the deserted atrium toward the doors to the street. "No more riding in elevators? That's going to be inconvenient. My office is on the top floor."

"No more *trying to kiss me* in elevators," I correct, still backing away from him like he's in possession of a deadly weapon.

Who am I kidding?

His lips are *a deadly weapon.*

To my great shock, he freezes, adopts a contemplative look,

and gives a slow nod of agreement. "Fine. I won't do it anymore."

I'm so surprised he caved without a fight, I draw to a halt, leaving about ten feet of space between us. I pretend not to notice the faint flicker of disappointment in the pit of my stomach.

"Really?" My voice is skeptical.

"Sure." He shrugs. "I'm not unreasonable."

I stare at him warily for a long time and find no signs of insincerity in his expression.

"Okay," I say finally, accepting the remote possibility that he's being serious. "Can we go get this over with, then?"

"Of course," he says, his tone totally professional as he walks to my side and falls into step beside me. I glance at him from the corner of my eye, waiting for the other shoe to drop.

He's strangely silent all the way to the doors.

Wow. Maybe he was actually being serious for once...

"Plus, it's not some great sacrifice," he adds, chuckling as he holds the glass door open for me to walk through. "I can live without elevators. You didn't say I wasn't allowed to try and kiss you anywhere *else*."

There it is.

"Ugh!" An incredulous scream bursts from my mouth. "You are the most infuriating human I've ever met."

"Ever?"

"Ever."

"Thank you," he says, his voice somber as he trails me out onto the street. "I take that as a high compliment."

I groan.

He laughs and takes my hand again.

It's going to be a long day.

"WHERE ARE WE GOING?" I ask for the thirtieth time. We're walking along the waterfront, still hand in hand — much to my annoyance. The winter wind whips at my face and I find myself wishing I'd brought a heavier jacket. My ankles have blisters from the shitty heels and my shoulder is aching from the weight of my laptop bag. I push the strap higher and sigh heavily as my feet wobble on the uneven cobblestone path.

Parker squeezes my hand. "I did offer to carry it for you," he reminds me.

It's true; he did offer. Twice.

I objected because I felt like being obstinate at the time. But that was ten blocks ago, when we were still in the Financial District and I was feeling high and mighty. Now, all I'm feeling is cold and I have the beginnings of a cramp in my side from lugging the heavy bag all this way.

I sigh again.

If I ask him to carry it, he will in a heartbeat.

I won't though — I'd rather suffer in silence than give him the satisfaction of knowing he was right.

Ass face.

"Want a piggy back ride?" he offers, dropping my hand and doubling over like a parent offering their six-year-old a lift. His eyebrows waggle in an obnoxiously cute way.

I roll my eyes and brush past him.

His long-legged strides catch up to mine in seconds. "Not even a smile. Jeeze. This is my best material."

"*This* is your best material?" I ask skeptically.

"I take it back — my best material involves a lot less talking and a lot fewer clothes." He winks.

I make fake gagging noises.

He bumps his shoulder into mine in retaliation. "If I were a lesser man, I'd be offended that you don't laugh at any of my jokes."

"Playboy, you don't seem to be offended by anything I say or do, so—"

My words are cut off by the sound of my phone buzzing noisily in the side pocket of my bag. I pull it out, glance at the screen, and frown when I see it's Luca calling. I don't want to ignore his call — he's insufferably overprotective about my "safety" — but I also don't want to talk to him while Parker West's side is fused against mine like superglue.

Just putting Luke and Parker in the same sentence makes me uncomfortable. I can't imagine what would happen if they were ever in the same room — the cage-fighting UFC-hopeful and the cavalier billionaire, breathing the same air.

Nothing good, probably.

"I'll call him back later," I mutter absentmindedly to myself, hitting a button to send the call to voicemail. Glancing up, I find Parker staring at me.

"Boyfriend?" His tone is light, but his eyes are sharp.

I shove the phone back into the side pocket. "Wouldn't you like to know?"

"Yes," he says immediately. "That's why I asked."

I roll my eyes. "Can we focus? You were supposed to take me to your house. Not for a stroll along the marina. It's pretty fucking cold out here, in case you haven't noticed."

"Hey, anytime you want to come a little closer, just say the word. You won't hear me objecting, darling."

"How thoughtful," I snap sarcastically.

He smirks as we round a bend in the path and I suck in a breath.

Twinkling white lights and red bows adorn every tree in the park. There's a man in a Santa hat collecting money for a local charity — every few seconds the sharp peal of his bell rings out, followed by his voice.

Merry Christmas! Ho, ho, ho!

A family walks a few yards ahead of us, the little girl holding both her parents' hands. She looks up at them with pure love in her eyes as they pull her toward the nearby carousel, which is blaring holiday music from every speaker. All three of them are signing off-key.

It's the most wonderful time of the year...

I drop my eyes and try to breathe through the stinging ache inside my chest.

"Seriously," I ask Parker when I think my emotions are under control. My voice cracks a bit, despite my efforts. "Are we getting close?"

I don't know how much more of this I can take.

He nods. "Yep."

"And?"

"Which part of *yep* did you not comprehend?"

I shoot him a look. "Just tell me where we're going."

"Sorry, I left your copy of the day's itinerary at home."

"I don't need an itinerary. I need basic facts."

"You are really fucking terrible at being spontaneous, you know that?"

"Spontaneity is irresponsible and overrated."

"It's also something else."

I raise my brows. "Reckless?"

"*Fun.*" His eyes narrow. "You ever do anything just for fun, Zoe? Ever let those wheels in your head stop spinning for long enough to enjoy yourself?"

No.

I look away. "That's none of your business."

"Guess that's my answer."

I scowl. "I have fun."

"Oh, yeah?" he asks. "Doing what? Plotting world destruction? Overthrowing governments? Sabotaging corporate businessmen?"

"Maybe I find that stuff fun."

"Maybe." He pauses. "But I have a feeling you've never really had fun in your life."

I slam to a halt and, since our hands are still interlocked, he stops too. "You don't know anything about me! And, for your information, I have plenty of fun."

He looks skeptical.

"I..." I trail off. "I run. Three times a week. That's fun."

"Running isn't fun." Parker shakes his head. "It's a mandatory activity one partakes in so they can continue to eat copious amounts of tacos."

I smile, despite myself. "Well, I do other fun things." My mind spins as I try to think of something — anything — I do for pure enjoyment. "Like... I do graphic design on the side, sometimes."

"A useful skill," he says, looking unimpressed. "Not a *fun* one."

"Well..." I trail off again. I feel a humiliating blush creeping up onto my cheeks. "Just... Give me a minute, I'll think of something."

"Wow. You really don't do anything for fun." His voice is incredulous. "That's just sad, snookums. Pathetic."

"I do so!" I protest. "And I am not pathetic!"

"I didn't mean *you* were pathetic," he corrects softly, his eyes going gentle in a way that makes me nervous. "I meant it's a pathetic state of affairs that someone like you doesn't have a single moment of her day reserved for pure, unadulterated joy."

"Not all of us have time for hobbies, playboy." My voice may be a tiny bit defensive. Caustic, even.

He doesn't seem to notice. "We're about to make time."

"What?"

"Come on," he says, tugging me after him once more.

"Wait!" I drag my heels but it's no use. "Would you just *stop!* You promised you were taking me to the flash drive."

"I am," he calls over his shoulder, never breaking stride as he leads me off the path onto one of the marina docks jutting out over the water. "Two birds, one stone, darling."

I sigh. Fighting with him is exhausting — especially since he seems to enjoy it so much. Then again, I'd be lying if I said there isn't a certain amount of attraction — Shit, I mean *amusement* — in arguing with the man.

"Oh, cheer up." He slows his pace a bit until I've caught up. "Humor me with this one, tiny detour, and then you'll get your flash drive back and be rid of me forever, snookums."

I turn my head to glare at him.

"I mean *Zoe*," he corrects, grinning unabashedly. His cheeks are red from the cold. His eyes are gleaming again. He's annoyingly good-looking.

"Fine," I mutter because, honestly, it's easier to cave at this point.

He pumps a fist into the air, victorious, like he's Judd Freaking Nelson in *The Breakfast Club*.

"*One tiny detour*," I add in a threatening voice. "That's all I'm agreeing to."

"Of course," he agrees readily — *he's so full of shit* — before tugging my arm so I stumble into him. We collide, our interlocked hands trapped between our bodies, our sides pressed together as we walk along the dock.

It feels distinctly couple-esque.

Definitely crossing into PDA territory.

And yet... he's warm. Like a human space heater.

At least, that's the reason I give myself for staying close to him as we make our way down the docks. There are only a handful of boats in the harbor this time of year — it's too cold, even at the heated marina slips, for most to remain in the water.

We eventually come to a stop at the end of the row, where a massive sailboat is docked. Its hull is starkly white in contrast to the lapping gray waves. It must be at least sixty feet long.

I eye the vessel warily. "Please tell me we're not going deep sea fishing."

He laughs. "You can't go deep sea fishing on a sailboat."

"I wouldn't know," I murmur. "I've never been on one."

"A sailboat?"

"Any boat."

I don't do boats. I don't know how to swim. Hell, I've only been to the beach a handful of times in my entire life, and frankly I would've rather eaten a bucketful of sand than actually enter those shark-infested waters.

Um, hello? They filmed Jaws *in Martha's Vineyard for a reason.*

Still — my aversion to water sports is a rarity, in a place like this. Boston is surrounded on three sides by water. If you grow up here, there's a good chance you'll spend your summers tanning at a beachfront cottage on the Cape, sailing between the harbor islands, zipping around on jet skis, tubing or water-skiing off the back of a motorboat.

Assuming, of course, you have parents who are alive to do those things with you...

I feel Parker studying me, but I keep my eyes trained forward. I don't want to see the curiosity — or worse, the pity — in his stare.

"Well," he says, his voice softer than usual. "Let's do something about that."

I swallow hard, determined not to broadcast the idea of getting onboard that thing scares the shit out of me. I've always been in favor of keeping both feet planted firmly on the ground.

But... The more time I spend with him, the more I'm getting the feeling Parker lives in total contradiction to that belief. His is a changeable, mercurial existence — flying on wind currents, skimming over waves. He, down to a molecular level, challenges everything about the person I've worked to become and the values I've tried to instill.

I'm careful. Cautious. Methodical.

He's bold. Brash. Free.

It's anathema.

It's addicting.

"Spend one afternoon with me," he whispers. For once, his voice is totally stripped of that wisecracking sarcasm he's constantly using.

I look up at him, straight into his eyes, and feel my heart thudding too loud inside my veins. I don't want to ask the question — I don't want to reveal any insecurity to him — but I can't seem to stop the words from tumbling out.

"Why are you so intent on spending time with me?"

"I like you," he says softly, hazel eyes roaming my face like a detective searching a crime scene for clues. "Is that so hard to believe?"

"You don't know me," I counter.

He thinks about that for a minute. "Thing is, that's not really an excuse. Because no one ever really knows anybody. Some people spend their whole lives with someone, only to find out after they're gone that everything they *thought* they knew was total bullshit."

I open my mouth to argue, but nothing comes out. I'm stunned to find... I actually agree with him.

His hand tightens on mine. "I've traveled a lot. Been all over the world. Seen places of immense poverty and immense wealth. For a long time, I wanted to see *everything*, just so I could say I'd done it. Climbed Kilimanjaro, walked among the moai statues at Easter Island, dived on an underwater volcano in Indonesia, seen the dragons on Komodo. But at a certain point, you realize you'll never see it all before you die—" He pauses. "—or before some petite, pretty-as-hell hacker frames you for murder and sends you to prison with a cellmate named Nacho."

"Diablo," I correct, laughing.

He shrugs. "My point is, you can't see it all. You have to pick and choose. Prioritize the places you want to visit, the way you want to spend your limited days on this earth. Life's too damn short to waste it with people who don't make you happy, in places that don't excite you, doing things that don't challenge you." He looks at me — really looks — and I get the oddest sense that he actually *sees* me. This person who, by all accounts, is nothing more than a partying playboy, a tabloid prince, a paparazzi favorite... somehow understands me.

Me.

Zoe Bloom, who's never been anywhere outside the Greater Boston Area, never even *heard* of half the places he rattled off with such familiarity.

"Zoe," he says lowly, snapping my attention back to him. "You travel that much, you get pretty good at sorting out the things you'll enjoy exploring from the places that'll leave your soul empty." His hand gives mine a quick squeeze. "Only took one look at you to know which category you'd fall into."

I suck in a sharp breath.

Only took one look...

"So," he says, before I have time to recover.

"So?" I echo, ignoring the racing of my heart.

"Spend the day with me. Let me take you on an adventure. Let me show you what fun looks like."

I take a breath.

Here it is. The tipping point.

I've been putting him off all day, telling myself I don't like him, don't want to spend any more time with him than I have to, that lingering in his presence is due to the flash drive, nothing else. Certainly not because I might actually *like* him.

That would be crazy. Right?

His expression is easy-going as he waits for my answer, but his eyes never lose that intent edge as they stare into mine. There's something simmering at the back of his irises that I can't quite define — I don't know him well enough.

But I want to, a voice in my mind stuns me by replying. *I want to know this man — want to see what lies beneath that facade of trust-fund entitlement and joking nonchalance.*

"Okay, Parker," I whisper. His eyes flare when I say his name — his real name, not *playboy* or *man-child*. "One day. One adventure. You'd better make it count."

"Darling... Something to know about me?" He leans closer. "I *always* make it count."

CHAPTER 7

THE BAD IDEA

WE WALK along the side of the boat until we reach a narrow wooden gangway extending over the water. One end rests on the dock before us; the other sits on the rail of the sailboat. It looks far too thin to hold Parker's body weight, but he doesn't even blink as he strides out onto the ramp like he's done it a million times before. He probably *has* done it a million times before.

He pulls me along behind him and I have to bite down on my lip to keep from yelling, *Wait just a goddamned minute! We don't all live like you, jumping into things without ever glancing at the ground.*

He must feel my hand go tense in his, because his grip loosens to release it. He stops in the middle of the gangway and glances back at me.

"You okay?"

My eyes dart down to the thin piece of wood suspending him over the water. There is no fucking way I'm walking on that thing in heels. "Peachy."

His eyes narrow. "Oh really?"

"Yep." I swallow. "I just don't want to plummet into the harbor, seeing as it looks about as warm as the White Witch from the Narnia movies and I'd rather not freeze to death."

"Narnia?" His mouth twitches. "Really?"

I cross my arms over my chest. "Yes, really. Why do you sound so surprised?"

"I just wouldn't have pegged you as a kids' movie fan. I kind of figured you only watched documentaries. Black and white silent films. Foreign flicks with subtitles. Shit like that."

"Well, you're wrong." My voice lowers. "And for the record, Narnia is *not* just a kids' movie."

"Whoa." He holds his hands up in surrender. "Happy to be proven wrong. Let's have a movie night, you can educate me on all things Narnian."

"We're not having a movie night."

"Why not?"

"We've been through this. *Multiple* times. I'm not going out with you."

"Technically, I was suggesting we stay in."

"Still not happening."

"Uh huh." His tone is amused. As though he doesn't believe a word I'm saying.

Idiot.

I strive for composure. "Listen. You really need to wrap your mind around this..." I make sure to emphasize every word, so he can't possibly misinterpret my meaning. "After today, we're never going to see each other again."

He thinks about that for a nanosecond. "You're very persnickety."

"This is me being *nice*," I inform him. "If you give me my flash drive back, you won't have to experience my truly disagreeable side."

"But, Zoe... I *like* your disagreeable side."

I look skyward and ask the heavens, "Why me? What did I do to deserve this?"

"Oh, don't be so dramatic."

My gaze returns to Parker. "I hate you," I say tiredly.

"Well, can you hate me from onboard?" He bounces a bit and the whole gangplank shakes like a tambourine. "You're shivering. It's warmer inside."

My eyes widen. "Don't bounce like that, you'll snap the wood."

"That's what she said."

I glare.

He grins. "Sorry. Couldn't resist." He bounces again and the board jumps beneath his feet. "Come on. It's perfectly safe."

"Would you stop that?!" I exclaim, watching the plank rattle precariously. Another good bounce and he'll be in the water.

"Why?" he asks, bouncing again. The board slips closer to the edge of the rail. "You worried about me?"

"No." I swallow. My eyes are locked on his tread-less leather shoes — sliding again and again — and I feel my stomach clench. "You're going to fall into the fucking harbor and I am *not* jumping in after you, man-child."

"Aw." He laughs. "You're worried about my welfare. It's cute."

I make an incredulous sound. "Only you would interpret that statement as *cute*."

"How much longer are you going to delay getting on the boat?"

"At the very least until you stop bouncing like a six-year-old in an inflatable castle."

He stops, but his boyish grin never wavers. "There — I've

stopped. Now, come on, scaredy cat. You won't fall in. I've got you."

My chin jerks up. "I'm not scared."

I'm not scared of anything.

"Prove it," he says, that challenging look back in his eye.

I grit my teeth and reach down to pull off my heels, one by one. Without saying a word, I shove them into the space between us and wait for Parker to take them.

His mouth opens, a question poised on his lips.

"Shut up," I cut him off, still holding out the shoes. "And take the damn heels before I change my mind."

He's silent as his large hands close around the slingback straps and even manages not to say anything as I grudgingly pass over my laptop bag. He can't quite hide the way his lips twitch, though, as he watches me jumping from foot to foot on the freezing dock, trying to stay warm.

"Not a word," I mutter in a threatening tone.

His eyes glitter with amusement but he remains silent.

Forcing a deep breath into my lungs, I make myself take a step onto the gangway. And then another. And another.

I'm watching my feet, entirely focused on not toppling into the water, so I don't notice Parker hasn't moved from the middle of the board. I bump straight into his chest, the jolt of my body against his throwing me off balance. For a split second, I actually think I *am* going to fall into that icy water and drown.

"Whoa," he whispers, his hands coming up to steady my shoulders. I can feel the warmth of his strong palms radiating through my thin blazer. My pulse is pounding like a kick-drum as we stand suspended over the water, eyes locked. Invading each other's space. Breathing each other in.

"There. That wasn't too hard, was it?" he asks in a soft, serious tone.

I pause and, equally serious, whisper, "That's what she said."

He throws his head back and laughs. "I could kiss you, for that," he says when he's done chuckling.

"You'd better not," I warn. "Or I'll push you in the harbor and leave you to freeze. And I've heard hypothermia isn't exactly a bucket of laughs."

"You happen to know the cure for hypothermia?" he asks, grinning.

"I have a feeling I don't want to know."

"Best way to warm up — climb inside a sleeping bag naked with the nearest available human." His eyes crinkle. "That would be you, darling."

"I think I'd rather let you freeze. I've heard your appendages turn black and fall off." My eyes narrow. "Fingers. Toes. Your pen—"

"AH!" He cuts me off with a grimace. "Don't finish that sentence."

Muttering something under his breath about me being evil, he turns and walks onto the sailboat. I keep my eyes on his shoulder blades as I follow him onboard, and with the warmth of his presence radiating through my chest, I don't spare a single bit of attention to the icy water beneath my feet.

"HERE." Parker shoves a ball of fabric at me almost as soon as we step down into the cabin — it looks vaguely like the suit the Gorton's fish stick man wears, but it's white instead of bright yellow. I stare at it like a venomous animal.

"What is that?"

"Just put it on." He moves closer and bends until we're eye to eye. "It'll be huge on you, but at least it'll keep you warm."

"Warm for what?" I ask suspiciously.

"I seem to remember you agreeing to stick around for at least one spontaneous adventure. That does not include asking a thousand questions."

"I didn't agree. You browbeat me until I caved in."

"Semantics." He grins. "Just put it on."

"It's about two degrees out. You don't really expect me to go sailing with you, right? People don't sail in the winter."

"How would you know?"

"Parker."

"What's the worst that can happen?"

My eyes bug out. "Windburn. Frostbite. Drowning. Exposure... Need I go on?"

"Live a little."

"I *am* living. It's the imminent death-at-sea that I'm worried about."

He grins as he places a set of rubber boots in front of me. "These will be way too big on your tiny little feet, but they're all I have. I'll have to get a smaller pair for next time."

"Next time? What do you mean, *next time?*"

He stares at my bare feet and for the first moment in my life, I find myself wishing I was one of those girls who keeps her toes perfectly pedicured at all times. Against the hardwood, they look pale and, I must admit, very small.

"Though, I don't know if they make these in kids sizes," he murmurs to himself.

"My feet are not tiny! They're a size six. That's a perfectly normal size."

He doesn't respond. He's busy moving through the cabin — which, now that I've taken the time to look around, I must admit is really fucking amazing for a boat.

Actually — not even *for a boat*. It's just plain amazing.

The stairs leading down here are so steep they're practically a ladder — it reminds me of climbing into a treehouse or a fort of some kind – but that's to be expected, I suppose. The space is about the same length as my loft but a lot narrower, maybe fourteen or fifteen feet at its widest point.

I thought the inside might feel claustrophobic, but I couldn't have been more wrong. It's all warm wood and white cushions. Natural light pours in everywhere, despite the cloudy day — skylight hatches cover the ceiling, round portals dot the walls.

From what I can see, there's a full master suite at the front, a small bathroom to either side, and a decent sized kitchen complete with a compact refrigerator and a stove top. On the right, there's a table that seats six and a desk covered with navigational equipment. The left is dominated by a low-slung white couch with a plasma TV mounted on the wall across from it. Turning to glance behind me, I see there are at least two more bedrooms in the rear of the boat.

It may float, but it's nicer than most apartments I've been inside.

And, to my surprise, it looks *lived in*. There's an open camera bag sitting on a shelf — from here, I can see several different lenses and a giant Nikon sticking out the top. There's a dirty coffee mug in the sink. A bread on the counter. A sweater draped over the back of one chair. A well-worn pair of Sperry's sitting by the bedroom door.

"Do you live here?" I ask, recalling that I couldn't find an address for him during my cyber-stalking. A sailboat wouldn't be listed in the Registry of Deeds or the RMV database... and I hadn't thought to check any boating registries.

"Yes." His reply is muffled — he's leaning into the closet, searching for something.

"Every night?" I pester.

"Yes."

"All year?"

"No more questions. You're stalling," Parker calls, pulling another water-resistant suit from the closet. It looks bigger than the one in my hands, and it's red instead of white. "Put on your foulies."

"Foulies?" I ask.

"Foul-weather gear," he responds, bending to undo the laces of his leather shoes.

Ignoring his command, I lean against the table and glance around the boat again. "I didn't know a boat could look like this."

"She's not just a *boat*." He scoffs, clearly offended. "She's a Swan 60."

"She?" I ask, amused.

"*Folly*." I hear one of his shoes drop to the floor.

"You named your boat *Folly*? Isn't that asking for trouble?"

There's another thud as the second shoe drops. "I didn't name her — the guy who sold her to me was an idiot, and I haven't had time to rechristen her with something better. I've only had her a few months. I was crashing at my friend Nate's place for a while, when I first moved here. My last boat was too small to stay on long-term, so I had to upgrade."

Nate. He must mean Nathaniel Knox, the best private security specialist in the city... and his sister Phoebe's boyfriend. Our paths have never crossed directly, but I know Luca has done some work with Knox in the past – hired him for surveillance work when we needed help on a few tricky cases, that sort of thing. I wouldn't call them friends, but they certainly know each other.

"Needed my own space," Parker adds. "Nate's a great guy, but his place has about as much color as a monastery."

"And you decided a boat was better than a reasonable one-bedroom because...?"

He chuckles. "Darling, what about me screams *reasonable?*"

"Point taken," I mutter, studying the navigational equipment at the desk and wondering how hard it would be to hack his GPS software.

Maybe I can send him sailing straight into the Bermuda Triangle... Then I'll never have to deal with him again.

"Plus, I don't know how long I'll be sticking around. I only came to Boston to help with the family business. Once West-Tech is stable enough, I'll hire a new CEO and sail off into the sunset. Literally."

A pang of something unfamiliar jolts through me when he mentions leaving. I steadfastly ignore it.

"Anyway, to answer your original question," he continues. "All boats and cars are women. Why do you think men love them so much?"

I look back at him, a comment about patriarchal stereotypes poised on my lips, and feel my mouth go completely dry. He's stripped off his suit jacket and his tie, leaving him in a tight-fitting white button down. His bicep muscles strain against the fabric each time his deft fingers move to undo the buttons at his wrists.

He grins as he reaches for his belt buckle. "Should I put on some mood music? Usually when I do a strip-tease, I like a background beat..."

"Ah!" I turn away swiftly. The sound of pants hitting the floor makes heat rise to my cheeks. "Why are you stripping?"

"Well, I'm not going to wear a two-thousand-dollar suit sailing."

"You seriously think we're going sailing? In *December?*" I'm so incredulous, I forget that he's practically naked and spin my head back around... only to find my eyes glued to the finest bare chest I've ever seen in my life.

Holy. Fuck.

A thin smattering of blond hair — just the right amount — covers his chest and trails down his abs into the elastic waistline of his tight, black boxer briefs. His skin is somehow bronze from the sun, even though it's the middle of winter. And his muscles — dear god, those muscles. I don't know whether to focus on his thighs or his abs or the corded veins in his forearms. I don't even dare a glance at the bulge in his boxers.

"Put some clothes on," I squeak, tilting my head back and staring at the ceiling as I try to banish all thoughts of taught, tan skin.

He laughs and it sounds like sin. "Why? Is this bothering you?"

"No," I snap. "I just don't want to catch chlamydia."

"Ouch! That wasn't nice, snookums. Even for you."

"Maybe I'm not a nice person," I tell the ceiling.

He thinks about my words for a minute. "Nah, I can't buy that."

"You can buy whatever you want, with a trust fund like yours." I swallow when I hear him walking closer. "So long as you put some freaking clothes on."

"Hmmm... Been researching me, huh?"

Damn. The trust fund slip-up gave me away.

I squirm a little. "No."

"I bet you Facebook-stalked the shit out of me."

"I did no such thing."

"I bet you saved a picture of me as your desktop background." His voice is smug. And close. Like he's standing less than a foot away.

Look at the ceiling. Don't look at him.

"You're delusional."

"I bet you think you know everything there is to know about me, don't you, hacker girl?" His voice drops to a husky whisper. "I bet you think you've got me all figured out, like everything else in your orderly little life."

Ugh!

I know he's baiting me, but I can't take it anymore — I have to glare at him.

As soon as my eyes land on his body, I wish I'd resisted the urge.

His chest is at eye-level — and, fuck me, it's even better up close. I watch his Adam's apple bob in his throat and tell myself it would be very, very wrong to sleep with him.

Even though it would be the best sex of your life... a voice whispers from the back of my mind. *Even though there's a very large, comfortable-looking bed just a handful of feet away... Even though you're insanely attracted to him... at least, when he's not speaking...*

Zoe! Focus.

Shaking myself back into sanity, I look up at his face so I'll stop drooling over his body. It's not much of an improvement — his gorgeous eyes are locked on mine, burning with heat and humor. I feel my stomach flip as desire threads through me.

Shit. I really need to steer this conversation into safer waters.

I clear my throat. "Judging from the *very brief amount of time* I spent stalking you on the internet—"

He chuckles lowly. Damn, that's a sexy sound.

"—I would have to concur that there's really nothing interesting to know about you, Parker West." I pause and lean toward him. "Except, perhaps, your middle name."

His grin disappears.

Gotcha.

My nose wrinkles. "*Gilbert?* What were your parents thinking?"

"It's a family name," he says defensively.

"Gilbert? *Gil-bert.*" I repeat, dragging out the syllables.

"I take it back," he mutters, his expression dark. "You're not a nice person."

I laugh, victorious, and turn away. "Put some clothes on, playboy."

Remarkably, he doesn't say anything as I slip into the nearby bathroom. I make sure to lock the door behind me as I reach for the zipper of my skirt and prepare to pull the sailor suit on over my underwear.

Somehow, I have a feeling I'll be safer inside a rubber rain jacket and boots than in my flimsy blazer and bare feet.

As I step into the ridiculously large pants, tightening the elastic suspenders as much as possible, I don't let myself think about why I've agreed to spend the day with this man I barely know. I don't let myself dwell on the lingering attraction in my bloodstream. And I don't let myself answer my phone, which is buzzing for the third time in an hour, because I know Luca will just try to talk me out of going.

For once, I'm not going to think; I'm going to live.

For one, single afternoon, I'm going to leap before I look.

For a fleeting, fragmented instant of my regimented life... I'm going to be free.

I'M FLYING.

Head thrown back, arms outstretched, torso leaning into the wind.

The boat slices through the waves like a knife through

butter, living up to her name — a swan. Majestic, graceful, powerful.

Parker's at the wheel at the back of the boat. Or, at the *stern*, as he calls it. I'm as far from him as I can get, pressed up at the front — sorry, the *bow* — like Jack in *Titanic*.

"I'm king of the world!" I yell into the wind, the words snatched away as soon as they pass my lips. Mist from a wave sprays up and coats my face, frigid and salty. That doesn't stop me from grinning like an idiot. I've never felt anything like this before — this rush of pure adrenaline. Even when I finish a particularly difficult hack or a tricky piece of code... it can't compare to this.

When Parker first pulled out of the harbor, switched off the motor, and put up the sails, I was nervous. But as soon as we were out of the main channel, flanked by open water and an outcropping of rocky islands, passing hundred year-old light-houses and flocks of white shorebirds... as soon as I felt the wind on my face and the rush of speed in my veins...

The fear disappeared entirely.

I glance back and, craning my neck, can just make out the grin on his face.

It's obvious he loves this. Everything about it.

The speed, the salt, the icy water.

And I kind of love that he's sharing it with me.

I replay his words back on the docks, when he asked what I do for fun, and realize he was right. I don't have any hobbies. Not real ones, anyway. I don't do anything just for fun — just for *me*.

It's a pathetic state of affairs that someone like you doesn't have a single moment of her day reserved for pure, unadulterated joy.

He's right. About all of it.

Not that I'll ever admit that to his face. The man is arrogant enough already.

After a while, I make my way back to the cockpit where he's standing, two large hands wrapped around the wheel and a grin on his face.

"Admit it," he yells when I'm within earshot. I can barely hear him over the roar of the wind. "This is pretty fucking great."

I can't help smiling as I scream back at him. "It's okay!"

His eyes narrow. "Just okay?"

I shrug playfully. "I thought it'd be faster!"

He takes my words as a challenge. With one hand on the wheel, he turns the boat so the wind blasts straight across our side, filling the sails to capacity. The boat responds instantly — picking up speed in a burst, heeling over until I think for sure we'll flip and sink to the bottom of the Atlantic.

A squeak of surprise flies from my mouth and I grip the rail to keep upright.

"Hold on, darling," Parker calls, eyes flashing as we fly over the waves like a rocket. "I'm about to take you for the ride of your life."

IT'S dark by the time we pull back into the harbor — well past sunset. Parker docks the boat with expert precision under the low lights of the marina, and I do my best to help with coiling lines and tying us off to the slip, even though I have no idea what the hell I'm doing. He doesn't mock my efforts — he just smiles and shows me how to make a proper figure-eight knot around a cleat.

We don't say much of anything as we make our way down

into the cabin, but I can't wipe the dopey grin off my face. I haven't had such a fun afternoon in... god, I can't even remember. Even after I've collapsed, legs aching, onto the plush white couch, internally I'm still riding the waves of adrenaline that crash through my system.

Parker flips on a light and flops down on the other side of the couch, leaving a few inches between our bodies. I feel the weight of his gaze on my face and turn to narrow my eyes at him.

"What are you looking at?"

"You," he says simply, leaning his head back against the cushion. His blond hair sticks up in several directions, even messier than usual due to the salt and the wind. I'm sure mine is equally crazy; not even a bottle of industrial strength hairspray can save me at this point, let alone my flimsy elastic.

"Well, stop it," I say softly. "It's creepy."

"Don't care." He shakes his head. "I like that look on your face. I've never seen it before."

I raise my eyebrows. "What look?"

"Happy. Relaxed. Satisfied." He pauses and his eyes go lazy with heat. "Makes me wonder what other faces I could get you to make."

I elbow him sharply in the side. "Don't be gross."

"Oh, relax. It was just a joke." He laughs and rubs the spot I struck. "Mostly."

I roll my eyes. "We had such a fun afternoon. Do you have to ruin it?"

"So you admit it was fun?"

"Did I say fun? I meant dys*fun*ctional."

"Come on." His tone is teasing. "Admit it."

"Fine," I say grudgingly. "You were right. It didn't completely suck."

"I'm sorry, could you repeat that?" He cups one hand around his ear. "I'd like to make sure it's on the record."

"You were right," I grumble.

"Once more?"

"Don't push it."

Grinning, he reaches up to unzip his heavy jacket, revealing a thin white t-shirt underneath. Discarding the coat and sliding his suspenders off so they hang around his thighs, he stands and looks down at me. I try — and fail — not to drool at the sight of the red pants riding low on his hipbones.

Hey — I never said I was perfect.

"I'm grabbing a beer. You want one?" he asks, crossing over to the fridge. "Sorry, I don't have any girly shit here."

My nose wrinkles. "Girly shit?"

"Cosmos, martinis... Wait, a cosmo *is* a martini, right? But not all martinis are cosmos... kind of like all squares are rectangles but not all rectangles are squares?" He shakes his head. "Fuck, I don't know."

I snort. "Does your brain hurt from that analysis?"

"Yes, wise-ass, it does." He narrows his eyes at me. "Now tell me what you want to drink."

"Still waiting for you to tell me what you have."

"Ah. Right." An adorable hint of red creeps up his collar. He turns away quickly so I won't see the blush, pulling open the fridge to look inside. "I have... beer. Beer. And, last but not least... more beer."

"Such variety. How ever will I choose?"

He grabs two Harpoon IPAs, pops off their caps, and crosses back to hand one to me. The glass is cool against my fingers as they close around the neck. I feel Parker watching as I take a long draw from the mouth of the bottle.

"You're staring again," I point out as soon as I've swallowed.

He sips his beer and flops down next to me — a little closer, this time. Our arms brush every time I raise the bottle to my lips.

I don't move away; neither does he. We just sit there for a while, sipping our beers, and I'm shocked to find I'm totally comfortable in a way I rarely manage around most strangers.

It's not easy for me to let my walls down. I absolutely hate when people demand intimacy they haven't earned. But Parker doesn't demand anything. He doesn't ask invasive questions, or pester me. In fact, since the moment we met, he's just let me be... *me.*

"How are your legs?" he asks, a knowing look on his face.

My thighs press together of their own accord and my features twist into a grimace. Truthfully, they're killing me. Just staying vertical while we were out there on the water was a tougher workout than any of my morning jogs along the Charles.

Who knew sailing was such a contact sport?

"I have a feeling I'll be sore tomorrow," I murmur. Glancing at him from the corner of my eye, I see his lips are pressed together to contain a laugh.

"Don't make the joke, playboy."

He chuckles. "It was too easy, anyway."

I settle back against the cushions, trying to get comfortable despite the rain jacket still engulfing me from head to toe. The stiff waterproof material is warm and durable as all hell, but it's not exactly lounge-wear.

"Here." Parker grabs the large black sweater draped over a nearby chair and shoves it in my direction. "This will be more comfortable."

I stare at the sweater, then let my eyes drag up his tanned forearm all the way to his face. The soft glow of the overhead light leaves his features in shadow, but I can still make out the plushness of his lips, the strong slope of his jawline, the dark slash of his brows. His eyes are warm gold, like melted honey, and there's an expression on his face that makes my heart squeeze inside my chest.

Tenderness.

No one's ever looked at me quite like that, before. I've never gotten close enough to give them a chance.

"Thanks," I murmur, tearing my eyes from his as my fingers close around the fabric. "Now, turn around so I can change."

He does, without a word.

In silence, I unzip the bulky jacket as fast as possible and slide the sweater over my head. It drapes well past mid-thigh, covering practically everything, so I shimmy out of the rain pants as well. Tugging at the hem to make sure none of my girly bits are exposed, I plant my hands on my hips and take a breath.

"All good," I say. "You can look, now."

When he turns back to face me, his eyes drop straight to my bare legs and hold there. In the space of a single heartbeat, I watch his jaw clench, see his eyes turn smoldering, recognize the way his posture changes from casual to carnal. I'm suddenly extremely aware that despite all his jokes and light-hearted comments... he's very much a man.

An attractive, straight-up *appetizing* man, who's looking at me with such heat, there's no logical reason I haven't melted into a pool of hormones at his feet.

His gaze flashes up to lock on mine. I see his intent a split second before it turns to action.

"Don't," I whisper.

He takes a step toward me anyway.

"We shouldn't," I say, not moving.

He prowls closer.

"No good can come of this," I point out.

His hands hit my shoulders and he hauls me into his chest.

"This is a bad idea," I breathe against his lips.

"This is a fucking great idea," he mutters.

And then I can't say anything else, can't even think of anything else, because his mouth is on mine.

CHAPTER 8

THE REGRET

THERE'S A LOUD BANG, like a door being kicked in, but I barely hear it. I'm buried in sensation — big hands in my hair, on my sides, beneath my shirt. Lips against my neck, my collarbone, the hollow behind my ear. Weight between my hips, pressing me into the cushions.

Parker's fingers have found the hem of the sweater and started to make their way up my ribs. Mine are wrapped around his neck as he hovers above me, my lips tasting the sea salt on his skin as they move down the broad column of his throat.

I'm not sure if we've been kissing seconds or minutes. All I know is, it's not nearly enough when we're interrupted.

"What the fuck is this?" a deadly voice growls. "Get off her!"

Parker's weight vanishes and I hear a thud, followed by a grunt of pain. My eyes fly open and I'm stunned to see Luca towering over me like a storm cloud. His dark auburn hair is disheveled, his light blue eyes furious.

"Are you okay?"

I nod, stunned silent by his sudden appearance.

He doesn't wait for me to say anything. He spins, strides across the room, and hauls a dazed-looking Parker to his feet. Before he can even find his footing, Luca's got Parker pinned against the wall with one arm pressed tight across his neck, compressing his windpipe until he can barely breathe.

"What the fuck do you think you were doing?" he hisses into Parker's face. His tone is downright scary. He looks like he's about to murder someone.

And by *someone* I mean a certain wise-cracking playboy who just had his tongue in my mouth.

"Luke," I call, springing to my feet. "Luke, stop!"

It's like he doesn't even hear me. He's entered full-on rage mode.

I've only seen him like this once before — the afternoon he saved me from those guys behind the group home. Parker would be wise to keep his mouth shut and let me deal with it before Luca's anger boils over.

But, of course, this is Parker we're talking about. When has he ever kept his mouth shut?

"Well?" Luca hisses, slamming Parker harder against the wall. "Do I have to shove my foot up your ass?"

"Buy me a drink before we talk ass-play, baby," Parker wheezes, defiant despite the fact that a savage is strangling the life out of him.

Ho boy.

The hand at Luca's side curls into a fist. Before he can lift it, I'm there — holding on for dear life to keep him from killing Parker.

"Luca! Luca, listen to me!" I yank harder on his arm; he doesn't move a single inch. I'm an ant trying to shift a mountain. "He wasn't hurting me. Okay? He was... we were..." I fidget as I search for the right words. My voice drops lower. "He wasn't hurting me, Luke."

Luca and I never talk about this shit. I've always tiptoed around the subject of men in my life, just as he's never shared details of the fan-girl hoes who line the front rows at his fights, their fake boobs spilling out of too-tight t-shirts. We don't talk about sex. Relationships. None of that shit.

Until now, apparently.

I see his posture change slightly as he processes my words. As the scenario in his head — me being assaulted — changes to something entirely different.

He shifts his arm so Parker can breathe, but doesn't move away. A muscle jumps in his cheek. "This guy? Really, Zoe?"

"Luca," I repeat softly. "Let him go."

He does, a disgusted huff of air blasting from his lips as he pushes away from the wall and strides toward the stairs, grabbing my hand and bringing me along with him. Hearing Parker drag a ragged breath into his lungs, I glance back to see if he's all right.

His eyes meet mine; there's a dark look in their depths. I get the sense he's about a second away from tackling Luca to the ground – which will not end well for anyone involved.

Great. I'm standing between two barrels of gasoline, holding a match.

With a rough yank, I pull out of Luca's hold before he can drag me up the ladder out of the cabin. He stops and looks down at me, features contorted into a stony mask, and I use both hands to shove his chest. *Hard.*

"What the hell was that, Luca?" I snap.

"That was me looking out for you, like I always do."

"I didn't ask you to look out for me!"

"That's kind of the point of looking out for someone — they

shouldn't have to ask. Ever." He doesn't sound remotely apologetic.

I try to remain calm. "What possible reason could you have for thinking I needed looking after at this exact moment in time?"

"You weren't answering your phone."

"So?"

"You always answer."

"Okay, sorry, apparently I'm not a perfect person!" I throw my hands up. "That doesn't give you an excuse to barge in here like some kind of psychopath and assault my..." I swallow. "My friend."

Parker snorts at my word choice. I ignore him.

"What do you even know about this guy?" Luca asks.

"More than you, I'm sure!" I hiss. "I don't need you to protect me anymore. I'm a grown woman."

His light blue eyes drop to scan my body, stopping on my bare legs. "I can see that."

I flinch. He's never said *anything* like that to me before.

"Just get out of here, Luca." I turn and walk back toward Parker, making it clear where I stand in this whole ridiculous show of masculine bravado. "I appreciate your concern, but it's neither wanted or needed here."

"I'm not leaving without you," he says flatly.

I stop halfway between the men and roll my eyes so hard I'm surprised they don't get lodged up inside my skull. "How'd you even find me?"

"Went to your place and used that *Find My iPhone* app on your computer."

"That is a total invasion of privacy!" My voice is incredulous. "You had no right to do that."

"Yeah, well, I was pretty sure I was going to find your

corpse rotting at the bottom of the harbor, so I don't really give fuck about invading your privacy."

My anger thaws a bit, at that. "I get it. You were worried. But now that you can see I'm totally fine, not remotely in danger, certainly not fish food in the marina... Can you please get the fuck out of here?"

He doesn't move an inch except to cross his arms over his chest. "Thought we didn't have secrets?"

"We don't," I say immediately. "But we aren't kids anymore, Luke. And, frankly... who I choose to spend my time with is none your business."

The muscle jumps in his cheek when he glances at Parker. "Thought, after that shit last spring, you were done with this family, Zoe. Why'd you lie?"

Fuck.

Parker doesn't know about last April, when I helped his sister get away from the MacDonough mob. I'd never intended for him to know. Never thought Phoebe would even come up in conversation, considering I planned to avoid him for the rest of eternity after today.

I dart a glance at Parker and see his eyes have gone intent.

"Last year?" he grumbles, his stare never shifting from mine. "What's he talking about, Zoe?"

"Nothing," I say quickly.

Luca snorts. "For fuck's sake, he doesn't even know? Jesus, Zoe. I don't know what the hell kind of game you're playing, but we need to leave."

My eyes fly back to my oldest friend. "This isn't the street. You don't make the rules anymore, Luke."

"I do if it means protecting you from scumbags like this." He jerks his chin at Parker. "Don't be stupid, Zoe."

I open my mouth to snap back, but Parker beats me to it.

"I've been pretty tolerant. Let you insult me, push me around in my own home. But you ever speak like that to Zoe again in front of me, you'll regret it," he warns in a deadly voice. "*Sorely.*"

"You don't even know her," Luca growls. "You think, because she let you fuck her, that you mean anything? You're *nothing.*"

Oh, shit.

Parker's control snaps. He lunges at Luca, fist swinging out like lightning. I'm shocked to see him clip Luke across the chin — most people never manage to hit him. He's too damn fast.

In a frozen moment, I see a small trickle of blood leak from the corner of Luca's mouth. His tongue darts out to taste it and I watch, terrified, as a familiar look creeps into his eyes. It's the look he gets before every match.

Excitement. Anger. Bloodlust.

He lives for this — the fight. The rush.

And he's great at it, if the three semi-pro heavyweight titles he's got under his belt say anything about his skill level. Parker may be tall and strong, but Luca's a professional. No way in hell will this be a fair fight.

"Didn't think you had it in you," Luca mutters, wiping the blood from his lip with the back of one hand. He's eyeing Parker like a snake about to strike. "This is going to be more fun than I thought."

"Luca, don't!" I rush to stand between them, holding my arms out to either side against their chests — as though my petite frame could possibly keep them apart. "This is insane!"

Parker's chest presses hard into my right hand; Luca's weight leans into my left. Combustion is imminent.

"I hope you're not expecting your security deposit back," Luca growls at Parker, jerking his hand around the beautifully furnished yacht. "This place won't look the same after I toss you through that table."

"You going to talk me to death or fight me?" Parker's grin has a decidedly dark edge. "I've had first dates with less conversation."

"Enough!" My head whips from one man to the other. "You want to kill each other, that's just fine. But don't do it on my account. Frankly, seeing this idiocy, I want nothing to do with either of you."

The pressure lessens slightly on both hands as they absorb my words, but neither backs away.

Testosterone-fueled imbeciles, the both of them.

"Luca, you so much as touch him and I will never speak to you again," I whisper hotly, zeroing in on his chiseled features. He's handsome, but not in an open, obvious way. His mouth is too severe. His nose has been broken one too many times and never reset properly. There's too much darkness in his light eyes.

Still — that doesn't deter most women from flinging themselves at him.

His eyes drop down and scan my face. He sees how serious I am — I can tell, because the weight against my left hand finally disappears as he steps back. He looks about as happy as a dad at a Taylor Swift concert, but at least he's in control of his rage.

"We'll talk later." His words are clipped — he wants to say more but he's holding back. For now. He shoots Parker one last withering look before turning and climbing up the ladder. Just before he disappears into the dark, I hear a gruff order.

"And keep your damn phone on."

I roll my eyes and feel my lips tug into an involuntary smile. Luca's a pain in the ass, but he's *my* pain in the ass.

The smile falters when I turn to face Parker and see the look on his face.

Gone is the carefree man I spent the afternoon with at sea.

He looks almost somber — eyes narrowed, mouth set sternly, jaw clenched. His hands are fisted at his sides.

"I'm sorry about Luca," I murmur. "I had no idea he was going to show up like that."

He doesn't reply.

I take a step toward him and, for once, he's the one stepping back from me. A pang of something that feels a lot like regret lances through me.

"Parker..." My voice cracks.

His eyes flare. "Don't."

I swallow and watch as he crosses over to the desk, pulls open a drawer, and extracts my flash drive. I'd completely forgotten about it — completely forgotten my reason for coming here in the first place. Being in Parker's presence swept me away entirely, until all thoughts of Luca's vendettas and memories of a blood-soaked Christmas eve slipped out of my mind. Until it was just him and me, together in the moment.

That, in itself, is the most precious gift I've ever received.

It's so quiet you can hear the faint whoosh of waves against the hull outside as he stops in front of me, leaving a careful distance, and offers me the USB.

"Take it," he rasps, hand extended. "It's why you came here, isn't it? The whole reason you're with me."

I don't move.

"Zoe." His hand shakes a bit. "Take the damn flash drive."

"No."

"No?" His voice goes down an octave. "You've been trying to get me to give it to you all fucking day. Now, when I offer it to you, you turn me down. What the fuck kind of logic is that?"

He's angry. Furious, even.

The emotion startles me; it's so contrary to everything I've seen from him before. As I study the expression on his features,

I realize this man is not a volcano, like Luca — dangerous from a distance, a clear threat to everyone in a ten-mile radius.

Parker is a hot spring, a geyser buried beneath a meadow. The kind that erupts through cracks you don't even see until you're standing over them, boiling up with the heat of it, too distracted by its beauty to notice its lethality.

"Just let me explain—"

"Explain?" He barks out a laugh. "Fine. Let's start with the fact that your boyfriend is *Blaze Fucking Buchanan*, the best underground fighter in the city, and then we can discuss whatever the fuck he meant when he said he thought you were done with my family after last spring." His jaw ticks. "Pretty weird, considering I was under the impression we didn't know each other until the Lancaster party."

I'm surprised to hear Luca's nickname come out of his mouth — *Blaze*, inspired by his deep auburn hair and the all-consuming way he fights, like wildfire — but I shouldn't be. Nearly every man in the northeastern United States knows who he is, watches his fights, follows his career.

"You knew who he was and you were still going to fight him?" I ask, my voice incredulous. Only a mad man would fight Luca willingly.

Tired of holding out the drive, Parker sets it on the table beside me and averts his eyes. "Does it matter?"

Yes, I think. *Yes, it matters that you knew you'd get the shit kicked out of you, but you were ready to defend my honor anyway.*

I take a breath, trying to stay calm. He glances back at me and, for a split second, I see the hurt in his eyes. It's gone in a flash, buried back behind a hazel shield of frustration.

"You know, it's funny..." His arms cross over his chest. "I don't hear you explaining."

"He's not my boyfriend." My voice is soft. "He's more like... my brother."

Parker shakes his head, as if he doesn't believe me. "Sure. Whatever you say."

"I'm telling you the truth."

"Zoe, that man is in love with you." Parker runs a hand through his hair. "He may not like it, hell, he may not even know it — but he's in love with you."

"That's not true."

"Fine. Whatever." He shakes his head. "But the other shit? You care to share how you know me? Because I'm pretty sure I asked you, point blank, if we'd ever met before, and you lied to my face."

"I didn't lie." My chest feels tight. "I just... left some things out."

"Such as?"

I *could* tell him — about Phoebe, about the mob, about the dank basement I found her in and how she sprinted beside me in her damn stilettos as we fled under the cover of darkness. How she'd called me her fairy godmother, nicknamed me *Tinkerbell,* and thanked me for saving her life when I left her alone on a strange street corner, with nothing but a burner phone.

Heroic? Not exactly.

I'm no hero.

At my core, I'm just a shitty person with some computer skills.

Sure, Phoebe thanked me in the moment... but she probably hates me, now that she's had a few months to reflect on what happened. I may've gotten her out of that basement, but then I abandoned her. Walked away. I might as well have left her for dead on that corner.

I don't want Parker to look at me like I'm a monster. I

don't want him to see that I'm not the girl he thinks I am. And even if by some chance he doesn't think I'm terrible, telling him about my connection to Phoebe will just make this thing between us — whatever it is — even more complicated.

And then, a small voice whispers. *When he sails his giant yacht off into the sunset in a few days or weeks or months... you'll still be here. Alone. Empty. And, quite possibly, broken-hearted.*

No. I can't tell him. Can't let him in any more than I've already done. Look what's happened in the span of a single afternoon — he's gotten me to strip out of more than just my clothes. He's stripped away my defenses. Obliterated every barrier I've built around my heart.

So... a week with him? A month? A year?

He'll take everything.

And I've spent far too long building myself up from nothing to let a guy walk into my life and reduce me back to rubble.

"Zoe?" Parker prompts, a pleading note in his voice.

I stay silent.

It's for the best, I assure myself. *This pain, right now, is nothing compared to what you'll feel if you let yourself fall in love with this man.*

Parker scoffs. "Know what, Zoe? Keep your secrets. Keep your walls up." He shoots me a look that's so disappointed, it breaks my heart. "I just hope you know, this life you're living — it's not worth shit if you live it alone. You call me a playboy, a man-child... maybe that's true. But at least I *live*. At least I grab life by the throat and take it for all it's worth. Can you say the same?"

He doesn't wait for me to answer; he just turns and walks toward his bedroom.

"You got what you wanted," he calls over one shoulder. "You can see yourself out."

The sound of his door clicking closed cuts through me like a knife wound to the stomach. Ignoring the tears filling my eyes, I reach out and grab the flash drive off the table. Collecting my bag from the couch, I'm up the ladder and off the boat before I have a chance to do something stupid.

Like follow him into his bedroom and beg him to change his mind about me.

I SPEND a week moping around my apartment, tying up loose ends on a few freelance programming (read: *hacking*) jobs I've been working on the side for cash. Luca calls several times; I never answer.

Parker doesn't call.

He doesn't have my number, so it's not like he could even if he wanted to.

That's what I tell myself, anyway.

Still, there's an ache of disappointment as I walk around my loft, staring out the windows at the snowflakes drifting down and feeling even emptier than usual.

When we were teenagers, still living at the group home some nights, sleeping in Luca's car others, we often spent holidays at a local church. They'd always give out candy on Easter and Halloween and Christmas but I never ate any. At first, Luca just shoved my portion in his mouth without question, happy to have double. Eventually, though, he asked me why never ate my share.

I don't want to know what I'm missing, I always told him. *I don't want to taste something once, see how good it is, and then spend the rest of my life wishing I could have it again. I'd rather stay in the dark.*

That's how it feels with Parker.

He's chocolate, the most delectable candy, the most forbidden of desserts. And once I sampled him — not just kissed him, not just felt his hands on my skin... but experienced the way he made me *feel*, the freedom he inspired, the reckless hope he instilled inside my heart in the space of a single afternoon...

I crave more.

And it damn near kills me to know I'll never get it.

I bury myself in work, praying the Lancaster Consolidated case will distract me from memories of his hot mouth, his big, callused hands, his thick, messy hair. It doesn't — not remotely. But at least I have something to do instead of mope and eat all the chocolate peanut butter cups in my pantry.

After all the damn work I went through to get it back, it chafes to find there's almost nothing of value on the flash drive. The only files of potential use are so heavily encrypted, even I can't decode them. And that's saying something.

Luca will be pissed — that means we have to get outside help. Probably from Knox Investigations or one of the other private firms in the city with a server big enough to run an algorithm program that can filter through the millions of possible password combinations until it finds the correct one to unlock the documents. My laptop's small brain isn't quite up to that challenge.

The only silver lining from my night spent as Cindy the cater-waiter is the fact that I managed to install my virus into the LC network before I got caught. The Clover. With each day that passes, the virus creeps a little further into their network, embeds itself a little deeper in the innermost workings of their computers.

Reaching out in four directions, it then cloaks itself to blend in with the rest of their files — one tiny green blade, indiscernible from the zillion others in the field. My little emerald Trojan Horse.

It's slow — painstakingly so — but I designed it that way on purpose. Any faster, a breach would be detected and I'd be up shit's creek without a paddle. So, I sit on my hands and wait. And wait, and wait, until I'm practically pulling my hair out by the roots.

Day by day, my access increases. File by file, folder by folder, terminal by terminal, from the lower-level office where I planted my bug all the way up to Lancaster's corner office. And the best part? It's not just the documents saved to their hard drives.

With my virus, I can see emails. Inter-office chat windows.

Live communications between Lancaster and whoever he's doing business with.

Almost a week after we went sailing, I'm eating peanut butter cups while I scroll rapid-fire through LC emails so boring they make episodes of *Seventh Heaven* seem dramatic, searching for *anything* that'll help prove financial misconduct, when my eyes catch on something interesting.

An email from Robert Lancaster to his Head of Security.

Linus,

The workers from the Lynn factory are striking outside the corporate offices tomorrow. Press will be all over it. Make sure there's adequate coverage for staff to enter and exit, but don't interfere. They can chant until they lose their voices, wave their little picket signs until their arms fall off; it won't change my mind. I'm not re-opening.

That said, did you handle the clean-up we discussed at the factory site?

Did the final transfer go smoothly with Birkin?

Let me know. The last thing we need is to give the fuckers grounds for a class action suit.

Bert

Okay, first of all, what self-respecting CEO goes by *Bert*? That's just wrong. And secondly, besides the fact that he's a total dick-wad for not giving a crap about his former employees, there's clearly something else going on with the Lynn factory closing down. Something more than just budget cuts or moving jobs overseas to save some company cash.

"I'm going to find out exactly what," I mutter, hitting a button to print out a copy of his email. "And use it to pin you to the wall, *Bert*."

CHAPTER 9

THE DISCOVERY

NEW ENGLAND IS KNOWN for many things — big lobsters, good clam chowder, bad accents, great movies, old Pilgrims, fantastic sports teams, terrible drivers.

It is not, however, known for its predictable weather.

So, when I step off the commuter rail in downtown Lynn the next morning and find it's nearly sixty-five degrees only a handful of days before Christmas, I'm pleasantly surprised but certainly not shocked.

I strip off my bulky sweater and tuck it into my bag as I make my way across a busy four-lane highway toward the waterfront. This area could be — *should be* — beautiful. A long stretch of coastline just north of Boston, Lynn abuts some of the wealthiest towns in the entire state. And yet, corporate greed and shortsighted planning turned paradise into parking lots and factories. There are no boardwalks or beaches, here. Instead, the waterfront is jammed with row after row of industrial warehouses, used car lots, tattoo parlors, fast food joints, and bowling alleys.

Lynn, Lynn, city of sin, you'll never get out the way you came in.

Everyone raised around here knows the anthem. And it's true — not just when it comes to driving routes, either. Living here changes people. Makes them a little more bleary-eyed when they look at the world and its possibilities. I don't know if it's the gangs or the drugs or the total lack of aesthetics, but the entire town is corroding like a metal lawn chair left out in the rain.

It doesn't surprise me in the least to know one of the factories here belongs to Richard Lancaster. He's exactly the type to take something beautiful and turn it to trash, just for the sake of lining his own pockets.

I cut down a side street, leaving behind the steady rush of commuters, and find myself abruptly alone. One block from the highway, there are no signs of life at all besides the occasional seagull waddling on webbed feet across the cracked asphalt. I've never been here before, so I'm not sure exactly where I'm headed, but I walk steadily toward the water, knowing I'll bump into the factory eventually.

Out of nowhere, I feel a chill go up my spine — a razor-edged awareness that makes all the hairs on the back of my neck stand erect as soldiers preparing for battle. There's no sound, no movement, nothing to indicate I'm being followed... but I can't help myself from turning around to check anyway. My breathing resumes when I see there's nothing trailing me except my shadow, elongated in the afternoon light.

You're being ridiculous, Zoe. Who would bother to follow you all the way out here?

I shake off the strange sensation and keep going. A few minutes later, when I pass a sleeping homeless man curled on a concrete bench, I reach silently into my bag, so as not to disturb him, pull out all the bills in my wallet and shove them into his cup. I don't bother to count them. He needs groceries more than I do this week.

I know from experience.

I'm breathing a bit heavier by the time I reach the water, warm from my quick-paced walk and the unusual weather. Craning my neck, I take in the sight of the closed LC factory, sitting like an aging beauty queen on the edge of the sound, her paint chipping in the elements, her front walkway riddled with trash. Most of the windows are boarded up. The parking lot is empty. It looks like it's been closed far longer than three weeks.

I turn in a circle, surveying the entire property. There's just... *nothing* here. The only movement is a plastic bag blowing in the wind, the only sound the faint whisper of waves crashing against nearby rocks. It looks desolate. Almost post-apocalyptic.

If the zombie apocalypse breaks out tomorrow, this will be ground fucking zero.

I try the front door and find — surprise, surprise — it's bolted firmly. And it's solid metal; there's no way I'm getting in. A quick walk around the perimeter leads me past the rocky water's edge, where garbage floats next to dead birds in the polluted water. All the windows I pass by are either too high to climb through or so thoroughly boarded up, I'd need a crow-bar to gain access.

I've almost given up hope of getting inside when I reach the litter-filled alley that runs along the back of the factory. I step around a discarded air conditioning unit, squeeze by a dumpster, and finally find a small back entrance, probably an emergency exit of some kind. It's still half-boarded over, but some of the plywood panels have been yanked off. Even from ten feet away, I can see the metal lock was wrenched open with brute force, probably by squatters or graffiti artists looking for a few blank walls to vandalize.

Before I can talk myself out of it — or pay attention to the small voice in the back of my mind whispering, *"Um, maybe you should've forgiven Luca in time to bring him on this exploration, you idiot"* — I steady my shoulders, push the groaning metal door wide enough to pass through, and slip inside the building.

It's dark.

Not just dark — pitch black.

I blink my eyes for at least thirty seconds, hoping like hell they'll adjust. They don't. Frustrated, I finally just yank out my phone and turn on the flashlight app. The first thing the beam of light catches is a huge rat, scurrying across the floor about ten feet away. It takes all my self-control not to curse at the top of my voice, but I'm not stupid enough to draw that much attention to myself. Not when I don't know what else is lurking in the dark.

I don't scare easily. With a past like mine, I suppose that's a given. But being in places with no visibility, no way of knowing who else is breathing your air, watching you move... that's one of the most terrifying things imaginable.

You never know who you'll meet inside buildings like this. I learned early, in my time on the streets, abandoned places don't stay that way for long. All manner of people find their way in — and they aren't always friendly.

Rubbing the goose bumps from my arms, I force myself to walk further into the factory. Honestly, I don't even know what I'm looking for. The deeper I get into the space, the more empty rooms I pass through, the more I begin to feel like I'm running a fool's errand.

They made jet engines, here. Perfected aircraft systems for military and private use. Most of the equipment is gone, of course, sold at auction to other companies or shipped to another of Lancaster's workshops in some distant part of the country.

All that remains is the faint scent of oil, hanging in the air like a mechanic's perfume.

There's a fine layer of dust along the concrete floors — if I shine my narrow beam of light behind me, I can see my footprints like tracks through snow. No one else has been here in a while.

The thought bolsters me enough to keep going.

I pass through a room scattered with empty spray paint cans, the white walls tagged with various gang signs and puffy-lettered slogans whose meanings I can never seem to discern. The teens left their mark and vanished, nothing but cigarette butts and empty beer cans as evidence of their presence.

I'm about ready to give up this crazy crusade and turn back when I cross through a wide archway and find the main assembly line. It's a cavernous room with staggeringly high ceilings — probably where they built the engines — and my pathetic little light barely illuminates the space around me. The dark seems to encroach from all sides. Shadows slither along the walls, the silence pushes back at me like a weight against my eardrums.

I've only made it a few steps inside when I spot them. Footprints, disturbing the dust coating the floor. I stifle a gasp as I make out the distinct shape of a man's boots, their treads perfectly in tact. They look crisp, fresh — no dust dulling their edges or filling in their borders. It's clear they're recent.

Someone's in here.

The panicked thought bursts into my mind without warning. I bite my lip and hold my breath, trying to regulate my racing heart. It's no use panicking. If someone really *is* in here with me, they've already seen my flashlight. The damage is done.

You used to be a badass, Zoe Bloom. What happened?

Swallowing hard, I grip the phone tighter in my suddenly

clammy fist and start to follow the boot prints across the room. They're concentrated almost entirely in one area, around a wall of pipes on the far side of the room.

If I had to wager a guess — which I wouldn't because I'm not a gambler — I'd say it's some kind of cooling unit. Dealing with superheated steel, molding engine parts, they'd sure as hell need one in here, somewhere.

The room doesn't look vandalized, like the graffitied space I was in earlier. In fact, the pipes are shiny silver steel, so bright they reflect my flashlight beams back at me when I approach. It's the oddest thing... they look almost *new* compared to everything else in the crumbling factory.

In the email Lancaster sent to Linus, his Head of Security, he talked about *clean up*. I don't know why but I get the unshakeable feeling that this, right here, is exactly what he was talking about.

I just don't know what any of it *means*. Which really pisses me off.

Following the footprints, I see they lead from the pipes to a window. I peer through the foggy glass and make out the shape of a fire escape in the alley outside, its metal corroded with rust, its ladder crumbling from disuse. Just looking at it inspires the need for a tetanus shot.

With a careful sweep of my flashlight, I turn back to glare at the gleaming pipes, willing the answers I'm seeking to materialize like a genie from a bottle.

Think, Zoe. What the hell is so special about these fucking pipes?

I'm staring at a puzzle, holding the final piece in my hand, but no matter how long I look I can't quite seem to figure out where the hell it goes.

My nonexistent knowledge of industrial factory equipment is exceedingly useless. So, eventually, I do the only thing I *can* do — snap a few pictures with my phone and high-tail it out of there before whoever was messing with the pipes comes back.

My pace is faster on my way out. I keep my legs moving and my eyes forward, suddenly desperate to be out of this place, out of this town, back in my safe, comfortable bed. I haven't felt like this for years — this nervous, haunting nausea swirling in the pit of my stomach. Some innate instinct is telling me *run, go, quick! Get out of sight.*

As though everything I've worked for could be snatched from my grip with a rogue gust of wind.

Feeling like that made sense when I was living on street corners. It makes almost no sense, now.

Still, I'm relieved when I burst through the back door into the light of day, blinking at the sudden brightness. I practically run through the alley and across the parking lot. I don't look back until I hit the street, nearly out of sight – just a quick glance over my shoulder at the factory, silhouetted by the sun sinking over the water.

Every muscle in my body goes tense.

Someone is standing in the shadows at the mouth of the alley, watching me leave. I can't see his face, but I know it's a man from his clothing, his build, his height. I'd bet my ass he's wearing size-nine boots with deep, dust-covered treads on his feet.

Maybe you're wrong, I tell myself. *Maybe he's just a homeless guy. Maybe he's a teenage graffiti artist. Maybe he's doing something totally innocent in that alley, like conducting a drug deal or soliciting a prostitute. Just because he's watching you now doesn't mean he's been watching you since you got here.*

My reassurances fall flat. This guy isn't some teenage derelict. He isn't a dealer or a creepy cheating husband.

He works for Lancaster.

As I watch, he takes a few steps into the abandoned stretch of parking lot, closing a tiny bit of the distance between us.

It's close enough.

I don't stick around another second to see what he plans to do about my trespassing. I turn on one heel and bolt toward civilization, never stopping until my ass is planted firmly in a plastic train seat and I'm barreling back toward Boston.

THE NEXT NIGHT, I'm sitting at my computer pouring over architectural plans of the LC factory I found on the flash drive, trying to figure out what those shiny pipes are — just like I've been doing since the moment I got back to my apartment — when the doorbell intercom buzzes.

I glance at my watch. It's nearly midnight on a Thursday.

Who the fuck is at my door, at this hour?

Luca and I still aren't speaking, so it can't be him. Plus, he has his own key; he wouldn't buzz up. And... I don't have any other friends.

The buzzer goes again, more insistently.

Grumbling under my breath, I rise to my feet and cross to the intercom panel by my door. The small screen shows a blurry, black and white video feed of a man wearing some kind of uniform, holding a box.

"Who is it?"

"Delivery for Zoe Bloom."

"I didn't order anything."

"The guy said to tell you it's from *Blaze*." The male voice sounds tired and somewhat nervous. "Listen, lady, he paid me double to deliver it tonight. And, to be totally honest, he's not the kind of guy I want to have to disappoint with news I couldn't make it happen."

I snort, but I'm not exactly surprised. Luca has that effect on people.

"Fine," I agree. "I'll buzz you in. You can put the package in the elevator. I'll call it up after you leave."

I wasn't born yesterday. I'm not about to let some random dude into my apartment in the middle of the night. In this old building, the elevator doors open straight into my living room. Yes, the keyed-panel system offers a layer of protection, but it's not exactly the same as having a concierge guarding the door at all hours. And my neighbors aren't the type to call the police if they hear a scream, what with the illegal pot farm the guys in the unit below mine are cultivating and the fake ID operation the lady on the first floor runs out of her living room.

By the time the elevator clangs to a stop on my floor, the delivery boy is long gone. When the doors slide open, I find a small, hot pink box labeled *Crumble* in curvy white letters sitting inside. I stare at it ominously.

I know exactly what's in the box — the same thing I order every time I stop at my favorite bakery in the city.

Double chocolate cupcakes with peanut butter frosting.

I have to hand it to Luca — the bastard knows my weakness and is shamelessly exploiting it to get me to forgive him.

Still... it would be a shame to let them go to waste...

I sigh as I grab the box and retreat back into my apartment. I only last about thirty seconds after setting it down on the counter before I cave and flip open the lid, inhaling the scent of chocolate with a soft moan. There are four perfect, frosted cupcakes sitting inside, crying out for me to devour them.

Damn.

There's a note tucked between two in the middle. I pluck it out and read it as I suck chocolate glaze off one finger.

I'm a dick. Forgive me anyway?

Got a fight tomorrow night — need you there, babe.

8PM. Lansdowne Gym.

He doesn't sign his name. Doesn't apologize.

Typical Luca.

But he knows I'll be there. Just as he knew exactly what kind of cupcakes would be most effective in leveraging my sympathies.

Parker may think Luca is in love with me, but he's wrong. Sure, we love each other — but it's familial, not romantic. We've seen all the ugly, awful parts of each other. We've hated each other. Pushed each other. Forced each other to carry on when the whole damn world seemed to be telling us not to bother.

You can't love someone who knows you like that.

Or at least... *I* can't love someone who knows *me* like that.

Luca and I both gravitate toward darkness. Distrust. Destruction.

And, the truth is, you can't drive out shadows in a window-less room. At some point, you have to let the light in. Find someone who glows bright enough to lessen the burden of your misfortunes.

Luca deserves someone who can bring that light into his life.

Out of nowhere, Parker's face flashes in my mind. And for the rest of the night, no matter how hard I try, no matter how hard I focus on financial data and executive email streams... I can't quite seem to banish it from my thoughts.

Later, when my eyes are drooping shut and I can no longer make out the words on my screen, I can't stop myself from crossing to my dresser, pulling his large black sweater from the back of the drawer where I hid it last week, and tugging it on before sliding beneath the sheets.

CHAPTER 10

THE INVITATION

I PUSH my way through the crowd, my *don't-fuck-with-me* expression firmly in place. It makes little difference — no one pays me a bit of attention. Everyone's eyes are on the center ring as the crowd slowly moves inward, jostling for better positions. This isn't an official fight, so there are no seats or press boxes; the UFC doesn't sanction underground bouts. But, for a twenty-five-dollar cover charge at the door, anyone can get in... so long as they know where to go, of course.

The gym is well over the fire marshal's designated capacity, but no one seems to care. Money flows freely as bets are exchanged last minute. Fans trash-talk about the competitors, discuss the odds. I overhear someone saying Luca is expected to take a heavy beating against Dean "Iceman" Bailey, a massive lunkhead from New Jersey with a killer right hook and a twelve-match winning streak under his belt.

Go ahead and underestimate Luca, I think, pushing past them. *You'll be eating your words by the end of the night.*

From what I hear, there's a shitload of money on the line.

I've never been one to place bets, but if I did I'd bet on Luca every time.

Times like this, being petite comes in handy. I duck under arms and between groups like a shadow, finding space to maneuver where there is none. By the time I make it to the ring — a raised, fenced-in octagonal platform surrounded by metal barriers to keep the fans back — the roar of the crowd has reached a crescendo.

Groupies push up against the metal fencing, their boobs straining inside see-through white t-shits. Bouncers make a half-hearted attempt at holding them back from the narrow ringside area where corner men, octagon girls, and coaches gather before the fight. The male fans in the crowd are a little more subdued, but not much — they eye the empty octagon with an anticipatory look, taking stock of the bets they made upon arrival.

They crave blood, tonight.

There's an uncomfortable flutter of nerves in my stomach; the same one I get every time Luca fights. No matter how often he goes up against impossible odds and makes it out alive, it never gets easier. Tonight, when he's battling one of the best fighters in the underground circuit, my heart is lodged firmly in my throat.

He's still backstage, likely getting psyched up and going over his strategy for the match. He likes to be alone, before all his fights. He's not the biggest fighter, not the strongest or the most muscular in the heavyweight division, but he fights *fast*, he fights *smart*, and he never goes into a fight blind. He says dominating in the ring is as much mental as it is physical.

His sparring partner, Colton, somehow spots me from where he's standing in the blockaded area by the ring. In a flash, he's there in front of me, nodding to the nearest bouncer before extending one huge hand and hoisting me over the barrier with a single flex of his bicep.

"Thanks, Colt," I say breathlessly, when he sets me down. I hear whines of complaint from the groupies along the fence.

"Hey, why does she get ringside access?" a busty brunette squeals.

"Take me, too!" a hopeful blonde suggests.

"What's so special about *her*?" a redhead sneers.

Colt shoots them all a withering glare. Despite his blond, surfer-boy good looks, he can bring the heat when necessary.

"*She* is with Blaze."

Without another word to them, he hooks one arm around my neck and walks me to the cluster of metal folding chairs reserved for the fighters' teams.

"He'll be happy you're here," Colt yells into my ear. I can barely hear him, over the din behind us. "He's been a total nutcase all week."

I shrug. "He's always a nutcase, Colt."

"Yeah, well, nuttier than usual. You two fighting or something?"

"Or something," I mutter.

His blue eyes crinkle. "Well, don't take it out on him too long. He needs to focus."

"What are his odds?"

Colt shakes his head and his eyes dart across the ring to where Iceman's coach is standing. "They're pretty evenly matched, if I'm being honest. Hard to say who will take it. Iceman is brawn and brute force... Blaze is speed and strategy. Totally different approaches. It's anyone's game."

I suck in a breath. It's one thing to hear shitheads in the crowd talking about Luca losing — it's another to hear one of his best friends discuss the possibility.

"Don't worry, Zoe." Colt smirks. "Fire always melts ice."

I hope he's right.

A few minutes later, the crowd has swelled to bursting. I keep my eyes on the ring as the announcer runs up the short set of stairs and hoists his mic into the air. His voice booms like a clap of thunder.

"ARE YOU READY, BOSTON?"

The crowd roars in response.

"I SAID *ARE YOU FUCKING READY?*"

Five hundred people scream at the top of their lungs.

"Then make some noise for our first fighter.... a man built like a glacier... a powerhouse with fists like icebergs... your undefeated champ.... *ICEMAN!*"

A rap song blares from the speakers overhead, barely audible over the cheers. From the left side of the gym, a bare-chested man in shiny black shorts cuts a swathe through the crowd, flanked by bouncers on all sides. Fans reach out to touch him as he passes by, but he brushes them off — he's watching the ring, hyper-focused and frigid as he makes his way up into the octagon.

I feel my eyes widen.

He's built like an eighteen-wheeler — at least 260 pounds of solid muscle. His head goes straight into his shoulders, foregoing a neck entirely, and his fists are each about the size of my face. Just before he climbs into the ring, he cuts a cold glance at Colt... and then his black eyes slide to meet mine.

I shiver when he stares at me, suddenly understanding his nickname. There's not an ounce of warmth inside him.

Dropping my gaze, I refuse to watch as he does his victory lap around the inside of the ring, hyping the crowd to new levels. They chant like druids at the alter of their god.

ICE-MAN!

ICE-MAN!

ICE-MAN!

The announcer's voice blares again. "And now, ladies and gents, your challenger this evening... your very own hometown hero... a man who'll bring the heat and try to burn his way to an upset... BLAZE BUCHANAN!"

Luca's entry music always makes me grin. What can I say? The Dropkick Murphy's *I'm Shipping Up to Boston* is an unbeatable soundtrack choice for a redheaded Irishman from the city. The crowd eats it up, singing along as Luca emerges from the back room and jogs to the stage, two beefy security guards at his sides to keep the fans back. Just before he hops up the steps into the ring, he spots me. His lips curl into a devilish grin.

I smile back and mouth, *Good luck.*

He winks and steps into the arena, all humor fading from his expression as his focus narrows on his opponent. He looks much, much smaller than his 210 pounds, up there next to the human ice sculpture.

Colt's shoulder bumps mine. "Breathe, babe."

I bump him back. "I'll breathe when it's over."

The announcer steps out. The referee steps in. The octagon door slams closed. The crowd screams. The fighters start to circle...

I hold my breath and force myself to watch as round one begins.

IT'S BRUTAL. Bloody.

Colt was right — they're pretty evenly matched. Luca moves quickly, ducking punches and striking out strategically whenever Iceman drops his hands, like the sun unleashing a solar flare of pure heat. I cheer as he manages to land several sharp blows to Iceman's head. Still, the sheer strength of his opponent can't be dismissed, because no matter how many times Luca hits him, the bastard refuses to go down. By the final round, Luca's bleeding from his bottom lip, and I'm relatively certain Iceman is actually made of stone.

The crowd is growing uneasy, the longer the match persists without a clear victor. They expected Iceman to take Luca out in one hit — now, with the clock ticking down to the finals seconds, they're not so sure about the outcome... or the security of their bets.

Both competitors are breathing heavily as they move around the arena. My eyes never leave Luca as he moves sharply to the left, attempting a knock-out uppercut to the jaw. I feel the breath seize in my throat as Iceman anticipates his strike and lunges back, so Luca's fist hits nothing but air. The forward momentum of the punch pulls Luca off balance, stumbling a few steps toward the closest cage wall. Iceman uses it to his advantage, effectively backing Luca into a corner in the tiny slice of time it takes the smaller man to find his footing.

Fuck.

Once you're pinned, it's almost impossible to escape — especially if your opponent is roughly the size of Mount Everest. The audience cheers as Iceman grapples for a solid hold. I watch his big hand flying out, preparing to deliver a fatal blow to the top of Luca's spine...

And then, the unthinkable — Luca ducks, quicker than I've ever seen him, pivots behind the lumbering hunk of ice, and swipes Iceman's legs out from under him with a perfectly placed roundhouse kick to the back of the thighs. The giant falls like a tree in the forest, face-first onto the canvas mats, and before he has time to find his feet, Luca's there, delivering a series of sharp jabs to his ribs. His arm snakes around Iceman's throat in a chokehold as he presses him into the mat, demanding submission.

It's over quickly, after that.

The ache of worry inside my chest eases as soon as Iceman's fist taps the mat, crying uncle. The crowd is stunned, their roars louder than ever — some are pissed to see their champion fall, but most are thrilled that the underdog dominated. It's akin to David taking on Goliath — albeit a bit bloodier. (And I'm relatively certain there were no bikini-clad ring girls pressed up against *David* after he won that biblical bout.)

Colt is whooping in celebration as he pulls me up the stairs into the octagon. We're barely on the canvas when Luca appears. Dismissing his corner men and clingy cheerleaders without a word, he grabs me in a giant bear hug.

"You did it," I yell into his ear, returning his tight embrace as he spins me in a circle. "Are you okay? You nose is bleeding."

"I'm fine."

"Are you sure? Because—"

"*Mom*, I said I'm fine."

I huff.

"Thanks for coming, babe," he says, pulling back so he can look down into my face. "I know I was a dick, the other day."

"You think?" I ask, arching a brow.

He smirks. "I'll make it up to you. You'll see."

"You can start by setting me down. You're so sweaty, I might actually drown standing this close to you. It's gross."

With a laugh, he sets me back on my feet. He turns to accept a back-slapping hug from Colton — but not before wiping a sweat-coated arm against my face just to taunt me, the rotten bastard.

"Ew!" I exclaim, dragging my sleeve against the sweat mark. "Now I have to go wash my face."

Luca rolls his eyes. "Priss."

Colt shakes his head. "Such a girl."

I flip them both off.

"Hurry back! We're going out to celebrate!" Colton scuffs his knuckles against Luca's head in a playful gesture. "Pretty sure this guy could use a few drinks."

I laugh as I turn away, calling back over my shoulder, "Oh, get a room, you two."

Luca's grin is the last thing I see before the mob of fans closes in around him.

It takes a while, but eventually I maneuver through the dozens of people crowding the octagon and make my way down the stairs. My eyes scan the crowd as everyone slowly funnels out the front doors onto the street — five hundred people trying to exit at once has resulted in a serious traffic jam. I'm searching in vain for a bathroom sign, eyes moving along the walls, when I see something that makes my heart clench inside my chest.

It's been a while, but I'd recognize her anywhere.

Long, dark hair. Impeccable clothing. Skyscraper heels.

And, most familiar, a set of hazel eyes so like her brother's it makes my heart twist.

Phoebe West.

She's standing with a group of girls about fifty feet to my left. A brunette with large blue eyes — who looks so strikingly similar to Phoebe she must be her sister — is telling a story, making everyone laugh. A petite woman with a platinum pixie cut is standing with her back to me. By her side is a willowy brunette who must teach yoga because, *damn* the girl has a rocking body. Rounding out the group is a curvaceous strawberry blond with big brown eyes I can see, even from this distance, are glossy and long-lashed.

They're all giggling and grinning, clearly having a great night.

I tell myself to walk away, to fade into the crowd before Phoebe has a chance to spot me, but it's like I've lost control of my senses. My eyes move of their own accord, seeking someone else in the crowd... someone with tousled blond hair and a broad chest...

I don't find him.

Instead, my eyes latch onto the man hovering just behind Phoebe. The way he's standing — feet planted, arms crossed, eyes hyper-vigilant as they scan the crowd — tells me he's guarding her from any potential threats. I know who he is without blinking twice.

Nathaniel Knox.

Parker's best friend; Phoebe's boyfriend.

Knox Investigations is well-known and well-respected by everyone in this city. Knox is smart, capable, and exceedingly good at his job. Which probably explains why he notices my scrutiny almost instantly.

Dark eyes lock on mine, a question in their depths. He takes a stride closer to Phoebe, never looking away from me, and as I see him bend to catch her attention, I finally snap into motion.

She can't see me. She'll recognize me. Confront me about abandoning her last year. Remind me what a shitty fucking person I am for walking away.

And somehow, it'll all get back to Parker... who I've determined to avoid for the rest of infinity...

I whirl and bolt in the opposite direction, cursing myself for being so incapacitated by just the thought of Parker, I let my guard down entirely. Spotting the small, illuminated bathroom sign at the far end of the gym, I race toward it, hoping Phoebe hasn't spotted me. My black Toms eat up the distance in seconds. When my hand curls around the knob, I ignore the tinge of disappointment in my stomach.

I made it without being spotted. That should be a relief.

So, why isn't it?

Just before the door shuts at my back, it happens.

"Holy frack!" a feminine voice shouts, her excited squawk is so loud I can hear her even from this distance. "That's *Tinkerbell!*"

Shit.

I step into the bathroom and shut the door behind me, even though I know it's futile. She spotted me. And, if she's anything at all like her brother, she's not going to let it go without a confrontation.

With nowhere else to go, I enter the nearest stall and quickly bolt the door behind me. I've barely gotten the latch closed when I hear the outer door swing inward. I wince as the sound of stiletto heels clack across the floor, coming ever closer. Two black shiny pumps come to a stop right outside my stall.

"*Tink!*" Phoebe's voice is impatient. "I know it's you! You might as well come out."

"You've got the wrong person."

"I don't think so."

"Seriously," I insist. "Just tying to pee in peace."

"Lying promotes wrinkles, Tink."

"Fuck off."

"Don't make me climb under the stall. These are Prada slacks."

I roll my eyes. "I see you haven't changed a bit, Princess."

"HA!" Her voice is triumphant. "I knew it was you!"

Resigned to my fate, I reach forward and flip open the lock. The door swings slowly outward, revealing a pretty brunette who's staring at me with something like adoration.

Wait... Adoration?

I don't even have time to brace myself before she's flung her arms around me and pulled me into a hug so tight I can barely breathe.

She's hugging me?

"I thought I'd never see you again!" she screeches. "I'm happy I was wrong."

"Um." I pat her back awkwardly. "You're touching me."

She snorts and pulls back a bit, but doesn't release my shoulders. "Yes, this is called a *hug*. I realize you may be unfamiliar with the concept. We'll take it slow. Baby steps. Work our way up to rocking hugs. Back-petting hugs. Bear hugs. And my personal favorite..." She pauses, eyes twinkling. "*Tackle* hugs."

I blink. "You're still touching me."

She smacks my arm lightly. "I've been looking for you for *months*."

My brows lift. "Why?"

Her pretty hazel eyes widen. "To say *thank you*, genius. You saved my life."

She's got it all wrong.

A squirmy, uncomfortable feeling fills my stomach. "Not really."

"What the hell do you mean?" She stares me down. "You're my savior. My fairy freaking godmother. I've been trying to get Nate to track you down for *ages* but he didn't have a lot to go on. Blonde, petite, swears a lot — not exactly enough details for a full criminal investigation."

"Listen, you're mixed up. I'm not your savior." I swallow hard. "I'm not who you think I am at all. Let's just go our separate ways and pretend it never happened, okay?"

Phoebe blinks at me. "Are you *high*?"

Without waiting for an answer, she shakes her head to dismiss my words, loops her arm through mine, and starts walking striding toward the bathroom door. "Come on, Tink, I have to introduce you to everyone. I made them wait outside while I came in to get you, but I swear half my friends think I made you up. Granted, I was a bit sleep-deprived and dazed when we met, but I wasn't *delusional* for god's sake."

I dig in my heels but it's no use — in those stilettos, she's got at least seven inches of height on me. I'm dragged along like a deflated birthday balloon on a string.

"Wait—" I protest, searching for the right words. "I'm not— this isn't—"

She ignores my babbles.

God, she's just like her brother.

"Phoebe, listen—"

"There's really no point arguing," Phoebe says placidly, stopping just in front of the exit. "You're going to let me thank you properly. Now that Nate's seen you, he'll just track you down if you try to disappear again. Isn't that right, Nathaniel?" she calls through the door. Her tone very clearly suggests he'd better agree with her if he ever wants sex again.

"Whatever you say, little bird." Knox sounds amused — and *close*, like he's standing right outside.

When Phoebe pulls the door open, I realize that's because he *is* right outside, guarding the entrance — much to the annoyance of several girls waiting to pee. As we clear the door, his dark eyes sweep over my face, intelligent and intense in their perusal. This man misses *nothing* — not one detail. I can tell from a single glance at him that he's everything his reputation boasts and more.

"Zoe Bloom," Knox murmurs lowly. "Should've known."

I startle — I can't believe he knows who I am.

"You know Tinkerbell?" Phoebe hisses at her boyfriend, voice ominous. "And you didn't tell me? You are in so much trouble!"

"Little bird, I know her name; that doesn't mean I knew she was your foul-mouthed rescuer from eight months ago."

"Oh," Phoebe says, somewhat calmer. "Well, how do you know her, then?"

"That's a good question. I'd like to know the answer, myself." My brows arch. "Have we met?"

Knox jerks his head in the direction of the octagon, toward Luca. "You're a friend of a friend. I like to stay informed, whenever I work with someone. Who they know, who they deal with." His eyes hold mine and I see thoughts stirring at the back of that dark gaze. "You know Blaze... that means I made it my business to know *you*."

There's another sentence in his eyes, one he doesn't say out loud.

And I don't like what I know.

I hold his stare unflinchingly. He may be intimidating to most people, but I was raised in back alleys and on shadowed street corners. He doesn't scare me.

I've seen that look he's giving me before, too many times to count. The one that says, *Get out, you're not wanted here. You're dirty and dangerous. A threat.*

I saw it from soccer moms and teenage girls and little kids and businessmen in fancy suits, who'd press their cellphones tighter to their ears as they hustled past my cardboard sign like I might leap up and steal their wallets. For some unfathomable reason I thought, when I left the streets, I'd never see that look again.

Apparently, I was mistaken.

"Zoe?" Phoebe says from my side, totally oblivious to the hostilities being exchanged two feet from her. "That's your name? Zoe?"

I don't answer. I'm too busy glaring at her boyfriend.

"Ahem!" The girl with long strawberry-blonde hair clears her throat. *Loudly.* "Phee, you ever planning to introduce us, or...?"

"Sorry, sorry! This is Tinkerbell!" Phoebe announces, grinning like a madwoman. "I mean, Zoe. And, Zoe, this is..." With a sweep of her hand, she points at the girls in the group, from the redhead, "...Lila," to the willowy brunette "...Shelby," to the platinum pixie "...Chrissy," to the girl who looks like her sister. "...and Gemma."

I give a half-hearted wave. They all wave back. In unison.

It would be creepy, if it weren't so cute.

"She *is* tiny," Gemma says, grinning.

"And you weren't lying — great hair," Lila adds.

"She's the hacker chick?" Chrissy's nose scrunches. "I was expecting goth and grunge, not jeans and a cowl-neck sweater."

I roll my eyes. "Sorry to disappoint."

"Oh, don't mind Chrissy." Shelby laughs. "She's hormonal and sleep-deprived. Two babies in one house does that to a person."

Chrissy elbows Shelby in the ribs.

Gemma shakes her head at both of them.

Lila glances at her phone and taps out a quick text message.

Phoebe huffs. "Nice, guys. Real nice. You decide to act like total screwballs the *one time* I have to introduce you to someone I'm trying my damnedest to keep from bolting."

"They're *always* screwballs," Lila murmurs, briefly looking up from her phone. "I'm the only sane one of the bunch."

Gemma, Phoebe, Shelby, and Chrissy all trade glances... and simultaneously burst out into uproarious laughter.

"Oh my god," Phoebe brushes a tear from the corner of her eye. "She's serious, isn't she?"

Gemma's holding her stomach, trying to catch her breath. "It's cute."

Chrissy and Shelby are chuckling too hard to say anything.

Lila glares at her friends. "I'll have you know, I'm the only one here who hasn't been involved in some kind of car chase, kidnapped and held for ransom, threatened at gunpoint, or run for my life in stilettos."

They all go silent for a second, adopting serious expressions as they contemplate her words...

"Give it time," Gemma says, shrugging. "Keep hanging with us, I'm sure you'll be kidnapped eventually."

That sets them all off again, cackling like hyenas. Lila scowls silently.

Is this what it's like to have friends? A whole group of people who know all your shit, even the dark, scary shit, and can still somehow laugh with you about it?

I'm feeling about as awkward as a horse at a glue factory, so I start to edge backward, trying not to draw any attention. They're so busy laughing, they don't seem to notice I'm about to vanish into the crowd. I take another step, relief flooding my system, and suddenly my back hits something solid. It feels like stone. For a minute, I think I've backed straight into a wall...

Until the wall *moves* and I hear a deep male voice close to my ear.

"Going somewhere?"

Damn Knox and his fucking spidey-senses.

My spine straightens. "No."

"Good. You disappearing would upset Phoebe. And I don't like her upset."

I bite my tongue to keep from snapping at him. Macho-man antics have never been my style, and this guy takes the freaking cake when it comes to bossy, alpha-male shenanigans.

He steps back — far enough that he's no longer pressed up against me, but close enough that I know I can't slip away into the crowd without him running interference. A few seconds later, Phoebe's eyes lock back on mine and my escape window slips away.

"Zoe! You're coming to my Christmas party tomorrow night. No excuses."

My hands clench. "Sorry, I have plans."

I have a full evening scheduled — Netflix in my pajamas, binge-watching the new season of House of Cards and eating too many peanut-butter cups to count.

"You do not," she counters, crossing her arms over her chest. "And it wasn't a request, Tink — sorry, Zoe. You're coming. Parker made me invite almost half the WestTech staff and we need some normal people in the mix, to break up the awkward work-bonding."

I go still at the mention of Parker's name. It's clear they don't know about my connection to him; that will certainly change, if I go to Phoebe's party.

"I really can't."

"Uh huh. Why's that?" she asks.

I hesitate, contemplate lying, and finally decide to just go with the truth. "I don't do Christmas."

"Are you Jewish?"

"No."

"Buddhist?"

"No."

"Wiccan?"

"Please don't go through every religion." I sigh. "Like everyone in Boston, I'm a lapsed Catholic."

"A lapsed Catholic who doesn't do Christmas?"

"What about this are you having trouble understanding?"

She stares at me incredulously. "Everyone does Christmas."

"Not me."

"Well, you do this year."

My fists clench tighter and I feel something like fear flip my stomach into somersaults. I can't go to that party, and not just because I can't stand to be around that much holiday cheer without curling into the fetal position.

I can't see Parker.

Feeling pressured, I lash out like a feral cat — a method I've used for years, whenever I'm feeling cornered. My voice drops to a scathing whisper. "Listen, princess, I don't know if it's a lack of brain cells keeping you from hearing me..." I feel Nate tense at my back; I keep going anyway. "...or just plain entitled ignorance, but I'm *not* going to your fucking party. *Comprende?*"

Instead of backing off, I see something flicker in Phoebe's eyes. It looks a lot like determination. She strides closer on those damn skyscraper heels, getting right up in my face, and glares down at me.

"I don't know what happened to make you so miserable, I don't know who hurt you so bad you think you have to lash out at everyone who wants to be your friend... frankly, I don't care. You want to treat me like gum stuck to the bottom of your shoe? *Fine.* Either way, you're stuck with me. I'm *sticking.* Deal with it."

My mouth drops open to retort, but a growling male voice intercedes before I can.

"What's going on? You okay, babe?" Luca steps into the ring of women surrounding me and inserts himself by my side. I hear appreciative feminine sounds from Shelby, Chrissy, and Lila as they take him in.

"That's Blaze Buchanan," Shelby whisper-yells.

"We know, dufus," Chrissy fires back.

Luca stares from me to Phoebe and back again. "Babe?"

I sigh. "I'm fine. Just a little misunderstanding."

"No misunderstanding," Phoebe clips. "I was just inviting Zoe here to my Christmas party. She was trying to squirm her way out of it."

Luca's mouth twitches. "Sounds about right."

"You're invited too, of course," she adds. "Though I think your presence at the party may incite riots among my friends." She gestures at the cluster of women flanking her sides.

Luca's eyes cut around the circle and lock on Knox. They exchange silent nods — bro-code for *hey, man, good to see you* — before Luca continues his sweep of the group. His gaze flickers past Gemma, Chrissy, and Shelby, then seems to freeze on Lila with particular interest.

To my surprise, she's not looking at her phone. Gone is her scowl.

Her wide brown eyes are locked on Luca with one hundred percent focus. And he's looking back at her with an intensity I've rarely seen from him — taking in her long, reddish blonde hair, her curvy figure, her delicate features.

"You going to be at this party?" Luca asks her in a low voice.

"Y-yes," she stutters, before getting her tone of careful nonchalance under control. "I mean, I was planning on it. Maybe."

Luca's grin is wicked. "Great. We'll be there."

"Luke!" I hiss, outraged. I try to punch him in the side but his large hand engulfs mine just before I make contact with his ribs.

"Address?" he asks Phoebe, ignoring my attempts to escape his grip and murder him with my bare hands.

Phoebe is grinning. "112 Commonwealth Avenue, in Back Bay. It's a brownstone with a mammoth wreath on the front door — you can't miss it. Starts at seven! Ugly Christmas sweaters are encouraged, but not required."

"Don't wait up," I say. "We're not coming."

Luca is still looking at Lila. "Seven. Sounds good."

"Great!" Phoebe exclaims.

"Seriously, we won't be there," I insist.

Phoebe laughs. "See you tomorrow, Tink!"

"Don't count on it!" I call as she turns and walks away, her friends all around her.

"Don't worry," Gemma calls back over one shoulder. "I've got an extra Santa hat you can borrow, if you don't have one."

I screech.

How the hell did that just happen?

CHAPTER 11

THE PARTY

"I LITERALLY HATE YOUR GUTS."

"Tell me something I don't know."

"If I was strong enough, I'd push you into oncoming traffic."

"Awww, babe, that's so sweet."

"Really, Luke, this is over the top. Even for you."

He shrugs and continues pulling me down Comm Ave. Every tree on the boulevard is covered in white Christmas lights. Despite the cold, there are more than a few people out walking — taking in the sights, enjoying the decorations. Our breath puffs in the air in front of us and I shiver inside my thin peacoat, as much from nerves as the cold. When Luca throws an arm around my shoulders, sharing his warmth, I grudgingly decide not to shake him off. It's too hard to stay mad at him.

"We'd barely stopped fighting about the last macho-man, out-of-control shenanigans you pulled on me. Then you have to go and do it all over again."

"You know what they say, babe." He grins. "Leopard, spots, all that jazz."

"I don't know why I'm still your friend."

"Yeah, you do. Now, tell me about Lancaster."

I sigh. "Found a weird email from our darling CEO to a guy named Linus, his Head of Security, talking about some kind of *clean up* at the Lynn Factory." I drop my voice lower, knowing I'm about to start yet another disagreement. "So, I headed over there to check it out on Wednesday afternoon, just to see if there was anything strange going on."

"What the fuck were you thinking, going there alone?" Luca explodes, stopping mid-stride. "Everyone knows Lancaster is a shithead. You find evidence he may be even *more* of a shithead than we originally believed, and you decide to go traipsing through his factory by yourself." He shakes his head. "You should've called me, babe."

"I wasn't speaking to you," I remind him.

"Yeah, well, I didn't say we had to sit down over tea and discuss our feelings. I said I would've come with you, provided a little muscle if you got into trouble."

"I didn't." My lips twitch at his words. "But I did find something weird at the factory. It looked like someone had been inside, messing with the pipes. Problem is, I wouldn't know a cooling system from a carburetor, so I sure as shit don't know why Lancaster would go to all the trouble of replacing pipes in a factory he just closed and is scheduled to knock down in a few months."

"Well, babe, for starters, carburetors are in *cars*, and no one even uses them anymore—"

"Luca. Save the mechanical lecture for another day." I hold his gaze. "I think there's something going on with the plant closing. Something more than just budget cuts and screwing workers out of pensions. Something... bigger."

His brow wrinkles. "I'll go take a look, when I get a chance. You don't go back there alone, you hear me?"

"I hear you, you big softie." I punch him lightly on the arm. "Let's go. We're already late for this damn thing."

"It might not be so bad," he says. "Hell, if that redhead is there, I'm thinking my night may actually be *excellent*."

"Do you ever think about anything but sex?"

He shrugs. "Maybe when I'm unconscious."

"I still don't know how I let you talk me into this," I mutter darkly as we pass a row of wreath-covered brownstones. We'll be at Phoebe's any minute.

"Babe, I know this time of year is tough for you. But you don't ever run from a fight. You don't let shit scare you." Luca glances at me. "I'm tired of watching you disappear every December. I'm tired of seeing that sad look in your eyes."

"You think it's easy for me, Luke? You think I'm not tired of it, year after year?" I ask, voice breaking a little. "You think it's as simple as just throwing on a Christmas sweater, singing some carols, and embracing the holiday spirit?"

"I never said it was gonna be easy. Nothing good in life ever comes easy — you know that better than anyone. But you keep closing yourself off from everything, you're gonna wind up as alone as the day we first met."

"Since when are you Mr. Well-Adjusted, Luke?" I shake my head. "I don't see you in any long-term, healthy relationships. You don't have any family. You can count all your friends on one fucking hand."

"Maybe I'm ready for something different." He stops walking and looks down at me. "Change is scary. I get that. But you're not required to be the same person you were ten years ago, ten weeks ago, ten days ago. Hell, you don't even have to be the person you were ten minutes ago. You're free to be whoever the hell you want, Zoe Bloom." His mouth curves. "If that person happens to be a bitchy, misanthropic, Christmas-hating curmudgeon, so be it. I'll still be here. But if you want to be someone different — someone who let's herself laugh, and have fun, and go sailing in the goddamned icy tundra we call home with some idiot who probably spends too long styling his hair... that's okay too."

"Is this — you dragging me here tonight — about *Parker*?" My tone has surpassed incredulity and gone straight to stunned disbelief. "You nearly killed the guy. Now you want me to see him again?"

Luca's eyes narrow. "It's not about what I want. It's about what *you* want, babe."

I pause. "How do you know I want him?"

"Ten years I've known you, we've never gone more than a day without checking in." His eyes darken a bit. "I ruin your date with the rich boy, and you freeze me out for an entire week. Not rocket science, babe."

I press my lips together, trying to come up with a retort. Nothing comes to mind.

Luca's big hand lands on my shoulder and squeezes. "I'm not saying I know what's best for you, or that he's the right guy, or even that I approve of the idiot. All I'm saying is, you're not required to suffer forever. Your parents would want you to be happy, Zoe. You have to know that."

My eyes are stinging. I tell myself it's from the cold. "I had no idea there was such a mushy, emotional girl hiding beneath that badass exterior, Luca. You want me to run to that convenience store we passed a few blocks back? Grab you a box of maxi-pads and a few chocolate bars?"

He grins. "Come on, you priss. We're already late."

I make a growly sound at the back of my throat and follow him down the street. A few minutes later, we come to a stop outside a beautiful brownstone, every light shining like a beacon, the sound of laughter and music pouring out onto the street.

"Think we're here." Luca looks over at me. "You ready?"

"As I'll ever be."

He gives me his trademark *you-can-do-this* nod as we walk up the stairs and ring the bell. The door opens almost instantly.

"You're here!" Phoebe yells at the top of her lungs. She's wearing what must be the singularly most unattractive sweater on the planet — garish red with a horrific sequined snowman on the front. There's a glass of what looks like eggnog in one hand and the tiniest dog I've ever seen in my life tucked under her other arm. My eyes widen as the ball of white fur leaps from her grip onto the hardwood floor and begins to bark at us like we're about to rob the place armed with AK-47s.

"Boo!" Phoebe scolds. "Be nice."

"Is it a cat or a dog?" Luca mutters under his breath.

"Not entirely convinced it isn't a Furby, back from the '90s to kill us," I murmur back.

"Come in, come in!" Phoebe reaches out, hooks her arm through mine, and yanks me inside. Luca follows close behind, closing the door with a gentle click. Boo trails after us, running dizzying circles around our feet. He's got a bedazzled red collar around his tiny neck, appliqué jingle bells chiming every time he moves.

"Everyone's in the living room, but the liquor is in the kitchen." Phoebe glances at me. "What's your poison? We've got spiked eggnog, rum punch, champagne, and whiskey."

I grimace. "Whiskey. Definitely whiskey."

"My kind of girl." Phoebe grins. "Knew I liked you."

"Eggnog for me," Luca chimes in.

I raise my brows. "Really?"

"What?" He shrugs. "Just because you're a scrooge, doesn't mean I have to be. I happen to like Christmas."

Phoebe laughs. "Knew I liked him, too."

I examine the space as we make our way toward the

kitchen, taking note of the expensive art on the walls and the gorgeous furnishings. The whole place looks straight out of a Restoration Hardware store, and I've never seen so many Christmas decorations in my life. Mistletoe hangs in every doorway, holly boughs wind up the stair bannister, frosted pine cones sit in baskets scattered on every table.

Once we've got our drinks, we follow Phoebe into the massive, high-ceilinged living room, where the party is in full swing. Despite what the noise from the street led me to believe, there aren't all that many people inside. Maybe fifty, at the most, eating from a makeshift buffet by the window, admiring the towering Christmas tree on the far wall, clustered on couches making small talk.

My eyes sweep the crowd, searching for him. Every corner, every face, every inch of the room. And...

He's not here.

I must make a tiny sound of disappointment, because Luca leans his shoulder lightly against mine, lending me his strength.

"The redhead isn't here either," he grumbles.

"And there it is, ladies and gents! His true motivation for dragging me to this..." I smirk. "You are such a bullshit artist, Luca Buchanan."

"Takes one to know one," he counters.

I spot Gemma — there's a tall, blond man by her side, looking down at her with adoration. Chrissy and a man I assume is her husband are busy chasing a towheaded toddler and a squirming baby around the room. Shelby is standing alone, sipping rum punch at an alarming pace and picking out songs for the Christmas playlist blaring from the speakers. Nate is standing by the door with a trio of badass, mega-hot macho men.

There are a few dozen people I don't know — WestTech employees, most likely — camped out on the couches... including, to my great delight, the Three Stooges from the IT Department.

"Moe! Larry! Curly!" I laugh and wave. "You're here!"

"Not *her*," Moe moans. "Anyone but her."

Curly and Larry both glare at me.

"You know them?" Phoebe asks quizzically.

"It's a long story," I say, laughing.

Before she can request further clarification, I hear Gemma's voice call out from the other side of the room.

"Hey, Zoe! Come meet Chase!"

"And Mark!" I hear Chrissy call from somewhere down on the carpet. "Also the kids, if we can get them to stop running around like trolls."

"And my invisible husband, who promised he'd be here two hours ago." Shelby takes another swig of punch and gestures to the empty chair beside her. "Isn't he handsome?"

"Very," I call back dryly, smiling despite myself.

"Babe, I'm gonna go say hello to Knox, Theo, and the rest of the boys. You good?" Luca asks quietly.

I force myself to smile. "I'm good. I think."

"Oh, she's fine." Phoebe plants both hands on Luca's shoulders and gives him a push. "Off with you."

And then, before I can say another word, I'm thrust full-force into the party madness.

"SO, Zoe, what's the deal with you and Blaze?" Chrissy asks, glancing over at the men. After a short introduction, Chase and Mark abandoned us to join them. That was almost a half hour ago — I'm surprised I've lasted this long, buffeted on all sides by girl talk.

"Yeah, are you guys together?" Gemma chimes in. "He keeps an eye on you, that much is obvious. And he's mega hot."

"I would *not* mind getting with that." Shelby nods appreciatively. "Not a damn bit."

"You're married," Phoebe reminds her.

"Theoretically." Shelby shrugs. "But the only thing that's been up close and personal with my lady business in the past five years is a pair of Spanx."

Phoebe and Gemma bust out laughing.

"Wait!" Chrissy interjects. "No tangents. The kids are finally asleep; I have *maybe* a thirty-minute window before one of them starts screaming again. I want to hear Zoe's answer about whether she's getting any from the sexy redheaded fighter."

"No," I say, shaking my head adamantly. I go to take another sip of my whiskey and find my glass is empty. *Damn.* "We're friends. Family, practically. We look out for each other, that's all."

"I know someone who'll be happy to hear that." Shelby grins. "Speaking of Lila, where is she?"

"God only knows what that girl does with her time." Chrissy snorts. "Does she even work? Or does she just professionally juggle boyfriends?"

"Hey! No tangents! We'll never get the truth out of Zoe if we keep getting distracted." Phoebe swings her head to me. "So, are you dating anyone?"

I rattle the ice in my glass. "I really need more whiskey if I'm going to continue this conversation."

"I need a refill too," Gemma says, nabbing the glass from my hand. "I'll grab you one while I'm in there."

"Thanks," I murmur.

She winks and walks away.

"So?" Phoebe persists. "Boyfriend? Fuck buddy? Husband? Crush?"

You mean, including your brother or...?

I shake my head, fighting the blush threatening to stain my cheeks. "No. None of the above."

"Then why are you blushing?"

"I'm not," I lie.

"She totally is," Shelby says.

"So, who is he?" Chrissy asks, leaning in.

"No one! There's no one." *Where the hell is Gemma with my refill?* "I'm definitely, one hundred percent single. And I'll probably be that way forever."

"Uh huh." Phoebe's grin is wider than ever. "That's what I said about two seconds before Nate and I got together."

"And what I said just before Chase swept me off my feet," Gemma adds, stepping back into our circle and passing me a full glass.

"Tall pour, much?" I arch my brows at the whiskey filling the tumbler nearly to the brim.

Gemma grins. "Figured you'd need it."

"Zoe." Phoebe snaps. "Back to the hot boy you're in love with."

"Listen, you've got things all wrong." I swallow a sip. "I'm not in love with anyone. I don't even date. And even if there is a guy I like — *and I'm not saying there is!* — I really wouldn't talk about it with you guys because A. I barely know you and B. there's no real chance of it going anywhere."

"So there *is* a guy." Phoebe claps excitedly. "Who is he?"

"Did you hear anything I just said?" I ask incredulously.

"Would we know him?" Gemma pesters.

Well, you do share DNA with him...

I gulp my drink and fling my hand in the general direction of the couches, where I saw the Three Stooges sitting not too long ago. "It's more likely I'd fall for *that* guy over there than actually find true love."

"That guy?" Gemma asks.

I nod and take another sip.

"You sure?"

I glance at her and find she's smiling *huge*. "Yeah, Moe—"

"You mean *Parker*," Phoebe corrects, laughing. "Our brother."

I snort whiskey through my nose. "*What?*"

"You said *the guy over there* and pointed..." Gemma's voice drops to an amused whisper. "That would be our brother."

My gaze flies toward the place I just pointed and, sure enough, I see Parker's familiar broad shoulders striding through the archway from the kitchen, a Christmas sweater even uglier than Phoebe's covering his muscular chest — emerald green with two red embroidered ornaments on the front, accompanied by the word *BALLS* in elaborate, glittery cursive.

Where the hell do they find these sweaters?

I'm still spluttering like a fool, the alcohol stinging my sinuses, so Shelby smacks me on the back in a helpful show of support.

"You okay, Zoe?" She hits me straight between the shoulder blades. "You're white as a ghost."

"I'd be better—" I gasp. "—if you'd stop—" I wheeze. "—fucking *hitting* me."

"She's fine," Shelby announces, grinning. "Just having difficulty breathing over your hot-as-shit brother."

"Ew!" Gemma and Phoebe whine simultaneously.

Finally catching my breath, I look up in time to see something that makes my throat feel a bit too tight. Parker's leggy receptionist, Patricia, enters the room just after him, grabs hold of his arm, and pulls him to a stop beneath the mistletoe hanging in the wide archway. Before he can react, she pops up onto her tiptoes and lays a kiss on his cheek.

An ugly feeling stirs inside me.

"What?" Shelby shakes her head at her friends. "He's sex on a stick, without all the alpha-male damage. What more could a girl ask for?"

"Maybe someone who doesn't get more ass than a toilet bowl at Fenway Park?" I grumble under my breath, my tone murderous.

Four sets of eyes snap to my face and I realize perhaps I voiced my thoughts too loudly.

Gemma's blue eyes get sharp. "Why would you say that?"

"Wait... do you know Parker?" Phoebe asks, head tilting.

I don't answer, because suddenly there's another set of eyes on my face. Eyes I can feel burning into mine even from across the room. Hazel, hot, and maybe, if I let myself believe it... hopeful.

Like maybe he wants me here.

Like maybe he's happy to see me.

Except he brought a date. A tall, perfectly proportioned brunette who looks like Adriana Freaking Lima.

The thought has barely formed when I watch her sidle up to Parker's side again and wrap her arm around his. He doesn't pay her any attention — he's still looking at me, frozen in place like he can't quite believe what he's seeing. And I'm looking at *her*, pressing so close her boobs are laying on his arm.

They're a perfect fit. He's funny and charming. She's perky and preppy. There's not a single jaded, cynical, damaged bone in either of their bodies.

I don't belong here. I was a fool to come.

"I have to go," I say instantly, turning to thrust my empty glass onto the closest table. "Thanks for the whiskey."

"Wait!" Phoebe cries. "Zoe! You can't leave, you just got here!"

"We still have to play *pin-the-balls-on-the-reindeer*," Shelby says somberly. "A time-honored tradition."

"I'm sorry." I turn and head for the archway by the front door, as far from Parker as I can get, cursing Luca for dragging me here and cursing myself for actually having hope that maybe I could open up to someone.

As soon as I turn to run, Parker finds his voice.

"Zoe!" He shouts, starting after me. "Zoe, wait!"

I keep moving, leaving the living room behind and rounding the archway into the front parlor. I hear angry words break out behind me.

"Get out of my way," Parker growls at someone.

"Free tip — when they run away like that, it means they *don't* want to talk to you." Luca's voice is threatening. "She doesn't want you near her, you're not going near her."

"Step *back*." Parker sounds pissed.

"You have a death wish, rich boy?"

"You have a hearing problem, *Blaze*?"

I picture them up in each other's faces, ready to do battle at a fucking Christmas party for god's sake, and my feet falter. My hand drops away from the doorknob and I hurry back into the living room.

"Stop it!" I bark at the two idiots, drawing all fifty sets of eyes at the party to me. "Luca, back off him. *Now*."

He does — grudgingly. He looks about has happy as a One Direction fan when news of the band's split broke.

Parker's eyes are on me as he steps around Luca and closes the gap between us. I backpedal as he approaches, out of the living room, through the archway, until I'm practically pressed against the front door in the foyer. He keeps coming until there's a tiny sliver of space remaining between our bodies.

My eyes hold his. He's breathing too hard, looking down at me with so many emotions it's hard to know what he's feeling.

"I should probably go," I say after a minute, trying to catch my breath. "I've done enough damage here. I ruined Phoebe's party – apologize to her for me, please."

"You're just gonna run again?" he asks, voice low. "Really, Zoe?"

I swallow. "I have to be somewhere."

"Where?" He scoffs. "Anywhere but near me, I suppose?"

I don't answer.

"Pretty strange, then, you showing up at my sister's Christmas party." His eyes narrow.

Before I can retort, there's a sound of commotion — whispers, footfalls, muffled curses — and then the entire damn West entourage bursts into the foyer, all wide-eyed and winded, jostling for positions in the archway, pushing each other for better views. I turn and see Phoebe, Nate, Mark, Chrissy, Gemma, Chase, Shelby, and Luca all staring at us. Nate's private security boys tower at the back, a head above the rest of the group. Even the Three Stooges are there, peeking around a corner to witness whatever's about to go down. And Boo is weaving between their legs like a cat, jingling with every step.

"What's happening?" Chrissy hisses.

"Do they know each other?" Shelby asks.

"Apparently." Gemma's voice is dry.

"*Woof!*" Boo barks.

"Parker, how do you know Tink?" Phoebe pushes free of the fray and steps up to my side.

There's a loaded beat of silence. Parker's voice goes gravelly.

"*Tink?*"

I don't look at him. I can't look at him. I'm afraid of what I'll see in his eyes.

"Yeah, Tink." Phoebe sounds exasperated. "The girl who saved my ass, last spring. You remember, don't you? That time your *only* sister, your flesh and blood, got kidnapped by mobsters?"

He pauses again. From the corner of my eye, I see his head swivel around to look down into my face. When he speaks, the words reverberate from deep inside his chest. "Yeah. I remember."

I press my eyes closed.

Shit, fuck, damn.

"Well, we bumped into her at that underground fight last night, the one you and Nate didn't want us going to because it was a quote-unquote *bad crowd*, or whatever. Thank god I never listen to anything you two say."

I feel Parker move closer. When he speaks, it's not to Phoebe.

"You're the one who saved my sister."

I still don't look at him.

"But, wait..." Phoebe's confused. "If you didn't know she was Tink, how'd you know her?"

Parker doesn't say anything.

Forcing my eyes open, I muster my courage and drag my gaze up to his face. Immediately, I see he's not angry. Alarmingly, he looks almost... *happy*. His eyes rove my features with new awareness, like a master thief who's finally discovered the right combination to crack open an impenetrable safe.

"You could've told me, you know," he murmurs, a hint of a smile touching his lips. "Saved me a week of thinking you weren't interested in me. My ego could've been permanently damaged."

"Seriously doubt that's possible." I counter immediately. "And I'm *not* interested in you."

"See, I don't think that's the case." He leans in a bit, eyes getting warm. "I'm thinking, if anything, you being here tonight means you're more than interested."

"You're wrong."

"You could've told me how you knew my family. One sentence of explanation would've cleared the air." His gaze is sharp. "You kept it hidden because you were looking for any excuse to talk yourself out of taking a risk on something that scares you."

"And what would that be?" I snap.

His eyes soften. "Us."

"There is no us," I whisper, heart clenching.

"Then why'd you come sailing with me?" he asks.

"You had something I needed." I try — unsuccessfully — to move out of his space. "You blackmailed me."

He grins. "That's not what happened and you know it."

"Wait!" Phoebe explodes. "Wait just a damn minute!"

We both look at her. She's got her hands planted on her hips and is glaring at her brother furiously. Nate, standing immediately behind her, looks like he's trying very hard not to laugh.

"*This* is the girl you took sailing?" Phoebe's gaze swivels back and forth between Parker and me. "*Tink* is the girl you've been talking about ad nauseam for the past week?"

My gaze swings to Parker. I feel my mouth tug up in an involuntary smile. "Oh, *really?*"

Parker looks a little red around the collar — it's actually pretty adorable, seeing him flustered. "No."

"You said she was *amazing,*" Phoebe reveals, grinning so wide I'm afraid her cheeks might split. "You said you'd never met anyone like—"

"Enough!" Parker cuts her off before she can reveal anything else, grabs my arm, and yanks open the front door. "We're leaving."

"We are?" I ask, arching my brows. "Are you sure you don't want to stay here? I think Phoebe has more to say…"

He grunts and pushes me out onto the steps. I manage to wave briefly at Luca before I lose sight of him.

"I'll call you, Zoe!" Phoebe yells as the door slams closed.

It's quiet and cold out on the narrow landing.

Parker runs a hand through his hair and chuckles incredulously under his breath before cutting a glance at me. I try my best to hold back my own amusement at the situation, but I lack the self-control. A giggle bubbles up my throat and bursts from my lips, and before I know it I'm doubled-over, laughing so hard I can barely breathe. Laughing like I haven't in… god, I can't even remember how long.

I'm still cackling like an asthmatic hyena when Parker strides across the stoop, invading my space until I'm pushed up against the railing. His arms reach out and close around the metal rail on either side of me, caging me in so I can't move.

"You like laughing at me, huh, Zoe?"

I giggle-snort. "Yep."

He leans in so his front presses against me and I gasp when I feel the length of him, hard and huge against my stomach. I'm shocked how ready he is for me without ever lifting a finger, without doing a damn thing except standing there laughing at him.

"You should know, that husky little laugh of yours is the sexiest fucking thing I've ever heard," he mutters, eyes on mine. "You keep it up, I'm going to throw you over my shoulder, take you back to my boat, and fuck you until you can't walk straight."

The laugh dies on my lips as a bolt of lightning shoots through my panties.

"I've been thinking about that mouth since you walked away from me last week." His lips are practically on mine.

"The sounds it makes. The way it looks when it shapes my name. What it's going to look like when I make you come for the first time."

I suck in a sharp breath.

"And I am going to make you come, Zoe." I feel his stubble against my skin as his lips skim over my jawline. "*Very* soon. I promise you that."

I think I moan a little.

"Still laughing?" he murmurs.

I shake my head.

"Good." His mouth brushes mine in a featherlight kiss that leaves me craving more. "Let's go."

"Back you your boat?" I breathe.

His eyes crinkle. "No. Not yet. We have some shit to say to each other, and if we go to my boat, your powers of speech will be limited to a few choice words. Namely: *harder, faster, please, oh my god, don't stop, Parker, you're a sex god.*"

Rolling my eyes at his ridiculously inflated ego, I try to muffle the sound of disappointment in the back of my throat. I'm pretty sure he hears it anyway, judging by the way his hand tightens on mine as he pulls me down the stairs onto the street.

CHAPTER 12

THE IMPACT

"WHERE ARE WE GOING?" I ask, staring ominously at the black Porsche.

Parker's busy sending a text to someone on his phone while he waits for me to climb into the deathtrap. When the iPhone buzzes and he reads the response on his screen, he smiles wide.

"What?" He looks up at me with warm eyes. "I didn't hear you."

"I asked where we're going."

"Somewhere to talk. I have things to say, and it can't be anywhere with a bed. I can't be trusted not to..." He trails off. He doesn't need to say more — the heat in his stare says more than any words could convey.

I gulp.

"Um." Deep breath. "But... *where* are we going to talk?"

"New rule." He tucks his phone into his pocket. "Humans named Zoe are not allowed to ask any questions for the rest of the night."

"I don't accept that rule."

"Sorry, too late to change it now."

"What the hell do you mean, it's too late to change it? You just *made* the damn rule!"

Parker chuckles. "Shut up and get in the car, snookums."

I shoot him a death glare. "Call me that one more time, and I'm going to start calling you *boo-bear* in front of everyone we pass on the street."

"Difference between you and me, darling?" His eyes darken. "I don't care what you call me, so long as we're not in my bed. When I'm inside you, I want you to know exactly who's fucking you. I want *my* name on your lips." His voice has gone deep. "Other that that, you can call me whatever you damn please."

I suck in a breath and decide now is a very good time to stop arguing.

He leans in. "Any more questions?"

I shake my head.

"Great. Get in the damn car."

I heave a heavy sigh... and then I get in the damn car.

TEN MINUTES LATER, I feel my eyes widen as he turns onto a familiar street.

"Why are we on Yawkey Way?"

He quirks an eyebrow. "That sounded like a question."

"Fine. I'll rephrase." I sigh deeply. "It appears, Oh Mighty Annoying One, that we are at Fenway Park."

"Very astute. You're much smarter than the girls I usually date."

I elbow him. Hard. "This isn't a date. And it's not tough to be smarter than girls who never read anything except nutritional facts on the back of their diet products."

His grin widens. "Have I told you I like it when you're sassy?"

"Several times. Flattery will get you nowhere."

"What *will* get me somewhere? Specifically, to third base?"

I scoff at him. "You're not getting anywhere near my bases."

"Zoe! I'm shocked and appalled." He shakes his head as if deeply disappointed, shifting into park just outside one of the stadium gates. "I was talking about bases on the actual baseball field. You know, where the Red Sox play. Clearly."

"Clearly," I echo dryly.

He chuckles as the engine falls silent with a low purr, throws open his door, and rounds the hood to open mine like I'm some eighteenth-century maiden climbing from a stage-coach. Before he can even reach for my handle, I'm out waiting on the curb with my arms crossed over my chest.

"Chivalry is dead?" he asks, brows raised.

"And buried," I concur.

"Great. Just checking." He grabs my hand before I can stop him and starts leading me toward the doors.

"I wish you'd stop tugging me around like a dog on a leash."

"You're so tiny. I'm worried I'll lose you in the crowd."

I glance around at the deserted street. Two days before Christmas in thirty-degree weather, there's not a soul to be seen.

"Yeah, that seems likely."

He laughs lowly as we walk along the gated entryway.

"Your snazzy car is going to get towed," I feel obligated to tell him.

"It's not mine, it's Nate's. And it won't get towed."

"This is Boston. Do you know how overjoyed it would make one of the demonic meter-maids to find a car like that parked illegally on the street?"

"Will you just trust me?" He stops and looks down at me. "Can you do that? Just for one night. Trust me."

I bite my lip to keep in all the bullshit reasons I shouldn't, all the arguments that I should never leap before I look... and give a slow nod.

"I think I can do that," I murmur quietly.

His hand tightens on mine. "*Finally.*"

When we reach a small green side door, Parker bangs a fist against the metal grate a few times.

"Jim!" he calls loudly. "It's Parker."

Almost instantly, the door cracks open.

"Bro! I didn't know you were back in the city till you texted me!" The gangly, bearded man in a Red Sox jacket reaches out and envelops Parker in a bear hug. "Haven't seen you in years! Thought you were off living the dream, exploring the world, banging chicks—" Jim seems to realize what he's saying, because he turns red and shoots me a bashful look.

I roll my eyes.

"Sorry." Jim hurries on. "What I mean to say is, never thought you'd come back to the city, after college. Guess it makes sense, though, after all that shit with your dad went down..." He gets red again. "Sorry, sorry."

Jim has a serious case of word-vomit.

Parker clears his throat awkwardly and takes a step back. "It's good to see you, man."

"You too. We gotta grab a beer sometime, catch up."

"*Definitely,*" Parker says in a way that makes me think he won't be following through on that statement anytime soon. "So, we all good?"

"Yeah, you got an hour before my shift ends. Just don't mess anything up or I'll be in a fuckload of trouble, feel me?"

"I feel you. Thanks, Jim."

"Nice outfit, by the way." Jim smirks and punches Parker

on the bright green arm of his BALLS sweater. "Not even going to ask why you're dressed like my seventy-year-old grandmother at a holiday party."

Parker laughs, returns Jim's arm punch, then leads me inside. I hear the sharp peal of the door slamming closed as we walk into the abandoned park. I must admit, it's a bit surreal to be here without the usual rush of crowds. Boston baseball fans are a boisterous lot — it's strange to see Fenway stripped of people pushing to find their rickety wooden seats, devoid of vendors calling out, "Peanuts!" at the top of their lungs as they cut through the rows, silenced of the strains of "Sweet Caroline" pouring from the overhead speakers.

The field is covered with snow; it'll be months before the season opens.

"We're definitely not supposed to be in here," I whisper-yell at Parker.

"I know," he says at a totally normal volume. "That's what makes it fun, Zoe."

I sigh.

A few hundred steps and ten minutes later, my legs are aching but my eyes are wide with wonder as we step through a door and I realize where we are.

"We're on top of the Green Monster," I breathe, spinning in a circle to get the full effect.

Fenway is the oldest MLB park in the country. Her Green Monster — the forty-foot emerald wall that towers over left field — is legendary. Even though I was raised in this city, I've never been up here before. Game tickets are too expensive for my meager salary; I can't imagine how much it would cost to take a private tour.

And yet, Parker made it happen with a single text message.

Laughing like a little kid, I drop his hand so I can spin around unrestrained. I don't care if I look like an absolute fool running between the rows; I take it all in — the snowy field sprawled out below us, the city skyline to the north, the infamous Citgo sign glowing red and white just behind the park. The stars are so bright and so close, I feel like I could reach out and grab one. Usually, with the stadium lights shining, you can't see them at all.

"This is amazing," I whisper into the dark, turning to look at Parker when I'm finally done admiring the view. "It's beautiful up here."

He's leaning against the rail, watching me.

"I admit, I'm impressed, playboy." I tilt my head and lean back against the rail. "You bring all your dates here?"

He smirks. "Darling, I'm getting the sense that somewhere along the way, you got the wrong idea about me. Probably during your little internet-stalking stint. Allow me to clear something up for you..." With measured steps, he closes some of the distance between us until we're only a handful of feet apart. "I don't date. I've never dated. I don't like long-term. Don't stay in any place long enough to get comfortable, let alone pick out china patterns with someone." His eyes lose their joking edge. "That tool Jim who let us up here? There's a reason he was surprised to see me. When I was a kid, I spent a decade looking after Phoebe, looking after my family. There was no one else to do it, so I stepped up; that didn't make it fun or easy. So, when Phoebe was finally old enough to take care of herself, I didn't hesitate."

"You left," I murmur.

He nods. "And I didn't ever plan on coming back, once I finally got out. Not for longer than a weekend, a holiday visit, a birthday. Until last spring, when my baby sister was kidnapped..." He glances at me. "I guess I have you to thank for saving her."

"It was nothing."

His eyes hold mine. "Not nothing to me."

I glance away, uncomfortable with the look he's giving me. Soft. Intimate. Ultra-warm.

I clear my throat. "Anyone would've done the same, if they'd known she was in trouble."

"How *did* you know?" he asks. "That she was in trouble? I mean... how did you know where to find her? Even Nate couldn't track her down, and he's the best in the business."

I bite my lip and look back at him. "It's complicated."

"More clandestine spy shit?"

"I'm not a spy."

"That's funny. In my fantasies, you're always tying me up..." His grin is sinful. "Strictly for interrogation purposes of course."

I snort. "I'm not a spy, or a CIA member, or any of the heroic titles you keep trying to give me. I'm just a girl with a computer."

He pauses. "You save people. Help people. Hate to break it to you, but that kind of makes you a hero, Zoe."

I shake my head, rejecting his words. "No."

"Fine." He chuckles. "But I wouldn't want to be Robert Lancaster right now, I'll tell you that much."

My eyes widen. "You looked on my flash drive!"

"Of course I looked on your damn flash drive. You think I'd give it back to you without ever glancing at it?" He chuckles. "I'm blond, but I'm not an idiot. Don't objectify me... Unless we're talking about sexual objectification. You can do *that* any time you want."

I roll my eyes. "Do you ever stop making jokes?"

"Not if I can help it."

"It's exhausting."

"*Liar.* Admit it — you laugh more with me than you do with anyone else."

"I'll admit no such thing."

"Stubborn."

"Stupid."

"Ooo, real mature."

I groan. "You're impossible."

"You think I'm cute."

"I think you have a hearing impairment."

"Possibly. But I'm gifted in other ways." He winks. "I could show you, if you want. Though, that particular tutorial would require fewer clothes."

I make a fake gagging noise. "Thanks, I'm good."

"I know you're good. That's why I'm happy I'm not the one in your crosshairs. Tell me, what are you planning to do to Lancaster? Cripple his computer network? Publicly shame his entire IT department? Harass his secretary?"

At the indirect mention of Patricia, I slide my eyes to his. "I doubt he cares as much as you do about his secretary's welfare. Frankly, she seemed to recover just fine from whatever *trauma* I inflicted on her during my visit."

Parker's grin gets wide. "Jealous, snookums?"

"No, *boo-bear*," I snap. "There's nothing to be jealous of."

"I agree." Parker's smile is almost blinding. "You know, Patricia and I have so much in common..."

I go tense.

"Mainly, the fact that we both fuck women," he adds conversationally.

I let that seep into my subconscious and ignore the simultaneous feelings of relief and embarrassment flaring through me.

"I don't know why that should concern me," I say in an uppity voice, when I think I've gotten my breathing under control.

"Of course not." Parker sounds thoroughly amused.

"Anyway," I say, latching onto a new topic with desperation. "Robert Lancaster is a bad guy. Trust me — he deserves everything he's got coming to him."

"I know. Just..." Parker pauses, his tone growing serious. "Be careful with him. He's a powerful guy, like it or not. You don't want him as an enemy."

"Maybe *he* doesn't want *me* as an enemy."

Parker's lips quirk up. "I'll bet that's true. Still... just be careful."

"I'm always careful. Plus, I've got Luca to help. He'll watch out for me."

The air gets a little tense.

"I'm sure he will," he says after a very long minute.

"Parker." I wait until he looks over at me. "Luca is like my brother. My family. There's nothing romantic between us."

Our eyes hold for a suspended moment and I can tell he's reading me to see if I'm being sincere. After a moment, he nods and I know he's accepted my words as truth. For now, at least.

"So..." I say, eager to change the subject to something less awkward. "What's the coolest place you've ever been?"

He dips his head back to look up at the stars and exhales sharply. "I could never pick just one. Though this place, right here with you..." His eyes find mine. "Top Five. No question."

I look away swiftly, focusing on the view and ignoring my thudding heartbeat. "You must be about ready to sail off into the sunset, huh? You've been here, what — seven, eight months?"

"Nine." Parker's voice is thoughtful. "You know, when my shithead father went to prison and the whole damn WestTech empire — an empire I've never wanted jack-shit to do with, mind you — was in jeopardy, I knew there was no choice but to come back. And then Phoebe asked me to stay. She needed me here. So I sucked it up and I stayed."

"I'm sorry," I say, meaning it. I know how it feels when

you're trapped in a situation out of your control. That cornered, inescapable feeling — it can drive you mad.

His voice gets lower. "Since I got here, I've been counting the minutes until I can leave again."

Inexplicable disappointment snakes through me at the thought of him leaving. I hope it isn't visible on my face, which I'm keeping carefully averted.

He slides a little closer. "Or... I *was* counting the minutes. Until I saw you."

I try not to let my knees quake as I feel the warmth of his side press against mine.

"Me?" I breathe, finally looking over at him.

His eyes trap mine immediately and I see they're dangerously soft again. He reaches out slowly, like I'm a horse who might buck if he moves too fast, and tucks a rogue strand of hair behind my ear.

"There's this thrill I get, when I go on an adventure. Climb a peak, explore a city, set down wheels on a dirt runway in a place I've never been before. I've spent my whole life chasing that feeling." He pauses. "You're the first person I've ever met who makes me feel that rush while I'm standing still. Looking at you, I don't need to chase some crazy whim. You..." He shakes his head, as if he can't believe he's saying this shit out loud. "You're a huge adventure in a five foot, hundred pound package."

For a minute, I don't respond. I can't. All I can do is stand there as his words wash over me, listening to the pulse pounding between my ears and trying not to let my eyes water.

Zoe Bloom doesn't cry over boys. Even boys who say things so sweet, she's worried she'll get used to hearing them and be miserable for the rest of her life when they inevitably stop.

I push that voice away. Force back the tears stinging behind my eyes. Brace myself for impact.

And then I take a tiny step forward, so there's only the smallest sliver of space left between our bodies. So I'm completely invading his space. He's so tall, I have to crane my head back to keep his eyes on mine.

"A good adventure or a bad adventure?" I whisper haltingly.

I watch his Adam's apple bob in his throat as he swallows, and I get the sense his control is hanging by a thread.

"You are my favorite kind of adventure," he says simply as his arms come up around me and he crushes his mouth down on mine.

Heat explodes between us. The fire that started burning last week when we met never truly went out. It was always there in the back of my mind, embers just waiting for a spark to reignite the inferno. Parker's mouth moves over mine in greedy, uncompromising sweeps and I return his kiss with equal fervor.

My hands grip his shoulders; his tug at my waist. I'm plastered against him, every curve, every atom in my body possessed by his, and it's still not close enough.

Sexual attraction is a powerful drug.

It's not something you can force or manufacture or hope to foster with enough time or practice or little blue pills. It's *elemental*.

I don't care how much you love someone's personality, their sense of humor, their compassion, their every redeemable quality... if you don't want to tear their clothes off, at the end of the day it's never going to work out. Without that fundamental attraction, two people can't last.

Longing. Desire. Lust.

Parker and I have it in spades.

We may not always communicate well with words, but our bodies speak a language all their own — that much is clear from just the way he touches me.

This sheer, unstoppable pull I feel for him is unlike anything I've ever experienced. It goes through me like a needle, threads into every part of my existence until I can't think of anything except the sensation of his hands against my skin.

I make a needy sound in the back of my throat as I push up onto my tiptoes, trying to deepen our kiss.

"Fuck," Parker growls, tearing his mouth from mine. "We're supposed to be talking. That's why I brought you here."

"Funny," I pant, clinging to his shoulders. "I thought you brought me here to see whether you could get to third base."

His eyebrows waggle. "What are my odds?"

"Slim to none."

"How about second?"

"Not likely."

"Figured as much." His mouth lands on the tip of my nose as he gently pushes me back to create a little distance. "Come on. Sit with me for a minute. And try not to be too grabby with the goods. I'm not a piece of meat, Zoe."

"You're the worst."

He laughs as he leads me down to the front row of seats, right on the edge of the wall. I don't fight him. As much as I'd like to get naked with him, the top of the Green Monster on a freezing December night is really not the appropriate locale for that.

We settle onto two metal seats, purposely leaving a few inches between our bodies. Our only point of contact is Parker's hand enveloping mine. His large fingers trace the small bones of my wrist as we settle in, and just that light touch sends flares of sensation through me like electricity. Trying to control my hormones, I prop my feet up on the rail and sigh as I take in the dark field below us.

"It's so fucking cool up here."

Parker nods. "When I was a kid, I always dreamed my dad would take me to a game here. He never managed to find the time." His shoulders lift in a small shrug. "That probably sounds totally cliché."

"It's not," I say softly. "There's nothing cliché about wanting good parents."

"I did my best, trying to raise Phoebe after our mom died. But when you're eleven years old and suddenly you've got to be an adult, a parent... you don't get to be a kid anymore."

I look over at him, this beautiful man who I've misjudged over and over since the first moment we met, and feel his words sink into me like a blade.

"I know what it's like to have your childhood taken away," I murmur after a few minutes. "And I'm sorry — about your mom. About everything."

Parker's thumb strokes the fragile flesh on the inside of my wrist. "It was a long time ago."

"Maybe," I murmur, staring hard at the pitcher's mound. "But there are some scars even time can't heal."

He doesn't press me for details, even though he could. He's revealed much more about himself than I expected, and I haven't returned the favor. Not remotely.

Instead, he just slides his arm around the back of my chair and tugs me closer. I let my head fall onto his shoulder, breathing in the scent of his skin and listening to the strong pulse in his neck, and for a while we don't say anything at all.

When Jim comes up and tells us his shift is over, we walk in silence down the steps back to the car. And this time, I don't complain that he's holding my hand. In fact, I twine my fingers tighter with his and tell myself I'd be an idiot to ever let go.

CHAPTER 13

THE FLOODGATES

"TAKE A LEFT."

Parker turns the car onto my street and I watch his jaw clench tighter.

"Just up ahead." I point out the old piano factory. "That's my building."

He glances at me. "That's not a building. It's a crack den."

"It's perfectly safe!"

"Zoe." He pulls the Porsche to a stop at the curb. "You shouldn't be living here."

"So, it's not the greatest neighborhood." I shrug. "Just because it's not a multimillion dollar yacht doesn't mean I have to move."

"There are two drug deals going on in the alley behind us."

I hesitate. "Three, actually, if you count the dealer behind the dumpster..."

Parker shakes his head. "I'm not leaving you here alone."

"You just want an invitation upstairs."

"That's true," he admits. "But only eighty percent because I want to see you naked. That last twenty percent strictly wants to check your windows and doors to make sure they lock properly."

"What a gentleman," I drawl, rolling my eyes.

"Zoe." His voice is soft. "I'm not going to push you. Ever. Yeah, I want you — your body, your mouth, your hands on me. I want you so bad it hurts. But I also want your mind. I want to know the secrets behind your eyes, and what makes you sad, and why you're so damn determined to walk through life alone. And I'm not going to do anything to jeopardize that." His heated eyes lock on my mouth. "I'll wait. Until you're ready. I might not be any good at it, but I'll wait."

By the time he's done talking, my thighs are pressed tight together and I'm feeling a little feverish.

Taking a deep breath, I lean into his space and whisper, "And what if I'm ready now?"

I see the flash of a grin, the flare of desire in his eyes, and then he's out of the car. I've barely gotten my seatbelt off when he yanks open my door and pulls me onto the curb.

"I was really fucking hoping you'd say that," he mutters as his lips close over mine.

THE ELEVATOR RIDE upstairs is a blur of hands in hair, fingers finding buttons, mouths exploring skin. His hands lift me as my legs go around his waist and my arms twine around his shoulders. Pressing me into the elevator wall, Parker's mouth dominates mine in a way that should scare me — too possessive, too needy, as if he already owns every facet of me, body and soul.

I'm a foregone conclusion in the circle of his arms.

"You told me not to kiss you in any more elevators," he reminds me, his voice muffled in the crook of my neck.

"Shut up," I say, tugging his lips back to mine.

When the ancient freight car clatters to a stop on the sixth floor, I barely have the mental wherewithal to remember to grab my key from the security panel as he carries me into the loft. He growls something against my mouth that sounds like *bed* so I unwind my legs from his waist and lead him there, walking backwards so my mouth never leaves his. We don't waste time finding the lights.

When my thighs bump the bed, I jolt back onto the plush white pillows — and Parker follows me down, his body settling over me with delectable, breath-stealing weight.

"It's fucking freezing in here," he grumbles against my lips, reaching back to tug off his sweater in one sharp motion.

"Someone once told me..." My fingers trace his bare chest and he groans. "...The cure for hypothermia..." I gasp as his fingers flick open the button of my jeans. "...Is getting naked with the nearest warm body..." My hips lift so he can slide the fabric over my hips. I'm barely holding onto my train of thought.

"Oh, really?" I feel Parker's grin against the skin of my stomach as his hands slide my shirt up.

"Yes," I breathe as he pushes my thighs apart. "Do you happen to know..." I pant as his head moves lower, so his mouth is poised over the lace triangle of my underwear. "...If there's any truth to that theory?"

The final words come out in a breathy squeak, because his hot mouth is suddenly *there*, pressed against the most intimate part of me, and it's all I can do not to come up off the bed at the sensation, even through the fabric.

"Darling, I'm happy to test any theory that involves me and you, naked in this bed." Parker's voice is a rumble. "But right now, I'm going to fuck you — first with my mouth, then with my hands, and later, when you're ready, with my cock. So let's save the discussion of our hypothetical findings until after you're done coming. You okay with that?"

"Yes," I whisper, my hands slipping into his hair as he tugs my underwear down to my knees.

"Good."

And then I don't say another damn thing, because Parker West and his dirty-talking mouth are all over me, keeping the promise he just made.

Multiple times.

NO ONE who's ever met me would make the mistake of calling me mushy. I'm not clingy or emotional. Certainly not one of those idiotic girls who stands in the mirror giggling at herself before a first date, trying out the sound of her crush's last name tagged on the end of hers.

Sex has always been something of a fun, yet ultimately substance-less endeavor for me. I pick up sexual partners at the bar with the same perfunctory selection I use to buy roses in a grocery store. You know, the commercially produced ones behind those glass doors that always look a little too perfect from their artificial coloring and are typically sanitized of any actual floral scent.

Sure, they're a pretty pick-me-up in a cheap vase on my kitchen table... for a few days. When their petals start to wither and fall, though, it's time to toss them in the trash and move on.

No sentimental strings attached.

Which is why it's so alarming to me that, with my limbs wrapped around Parker, with his body driving into mine in powerful, passionate thrusts that make my head spin, there's nothing perfunctory about it. Just like everything else in my orderly life, Parker took one look at my rules of intimacy and chose to break every single one.

"Zoe," he rasps, moving faster. "Open your eyes."

I don't fight him — my lashes flutter open at his command. In the past two hours he's possessed me entirely, orgasm by orgasm, stripping away my armor until I'm laid bare beneath him. Utterly defenseless.

"Look at me, Zoe."

Through the cloud of lust, I force my eyes to focus. His gaze traps mine, razor-sharp. The hazel of his irises is so bright, so intense, I feel like I could drown in the depths of his stare.

"Who's touching you?" he asks, pounding into me.

I gasp. "You are."

"Say my name, Zoe."

"Parker," I breathe, arching my back.

His forehead drops to my neck when he hears his name on my lips and he groans. "That's right, baby. I'm fucking you. You're mine, now." His mouth crushes mine in a carnal, brutal kiss. "This is where it starts. You and me." His strokes are getting faster, deeper, harder. "You hear me? No more running."

His hips move in a circle and I nearly shatter. I feel it building again inside me — I don't know how much more I can take before I explode under his hands.

"Say it, Zoe."

"No more running," I manage to gasp as he pushes deeper.

"You and me," he repeats. "Together."

I nod and pull him closer, nails digging into his back so hard I'm afraid I'll break the skin. "Together."

"That's right baby."

He drives deep one last time, his shoulders shaking as he finds release, and I cry out his name as my world flips on its axis again.

It's just sex, I think as I lay beneath him, trembling from the force of my attraction, from the things he made me feel, from the boundaries he pushed, both physical and emotional.

Just sex.

So... why is it suddenly so unimaginable to think about having another throwaway one-night-stand ever again? And why don't I protest when he cradles me close to his chest, his lips in my hair and his hands splayed across my skin, like he can't quite bring himself to let go?

I don't know.

All I do know is...

Lying inside the span of his arms is the safest place I've spent a night since my parents were killed. And that's not something you question.

It's something you treasure.

I DON'T WAKE him when I slide out of bed a few hours later and pad my way over to the bank of computers by the far wall, tugging his giant black sweater on over my head as I go. I've decided I'm not returning it; after a week in my possession, I've grown too fond of it to let him take it back.

Possession is nine-tenths of the law.

I make sure to toggle off the volume as the monitors power up, so as not to wake Parker. I can't sleep. No matter how I've tried to quiet my mind, thoughts of Lancaster and the Lynn Factory keep haunting me, playing over and over until I have no choice but to confront them.

It's late, so Luca's probably asleep, but I send him a quick text anyway, reminding him to check out the factory pipes if he has a chance tomorrow. Then, I crack my neck, flex my wrists, and dive down the rabbit hole.

The Clover virus has spread completely through the LC network, by this point — I have access to almost all their files and servers. Which is *great*... but it's also a lot more information than I thought it would be. It'll take me several years to pour through all of it.

I feel like Sisyphus pushing a damn boulder up a mountainside as I attempt to read through emails and business contracts, ledgers and financial reports. Any headway I make feels imperceptible in the face of so much material.

An hour ticks by, then two. Legal jargon blurs before my bleary eyes as they fly over the screen. I'm practically asleep on my keyboard when I finally discover something — well, I *think* it's something.

Deep in the archives of permits and safety inspections, there's a bevy of deleted documents, left behind like invisible strands of DNA at the scene of a homicide. The average computer user will drag and drop a file into their desktop trash bin and assume it's gone forever.

That's rarely the case.

The file still exists until it's been permanently scrubbed from the hard drive. If you're looking for something suspicious on a computer... My advice? Search for the things they tried to delete from existence. That's usually a good place to start.

And it's exactly where I find the first clue in the LC case.

The single-page document looks like a hundred other documents I've scrolled past, tonight, but a short, four-letter word catches my eye.

PIPE

My eyes widen as they read. It's a work order for new pipes to be installed at the Lynn Factory.

In itself, that's not particularly earth-shattering.

The weird part is... it's dated two days after the plant closed for business. Those shiny pipes I saw when I snuck in were brand new.

So, Lancaster replaced them after closing the place down.

But why?

The question nags at me like a paper cut on a knuckle, refusing to heal over no matter how long I stare at the screen. When Luca suggested we take down Lancaster, I was hesitant. Now that I've started digging, I'm too invested in the project to turn back. I have to know the answer, have to solve the mystery.

Before I fall asleep at my desk, I email a PDF of the work order to Luca and print out a copy for my own files. I've just popped the last Reese's cup from my stash into my mouth when I feel two hands settle on my shoulders and a warm, wet set of lips hit my neck.

"Come back to bed," Parker murmurs, his voice still husky from sleep.

"Can't," I say around a mouthful of chocolate. "I'm working."

"It's two in the morning."

I shrug.

He sighs and crouches down beside me to peer at my screen. "This the Lancaster case?"

I dart a wary glance at him and nod.

Parker's eyes are still on the screen. "What are you looking for?"

I pause, searching for the right words.

He must notice my hesitation, because he looks over at me with a small smile playing on his lips. "Still don't trust me?"

"It's not that I don't trust you." I swallow. "I just don't know how much of this I should share with you. WestTech has done business with Lancaster Consolidated in the past. Anything I say could complicate business matters for you."

"My father is the one who worked with scumbags like

Robert Lancaster." Parker's lips twist. "Since I took over, I've been weeding through our corporate partners a bit. Clearing house — quietly, of course. Don't want investors to panic or stocks to take a tumble. But I'm hoping within a year, WestTech will be free of its less-than-upstanding connections, for the most part. It's one of the priorities I brought into the company, when I decided I was taking over. I refuse to run our family business the way my father did — through schemes and manipulation and bribery."

I stare at him in silence, a little awed.

"What?" he asks, brow knitting.

"Sometimes I forget that you're kind of a big deal," I whisper, laughing lightly. "You're such a—"

Playboy. Man-child.

His brows lift.

I bite back the word. "I mean, you don't act like a normal CEO. Most of those guys are total tool bags."

He shakes his head, grabs the seat of my rolling desk chair, and spins me toward him so he's kneeling between my legs with his hands on either armrest.

"Darling, a lot of people mistake being a dick for being in charge." His eyes crinkle. "But I've found you don't have to stomp around like a tyrant to earn respect. Life as a CEO isn't all that different from life on the road. Bottom line — you treat people like shit, they'll be shit workers. Treat them like gold..."

"Let me guess," I interject. "Everyone gets gold stars?"

He grins. "I was going to say *and you all make a fuckton of money,* but that works, too."

"A CEO who doesn't have a god-complex, power-trip, or obsession with belittling people," I marvel. "What is the world coming to?"

He chuckles and before I can react, he leans in and kisses me — hard, uncompromising, his tongue invading my mouth.

"You taste like peanut butter," he murmurs as he pulls away. I watch his eyes dilate as his hands slide around my waist beneath the bottom hem of his sweater. "This is mine."

"It *was*," I correct. "I'm confiscating it."

"Looks better on you, anyway." His gaze flickers down to my mouth. "I like you in my clothes. Almost as much as I like you out of them..."

A pulse of heat shoots between my legs. "I have to work."

"Uh huh." His hands slide higher, up my ribcage. The sensual scrape of his calluses against my skin makes my teeth sink into my bottom lip.

"Parker," I protest weakly.

It's the wrong thing to say, if I was hoping to deter him. Hearing me breathe his name only seems to make him more desperate for me. And apparently I'm equally desperate, because when he guides me to the floor and pulls the sweater up over my head, there's not an ounce of hesitation in my mind as I wrap my arms around his back to bring him closer. All thoughts of conspiracy theories and corruption disappear from my head as he makes slow, sweet love to me beneath my desk.

"WHAT ARE YOU DOING TOMORROW?" Parker calls from the next aisle over.

Waking up this morning to discover there was absolutely no food in my refrigerator besides some expired milk and what, at one point in the distant past, we think may've been a banana, he dragged me down the street to the small convenience store where I occasionally stock up on groceries.

And by *groceries* I mean chocolate peanut butter cups and Diet Coke.

Breakfast of champions.

But of course, Parker is some kind of crunchy granola health-nut who likes to start his day eating cereal that looks like it was made for rabbits while drinking organic pomegranate juice out of an eight-dollar plastic bottle. Needless to say, he doesn't exactly approve of my highly-nutritious eating habits.

"Tomorrow?" I call back, staring absentmindedly at the small selection of flowers behind the glass doors in the corner.

No more grocery store roses for me.

"Yes, tomorrow." Parker rounds a corner with one of those little plastic carriers in his hands. It's filled to the brim with things I will never eat.

"What is all that?" I ask, staring at the groceries.

"Ho boy. We're going to have to start from scratch with this one, aren't we?" He shakes his head, like a kindergarten teacher with one of his students. "This green stuff is called *lettuce*. And the other stuff, right here, is called *broccoli*. Can you say *bro-cco-li*?"

I shoot him a death glare. "Shut up. You know what I meant."

"Did I?" He grins.

"Why are you getting all that food?"

"To *eat*." His head tilts. "Why? What do you usually do with your food? Do you have some weird fetish I should know about, where you strip naked and cover yourself with—

"Seriously, don't finish that sentence."

His lips clamp shut to hold in a laugh. "Fine."

My arms cross over my chest. "I'll never eat all that."

"Maybe it's for me. Not all of us subsist on caffeine and chocolate alone."

"You planning on bringing it back to your place?" I ask.

"No, but I am planning to spend a lot of time at *your* place, now that we'll be having sex every night."

"You're delusional." I snort. "And you also need a carriage. The handles on that thing are about to snap."

He scoffs. "Men don't push carriages. It's against the laws of nature."

"So you'd rather walk around giving yourself carpal tunnel from carrying all that?"

"Absolutely."

"You're an idiot."

"Aww, snookums, what have I told you about being so sweet to me in public?" He makes eye contact with the woman shopping for applesauce ten feet down the aisle and winks suggestively at her. "You should hear her in the bedroom." He gestures at me. "Total drill sergeant, this one."

The woman glances at me with wide eyes, then turns her back and quickly walks away. She doesn't even take her applesauce.

"I hate you," I hiss, fighting off a blush as I whirl to face Parker — who, I might add, is grinning like he's just won the lottery.

"Come on." He laughs. "Grab your peanut butter cups. I'll meet you up front."

There's really nothing to do but roll my eyes as he pivots on one heel and strides to the front of the store, somehow looking handsome and put together after very little sleep, while wearing his raunchy holiday sweater from yesterday. I follow at a slower pace, stopping to grab a six-pack of diet soda and a jumbo bag of Reese's on my way. When I reach the front, I make sure to get into a different checkout line so Parker can't pull any macho crap by attempting to pay for my groceries.

There's an old lady in front of me, struggling with the credit card reader. The conveyer-belt is practically empty, except for some cans of soup, a box of crackers, and a few rolls of toilet paper.

"Ma'am, as I told you, starting last week we only accept cash or chip-enabled credit cards." The cashier crosses her arms over her chest impatiently. "You can't use that card here."

"Chip-enabled?" the white-haired woman asks. "I don't know what that is."

The cashier sighs. "Call your card company. They'll send you one."

"But I need these groceries today. Even if they send a new card, it'll take at least a week to get here." The woman's voice trembles a bit. "What am I supposed to do in the meantime?"

"Come back with cash."

"All— all right." The woman is visibly distressed. "I suppose I'll have to do that."

"Ma'am, I'm sorry, but I have a line." The cashier looks pointedly at me and the three other people waiting. "So, I'm going to need you to—"

"Here," I say without thinking, reaching into my wallet and pulling out a twenty. "How much are her groceries? I'll pay for them."

"It's $17.50," the cashier tells me.

"Perfect." I pull out another twenty. "Just throw it all in with mine, I'll pay for it together."

"Oh, no," the elderly woman protests quietly, grabbing my arm. "I couldn't possibly—"

"It's already done." I pass over the money and smile at her.

"Thank you," she whispers, clearly embarrassed. "I usually have cash with me, but I was in a hurry this morning and—"

"Don't worry about it." I shrug and toss my stuff in a clear plastic bag. "The new chip technology is a big pain in the ass, if you ask me. But if you call the number on the back of your card, they'll send you an updated one."

She smiles and takes her bag from the cashier. "I'll do that when I get home. Can I at least pay you back?"

I shake my head. "Absolutely not."

Her hands curl around the bag handles. "I don't know how to thank you."

"Then don't." I smile at her as she nods, turns, and walks out of the store.

I'm still smiling as I shove my change into my purse. When I go to grab my bag, I find Parker's already got it looped around his arm alongside his own groceries. He's waiting right at the end of the checkout line, watching me carefully.

"What?" I narrow my eyes at him. "Why are you giving me that look, playboy?"

"No reason," he murmurs, suppressing whatever emotion I just saw in his eyes. "Come on, Zoe. Let's make like a tree."

"And leaf?" I snort and hold open the door for him — his arms are full of groceries. "I didn't realize you were in fourth grade."

"What do you have against a good pun?"

"Besides the fact that they're the lowest form of humor?"

"Baby, I'm the pun master. I've got puns for days."

"How nice for you."

We walk in silence for a half block. That's as long as he can contain himself.

"You know, sometimes when I get naked in the bathroom, the shower gets *turned on*."

I sigh. "Stop."

"I couldn't remember how to use a boomerang, but don't worry, it *came back to me*."

"You're getting less attractive by the second."

"My grade in Marine Biology was below *C* level."

"That, I can believe. You're not the brightest bulb."

"Two peanuts were walking in a rough area. One was *a salted*."

"That's it! I'm never sleeping with you again."

"Fine. I'm done." His voice is strangled, like he's trying desperately to hold in a laugh.

Glancing over, I see his lips are clamped together to hide his smile.

"Oh, just say it," I grumble. "I'm worried your brain will explode if you hold it in any longer."

He laughs. "Never trust atoms. They *make up everything.*"

I roll my eyes. "It's a good thing you're hot. Otherwise, you'd have no redeeming qualities."

"If I wasn't weighted down by so many groceries right now, I'd probably kiss you."

"If you weren't such a pain in the ass, I'd definitely let you."

"Just for that, I'm not making you a kale smoothie when we get to your place."

"Considering I don't have a blender, you're not making *anyone* a kale smoothie."

"God, it's like dating a heathen."

"Except, we aren't dating."

He shakes his head in faux disgust. "Diet of pure sugar, no working heat, doors that don't lock... I know how Jane felt when she met Tarzan. Except, obviously, I look much more dashing in a petticoat than Jane."

I raise my brows. "Not even going to touch that one."

"You said you love kids' movies. Figured you'd appreciate the reference."

We're almost back at my building. "Yeah, well, Tarzan was never my favorite. I was all about *Beauty and the Beast.*"

"Let me guess." His brows waggle. "You wanted a beast to call your own?"

"Um, no." I punch in the code to the outer door and follow him inside. "I wanted the cool-as-shit castle with the talking furniture, huge library, and enchanted closets. Obviously."

"Ah." He grins at me as we wait for the elevator to return,

clanging and groaning as it descends down the shaft. "Phoebe loved that one, too. She made me watch it a thousand times with her when she was seven. And then they made the damn Christmas-themed sequel, which wasn't nearly as good."

I bite my lip to keep in a laugh.

Playboy billionaire Parker West is discussing Disney movies with me.

It takes a moment for that to sink in.

Parker sighs. "The snow, all the decorations on the damn castle... I think that's why she's so obsessed with Christmas, to be honest. I place one hundred percent of the blame on Disney."

I slide up the wooden lift gate and wait for the heavy metal doors to edge open. "Good to know."

"Speaking of Christmas, you never answered my question."

"Hmm?" I follow him into the elevator and slide my key into the panel. The car jolts into motion.

"Earlier, in the store, I asked what you're doing tomorrow."

I stare hard at the illuminated buttons on the panel. "Tomorrow?"

"Yes." He pauses. "Christmas Eve. Prequel to the most widely-celebrated holiday in our nation. Maybe you've heard of it."

"Ah." I swallow and keep my eyes averted. When the doors slide open, I step into the loft and practically run to the kitchen. "So, yeah, you can put those anywhere. I suppose I'll have to make room in my fridge for your healthy crap — that moldy banana is taking up *so* much space—"

"Zoe."

Damn. He's using his quiet voice. That gentle, cajoling one that makes me shiver and sigh at the same time.

I look over at him. He's dropped the grocery bags on the

counter and is staring at me with questions swimming in his eyes.

"You want to tell me about it, or you wanna keep pretending it's not an issue until it breaks you down?" He steps toward me, eyes wide with trust. "Your call, darling. But you should know, whenever that happens — you falling apart — whether it's right now or tomorrow or next week or next year... if you'll let me, I'll be here to pick up the pieces."

And just like that, for the first time in years, staring at this man who never pushes or pries, this man who's just *there* for me even when I don't deserve it... maybe especially when I don't deserve it... I feel the damn floodgates crack wide open and tears spill down my cheeks in a relentless torrent of bottled-up despair.

CHAPTER 14

THE LONE WOLF

ONCE I START CRYING, I can't seem to stop.

I weep and weep and weep until my throat is burning and my lungs are aching, until there isn't a single ounce of moisture left behind my stinging eyes. I weep for all the years I never allowed myself to, for all the days when I didn't have the luxury of falling apart. Because you can't cry when you're sleeping on a cot in a church basement surrounded by strangers. You can't let it show how much it hurts when your foster mother turns a blind eye to her husband's wandering hands. You can't be meek or weak when there's a whole world of wolves out there, circling in the darkness, picking off the sheep one by one.

You do the only thing you can do: You become a wolf, too.

A wild thing.

It's better to have battle scars and sharp edges than wind up dinner on a predator's table.

But in this moment, I don't want to have claws or teeth. I don't want to lash out.

Inexplicably, I want strong arms around me.

I want lips on my hair, murmuring reassurances.

I want someone else to hold back the shadows that circle close, just for a few minutes, so I can finally, finally, *finally* drop my guard.

Parker doesn't say a word. He just holds me together when everything is spiraling into pieces, just like he promised he would. He lends me the strength I need to allow myself to be weak.

His shirt is wet when I finally fall silent, my ragged sobs settling into something resembling proper breath.

"Guess you picked now," he murmurs against my hair.

"I'm sorry," I hiccup. "I'm not usually this girl who gets all weepy and needs a guy to hold her and—" I hiccup again. "—to tell her it's all going to be okay."

"I know, Zoe." His arms tighten a bit.

"It's just this time of year, you know? The lights and the ornaments and the decorations and all the people out on the streets smiling and singing and acting like they actually enjoy each other's company. It's exhausting! I'm just... *exhausted*. I try to avoid it, to keep to myself, but this year..." I breathe deeply. "I'm sorry."

"Shhh." He pets my hair in long strokes. "Stop apologizing. You never have to apologize to me."

I pull back to look up into his face. There's no pity in his gaze – nothing but compassion and sympathy and maybe a bit of worry.

"Thank you," I whisper.

"I didn't do anything, darling."

"You were here." I shrug. "That's everything."

He pauses and I can tell there's something on his mind, something he wants to say but can't quite put into words.

"Say it," I whisper.

"You might feel better... If you talked about it."

I swallow. "I..."

"I don't mean right now," he says gently. "I don't even mean with me. But you should talk to someone, Zoe. You can't keep all this emotion locked up forever. It'll kill you. There are people out there, qualified people with fancy degrees, whose sole purpose is to help with shit like this. Believe me, I'd know – after everything that happened with my mom's death, my father's total inability to be a parent, I've got the therapy bills to prove it."

My brows lift. "You?"

"I know." His smile is wry. "Parker West, the cavalier adventurer, in therapy. Who'd have guessed?" He shrugs. "There's nothing wrong with admitting you need help, reaching out and taking it from someone who's offering. There's no shame in admitting you can't do it all yourself."

Where did he come from?

How did I find him?

Seven billion people on this earth... and somehow I find the exact one I need.

"I think..." I trail off. It takes a minute, but I somehow muster my courage. "I think... *You're* the person I want to talk to about it. Not some stranger on a couch in a stuffy office who'll shrink me for $400 over the course of an hour. I'd rather talk to someone who..."

Cares about me.

Understands me.

Accepts me.

I don't finish the rest of the sentence; neither does he. But his eyes fill with something warm and his voice is barely audible when he rumbles, "All right, Zoe," with so much emotion it nearly makes me cry again.

I take him by the hand and lead him to my desk. Opening the bottom drawer, I pull out the frame I keep hidden in the depths, where I don't have to look at it because it hurts too much. I barely glance at the image behind the glass as I pass it to Parker.

I don't need to — it's been burned into my memory for years. I can see it with my eyes closed, every perfect detail.

A little blonde girl in her ballerina costume, clutching a bouquet of red roses. Her proud parents, one on each side, their smiles so wide you'd think their daughter had just nailed her audition for Juilliard, rather than completed a rather halting rendition of *The Nutcracker*.

"These are..." Parker trails off. His finger hovers just over the glass surface.

"My parents." I nod. "And me. I was five."

He looks up at me as I pass him the other document from the drawer. It's a weathered sheet of newspaper, the front headline faded after nearly twenty years but still legible.

HOLIDAY DOUBLE-HOMICIDE: COUPLE SLAIN ON CHRISTMAS EVE

I watch his eyes move over the words, see the way his face sets into grim lines of grief as he reaches the smaller caption below the picture of bloody snow and rose petals outside the opera house. I memorized it long ago.

Rebecca and Luther Bloom, killed outside a recital hall on Christmas Eve by a suspect still-at-large. Their daughter Zoe Bloom, age 5, who witnessed the gruesome attack, remains in stable condition at Boston Children's Hospital, where she is expected to make a full recovery.

"Oh, Zoe." Parker looks up at me, ghosts swirling in his eyes, and I feel my heart clench like a fist inside my chest. There's nothing he can say. I know that — it's why I've never bothered discussing this with anyone. Even Luca knows only the smallest of details.

But, I'm stunned to discover, I don't *need* him to say anything. It's enough to have him reach over and twine his fingers with mine, his warm grip saying everything he can't find words for.

I feel my eyes fill with tears again, but I manage to keep them at bay this time. He only asks one question.

"Did they catch the scumbag who did this?"

I shake my head. "No. But... I've been trying to figure out what happened since I was old enough to turn on a computer."

His eyes flash. "That's why you do this. The hacking, the coding skills..."

I nod.

"So..." His hand fists in frustration. "The police have no leads? Nothing?"

"It's a cold case," I say, feeling hollowed out from my crying jag. "Back then, when it happened, there was an entire department trying to solve it. But as years went by with no suspects, no clues, no new evidence..."

"They stopped looking." His face contorts into a scowl. "That's bullshit. I don't care how long it takes, the BPD should be all over this."

"It's complicated."

"What do you mean?"

"The FBI was involved somehow. I don't know what prompted them to look into my parents' deaths, but last year I hacked into their database as a last-ditch effort to find a possible lead and..."

"You found something?"

"Maybe." I shrug. "There's a file that comes up, when you type my father's name into the government system. It's almost entirely redacted, so it's been pretty useless to me."

Parker's eyebrows lift. "That's weird."

"That's what I thought." I swallow. "Why would my father's name and details of his murder be in an FBI file, unless there's more to his death than some random act of violence?

Some crazed, Christmas-hating murderer on a senseless rampage?" My voice breaks. "I've spent so long wondering, so many years questioning why they were taken from me. And not having answers..."

Parker's silent for a minute. When he speaks, his voice is a vow.

"I'll help you. We'll find out. I promise you, Zoe. This is the last Christmas you'll spend wondering what happened to your parents."

"How can you promise something like that?" I whisper brokenly.

"My best friend is the best private investigator in the city." His eyes are somber. "Plus, my sister's abduction last spring and my father's testimony served Boston's biggest mob boss to the FBI on a silver platter. They owe the family a favor, trust me."

Something dangerous swirls to life inside me. It feels an awful lot like hope.

His eyes hold mine. "You aren't alone anymore, Zoe."

There's a lump in my throat too big to talk around, so I don't even try. I just reach for him and, when I do, he's there to hold me close.

LATER THAT AFTERNOON, I'm sitting in the passenger seat of the Porsche with my arms crossed over my chest, staring straight ahead and wondering why I ever agreed to this.

"Are you sure I have to go?"

"You don't have to do anything you don't want to, darling," Parker says. "But I'd say there's a seventy-five percent chance if you stall any longer out here with me, Phoebe's gonna burst through those doors and drag you inside with her bare bands."

Damn. Figured as much.

"Fine," I mutter, grabbing the door handle. "I'll go. But I won't like it."

"Hey." His voice is soft; when I glance back at him, I see his eyes are, too. "Forgetting something, aren't you?"

My brows lift. "What?"

He leans across the center console and kisses me — a no-nonsense, domineering possession of my lips. His hand slides into my hair at the nape, his tongue sweeps into my mouth, and by the time he's done, I'm panting.

"Oh," I reply breathlessly. "That."

"Yeah, *that*." He grins at me. "Now go, before I decide you should blow off this whole *lunch with the girls* thing, and take you back to my boat to make you my sex slave."

I tilt my head. "Actually, that doesn't sound half bad..."

His eyes darken. "Don't tempt me."

I laugh, push open the door, and hop out. Bending down, I blow him a kiss before I slam the door.

"See you later, sailor."

The grin on his face is hot enough to leave scorch marks. "Count on it, darling."

The Porsche tires squeal as he rockets away from the curb, barrels down the road, and turns out of sight... leaving me alone on a sidewalk, chewing my lip and staring up at the cheery pink awning of my favorite bakery. Never has a cupcake shop looked so ominous.

Though, admittedly, that has more to do with the fact that there's a group of women inside waiting to pick my brain for details of my sex life, and less to do with their top-notch pastries.

Phoebe called shortly after my meltdown, insisting I come to lunch with her and "the girls" — a group I must assume includes Gemma, Shelby, Chrissy, and Lila. Resistance seemed futile, especially when Parker suggested he'd use the time to meet with Nate and discuss my parents' case.

I heave a deep, martyred sigh and force myself to walk inside, thinking it's probably a bad sign I'd be happier talking with the guys about a grisly crime than deconstructing my somewhat baffling relationship status with these girls.

"Zoe!" Phoebe yells as soon as I walk through the door, hopping to her feet — which are, of course, clad in fabulous stilettos. "We're over here!"

She waves like a lunatic, as if there's a remote chance I haven't seen their group occupying the large table in the corner. Unlikely, considering the rest of the cafe is pretty much empty.

I wave awkwardly and walk toward them.

"Hi, Zoe!" Gemma says, grinning at me as she scoots over to make room in the booth. "Come sit."

"What do you want?" Phoebe asks as I settle in. "Latte? Coffee? Cronut?"

"I'm fine." I try to smile. "Really, not that hungry."

Phoebe thinks about that for two seconds. "I'm getting you a chocolate cupcake. They're out of this world."

"But—" Before I can get the protest past my lips she's already gone, striding to the counter across the room with the determination of a soldier heading off to war.

"My advice? Don't fight it," Lila says, smirking at me. "When it comes to the West family, it's easier just to cave. Trust me."

"I'm starting to learn that," I murmur. Glancing at the women clustered around the table, I try not to panic. "Anyway... thanks for inviting me to your girl date, or whatever this is."

"Happy to have you," Gemma says.

"Totally," Chrissy agrees. "We could use another sane person around here."

"You had sex!" Shelby announces, narrowing her pretty brown eyes at me.

My mouth drops open.

"Shelby!" Chrissy scolds.

"What? She's practically *glowing*. It's obvious she had an encounter with *el peen de Parker.*"

"Was that supposed to be Spanish?" Lila's nose wrinkles. "Because that's not the word for penis. Just for the record."

"That's rude!" Chrissy elbows her friend. "You can't just go around telling people they have sex-glow."

"Not the point." Shelby looks undaunted, smiling over at me like we're long lost pals instead of virtual strangers. "You totally had sex with Parker."

"Can we please keep in mind that this is my *brother* we're talking about?" Gemma grimaces. "Seriously... there's an ick factor."

"Sorry!" Shelby throws up her hands, not sounding sorry in the least. "Screw me for being excited that *someone* around here is getting... well... screwed. I'm just happy to hear Zoe is getting some. Any more sex-less women in a single place, stray cats are going to start following us around."

"Uh huh, I'm going to stop you right there." Lila's perfectly-plucked eyebrows rise in graceful twin arcs. "I have many problems in my life; celibacy is not one of them."

"To be honest, I get more than I can handle." Gemma's smile is wistful. "Chase makes sure of it."

"I also get it on the regular," Chrissy adds. "Well, if you consider *on the regular* the rare five-minute intervals that occasionally pop up when both kids are miraculously sleeping, Mark and I are both home, and one of us isn't covered in some kind of baby spittle."

We all look at her.

"I will pray for you," Lila tells her very seriously.

I snort.

"What are we talking about?" Phoebe asks, returning to the table loaded down with three different kind of cupcakes and two iced lattes balanced in her hands.

"Getting some," Gemma informs her cheerfully, snagging a chocolate cupcake off the plate.

"Oh, Nate gives it to me on the regular," Phoebe informs us happily.

"Fine! Whatever!" Shelby crosses her arms over her chest. "So, I'm the only celibate one. Fabulous."

"Have a cupcake," Lila suggests.

Shelby looks aghast. "Oh yeah, an extra five hundred calories that'll go straight to the cellulite on my ass will certainly help matters."

"Wait..." Phoebe pauses mid-bite, her large red velvet cupcake poised in the air, and glances at me. For a second she looks elated... but then her face contorts into a nauseous twist. "That means you and Parker.... *Oh*. I don't know whether to be happy or grossed out."

"A little of both," Gemma says around a massive mouthful of chocolate.

"That was supposed to be for Zoe," Phoebe tells her sister.

"I can't help it." Gemma licks her lips. "I'm starving today."

There's a beat of silence before they all explode. I feel utterly confused as every other woman at the table except Gemma starts bouncing in her seat and practically squealing.

Gemma looks at me and rolls her eyes.

"Dog whistle?" I ask.

She laughs. "They do this every time I eat anything in front of them. They all think I'm pregnant." She glares at her friends. "Which I am *not*. For the record."

The squealing stops.

"So..." Phoebe looks at me. "Guess this means you're officially part of the fam, Tink."

I blanche. "Don't get ahead of yourself. It's just sex."

Gemma looks thoughtful. "I doubt that. If it was just sex, you wouldn't be here trying to befriend his crazy family."

My mouth opens; I search for a reasonable explanation and come up empty.

"You like him!" Phoebe starts bouncing in her seat again. "This is the best day ever." She pauses. "Well, no, best day ever included Nate taking my virginity. But this is a close second."

"Wait," I protest. "Just—"

It's no use. Phoebe is on a roll.

"This is great. Parker's finally in love." She sighs happily. "Do you realize what this means?"

"Phoebe, just—"

She cuts me off. "Parker will finally settle down and stay here! He'll actually be around! *Permanently!*"

"That would be pretty awesome," Gemma chimes in.

"So, Tinkerbell lands the man-child." Lila shakes her head. "Impressive. I didn't think it was possible, after the nonstop bimbo parade we've had to watch for the past two decades."

My throat feels like it's closing.

What is wrong with this family?

Why do they insist on doing everything at hyper-speed?

"It almost won't be the same, without the Victoria's Secret models to mock on a regular basis," Chrissy murmurs. "Who will make us feel bad about ourselves, without Parker's stream of skanks?"

"Should we send out a memo?" Shelby wrinkles her nose. "ATTENTION, slutty Instagram girls everywhere: Parker West is officially off the market."

I can't breathe.

"This is just so exciting!" Phoebe claps. "Parker is in love. All is right in the world."

"It's a Christmas miracle," Lila drawls.

"Do you think—"

My hands slam down on the tabletop, cutting off Gemma's statement.

"STOP!" I yell, heart pounding too fast. Everyone looks at me with alarm, including the two couples at other tables across the cafe.

"Sorry," I say much more softly. "But please... just stop. You don't understand." I swallow hard. "Parker and I haven't even talked about this. For all I know, he's leaving tomorrow."

Phoebe's face contorts into a concerned mask. "Oh, Zoe, I'm sure—"

"I'm sorry." I push back my seat and rise to my feet. "You all seem very nice. But don't pin all your hopes and dreams on me for keeping your brother around. As far as I know, him dating me, seeing how fucked up I am? That could be the thing that makes him leave here for good."

With that, I turn and walk out — away from the women who've offered me their friendship, away from the first real shot I've ever had at a female support system, away from something that, for all intents and purposes, would be a good thing. A great thing, even.

The saddest part is, as I let the cafe door click closed at my back, I know it's fucked up.

I know *I'm* fucked up.

But recognizing a problem and actually changing it are two entirely different beasts.

I wander down the street, ignoring the buzzing of my phone and feeling more alone than I have in a very long time.

See, a tiny voice whispers at the back of my mind. *This is what happens when you let people in. It gives them power over you.*

You're better off without them.

A lone wolf.

Retracting your claws and playing nice for a day doesn't make you one of the dogs. You're just as dangerous as you've always been.

They don't need someone like you in their lives.

No one does.

As hard as I try to drown out that voice, I can't seem to muffle it as I walk through the park toward my apartment, eyes unseeing and feet on auto-pilot.

Maybe that voice is right.

Maybe I'm better off alone.

CHAPTER 15
THE FLASHBACK

SOMETIME DURING MY WALK HOME, the skies open up.

It's just a drizzle, at first, but it quickly turns to a downpour and before I know it, I'm soaked through from the Toms on my feet to the heavy mane of my hair, dripping steadily down my back.

Boston isn't a big city — that's one of the things I love about it. No matter where you are or where you need to go, for the most part you can get around on foot in less than an hour.

Somehow, I turn what should be a twenty-five-minute walk through downtown into a four-hour trek.

I wander alone through the streets — cold, wet, shivering — until I've walked from the North End down through Back Bay, over the foot bridge to Seaport. By the time I finally circle back to my neighborhood, the temperature has dropped with the sunset, turning rain to sleet and sleet to snow.

I trudge through a slushy puddle, barely feeling the icy water through my thin shoes. Rounding a corner, my building comes into view, its sagging profile dimly illuminated by snow-covered street lamps.

There's an edge of panic in my thoughts.

Maybe it's the timing, maybe it's the lonely feeling inside my gut, maybe it's the damn snow falling on a street the day before the anniversary of my parents' murder. I don't know, exactly. But paranoia settles over me as flurries coat the shoulders of my jacket. Whispers from the back of my mind say I'm being followed, stalked by some unseen predator.

The thoughts are absurd — every time I glance back, I'm alone on the desolate streets. No one is out in this weather. Especially in my neighborhood.

Pull yourself together.

When I finally reach my door, I'm shaking from more than just the cold. My mind feels as numb as my frozen body. I'm reaching for the entry panel to punch in the security code, willing my blue fingers to cooperate, when something slams into me from behind.

Hard.

I'm not a big woman. Most people would call me petite, and they'd be right. It doesn't take much force to lift me or send me flying. So I know it's intentional when a palm lodges between my shoulder blades and shoves me up against the brick wall of my building like a bug against a windshield.

The impact forces all the air from my lungs. My scream comes out as a rasp, barely echoing in the snow-dampened air. Hauling in a breath, I try again but a giant hand clamps over my mouth and muffles my cries before any sound escapes.

"Shut up," a deep, unfamiliar voice growls by my ear.

I feel my eyes moving frantically inside their sockets, whites flashing with fear as his body presses into my back. I'm flattened so tight I can barely draw a breath through my nose.

His grip has constricted all air flow and I feel myself starting to get light-headed, the longer I go without a proper breath.

I struggle against his hold, but it's no use. My thrashing limbs are no match for the strength in his. He's too strong.

My struggles cease completely when I feel the razor-sharp edge of a knife press into the hollow point at my throat. The blade cuts into the thin skin at my jugular, precariously close to my carotid. The slightest slip and I'll bleed out into the snow.

Just like my parents.

The pressure increases fractionally, slicing into my flesh, and I feel a stream of warmth against my chilled skin as a rivulet of blood starts to drip down my neck, into the collar of my jacket.

If I could speak, I'd tell him to take anything. Everything.

Money.

Phone.

Purse.

Laptop.

Anything.

But there's no way to tell him that with his hand over my mouth. There's no way to form words or even coherent thoughts as panic overrides my system, blending reality with memory. Flashes of another night are seeping into my consciousness — fragments of another time, almost twenty years to the day, when blood ran red into the snow.

I can't block them out. Can't separate *then* from *now*.

The man shifts closer, knife tightening against my skin.

I'm five again, clutching my bouquet as though the petals can protect me from the stranger in the dark.

Blood drips faster. My lungs are scream for breath.

Or is that a woman screaming?

The man at my back shifts closer. "Don't fight me."

"Run, Zoe!" My mother's hands, pushing me to safety. "Run, honey, run!"

His mouth scrapes my earlobe. His breath is hot against my frigid skin. "Listen. You listening, bitch?"

"Run, baby!"

His knife shifts.

Or is it a gun? A black, blunt weapon, firing in the dark. One, two, three, four, five, six shots. First Dad, then Mom as I duck between two parked cars.

"I don't want to hurt you." The growling voice is back. "But I will."

People rush outside, drawn by the sounds of gunfire. The man stops chasing me before they spot him. Vanishes into the dark.

"If you know what's good for you, you'll stop digging."

A stranger in a uniform pulls me from between the cars. Picks me up, puts a hand over my eyes.

"You're messing with the wrong people. Powerful people."

He tries to block my view, so I don't see them there, butchered in the snow. But between cracks in fingers, over shoulders, under flashing ambulance lights... I see the blood and I know. They're gone.

"You want to make it through this Christmas, don't go back to the fucking factory. Don't send any more of your boyfriends there. You hear me, bitch?" The knife presses in again. "Nod so I know you hear me."

Mommy. Daddy. Gone.

"I said *nod* if you hear me, bitch!"

I try to nod, but the world is going black around the edges. I can't breathe. Can't move. Can't see.

They're gone.

"Good." The knife pressure lessens slightly. "You tell your

damn boyfriend to stay away. Stay out of it. Make sure he knows, he tries anything, you'll pay the fucking price."

Gone.

Then, before I can turn to get a look at him, the weight at my back vanishes and he disappears. I fall to the ground, gasping for air, my eyes pressed tight closed as I curl into a ball in the snow.

Weeping.

Bleeding.

Remembering.

A voice in my head is telling me to get up, to call for help, to go inside so I don't die here from frostbite and exposure... but it's faint. And it's getting farther away by the second, replaced by much darker thoughts that whisper maybe I should've died with them, all those years ago.

They're gone.

Maybe you should be, too.

I curl in on myself a little tighter.

Feel the shadows close in a little darker.

And for the first time since I was five years old... I stop fighting.

"NO, no, no, no, no. Zoe! Goddammit, Zoe, open your eyes!" Arms are sliding around me. Lifting me from the snow. Cradling me tight against a chest. "Honey, look at me! Are you still with me? Fuck!"

The voice sounds desperate. Almost shattered. There's something about hearing that voice breaking on words, filled with worry and panic, that makes me sad.

His voice was made for laughter and light. He shouldn't ever sound sad.

I can't focus on much of anything as I shiver and shake in a set of strong hands, hands that feel like fire against my cold skin. There are more words, but I'm slipping in and out of consciousness, barely able to hear over the rush of blood inside my aching skull.

"Nate? It's Parker..."

We're moving. He's holding me one-handed like some kind of superhero and muttering frantically into his phone. I only catch some of what he's saying.

"...snow... blood... shivering... skin is fucking blue... like ice... Luca... okay... see you soon."

I hear the distant clanging of my ancient elevator. Feel the warmth of a man's mouth at my ear, the pressure of his big hands on my back as he whispers words into my neck. I know, even in my disoriented state, that he's not talking into the phone anymore. He's talking to me.

"I've got you, honey. I've got you." There's a pleading note in his voice. "Don't you fucking leave me. Didn't even know what I was looking for, until I met you, Zoe. I didn't even think it was possible to feel like this about someone. So you stay with me, okay? *Stay.*"

I open my mouth to tell him I'm still here, that I won't leave him, that he makes me feel more alive than anyone I've ever met, that his presence is enough to remind me why living in this brutal, ugly world is worth it, despite the pain and the heartbreak...

I find I can only manage one word.

"Parker."

My murmur is so quiet it barely makes it past my numb lips. But he must hear me, because his arms crush me a little tighter against his chest and I hear his voice crack with emotion again when he says, "That's right, Zoe. I'm here. And I'm not ever letting you go."

The last thing I feel before I slip unconscious once more is his mouth ghosting over mine in a kiss that feels like a promise.

———

WHEN I FINALLY WAKE UP, I'm in my bed. Every lamp in the loft is lit, basking the space in light as if to banish the shadows outside. Blinking to adjust to the sudden brightness, I hear several voices nearby, speaking in low whispers. The hostility in their tones is apparent despite the controlled volume.

Beneath the mound of blankets swaddled around my body, my hair is wet. They must've put me in a warm shower, at some point, but I don't have any memory of that. Nor do I recall putting on the pair of yoga pants and sweater covering my limbs, which means they probably dressed me.

I don't have the energy to feel embarrassed that any number of people potentially saw me naked.

There's a bandage of some kind stuck to my neck, taped over the spot where my assaulter's knife dug into my skin. It's sticky and uncomfortable, placed at the point where my jaw curves beneath my ear, and I plan on removing it as soon as I can find my way out of the stack of blankets pressing me into the bed.

The voices are angry, biting words at each other in clipped, quiet tones.

"...maybe we should take her to the hospital..."

"...think I know what she wants better than you do, rich boy..."

"...need to focus on whoever attacked her..."

I can barely move, what with the seventy-five blankets on top of me, but I somehow struggle into a sitting position. The conversation across the loft goes silent instantly as the three men notice my movement and stride to the side of the bed.

Parker, Luca, and Nate.

They're wearing identical expressions of anger and concern as they approach.

Parker reaches me first, settling in on the bed at my side and wrapping an arm around my back with such care, you'd think I were made of glass. Luca comes around my other side and stands by the edge of the bed, looking down at me with a mix of disapproval and worry. Nate stops at the footboard with his arms crossed over his chest and his eyes locked on my face, hyper-alert and highly intelligent.

"Hi," I croak, attempting to smile at the trio of badasses surrounding me.

They all frown deeply.

I sigh and feel Parker's arm tighten around me. "Are you okay?" he asks intently.

"I'm fine." *I think.* "How long was I out?"

Parker's expression is still worried. "A few hours."

"Babe." Luca shakes his head. "Scared us."

"What happened?" Nate asks.

I look up at the dark-haired investigator, straight into his black eyes, and feel my throat clench. Nathaniel Knox is *intense.* It's miraculous to me that a man like him could love a woman like Phoebe, who can't go ten seconds without cracking a joke.

Sometimes I guess two people really do complete each other — the jagged, broken pieces of their souls aligning perfectly, to create an undamaged whole.

The thought makes a fluttery, uncomfortable feeling stir inside my stomach.

"Zoe."

Parker's voice pulls me back to reality, and I realize I've been spacing out.

"Sorry." My voice feels raspy and sore, so I swallow and try again. "I was walking home. It started raining, then snowing. I kept feeling like someone was following me, but every time I looked back I was alone on the street. And then... he grabbed me right when I reached the doors."

They don't interrupt. They just watch me in silence, waiting for me to finish.

"I never saw his face. He was big. Strong. Southie accent. That's all I know." I swallow again. "He had a knife. He — he put it to my throat so I couldn't struggle."

The air gets a little tense, when I say that. Parker's arm tightens again.

"And..." I dart a glance at Luca. "He said..." *Breathe.*

"What?" Nate prompts softly. "What did he say, Zoe?"

"He said to stay away — to tell my boyfriend to stay away. And to make sure he knows if he tries anything, I'll pay the price."

Before I can explain, Luca's rounded the bed, grabbed Parker by the lapels of his button-down, and hauled him to his feet.

"*What the fuck did you do?*" he hisses.

"Go on, just give me an excuse to hit you," Parker returns, his voice vibrating with anger. "Please."

"Luca!" I yell, jumping to my feet – *ouch*, every bone in my body aches like I've been hit by a truck – and pushing my way between them. "Stop!"

Thankfully Nate is there to intervene, because there's literally no chance of them listening to me. Emotions are running too high for either of them to see reason, at the moment.

"Come on," Nate says, shoving the men apart with a rough

jab to both their chests. "This really how you two want to play this? Upsetting Zoe even more, after what she's been through?"

His words snap the two brutes out of it — they back off, but still eye each other with wary glares and angry expressions, each ready to go for the jugular at the slightest provocation.

"Knew you were terrible for her," Luca mutters darkly. "Should've stopped it. Should've locked her up until she forgot about your stupid ass."

"Zoe makes her own decisions," Parker volleys back. "Always will, when she's with me. That's exactly why she'll never be with someone like you."

"Enough," Nate growls. "Both of you. Or I'll make you leave."

They shut up. Grudgingly.

For a moment, there's total silence in the loft. I sink back onto the edge of my bed, feeling exhausted down to my marrow from the attack, the onslaught of emotions, *everything*.

"Luca," I start in a soft voice that makes the three of them focus on me. "He wasn't talking about Parker."

"What?" they all say in unison.

"The man... he was talking about you." I look at my best friend, hating to see the guilt filling his eyes as he stares back at me. "The factory. He must've seen you there, when you went to check it out."

The blood drains out of Luca's face as he realizes what that means — that he's the one who endangered my life. Not Parker, who he was so quick to blame.

"What are you talking about?" Nate asks. "What factory?"

"Does this have to do with the Lancaster case?" Parker adds, sitting down by my side again.

"Lancaster?" Nate's voice is dark. "Robert Lancaster? The CEO of Lancaster Consolidated?"

"I think so." I chew my lip. "Luca and I... well, we were

investigating some of the LC financials, after they screwed all their employees out of their pensions and closed the factories without warning. But... I think we found something." I glance at Parker. "Something bigger."

"Explain," Nate says in a no-nonsense tone.

I do a quick run-through of my trip to the Lynn factory, the pipes I found, the man who was watching me from across the parking lot as I left.

"You didn't tell me about that," Luca growls angrily. "You never fucking said there was some LC goon keeping tabs you. Jesus, babe, what were you thinking?"

"I wasn't sure he was watching me! Not really!" I protest. "How could I know something like that?"

"Still should've told me," Luca grumbles.

"I'm sorry," I whisper. "I think..."

"What?" Parker asks.

"I think it might've been the same guy. The one watching me at the factory and the one who attacked me." I expel a sharp breath. "I'm not positive. It's just... a gut feeling."

The three of them are silent for a few moments, each lost in their thoughts.

It's Nate, who finally breaks the silence. "So, you think Lancaster is covering something up."

"I don't just *think*," I say, rising shakily to my feet and crossing to the desk where I keep the file with all my notes from the investigation. "I found a work order, proving the pipes were installed after the plant closed."

I pass the document to Nate, and he studies it for a long moment. "Could be asbestos, some kind of toxin he exposed his employees to, while they were working at the factory. No other reason to go in and change out the pipes after closing things down. Especially if he's just going to demolish it in a few months."

"He's covering his ass," Parker mutters.

"That's the sense I got, when I went to the plant," Luca says, nodding. "Air ducts had been scrubbed, too. And the water pipes had been rigged to pump shit straight into the bay. Highly doubt that's compliant with EPA guidelines, but in a pinch, if you're trying to flush your system and get rid of evidence..."

"It's all circumstantial." Nate shrugs. "We don't have anything besides the work order and a sense of suspicion."

"And the fact that Lancaster is a shitty, corrupt fucking asshole." Parker sounds pissed beyond belief.

"Agreed," Luca mutters.

"Did we just agree on something?" Parker's eyebrows lift.

Luca's mouth twitches. "Don't push it, rich boy."

"Wait. Asbestos..." My voice is soft. "That would cause medical problems, right?"

Nate nods. "Anything from mesothelioma to lung cancer to immune system disorders."

"Hold on a second," I whisper, limping over to my computer. It takes a minute, but I pull up the document I was looking for and scroll down until I find it. "There! Right there." I jab my fingers at the screen and the three of them lean close to read the name on at the bottom of the staff list.

"Doctor Charles Birkin," Nate mutters, staring at the thumbnail image of the middle-aged man in a white lab coat. "Who the hell is that?"

"And why did Lancaster need a full-time doctor onsite at the Lynn factory?" Parker adds.

"I found an email from Lancaster to his Head of Security, a guy named Linus... he mentioned Birkin in the message, along with some kind of transfer – I'm guessing it was a payoff." I feel puzzle pieces starting to snap together in my brain. "I did a little digging to see what I could find on Birkin. Turns out,

Lancaster was a big proponent of in-house medical visits for his workers. Oddly considerate, since he paid most of them minimum wage. Don't you think?"

"He knew they were sick. Or... that they'll get sick eventually." Luca sounds disgusted. "I can't fucking believe this."

"He thinks if he makes it look like he fired ten thousand workers because of budgetary issues, he'll be able to avoid paying out millions in healthcare costs for workers he poisoned." My voice is dark. "That fucking asshole."

"If he gets rid of them now, he's less liable in their lawsuits when they finally start getting sick and realize what's happening." Parker's hand squeezes my shoulder. "From a business standpoint, he's covering his ass."

"We'll need to talk to some of the workers to confirm," Nate says. "See if any of them are exhibiting health symptoms, find out exactly how many times they saw Lancaster's doctor and what he told them about their health. Maybe get them in to see an actual, unbiased health professional."

"Shouldn't be tough. Most of them live locally," Luca mutters. "I can start making house calls later today."

"Tomorrow's Christmas Eve," I remind him. "Not exactly the gift most of them were hoping for."

Luca shrugs. "If you had cancer, wouldn't you want to know sooner than later?"

"Point taken." I push away from my computer and start to pace. "Lancaster is not going to get away with this. I'm going to pin that bastard to the wall, so help me god."

"Whoa, whoa, whoa." Parker steps in front of me and places his hands on my shoulders to stop my pacing. "Let's keep in mind for a second that literally three hours ago, Lancaster sent some thug from his security team to attack you, right outside your home. If you think you're still going after him, you're dead wrong, darling."

My mouth drops open to retort, but Luca jumps in before I can.

"He's right, babe."

I whirl to face my best friend. "You're fucking kidding me, right?"

He stares back stonily.

Parker's expression is identical.

"Great! You two finally start agreeing on shit at the worst possible time." I scream in frustration. "How can you even think I'm going to consider walking away from this? That I'd let Lancaster get away with what he's doing? It's my case! My investigation! You can't take it from me."

"No one's expecting you to let Lancaster get away with this," Nate says in that deep, intense voice of his.

I glance at him and see he's totally serious. My brows lift. "You aren't?"

His head shakes. "I'll take over on the investigative end. Do some surveillance, put ears to the ground and see what I hear. No offense, but it's what I do for a living, and I'll find out more in a shorter time frame than you could anyway."

I scowl. *He's a patronizing ass.*

Unfortunately, he's also right.

"And I suppose you just expect me to sit on my hands and do nothing?" I ask in a scathing tone.

Nate's head shakes. "No. I expect you to do what you're best at — keep pouring through his files until you find things we can use against him."

"Nothing I find is going to be admissible in a court of law. Hacking a server isn't exactly the same as possessing a search warrant," I point out. "You do realize that, right?"

Nate's lips slowly curl into a scary smile. "Who said anything about a court of law?"

A shiver goes up my spine. This boy does *not* fuck around.

"I'll go get started." Nate nods at Parker. "Let you know what I find out." His gaze moves to Luca. "It would be helpful if you could come back to headquarters, discuss some of the shit you found at the factory in more detail with me and my men. I'm sure Lancaster has the area locked down, now that they know you and Zoe are digging into things. We might not be able to get in a second time."

Luca nods. "All right." He glances at me, then Parker, then back at me. "You gonna be okay?"

I roll my eyes. "Luca."

He holds his hands up in surrender. "Fine. Got it. I'm going." He turns and starts for the elevator, gets halfway there, stops in his tracks, and stomps back to me. Before I can ask what he's doing, he hooks an arm around my neck, hauls me close, and plants a kiss on the side of my head. "Scared me today, babe. Don't do it again."

"I'll do my best," I whisper, telling myself not to cry.

He nods, turns, and follows Nate into the elevator. I wave as the doors slide shut and they rattle away. When the sound of the elevator fades, the loft is abruptly silent. Parker Can't-Stop-Babbling West is uncharacteristically quiet. I look at him, fully prepared to ask if he's feeling feverish, and feel my eyes widen.

He's sitting on the edge of my bed with his face in his hands.

My feet falter. The words dry up on my tongue.

I've never seen him look so utterly... *Defeated.* That's the only word for it. It sends an awful, gut-wrenching sensation through me.

"Parker?" My voice is shaky as I walk slowly toward him and sink down by his side on the edge of the mattress. "Honey... are you okay?"

He heaves a sigh and pulls his hands away to glance over at me. "Are you?" he asks in a broken voice.

I blink. "It's just a cut. It'll heal. I'll be fine."

"I'm not talking about the cut, Zoe."

"Then..." My mouth gapes a bit. "I... I don't know what you mean."

He looks away. "I talked to Phoebe."

A lump forms in my throat. No matter how many times I swallow, I can't seem to dislodge it. "Oh? And?"

He looks back at me and his hazel eyes are so sad it steals my breath. "And she told me what happened. You storming out of lunch with the girls."

"So, I didn't want to sit around gossiping over cupcakes. Sue me."

"We'll get to the reason you stormed out of there later." He straightens so he's no longer hunched over and stares down into my eyes. "Point is, that was hours ago, Zoe. Phoebe called me at two. I found you at six. Lying in the snow, half frozen to death. You were fucking blue. I thought..." His voice breaks, and it damn near kills me to hear it. He runs a hand through his hair, clearly frustrated, and when he speaks again his tone is low, like he's barely hanging onto his control. "I thought you were dead."

I suck in a breath. With a tentative hand, I reach for his. He flinches when my fingers curl over his knuckles.

"I'm happy you found me," I whisper. "You saved me."

He pulls his hand from mine and I feel something painful fissure through my heart.

"Are you really happy?" he asks, a note of disbelief in his voice.

"Of course I am. What, do you think..." I swallow. "Do you think I wanted to die out there? That I wanted to be attacked and left out in the snow?"

He rises to his feet and starts to pace. "I don't know what the fuck to think, Zoe. All I do know is, at any point in the four hours you were out there wandering in a fucking blizzard, sad and scared and upset... you could've called me. I would've dropped anything to come find you. No matter what." A muscle jumps in his cheek. "You chose not to do that. And then, some man attacks you..." He looks at me with ghosts in his eyes. "You're a fighter. I've known it since the second I clapped eyes on you. And yet, today, when you were cornered, when you were knocked down... You didn't get back up. Didn't call for help. Didn't *fight*."

My heart is pounding too fast and I feel dangerously close to falling apart. "What are you asking?" I force myself to say.

His eyes hold mine captive. "Did you stop fighting? Is there a part of you that wanted to slip away, out there on that street?"

Horror surges through me as I feel my eyes start to fill with tears. They spill down my cheeks in a rush, but not a single one of them has a chance to hit the floor because suddenly Parker's there, his hands cupping my cheeks, his face a hairsbreadth from mine.

"Shhh," he breathes. "It's okay, Zoe. It's okay."

"I just..." I cough on a sob. "I was just so tired. It was too much. My parents. That night. Replaying in my head like a horror film, over and over. It rattled me. And so, when he dropped me into the snow... I guess there was a part of me that was just too damn tired to get back up."

Parker's big hands hold my cheeks, so I can't look away. "Zoe." His voice breaks on the word. "Next time, you call me. You can't find your feet? I'll be there to pull you up. You can't walk? I'll fucking carry you." He comes closer, until I can't see anything except his eyes, and I'm pretty sure they're the most gorgeous thing I've ever seen in my twenty-four years of life. There's redemption and forgiveness in his gaze — no judgment or fear.

My broken pieces don't scare him.
He doesn't pretend they don't exist.

He sees me for exactly who I am... and he's here anyway.

"You think the world is too ugly to exist in anymore? I'll be here to remind you how fucking beautiful it can be." His voice is a vow. "I promise, darling. I'll be here. But I can't help you if you won't let me."

"I'm sorry. I should've called. I should've..." More tears spill.

He stares at me and I can't decipher the look in his eyes. "Do you want this, Zoe? This beautiful, messy, crazy life? Because I've seen what depression does to people. I've watched it tear families limb from limb. My family... When my mom..." His jaw clenches tight as he bites back words he can't let himself speak. "I have to know you want to be here. That you're still willing to fight. Everything is fixable... but you have to *want* to fix it. You have to *want* to be here." He hauls in a breath to steady himself. "You have to want it, darling. More than all the shitty days and the heartbreaks and the awful fucking horror of losing people... you have to want to live anyway."

"I do." My voice is shaky, but it's full of truth. "Parker... I want it more than anything."

He doesn't respond and, for a moment, I worry he doesn't believe me. But then, his arms come up and he crushes me against his chest in an embrace that steals my breath.

"Okay, Zoe," he murmurs against my hair. "It's going to be okay."

And as he holds me close, reminding me of all the reasons the world is pretty fucking amazing, I feel the weight of something I've been carrying around for twenty years lift off my shoulders.

This beautiful, messy, crazy life with this beautiful, messy, crazy man?

I want it.

CHAPTER 16
THE HERO

LATER THAT NIGHT, I wake to Parker's head between my legs. It's late, the middle of the night, but any sense of fatigue or residual anxiety from the day before is driven out by the sensation on his mouth, moving with expertise. I feel needy under his touch, with my hands in his hair and my body totally at his mercy. It doesn't take long for him to send me barreling toward the brink of pleasure. My toes curl, my hips arch, and I feel myself starting to losing control.

"Come up here," I pant, trying desperately to form coherent thoughts as my orgasm builds.

He grunts something unintelligible, never pausing in his efforts.

Holy shit.

"I want to see your eyes when I come, honey," I breathe. "*Please*, Parker."

At that, he goes still.

"Fuck," he mutters, crawling up my body, planting kisses as he moves from my thighs to my stomach to my breasts to the column of my throat. When his face comes level with mine, I see restraint and passion warring in his eyes.

"You can't say my name like that and expect me to stay in control." His voice is thick with need.

"I want to finish together," I tell him honestly. "I want you inside me."

"This is supposed to be about you." His voice is hoarse. "I'll survive."

"I know you'll survive. That's not the point." I arch up and kiss him. And then, I say something I've never said before. Something, if I'm being entirely honest, I never thought I'd find myself saying.

"Make love to me, Parker."

His eyes darken as his control snaps. A few seconds later, he pushes inside me, holding my gaze the entire time, and I look up at him knowing we can never go back to being strangers. It's not just sex. Not just passion or pleasure.

It's *Parker*.

Somehow in the space of a week, he's got both hands wrapped firmly around my heart.

I have a feeling he's not going to let go.

Not ever.

And strangely... I'm okay with that.

CHRISTMAS EVE DAWNS bright and cold outside the loft windows. I leave Parker asleep in my bed and make my way into the bathroom. In the fluorescent light, the faint bruising around my neck from where my attacker held me looks even uglier than it did last night. Thankfully, the thin slice wound just below my jawline isn't visible unless I tilt my head back.

I hop in the shower, turning the water almost as hot as it

will go, and stand under the torrent for a while. It's the anniversary of my parents' death – by all accounts, the worst day of my year.

And yet... the dreadful weight that usually fills my chest from the moment my eyes open on this day simply isn't there. Instead, there's a light, fluttery feeling inside my soul, crowding out the sadness.

I know that feeling has everything to do with the tall, bronze-haired man sleeping in my bed.

As though he's heard me call him in my thoughts, a few seconds later Parker steps into the shower behind me and slides his arms around my stomach.

"Good morning." His voice is still husky with sleep as he plants a kiss against my neck.

"Morning," I breathe, leaning into him.

"Are you okay?" He pulls back. "Sorry. Stupid question. I know today is impossible for you."

I turn in his arms and loop my hands around his neck. "Surprisingly... I'm okay."

His brows lift.

"Really." I push up onto my tiptoes and try plant a kiss on his lips — except I'm too short to reach. "Bend down, you giant human, so I can kiss you."

His eyes flash. "I'll do you one better."

Lifting me so my legs go around his waist, his hips pin my body as he backs me up against the tile wall. His lips find mine and I get my kiss... plus a hell of a lot more, as his hands move against my wet skin.

After our shower, we towel off in silence. I'm still grinning like an idiot from the after-glow of my orgasm.

"So, you're gonna have to pack at least a week's worth of clothes," Parker says casually, running the towel over his damp hair to remove most of the moisture.

The grin falls off my face. "Excuse me?"

"Clothes." He drops the towel. "Enough for a week."

"I'm not following."

"You can't stay here alone."

"Why the hell not?"

"Because someone followed you here. It's obvious they know where you live. Which means it's not safe for you to be here."

"I'm not leaving." I swallow. "This is my home."

"Fine." He shrugs. "Then I'll move in."

"What?!" I gape at him. "You'll do no such thing."

"Oh, darling, don't test me." He smiles, but there's a dangerous edge to it. "You're not going to be out of my sight until this shit with Lancaster is resolved." He pauses. "Maybe even after that."

"What?!" I exclaim again.

He doesn't answer. He just takes a few steps closer, bends down, and kisses me hard and fast. "I'm hungry. You want breakfast? I'll make breakfast."

Without another word, he strides naked out of my bathroom, leaving me slack-jawed and reeling.

"But—" I call after him, feeling totally helpless. "You can't move in. I mean it, Parker!"

"You like bacon, right?" he calls back.

I sigh.

Fuck.

WHEN MY PHONE rings later that day, I grimace as I glance at the screen.

Parker looks up from his spot on my couch, where he's been camped out watching old Christmas movies on my spare laptop for the past four hours as I pour over Lancaster files. He pulls off his headphones and raises his brows when he sees my expression.

"Who is it?"

I sigh. "Phoebe. Who on earth gave her my number?"

He laughs. "You do realize she'll just keep calling until you answer, right?"

"I was afraid you'd say that."

He pops his headphones back in to give me a little privacy and returns to his movie as I connect the call.

"Hello?"

"Holy frack, I can't believe you answered. I was pretty much positive you were going to ignore my calls until I was forced to come over there bearing cupcakes and scale the walls into your apartment with my bare hands." She hauls in a breath. "Really happy you proved me wrong, though, because I don't think many cupcake stores are even open today, what with it being Christmas Eve and all. Plus, I think channeling my inner Spiderman may be a challenge in Louboutins."

"Hi, Phoebe." I say dryly when she stops babbling.

"*Oh*! Sorry. Probably should've said hello before launching in like a lunatic." She sighs. "Anyway, Nate gave me your number. He didn't want to, but I was in a..." She pauses and her voice drops to a sultry whisper. "*Persuasive* mood."

"Gross."

She laughs. "Anyway, I just wanted to call and tell you how worried we all were about you. And also to apologize for yesterday. I feel fully responsible. We totally freaked you out with all that talk about relationships and true love. Seriously uncalled for, I see that now. Trust me, Parker was so unbelievably pissed at me when I called to tell him we'd scared you off, I'll be surprised if he ever talks to me again."

"You don't need to apologize, Phoebe." I glance at the man

across the loft; he's fully engrossed in his movie. "And he shouldn't blame you for a thing. I think he was just..."

"Scared," she murmurs. "Yeah, I figured that from the way he reamed me out last night."

I sigh. "I'll talk to him."

"You don't have to. That's not why I called." She pauses. I can tell she wants to say more, but is worried how I'll react.

"Just say it," I murmur tiredly.

"Say what?"

"The real reason you called. Just tell me. We both know you're dying to get it out."

She makes a grumbly sound of protest. "So sassy. Maybe I just called to apologize."

"Phoebe."

"Okay! Okay." She clears her throat. "Is Parker, like, right there hovering over you?"

"No. He's watching a movie."

"The boy does love a good Charlie Brown Christmas marathon."

"I'm getting that."

"One year, he made us watch it seven times in a row because he said there weren't enough—"

"Phoebe."

"Right." She clears her throat again. "The thing is, I really am sorry that I upset you yesterday. It wasn't my intention *at all*. Clearly, all the talk about love and relationships made you bolt faster than Boo when he sees a squirrel in the Public Garden. And that makes me somewhat nervous to say what I have to say."

I wait, knowing there's more to come.

"But it's Christmas Eve, and I think I'd hate myself if I went to sleep tonight without doing everything possible to make the people in my life happy. Because that's what this

whole damn holiday is about, isn't it? Joy. Love. Togetherness."
Her voice gets lower. "That's why I have to tell you that, even
though it totally freaks you out... I don't think I'm wrong. About
any of it."

I take a breath.

"You said you're fucked up. That if Parker sees that, it
might make him leave for good. And I just have to flat-out
disagree with you on that point, Tink." Phoebe's words come
out in a rush, as though she expects me to cut her off at any
given moment. "The thing is, you're kind of my hero. Maybe
that's weird for you, but I refuse to hide that fact. You saved my
life. Nate says you're trying to save thousands of other lives, in
this case you're working on with him. Parker says, beneath that
tough shell, you're a big softie who pays for strangers' groceries
and gives money to people on the street who need it more than
you do." She takes a quick pause. "In my book, that makes you a
pretty big hero."

My heart clutches inside my chest.

Wow.

"Thanks, Phoebe," I whisper when I think I have my voice
under control. It shakes anyway.

"Don't thank me. Just... *see yourself*. See the woman you
are. You're pretty amazing. And, I won't apologize if I want
someone like you for my big brother."

My hand tightens around my phone. I have to keep my eyes
averted from Parker, afraid if I look at him I'll start crying again.

"Still there?" Phoebe asks a minute later.

"Yeah," I say, voice breaking. "I'm here."

She pauses. "For the record... you'll always be Tinkerbell to
me. And Parker... well, he's the perpetual man-child. The boy
who never grew up. He's *Peter Pan*." I hear the smile in her
voice. "That makes you guys Peter Pan and Tinkerbell. A
perfect pair, if there ever was one."

I laugh. "You're crazy."

"Peter and Tink were an unstoppable duo. A team. They were totally different... but they somehow completed each other." She sighs happily. "Just think about it, okay?"

I roll my eyes. "Goodbye, Phoebe."

Her voice is warm. "Merry Christmas, Tink."

I swallow and make myself say it. And, surprisingly, it's not as tough as I thought it would be to get the words past my lips.

"Merry Christmas, Phoebe."

As soon as she clicks off, I set the phone down and walk across the loft to where Parker is sitting. Pulling the computer from his lap, I straddle his legs, push his headphones off, and wind my arms around his neck. Before he can say a word, I plant a soft kiss on his lips.

"What was that for?" he asks, smiling at me. "Not that I'm complaining."

"Do I need a reason?" I shrug.

"No." His eyes narrow. "But you never kiss me first."

"I don't?" I ask, genuinely surprised. I hadn't realized.

He shakes his head. "No. You don't."

I stare at him and swallow hard, feeling like a terrible person. "Well... I'll work on it."

His brows lift. "Did Phoebe brainwash you during that call?"

I flick him on the forehead. "Oh, shut up, idiot."

"It's so sexy when you shower me with compliments."

I laugh and snuggle into his chest. "It's sexier when we shower together. Period."

"Not arguing with that."

Tilting my head, I meet his eyes. "I'm sorry if I ever made you feel like I don't want to be with you. This is... new to me."

"It's new to me too, darling." He shrugs. "Just because something's new doesn't mean it has to be bad."

"So wise, in your old age."

"Old!" He scoffs. "I may be nearing thirty at an alarming pace, but I'll never grow up."

"Phoebe said..." I hesitate, not sure whether I should tell him.

His tone is amused. "Phoebe said...?"

"She called you Peter Pan," I say quickly, before I chicken out.

His eyes get warm as he thinks about it for a minute. "Peter Pan and Tinkerbell." A kiss lands on the tip of my nose. "I'd be lying if I said I didn't like that."

My heart flips. I bring my mouth to his and kiss him.

"I'll never admit it if you tell her," I whisper. "But I like it, too."

"Don't worry, darling." He grins against my lips. "Your secret is safe with me."

His arms tighten around me and his mouth lands in my hair. He doesn't say anything else, and neither do I — we don't need to. He holds me close and hits *play* on the movie, and I feel something warm inside my chest in a place that used to be iced over with sadness and fear.

"SHIT." My eyes widen. "Holy fucking shit."

"What is it?" Parker walks toward me and crouches beside my computer. "You find something?"

I glance at him. "I found the employee medical records. All of them." I swallow. "If you believe these reports, every Lancaster Consolidated worker is the perfect picture of health."

"Can you put them all on a flash drive so we can show Nate?"

"Already done."

Parker pulls me from my seat. "Come on, then."

"Where are we going?"

"Knox Investigations."

"It's Christmas Eve," I say dumbly. "Isn't Knox busy with Phoebe or something?"

Parker shrugs as he hands me my black peacoat and a scarf. "Nate doesn't take time off. He's a workaholic." He shoots me a pointed look. "Kind of reminds me of someone else I know."

"I'm not a workaholic," I protest.

His brows lift.

"Okay, so I keep busy." I shrug and slide my arms into my coat. "Is that such a crime, Mr. CEO?"

"No — not technically illegal, just heavily frowned upon."

I roll my eyes.

He reaches over and starts doing up the buttons on my coat, which is such a boyfriend-like task it should totally repulse me. Instead all it does is make my insides melt.

Shit.

"Speaking of you being an all-important CEO, don't you have lots of work to do?" My nose wrinkles as he gently wraps the scarf around my neck. "By my account, all you've done for the past few days is watch a Christmas movie marathon," I tease.

"And given you multiple orgasms," he says seriously. "Don't forget the multiple orgasms."

"I don't recall any orgasms."

"An insult to my manhood?" He gasps in outrage. "I'd be worried, if you hadn't spent all last night crying out my name."

I laugh. "Oh, that was *you* doing all that work? I thought it was the other Parker I've been spending time with..."

"So much evil in such a small package." He grimaces. "Are

your other boyfriends also worried you'll kill them in their sleep?"

"What other boyfriends?" I scoff... and then proceed to turn beet red as I realize I've just admitted he's the only man in my life. "I mean— that came out wrong," I protest, watching a shit-eating grin light up Parker's entire face.

"Oh, no, Zoe." His eyes are bright with humor and happiness. "It's too late. You can't take it back now."

"Yes, I can." My voice is a grumble. "In fact, that's exactly what I'm doing. I'm taking it back."

"Nope." He grabs my hand and places it over his heart. "I already know the truth. We're dating." His eyebrows waggle. "*Exclusively.*"

"Gross."

"Do you want to wear my letterman's jacket?"

"I'm going to vomit."

"Should I buy you a corsage?"

"Seriously. Gagging."

"Okay, no corsage." He laughs. "Just the matching tattoos, then?"

"Seriously." I fight the urge to stomp my foot. "*Let it go,* Parker. Let it go."

"Hey, Elsa, don't quote *Frozen* to me unless you're prepared to listen to the entire soundtrack in my car on the way to Seaport."

I stare up at him. "I'm not sure whether I should be disturbed or turned on by the fact that you know all the words to *Let It Go.*"

He grins. "Definitely turned on."

"Downloaded in your iTunes library, no doubt." I shake my head. "This is nearly as disturbing as the time I learned the song *A Whole New World* from Aladdin is a metaphor for mind-blowing sex."

"I'm sorry, *what?*"

"I can open your eyes? Lead you wonder by wonder? *Over, sideways,* and *under?*" I snort. "Come on. That's basically soft-core porn."

"Thank you, Zoe, for ruining a beloved Disney classic for me."

"Anytime."

"For the record..." He trails off.

I wince, anticipating the worst. "What?"

"I'll take you on my magic carpet ride any time you want, snookums."

"Pass."

"So, that's a no on rubbing my lamp then?"

"You know, I think I'll just find my own way to Nate's..." I turn and start walking to the elevator.

"Oh, come on." Parker twines his fingers with mine and pushes the call button, humming under his breath. "I'm a genie in a bottle, baby, gotta rub—"

"AH!" I stare at him in horror as the elevator arrives. "So help me god if you start singing vintage Christina Aguilera lyrics right now, I will murder you with my bare hands."

"With these dainty things?" He grabs one and pulls it to his lips, depositing a quick kiss in the center of my palm as we walk onboard.

I use my free hand to flick him in the temple.

"Ow!" He drops my hand and rubs at the spot I flicked. "What was that for? Christina, Aladdin, or Frozen? I'd like to narrow it down, so I know what most annoys you, in the future. It's still a bit of trial and error when it comes to driving you totally nuts in the shortest amount of time."

"I hate you."

"Keep telling yourself that, darling." He pulls me close and kisses me softly. "I hate to break it to you, but I'm not buying what you're selling."

My lips move under his, returning his sweet kiss, and I try to muster up some kind of protest. Funnily enough, as his tongue sweeps into my mouth, I can't think of a single thing to say to contradict his words.

A HALF HOUR LATER, we walk into a brightly lit brick building in the Seaport district, where Knox Investigations headquarters are located. Nate, Luca, and two other badass-looking dudes I recognize from Phoebe's Christmas party all look up when we enter.

"Long time no see," Luca jokes, coming forward to ruffle my hair. "You miss me already, babe?"

I punch him in the arm with my free hand. "Shockingly, this visit has nothing to do with you."

"Did you bring the files?" Nate asks, approaching with a serious expression on his face.

I nod and glance around. "Is there a computer I can use?"

"Here." A tall, gorgeous guy with dark hair, caramel skin, and stunning green eyes stands and offers me his desk. "Use this one."

"Thanks..." I trail off questioningly.

"Theo," he says, grinning in a way that probably makes panties all over the Boston area burst into flames.

"Zoe," I return, dropping Parker's hand as I move toward the empty chair.

My eyes lock on the towering blond man with bulging muscles and a crew cut leaning against a nearby desk.

"Owen," he offers, narrowing his eyes at me. "Gotta admit, I pictured you taller."

I glance at Nate. "I see my reputation proceeds me."

His eyes crinkle in a smile that doesn't touch his mouth. "Just show us what you found."

I sigh and settle into the chair, plugging in the drive and pulling up the documents as fast as possible. Parker, Luca, Nate, Theo, and Owen all line up behind me. It's only *slightly* intimidating to have five mammoth men hovering, their eyes watching my every keystroke.

"You're hovering," I murmur at them as my fingers fly over the keyboard.

None of them moves so much as a muscle. *Damn macho men.*

I do my best to ignore them as I pull up the files.

"Look. See here?" I point at the screen. "Almost every employee has a clean bill of health. Not just clean, actually — perfect. Not even a case of the sniffles, among ten thousand employees. The files are almost *identical.* As though someone just changed the names but copy and pasted the rest."

Nate leans closer. "What do we know about the doctor?"

I shake my head. "As far as I can tell, Dr. Charles Birkin isn't even a licensed physician. Not anymore." I hit a few keys and pull up another document. "I found an old court case from ten years ago — he was disbarred from practicing medicine for fabricating lab results during a clinical trial."

"Sounds like a real standup guy," Parker mutters.

"I haven't even told you about his arrest for writing himself dozens of unauthorized prescriptions for morphine and Vicodin." I sigh. "Wouldn't have been difficult for Lancaster to convince this guy to pose as his company doctor."

"Lancaster needed someone with enough medical experience to convince his employees they were being cared for," Nate mutters. "Someone who could play the part."

"Someone who wouldn't have any qualms about telling

people they were healthy when, in fact, the opposite is true."
Luca's voice is dark. "I paid a visit to a few former Lancaster
Consolidated employees. Of the six houses I stopped at this
afternoon, two of them have family members with lung cancer.
Another was just diagnosed with an auto-immune disorder —
she's spending her holiday at the hospital, in the ICU."

"So, what's next?" I ask, spinning my chair to look up at
Nate. "We find the doctor, lean on him a little, get him to
confess?"

Nate's mouth twitches. "This isn't a Jason Bourne movie."

"Well, excuse me for wanting to put an end to this." I rise to
my feet and cross my arms over my chest. "What's your grand
plan?"

"I make a call." Nate reaches into his pocket, pulls out his
cellphone, and walks away without any further explanation.

I glance at Parker. "Is he always like that?"

"Since he was eight." He grins. "Believe it or not, Phoebe's
had a calming effect on him. If anything, this is him being
chill."

"That's somewhat terrifying." I glance at Luca, Owen, and
Theo. "Any idea who he's calling?"

The three of them shake their heads in unison.

I sigh and turn back to the computer. My angst is short-
lived — a few minutes after Nate makes his mysterious call, the
front door to the offices swings wide and a man in an ill-fitting
suit steps inside, his black hair disheveled and in desperate
need of a cut, falling over piercing blue eyes that sweep the
room, taking everything in. He's got a coffee stain on his tie,
bags under his eyes from lack of sleep, and a pissed off attitude
to rival Nate's. There's something in the way he carries himself
that screams law enforcement.

"This is Conor Gallagher," Nate announces, gesturing to
the man. "He's with the Boston Bureau."

Fuck. Nate called the Feds.

The same Feds who would like nothing more than to arrest "Clover," the hacker who's infiltrated their networks on more than one occasion during the past two years and who they – rightly – suspect is responsible for taking down at least four corrupt companies in the Boston area by emptying out the CEOs' private accounts in the Cayman Islands.

Whoops.

Why do I have a feeling this isn't going to end well for me?

CHAPTER 17

THE LIGHTHOUSE

"NATE," I hiss under my breath. "Can I talk to you for a second?"

He ignores me.

I fight the urge to hide beneath the desk as the FBI agent walks a little further inside, stopping a handful of feet from me with his hands shoved deep in his pockets.

"This better be fucking good, Knox." He glances from me to the screen to Nate, taking in every detail. "It's Christmas Eve."

"Gallagher, we all know you have nothing better to do," Nate fires back at him. "I'm the only person you know in this city who doesn't work for the Bureau. Who else would you be spending the night with?"

The man smirks. "I'd rather be home alone than here with you, doing you yet another favor."

"Pretty sure we're square up on favors, after I helped you nab the MacDonough gang." Nate's eyes narrow. "That scored you a pretty sweet promotion, if I recall correctly."

The agent runs a hand through his too-long hair. "Just tell me why I'm here."

Nate gestures at me. "This is Zoe Bloom. She has some information we thought you might be interested in."

The agent's sharp blue eyes move to me. I try not to shiver under the frost in their depths.

"Zoe Bloom," Conor says, stepping toward me, his eyes narrowing. "Why do I know that name?"

I shift from foot to foot, feeling nervous, and Parker edges slightly in front of me. Luca moves to my other side in a show of force. Their message is clear.

Do not fuck with our girl.

At least they aren't at each other's throats, anymore.

Ignoring the pointed question, I look at Nate. "You sure we can trust this guy?"

Nate nods.

Conor's eyebrows lift. "Pretty paranoid, considering we've barely been introduced."

I glance back at him. "Yeah, well, FBI agents aren't generally at the top of my list of favorite people."

Conor's stony gaze never shifts. "Funny. Criminals aren't usually at the top of mine."

"Watch it," Parker growls.

Conor's eyes move to him. "Parker West. Surprised to see you here." His eyes move to Luca. "And Blaze Buchanan." He glances back at Nate. "Crack team you've gathered here, Knox. A CEO, an underground fighting champ, and a brash pixie with authority issues."

I cross my arms over my chest and step toward him, getting up in his face.

Well, if I were taller I'd be in his face. As it is, I'm more in the general vicinity of his chin.

"Listen, we don't need your assistance, so if you're going to be an asshole, why don't you just leave? It's clear you don't want to be here and, anyway, I highly doubt you can help."

Conor's lips twitch, just the tiniest bit — a chink in that icy, impenetrable armor he's shrouded himself with. "If I promise not to be an asshole, will you show me whatever's got you so riled up?"

I glance at Nate again — he gives me a slow nod and, I can't help but notice, he's grinning at me like I'm the funniest thing he's seen in a while.

Idiot.

"Fine," I grumble. "Though I still don't understand why we have to involve the damn Feds."

Conor follows me to the computer. "Are you always this unpleasant?"

"Said the corporate government drone," I retort.

"Zoe," Luca warns in a disapproving tone. "Don't push it."

"Whatever," I mutter, pulling up the vital documents so I can lead Agent Gallagher through our investigation from the beginning. When I meet his eyes, I'm pleased to see he's taking this seriously — there's not an ounce of humor in the depths of his gaze.

I clear my throat. "What do you know about Robert Lancaster?"

IT TAKES a while to tell him everything, from how I hacked the LC network to the files I found to the trip to the Lynn factory to our discovery of the healthcare cover-up with the fired employees. He doesn't ask me a zillion questions — he just listens in that intent way of his, occasionally jotting down some pertinent piece of information in a small notebook. When I finally finish showing him the documents on the LC server and fall silent, he takes a seat in the desk chair beside me with a heavy sigh.

"Well... fuck me." He runs a hand through his hair. "That's not what I expected."

"Can you help us get him, or not?" I ask.

For the first time, Conor cracks a smile. "Oh, we'll get the fucker. Don't worry about that."

My lips curl into a tiny grin and some of the anxiety in my stomach dissipates. Surely he's not going to toss me in jail for hacking after he's agreed to help.

Parker, Nate, and the rest of the boys are over by the surveillance computers, monitoring the tails they placed on Lancaster, Linus, and Birkin this morning. I push back my chair, fully intending to go join them, when I feel Conor's strong hand clamp down on my forearm. The force of his grip halts me in my tracks.

"It's strange," he says conversationally. "I thought when we finally met, it would be under different circumstances. You know — me on one side of an interrogation room and you shackled to a stainless steel table... *Clover.*"

I tug my arm away and glare at him. "I don't know what you're talking about."

"Sweetheart, don't play me for a fool." His eyes narrow. "I recognize your virus. Never seen anything else like it — no one at the Bureau has. Whether you want it or not, it's your trademark."

I bite down on my lip. "So, what, you're going to arrest me?"

"No." He rises to his feet. "Though I'd like to talk to you about a job."

A laugh bursts from my lips. "You're kidding."

He shakes his head, deadly serious.

"You want to offer me a job? At the FBI?"

He nods slowly.

I throw my head back at laugh. And laugh. And then I laugh some more.

"This is not the reaction I was expecting," he mutters lowly.

"I'm sorry," I say, wiping the corner of my eye. "What were you expecting?"

"Maybe 'Oh, thank you Conor, for agreeing not to arrest me and offering me a stable job with a 401k and benefits.' Something along those lines."

I try to contain my mirth, but it escapes again.

Nate's voice interrupts. "Don't tell me he's trying to recruit you."

Still giggling, I glance at him. "Totally."

Nate grins at Conor. "Hate to break it to you, but if she's working for anyone, it's going to be me."

My laughter dries up as I stare at him. "Wait... are you serious?"

Nate nods.

"You want me to work here?" I ask incredulously, glancing around the immaculate office. "At Knox Investigations?"

"Why is that so hard to believe?"

"Is this like... a pity thing?" I dart a glance at Parker, who I find is watching this entire exchange with alert eyes. "Did Phoebe or Parker force you to offer me a job?"

Nate's already dark irises seem to get even darker. "Let's get something straight. You're trouble. Knew it the first time I saw you. And I don't like trouble. Not around me, not around my best friend, not around the woman I love."

"Gee, thanks," I mutter.

"Turns out, doesn't matter what I like," he continues. "Phoebe and Parker both claimed you. They want you around. That means I'm claiming you, too." His eyes narrow a fraction. "Sure as shit doesn't mean I have to offer you a job, though, even if they begged me. This place, the work we do here – it's not something I'd risk fucking up for a friend who wanted a favor."

I blink.

"So, no, Zoe – it's not a *pity thing*. You're better with computers than anyone on the East Coast. If you worked here, you'd be doing *me* a favor. Not the other way around." His voice goes soft. "Why do you think Gallagher here is so eager to add you to the FBI ranks? The government doesn't have half your skill – nor do they have the same employee benefits I can offer, for the record."

Conor glares at Nate. "We have dental."

Nate grins wider. "We have actual salaries." His eyes cut to me. "Six figures, to start. Think about it."

I swallow hard, all laughter replaced by shock, and force myself to nod. "I will definitely think about it."

"Good." Nate turns to Conor. "So, let's talk logistics. I imagine you have an idea how you want this to go down."

The agent nods. "Give me a few days. I'll set things in motion on my end, then touch base. We don't want to spook Lancaster or have him send more cronies to attack Zoe." He looks at me with those piercing blue eyes and I see the hint of something almost warm in their depths, if only for a sliver of an instant. "Nice meeting you, Clover. You ever change your mind about that job, want to make an actual difference in the world... you give me a call."

"I'd be more inclined to consider it if you'd stop calling me *Clover* in the official FBI database."

His lips twitch. "You don't like the nickname?"

"Something slightly more badass would be preferable."

"Sorry." Conor shrugs. "Too late to change it now. You're already branded."

"Don't worry, darling." Parker wraps an arm around my

waist. "I'll call you all the badass nicknames you want." He pauses. "So long as the nickname you want to be called is *snookums*, of course."

I elbow him in the side. "Ignore him," I tell Conor a little desperately.

"*Snookums*?" Conor smirks. "Definitely badass."

I glare up at Parker. "See what you did? You're ruining my street cred."

He leans down and kisses me. "Uh huh."

"I'm serious, playboy."

"I can see that, darling."

I plant my hands on my hips and glare at every man in the room, my gaze sweeping from Parker to Conor to Nate to Luca to Owen to Theo. Infuriatingly, they're all grinning at me.

"I hate you all," I inform them, turning and stomping for the doors. "And I will not be accepting *any* job offers if it means my bad-assery is called into question on a regular basis."

The sound of muffled laughter chases me all the way to the doors.

PARKER'S in an annoyingly good mood all the way back to my loft. He gropes me playfully in the elevator, whispering scandalous things in my ear to make me laugh the entire ride up to my floor.

His joking, happy mood disintegrates as soon the doors slide open and we see the disaster site that used to be my apartment.

My laptop is cracked in two, lying in pieces on the cold concrete floor. Someone's smashed every one of my computer monitors with what looks like a baseball bat — there's no way they can be salvaged. My coffee table has been flipped on its side, scattering documents everywhere. Even from my spot by the door, I can see the hard copies from the Lancaster investigation are missing. The folders I painstakingly organized with printed copies of all the evidence I've spent weeks gathering are gone.

My bed is in tatters, gutted with some kind of sharp blade, as are my sofa cushions. Most disturbingly, though, are the photographs taped my my refrigerator.

Whoever is trailing me has been busy. There are pictures from the day I visited the Lynn factory, from my walk home in the snow, from my lunch with the girls at *Crumble*. There are even stills from the surveillance tape at Lancaster Consolidated, the night I dressed as Cindy the cater-waiter.

I suppose it was only a matter of time, before they put that together.

Each photo was taken from a careful distance, but it's clear they're the work of a professional. Especially given the photoshopping treatment they've received: every frame contains the bright red crosshairs of a sniper rifle over my profile.

As threats go, it's not a subtle one.

Keep this up and we'll kill you.

Parker shoves me behind him as his eyes move around the space, searching for intruders.

"They're long gone," I say quietly.

"Fuck," he curses lowly, running a hand through his hair. "At least you weren't here when they did this. If you'd been here..." His eyes move to the monitors, destroyed with brute force by someone with a significant amount of strength. "I don't even want to think about that."

I step up to his side and lace my fingers with his. "Don't think about it."

His furious hazel eyes lock on the photographs of me taped

to the fridge and I see whatever sense of calm he was hanging onto slip from his grasp like a handful of sand.

"I'm going to fucking kill them."

"Parker." I squeeze his hand. "They wouldn't be going through all this trouble to scare us if we hadn't rattled them. Don't you see? In a sick, weird, twisted way... this is a good thing. It means we're getting close to nailing them."

My words seem to soothe him — fractionally. His jaw unclenches a bit as he surveys the damage, but he still looks about ready to blow a gasket.

"There's no way they got in through the elevator without a key." He looks at me. "Who else has access? Your landlord? An ex? A previous tenant?"

I shake my head. "No. Luca has one, I have one. That's it. Whoever did this must've climbed the fire escape."

Parker strides to the opposite side of the loft, tugging me after him. Sure enough, when we reach the windows by the fire escape we find two of the panes are bashed in. The flimsy brass lock is snapped like plastic.

I suck in a breath.

Abruptly, Parker drops my hand and paces away, leaving me by the window. I don't follow him. My eyes are stuck on that broken lock, and I can't seem to look away. All at once, my careful sense of calm evaporates as reality sets in.

Someone was in my home. In my private space.

Sure, the loft leaves much to be desired. But it's always been mine. And now, someone's invaded that space. Taken my sanctuary and dirtied it, violated it, until I no longer feel secure in the only place I've ever been able to call home.

That fucking *sucks*, if I'm being honest.

I look around for Parker, assuming he's on the phone with Nate, and instead find him by my dresser, indiscriminately jamming clothes into a bag.

"What are you doing?" I screech, watching as three of my sweaters and a faded pair of jeans are shoved inside the duffle.

"I'm fucking packing," he snaps, never pausing. "Someone was in your home. Someone destroyed everything you've built here. Your work. Your life." His voice is a growl. "You're not spending another night in this place until this shit is handled."

"But—"

"In fact, even after it's handled you're not coming back here," he mutters. "If you never spend another night in this place again it'll be too soon, the way I see it."

"No one asked how you see it!" I exclaim, walking toward him and trying to pull the bag from his grip. He just lifts his arm so I can't reach and, damn it, I'm too proud to jump like a kid playing keep-away.

"Parker—"

"Hush."

"Don't tell me to hush, playboy!" I hiss. "Just where exactly do you expect me to stay? This is my home. We don't all own property on three different private islands."

"You're staying with me," he says succinctly.

I scoff. "I am not staying with you."

He drops the bag to the bed and turns chilly hazel eyes to mine. "Remember last night, when I fucked you until you couldn't move and you fell asleep in my arms? That moment — you became mine. I protect what's mine, darling. I protect it with every breath. Bottom line, I care about you... And I don't really give a shit whether you want me to or not."

I suck in a breath. "I'll stay with Luca."

His eyes narrow. "Like hell you will. That man has no concept of boundaries when it comes to you."

"He's my friend!"

"And I'm your—"

"My what?" I cut him off. "What exactly are you to me,

Parker West? Boyfriend? Bossy asshole? Annoying man-child who refuses to listen to reason?"

"You need a word or a definition for what I am to you, that's your problem. I'm not your *fill-in-the-blank* bullshit label. I'm just *yours*. And you're mine." He leans down and presses a hard, angry kiss against my lips. "That means you don't get to run off to some other guy's arms or bed."

"You're being outrageous!"

"This is me being reasonable, darling. You'd better fucking get used to it, because I'm not going anywhere." With that, he slings the packed duffle over one shoulder, grabs my hand, and hits a button on his phone to make a call, all while tugging me across the loft in long-legged strides. We're not even at the elevator when his voice cracks over the line.

"Nate? It's me. Change of plans..."

THIRTY MINUTES LATER, I'm standing in the cabin of *Folly*, trying to keep myself from bursting into tears. My outrage at Parker's bossy behavior has been replaced by a much more alarming emotion. I swallow once, twice, three times trying to dislodge the lump in my throat as I stare at the set of light blue foul weather gear in a woman's petite size small sitting on the table. Beside the suit, there's a set of tiny rubber boots that look about my size.

God dammit. Do not fucking cry, Zoe Bloom. Get your shit together.

"What?" Parker asks, catching sight of my expression as he climbs down into the cabin after me. "Do you not like the color? I can get that same gear in pink or red or white if you like that better. Just don't pick anything dark — the whole point is to wear something bright so I can see you if you fall overboard."

I pull a deep breath in through my nose and manage to get a hold of myself.

"I like the color," I murmur, staring at Parker.

"Then what's wrong?"

"Nothing."

His expression is wary. "The look on your face says otherwise."

Steadying my shoulders, I walk to him and slide my arms around his waist. "I promise, nothing's wrong. In fact... it's alarmingly close to perfect."

"Oh, dear god, no! The *horror!*" He grins. "We can't have that! Don't worry – twenty minutes ago you wanted to kill me. I'm sure I'll do something to fuck things up or piss you off again soon."

I stretch up onto my tiptoes and kiss him softly. "Undoubtedly," I whisper against his lips, enjoying the sensation of his smiling lips curved against mine.

"Come on." He squeezes me tight one last time, then pushes me away. "Put them on. We have to cast off soon or the sun will set, and it's no fun sailing in the dark. Plus, we'll miss our reservation."

"Reservation?"

He nods.

"When in the world did you have time to make reservations?"

His eyes narrow. "You know, if I didn't know any better I'd think you were surprised by my ability to provide for my woman."

"Your *woman?*" I roll my eyes. "What is this, an episode of *Outlander?* Because the only person allowed to refer to me as his *woman* is Jamie Fraser and you, my friend, are not wearing a kilt."

"I understood literally none of what you just said."

I grin, turn away, and grab my gear off the table. "Oh, never mind."

"See?" he calls, just before I close the bathroom door. "We're already fighting again! What'd I tell you?"

I laugh as I strip down to my skin and pull on the sailor suit.

It fits perfectly.

"TAKE THE WHEEL."

"What?"

"I have to put the sails up." Parker's voice is patient. "Take the wheel."

"Last time you put it in that auto-pilot mode. Why can't you do that again?"

"That was last time. You were new. Now, you're a seasoned sailor. Take the wheel."

"I don't know how to steer this thing!"

"Zoe. Just hold it steady in one direction. It's basically like driving a car, just... in an ocean. With no lanes or speed limits."

"That's really comforting, considering I never got a fucking driver's license."

"Seriously?"

"Seriously."

"Huh. Well... luckily, you're a quick learner. Just head for that green buoy in the distance."

Before I can object again, he lets go of the wheel and scurries up onto the top deck.

"Parker!" I yell, watching the wheel start to spin off course.

He doesn't respond — he's busy putting up the sails.

"Fuck," I mutter to myself. With no other choice, I grab the wheel and attempt to straighten our course.

Head straight into the wind, Parker advised me before

throwing me to the fucking wolves. *Once the sails are up, I'll come turn off the engines.*

I grit my teeth and try not to panic. A few nail-biting minutes pass before he returns.

"See?" His smile is a mile wide and his hair is adorably mussed from the wind. "You did great. I knew you would."

"I didn't sink us at the bottom of the Atlantic. That's not exactly the same as doing *great*."

He just shakes his head as he walks around behind me and grabs the wheel, so his chest is pressed up against my back and his arms cage me in.

"Where are we going?" I whisper as he makes an adjustment to our course, reading the compass mounted on the wheel.

His mouth scrapes my earlobe, the faint stubble of his beard ticklish against the sensitive skin there.

"Second star to the right and straight on till morning."

I smile and lean back against him, allowing the heat of his body and the gentle sway of the boat as she cuts through the waves to calm me. Thoughts of wrecked apartments and corrupt billionaires and evil henchmen and job offers fade away until it's just me and Parker, sailing away from the world. Leaving it all behind.

It's the best thing I've experienced in a long, long time.

We chase the sunset for just over an hour, then turn east and head straight out to sea. It's funny — a week ago, in this same situation with Parker West, I would've been freaking out. Asking a million questions about our destination, demanding to know his motives, wondering why on earth he would possibly want to spend time with a girl like me.

Now, all I feel is an unflappable sense of calm.

Because I trust him, I realize in a flash. *He won't hurt me.*

I'm totally safe with him.

I'm... home.

And, for me, a girl who never had a home...

That means everything.

The sun has almost set by the time the lighthouse comes into view. The sole structure on a tiny outcropping of rock in the middle of the sound, the pillar of granite looks ancient and weather-beaten, its stones caked with salt and brine from the ever-constant waves that crash with the tides. Every few seconds, a bright beacon flashes in the night from the top of the tower, the beam moving rhythmically across the darkening water to warn incoming ships of the small island and guide them into the harbor.

There are no other buildings on the island. Just a narrow dock, which Parker maneuvers the sailboat toward with expertise, cutting the motors at exactly the right moment so we glide to a smooth stop along the pier.

"This can't be where we're going," I murmur, eyeing the towering stone lighthouse with wide eyes. It's a lonely gray sentinel, guarding the city from afar.

Parker grins. "Help me with the lines, will you, lazy bones? I told you — we've got a reservation."

"At a lighthouse," I say flatly.

"Yep. Unless you plan on swimming back." He tosses me the stern line and scrambles toward the bow. "Tie us off, darling. Don't want the Swan drifting out to sea in the middle of the night."

"But..." I stare at the rope in my hands. "You can't mean... We can't be staying here! Parker?"

He doesn't answer; he's busy securing the front of the boat to a cleat along the pier.

Cursing under my breath, I hop over the rail onto the narrow wooden dock and try my best to replicate the knot

Parker demonstrated last week. I've barely coiled the ropes when he appears by my side.

"Perfect," he announces, reaching down to snug the knot. "You're a natural."

I meet his eyes, feeling wary. "Are we really staying here?"

His gaze is warm; his cheeks are red with cold.

"Safest place I could think of, on short notice."

"But how?" I shake my head. "How did you possibly make this happen?"

He grabs my hand and tugs me to my feet. "They were going to knock this place down, about a year ago. Let it crumble into the ocean. Lighthouses are mostly automated nowadays — they don't need light keepers, anymore." He shrugs. "I didn't want to see it fall into disrepair, dependent on some shitty state park budget to keep it up and running. So I bought it."

My mouth gapes. "You bought a lighthouse."

He glances over at me. "Did I mention my family has a lot of money?"

I blink. "I knew it was a lot. I just didn't realize it was *buy-a-lighthouse-with-your-trust-fund* kind of money."

"If it makes you feel better, this purchase put a rather large dent in my trust fund." His hand tightens on mine. "Will you still come sailing with me if I'm poor?"

"You'll never be poor," I inform him dryly. "WestTech is valued at over two billion dollars."

His eyes hold mine. "That wasn't my question."

"Yes." I sigh deeply. "I'll still go sailing with you if you're poor. I don't even know why you have to ask that question. Have I ever given you the impression that money is important to me?"

"Money is important to most people. I'd say every relationship in my life, with the exception of Nate, Phoebe, Chase, and Gemma, is driven almost exclusively by financial motives.

People who want my lifestyle, who crave a stake in my company, who want to work their way up the social ladder using the West name."

Hearing him say that in such a matter-of-fact tone makes my heart clench.

"Would it make you feel better if I told you I have no interest in your money? In fact..." I whisper, moving closer. "I'm really just using you for sexual favors."

"That's what I like to hear!" He grins. "Now let's go. It's fucking freezing out here. I don't know if you've noticed, but we're in the middle of the ocean on Christmas Eve."

"This was *your* crazy idea," I remind him.

"True." His eyes dance with humor. "I have no idea why you went along with it."

"I must be crazy, too."

"Must be."

Before we freeze to death, Parker slings our duffle bags over his shoulder and hurries me inside the lighthouse. It's the strangest thing — it should seem totally uninviting, this rock castle in the middle of the Atlantic... and yet, I've never felt more protected or secure than I do when the heavy door closes behind us, the thick metal screeching like a submarine hatch as Parker spins the bolt closed.

The lighthouse is narrow — maybe twenty feet wide — but it's well over a hundred feet tall. Parker never drops my hand as he leads me up a spiral staircase from the entryway into a tiny living room.

"This place has everything — kitchen, bathroom, bedroom. It's just..." He trails off.

"Vertical?" I supply, laughing.

"Pretty much. The rooms are stacked like a layer cake, the stairs hug the walls and wind all the way up. I put the bedroom at the top. You won't believe the view in the morning."

"I'll bet," I murmur, looking around.

It really is incredible. I feel like a princess, making her way up to the tallest turret in some kind of fairy tale. Through the thick-paned windows, I can see the last bit of sunset slipping over the horizon. My face must show my awe, because Parker sounds almost worried when he speaks next.

"I know this probably isn't what you were expecting."

"You're right. It's not what I was expecting." I pause. "It's better."

"Really?"

"Are you kidding me?" I marvel, turning to take it all in. "This is the most amazing place anyone has ever brought me. Ever." I grin. "You never do anything by the rules, do you, playboy?"

"Nope."

"Good." I step closer to him, craning my neck back to keep our gazes locked. "That's what I like most about you."

His eyes soften. "Come on. I want to show you the top."

Like little kids running through a jungle gym, we race up the stairs as fast as our legs can carry us, passing a kitchen, a small office, a bathroom, and eventually barreling to a stop when we hit the bedroom. Parker tosses our bags on the bed and pulls me toward a ladder that leads up through a portal in the roof.

"Let me go first." He grabs a rung and starts to hoist himself up. "The hatch is heavy."

Once he's got the narrow skylight door open, I watch his legs disappear out onto the top landing. Heights have never exactly been my favorite thing in the world, but I tell myself to stop being such a chicken as I grip the ladder rungs with shaky hands.

"Don't tell me you're scared, snookums." Parker's voice

drifts down to me. "It may cause irreparable damage to your so-called *street cred.*"

"Have I mentioned that I hate you?" I call back, climbing slowly up the ladder. As soon as my head pops out into the brisk air, Parker grabs me under the arms and lifts me up onto my feet.

"Only about a million times," he says, kissing me until I'm breathless and panting against his lips. When he pulls back and whispers, *"Look,"* I turn around and lose my breath all over again.

The entire ocean is at our feet, stretching for miles as far as my eyes can see. We're so high, Parker's sixty-foot sailboat looks like a toy, bobbing along the dock far below. The giant bulb flashes just above our heads, illuminating the coastline in rhythmic intervals like a massive flashlight shining in the dark. Boston glows in the distance, small and insignificant. Beyond that, a million stars blanket the sky — far more than you can ever see inside the city limits.

It's the most incredible thing I've ever seen.

"You live here," I say, laughing as I spin in a circle. "You literally *live* here."

Parker shoves his hands in the pockets of his waterproof jacket. "I *could* live here. Right now, I mostly live on my boat in the harbor and come check on this place every few weeks. I pay a guy to keep an eye on it, the times I can't get here."

I stop spinning and look at him. "Why wouldn't you stay here all the time?"

He smirks and gestures out at the ocean surrounding us on all sides. "Don't know if you've noticed, Zoe, but it might get kind of lonely out here. They say *no man is an island* but, in this case, I would have to disagree."

"True," I murmur. "Still... it seems a shame, to have a place like this — a *view* like this — and not wake up to it every single day."

"Maybe..." He trails off, as though he's afraid to finish the thought.

"Maybe what?" I ask softly.

"Nothing."

"Please... tell me. I want to know."

His eyes find mine through the darkness and even in the shadowy light I can see the stark longing in his eyes. It's enough to make my knees buckle.

"Maybe it wouldn't be so lonely if I had someone to share it with." He takes a step toward me. "If I'm being honest, since the moment I found out you were in trouble, the only thing I've wanted to do was pick you up in my arms and bring you out here, where I know nothing can get to you."

I close the last bit of space between us. "And now that you have?" I murmur.

His eyes flare. "I might never let you go."

I wind my arms around his neck. "Good answer, sailor."

His mouth crashes down on mine — a warm contrast to the cool wind. I don't care that it's freezing, or that there are a million things I should be worrying about.

Because I'm standing on top of the fucking world, kissing a man I'm dangerously close to falling in love with, and nothing else matters.

Not one damn bit.

CHAPTER 18
THE REASON

WE'RE LOST in each other, devouring with lips and hands and teeth against the rail of the lighthouse, until the sun sets entirely.

Parker pulls back to look at me. "It'll be Christmas in a few hours."

"Think we'll be able to see the sleigh go by from up here?"

"Oh, definitely. I slipped Santa a twenty – he's going to do a fly-by, just for you."

I roll my eyes.

"What do you want for a present, Zoe?" He nuzzles my neck. "Jewelry? Lifetime supply of chocolate peanut butter cups? A new computer strong enough to hack the CIA?"

"Nothing." I laugh. "Nothing at all."

"Well, *I* fully expect a gift of some kind." His tone goes husky. "Want to give me my present now or later?"

"Definitely now," I say, arching up to kiss him again. "Right fucking now."

I feel him grin as he scoops me into his arms, throws me onto his back in a fireman's carry, and proceeds to climb down the ladder like a crazy person with me draped over one shoulder.

"You're going to drop me!" I screech, watching the ground get closer as I hang upside down. I pound a fist against his back. "You caveman!"

He chuckles, never breaking his careful strides. When we hit the ground, he sets me gently on the bed. "I'd never drop you, darling." His grin is wicked. "Back in a flash."

He scampers back up the ladder to close the hatch as I lay there contemplating my near-death experience.

He almost killed me, the idiot!

I'm going to murder him.

That's clearly the only option.

Shockingly, as soon as Parker's frame hits the mattress beside me, all concerns of mortality vanish. He unzips my insulated jacket in one swift tug and rids me of my suspenders and weatherproof pants in record time.

"If I'd known you were only in underwear beneath those, I would've crashed the damn boat against the rocks," he growls, his hands making quick work of removing his own coat and pants.

I grin in the dark.

His hands slide over my skin like they were made to fit my curves, playing me like a song, shaping me like a memory, breaking me like a promise. I explore his skin with equal passion, tracing my lips along the muscular planes of his chest as his silhouette hovers over mine, his hazel eyes glowing gold in the shadowed room.

And as he makes love to me — hands and lips and hips all working in tandem to drive me to the brink of pleasure — I wonder how I ever lived without this sensation of total completeness. As he fills me, body and soul, I cry out at the feeling of utter fulfillment.

Long after our heartbeats have slowed to normal, I lay wrapped tight within the expanse of Parker's arms, his mouth pressing soft kisses into my temple, and revel in the sensation that for once in my life I'm incredibly fucking lucky to be exactly where I am.

I can only hope he feels the same.

"Did I ruin your Christmas?" I force myself to ask in the darkness.

"What?" I feel him shift to look at my face. "Why would you say that?"

"This holiday... It's clearly a big deal in the West family. I saw the size of Phoebe's tree, not to mention your ugly sweater collection and your obsession with Christmas movies."

"Zoe." Parker shakes his head. "Trust me. You didn't ruin a thing."

"But you're out here in the middle of the ocean, instead of spending the day with your family." I chew my lip. "I definitely ruined your Christmas, playboy. It's okay — you can tell me. I can take it."

He rolls, so he's staring straight down into my face. "Listen to me, Zoe. *You didn't ruin anything.* I mean it." His eyes are intense. "In fact... this is probably the best Christmas I've ever had. Screw the tree, the ornaments, the whole damn thing. Being here with you... that's the best gift I could ever fucking ask for. I mean it."

My eyes start to burn with telltale tears; I blink rapidly to clear them. "Yeah?" I ask after a minute.

"Yeah," he whispers, kissing me. "I know this isn't your favorite holiday. But I'm hoping, after this year... you might see that it isn't always so bad."

I swallow and press my face into his chest so I won't cry. After a while, his arms come around my back and he pulls me close.

"Parker," I whisper a few minutes later, desperation in my tone.

His body tenses. "What is it, darling?"

"Earlier... you asked me what I want for Christmas."

"Yeah."

"I think I know, now."

"Name it, Zoe." He tucks a strand of hair behind my ear. "Anything you want, I'll give it to you."

I choke back the emotions threatening to overwhelm me. "I need you to stop being so wonderful."

He pauses. "What?"

"Stop being nice to me. Stop being so damn sweet and funny and kind." I try to breathe normally and fail miserably. "Because..."

"Because what, darling?" His voice is infinitely soft.

"Because I don't think I'll be able to handle it..." My voice cracks pathetically. "...if you make me fall in love with you and then leave me behind."

He rolls so I'm pinned beneath him and he's staring down at me, his expression more serious than I've ever seen it. I press my eyes closed so I don't have to look at his gorgeous fucking face.

"Zoe. Look at me."

My eyes crack open a sliver.

"There's only one reason I've spent my life running," he says, his voice intent. "You know what that is?"

I shake my head.

"I've never had a good reason to stay."

I feel my eyes fill with tears.

"But you — you're my reason, darling. Now that I've met you..." He brushes his mouth against the tip of my nose. "I'm not going anywhere. You hear me?" Another kiss lands against my forehead. "I'm not leaving you."

I can't breathe.

"Zoe Bloom." His hazel eyes burn into mine. "There are some things I'd like to say to you. Things I'm pretty much dying to say to you. But I'm afraid if I tell you out loud that I care about you, that I want to wake up to your face every morning for the next week, next month, next year... you'll bolt. I'm afraid if I say that, in the span of a single fucking week, you've come to mean more to me than anyone else in my whole unfortunate existence... you'll run before I can catch you and convince you to stay."

I press my lips together to contain a sob.

"So," he whispers, his eyes still holding mine. "Right now, I'm not going to tell you that I'm pretty sure you're the one woman on this planet who was made for me. I'm not going to say that I think I could spend a whole lifetime exploring you, and have that be a sufficient adventure. I'm not going to admit that I think I love you." His lips twist. "Not yet. You're not ready for that."

My heart beats double-time inside my chest.

"But..." He brushes his lips against mine again, soft and sweet. "One day, you'll be ready. And, darling, for the record... I plan on sticking around until that day. And for all the days after."

My eyes are suspiciously wet.

"You feel like running, yet?" he asks gently.

I shake my head because I can't form words.

"Good. Because, honestly, we're in the middle of the ocean. And it would make for a pretty awkward sail home if you decided you wanted to leave after that speech."

A laugh bubbles up from my stomach and collides with the lump in my throat, resulting in a choked sob-giggle conglomeration.

"I..." I try to speak, but can't seem to form any words. "I..."

"Shh." Parker's arms wrap around me as he tugs me close and tucks me into his side. "Sleep, darling. You don't have to say anything right now."

"But..."

His mouth presses a kiss into the hollow of my neck. "I know, Zoe. I know."

He knows.

And so, I fall asleep in the arms of the man who maybe, possibly, definitely loves me, not worrying about the future or the past or anything except this moment.

Here.

Safe.

Home.

THERE'S a magical quality to the five days I spend at the lighthouse with Parker. We stay in bed all day, talking about nothing and making love. He cooks terrible, semi-charred grilled cheese sandwiches on the tiny kitchen stove and I don't complain, because it's highly unlikely I could manage to produce anything remotely more edible if I tried.

Sunsets blend into sunrises as we stay up talking about everything and nothing. I tell him about my childhood bouncing around foster homes; he reveals the horror of losing his mother at a young age and raising his sister in the absence of a reliable father figure.

He doesn't tell me he loves me again.

I don't say it either.

And yet, it doesn't matter.

There's no awkwardness or stilted conversation. We never fade into small talk.

Every moment with him *matters*.

On our fifth day out at sea, we're lying in bed after an afternoon session between the sheets when his phone rings. The chime is a harsh intrusion into our bubble of solitude; until I hear its piercing toll, I'd nearly forgotten the world existed outside this narrow pillar of stone.

"Nate?" Parker says into the speaker, forehead creasing in a frown. "What is it?"

Reality rushes back in a snap — Lancaster, the case, my trashed apartment. I can't believe I'd nearly forgotten, lost out here in the throes of lust and isolation.

"You're sure?" Parker asks, his tone serious. "Okay. Fine. See you soon."

My teeth sink into my bottom lip as I watch him hang up the phone.

When his eyes meet mine, there's a serious look in their depths.

"Agent Gallagher came through. Robert Lancaster was just arrested. So was Linus, his Head of Security – according to Nate, the fucker has a Southie accent, which means he was probably the one who attacked you last week." Parker's expression darkens. "Don't worry, we'll make sure he faces assault charges for laying a fucking hand on you."

"What about the other charges?" I ask, eyes wide. "The factory workers..."

"Their case has been passed over to the DA. Nate says any family suffering from any kind of health issue related to the asbestos poisoning will be part of a class action lawsuit against Lancaster Consolidated. It'll be a billion-dollar case."

"And the doctor?" I ask. "Charles Birkin?"

"Apparently he took his payoff and fled the country. No one has seen him in days, though Nate won't stop looking until he finds him. You can count on it."

I suck in a breath. "So it's over?"

A slow, sexy grin breaks across Parker's face. "It's over."

"Wow." I tilt my head. "Is it wrong that I'm a little disappointed?"

"What do you mean?"

I shrug. "I don't know. I just feel like we missed out on the action."

"Adrenaline junkie," he says accusingly.

"Takes one to know one."

"Touché." He smiles. "But, honestly, I refuse to be sorry that we missed the action if it means you're safe."

"And there will be more cases, right?" I ask.

"Of course, darling. Thought I'd prefer it if you'd give up trying to tackle every criminal in Boston single-handed. You're very little, and it worries me."

"But it's not single-handed." My lips twist. "I have you. And Luca. And, if I accept his job offer, I'll have Nate, plus all his boys. That's basically a posse of badass macho men to help me kick ass. I'm like Scarlet Johansson in The Avengers, surrounded by a group of superheroes."

His eyes get warm. "Does this mean you'll be modeling a tight spandex leather suit for me? Because, I have to tell you, I'm still having fantasies about that black wig you were wearing when we first met..."

"You're gross. For the record."

"Noted." He cracks a grin. "You ready to go home, Superwoman? I have a feeling there are some people who want to see us."

"Funny. *I* have a feeling those people are your sisters."

His smile turns to a smirk. "Not just my sisters. Doesn't Luca have a fight tomorrow night?"

"Shit!" I scowl. "I'd nearly forgotten."

"It's a big one, if my bookie is even remotely correct." Parker collapses back against the pillows, pulling me down on top of him. "I don't particularly like the guy, but that doesn't mean I don't respect his fighting skills. And I'm sure he'd be happy to have you there in the crowd, cheering him on."

I sigh. "He's my family. Sometimes I don't like him, but I always love him."

"I know." Parker kisses my forehead. "This is me playing the supportive boyfriend. How am I doing?"

I raise my eyebrows. "Boyfriend, huh?"

He grins. "You caught that, did you?"

"Uh, yeah."

"Freaking out?"

"Surprisingly no."

"Good." He kisses me. "What do you say we hide out here for one more night and sail back in the morning?"

I run my hand down his bare chest, loving the way his muscles tense beneath my touch. Pressing my lips to his skin, I follow the same path with my mouth and revel in the sharp intake of air that escapes him.

"I think," I murmur, pressing kisses along the trail of hair leading south of his belly button. "If we only have one more night...." My hand wraps around his length and I guide him toward my mouth. "...We'll have to make the most of it."

He groans. "You're evil."

I grin. "Honey... I'm just getting started."

WE DON'T TALK MUCH as we sail back to Boston.

I breathe in the arctic salt air as I watch our lighthouse grow smaller and smaller on the distant horizon before disappearing entirely.

"Don't worry." Parker wraps an arm around my waist and

presses a kiss to my temple. "That lighthouse has been there a couple hundred years. It isn't going anywhere."

I smile as I lean into his chest and let him steer us home, our breaths puffing in the air before our faces, our hearts beating a little too fast.

We've barely docked in the harbor when my phone starts ringing.

"Babe. You back on dry land, yet?" Luca grumbles into the phone.

I roll my eyes as I tie off a dock line. "Barely."

"You coming to my fight tonight?"

"Depends. You planning on winning?"

He scoffs. "Babe. I always win."

"Then I'll be there." I pause. "With Parker. Try not to be a dick."

He sighs audibly. "I'll do my best."

"Luca."

"Fine! I'll be *nice*." He spits out the word like a curse. "Whatever."

"See you at seven," I say cheerfully.

He clicks off without another word.

Typical.

Before I can even set the phone down, it starts ringing again.

"Hello?"

"Tink!" Phoebe yells. "Please tell me you're back from your adventures on the high seas now that Lancaster and that Hermès guy are behind bars."

"Hermès?"

"Birkin."

"I don't follow."

"God, you know nothing about fashion, do you?" She sighs.

"*Birkin*. As in Hermès *Birkin bags*. As in the most expensive, desirable purses on the market."

"Uh huh."

"No one appreciates my fashion references."

"How sad for you," I say wryly.

"Shut up. Are you back, or what?"

"Um." I glance up at Parker, who's hovering over me with an amused expression. "Yes, we just docked."

"Great! I'm having an impromptu New Years Eve get together this afternoon. Just the girls. Obviously, we're all going to the fight tonight—"

"Wait, what?"

There's a brief pause. "Of course. We're all going to see Blaze fight. It's, like, the hottest NYE gig around this year." She pauses again. "Plus, my friend Lila really has the hots for him."

I ignore the last part of her statement. "Who's *we*?"

"All of us. The whole gang."

I'm silent.

She sighs, then explains. "Me, Nate, Gemma, Chase, Shelby, Chrissy, Mark, Theo, Owen, and some of Nate's other boys, if he decides to give them the night off. Which is unlikely, but a girl can dream because hot damn, those boys are gorgeous. Oh, plus Shelby's husband, if he can *bear* to pull himself away from work." She sighs. "But, anyway, we'll all be there to cheer on Blaze! Apparently the guy he's fighting is a real douche. The boys have been betting and discussing odds all day."

"But..." I glance at Parker a little desperately. He just grins at me, the bastard. "Don't you all have better plans for ringing in the New Year than an underground UFC fight at a crappy gym?"

"Nope!" Phoebe says happily. "No plans at all!"

"Oh. Imagine that."

She laughs. "Anyway, come by my place if you have a

chance. Any time! I have big news, and I want to share it with all my favorite girls at once."

Holding Parker's warm gaze, I find the strength not to panic at this show of sisterly affection.

"Okay," I murmur into the receiver. "I'll be there."

"Fabulous!" she exclaims. "See you soon!"

She clicks off before I can say anything else. I stand and wrap my arms around Parker's waist.

"Your sister is alarmingly pushy."

"I know."

"A quality you share," I note dryly.

"Well, I did raise her." He shrugs and tucks his chin on top of my head. "When we have kids, they'll probably be pushy, too."

"What?!" I practically screech at the top of my lungs.

"Shhh." I can hear the smile in his voice. "I was just kidding. Maybe."

"Parker!"

"You're right." He laughs. "I totally wasn't kidding."

"*Parker!*"

"Zoe!"

"This isn't funny."

"Actually, it's kind of hilarious."

I sigh deeply. "Why do I get the sense it'll be easier to give in than keep arguing with you?"

"Because you are very wise, Oh Tiny One."

I snort. "I have to go get ready. Apparently, I'm being subjected to another girls' day at Phoebe's place. No doubt there will be gossip and naked pillow fights galore. When these women get together, anything is possible."

"Please keep in mind that you're talking about my sisters." Parker grimaces. "Not a good image."

"After the kid comment, it's really all you deserve."

"True enough." He hooks an arm around my waist and starts leading me down the docks. "Come on. I'll drop you at Phoebe's and go check in with Nate. I want to get the details of all the shit that went down with Lancaster first hand."

"You'll tell me everything," I demand instantly, my tone booking no room for argument.

"Of course." Parker's mouth hits my temple. "None of this would've happened without you, darling. I know it, Nate knows it, the damn FBI knows it, and I'm sure Lancaster knows it. Hell, he'll be spending the next twenty-five years in his prison cell knowing it."

I grin at the thought. "It's a Christmas miracle."

After a quick change of clothes from foul weather gear to jeans, flats, and a comfortable sweater, Parker bustles me into the Porsche and drives me across town to Back Bay. When we pull up outside Phoebe's brownstone, he leans over and kisses me soundly on the mouth.

"I'll be back in an hour or so to take you to the fight." His hand grips my chin so he can look deep into my eyes. "Don't do anything to put yourself in danger."

"All the bad guys are in jail, remember?"

His eyes are serious. "And yet, I still want nothing more than to put you back on my boat and lock you away in my lighthouse for the rest of eternity, where I know you'll be safe."

"That's kidnapping," I say lightly, leaning forward to nip his bottom lip with my teeth before I turn and push open the door.

"Not if the captive is willing!" he calls after me.

I bend back down to blow him a kiss. "When it comes to you, Peter Pan, I'm always ready and willing."

"That sounded like an innuendo, Tinkerbell."

"That's because it was."

His eyes flash with heat. "You'd better go, before I change my mind about letting you out of my sight."

I'm still smiling as I slam the door and turn to face the brownstone. Before I can do something logical, like run for my life, the front door swings open and Phoebe appears in the entryway, Boo a white blur at her feet.

"*There* you are!" she yells, running barefoot down the snowy stairs and grabbing my hand. "Come on! Everyone else is already here and I'm dying to tell you my news!"

I don't fight her as she pulls me into the house, though I do cast one last longing look over my shoulder at Parker, who's idling at the curb to ensure we make it inside safely.

Unnecessary, but rather nice of him, I must admit.

Phoebe practically sprints into the house, dragging me behind her like a rag doll. I do my best to keep pace with her, but by the time we burst into the kitchen where Shelby, Gemma, Lila, and Chrissy are gathered around the granite island drinking wine, I'm breathless.

"Hey, Zoe!" They all smile at me.

"Hi," I croak, bending at the waist and hauling in air.

"Jesus, Phoebe, you've nearly killed the girl," Lila chides. "We already scared her away once, let's try not to do it again."

"I can't help it. I'm excited. I have news!" Phoebe settles on a barstool and I follow suit, happily accepting the glass of wine Chrissy slides my way.

I bend down and scratch Boo behind the ears so he'll stop sniffing my shoes like a maniac.

"I have news too!" Gemma announces.

Phoebe's grin widens. "No way will it beat mine."

Gemma's head tilts. "Oh, I think it might."

"As fascinating as this conversation is, can someone just spill the fucking beans already?" Shelby says, taking a big sip of wine. "I'm getting wrinkles just sitting here listening to you two debate whose news is better."

I hide a laugh behind my wine glass.

The two sisters stare at each other, eyes locked in challenge, both totally convinced they're about to out-do the other.

"On three?" Phoebe suggests.

Gemma nods. "One... two..."

"Nate proposed on Christmas!" Phoebe screams at the same time Gemma yells, "Chase and I are pregnant!"

And then, quite suddenly, everyone is jumping up and down, alternately screaming and crying, touching Gemma's entirely flat stomach as if there's already a full-blown baby doing jumping jacks in there and fawning over the mammoth rock Phoebe's just pulled from her pocket and placed on a very important finger.

I barely know these women, but their excitement is infectious. So I don't let myself hold back — I scream right along with them, just one more lunatic in the flock of crazies, and it doesn't feel forced or weird. I don't feel like an outsider. I'm just... one of the girls.

And it's pretty fucking great.

When the collective freak-out cools from a boil to a simmer, we all sit in silence around the island, grinning until our cheeks ache.

"Suddenly, the spa gift card Mark gave me seems a bit underwhelming." Chrissy shakes her head. "Though, Winston made me an ornament out of macaroni noodles and a paper plate at daycare. That was pretty sweet."

"If it makes you feel any better, all I woke up to was a hangover from the tequila shots I did on Christmas Eve," Lila says, grinning. "Not exactly the most magical day of the year."

"I received multiple orgasms," I blurt, drawing all their

gazes to me. "Which pretty much makes it my best Christmas ever."

Lila, Shelby, and Chrissy silently high-five me while Phoebe and Gemma make gagging sounds.

"*Brother*," Phoebe reminds me. "Practically raised me. Gross."

I shrug. "Your brother is hot."

I receive more high-fives all around.

Shelby sighs and looks from Phoebe to Gemma. "Nate gave you an engagement ring. Chase gave you a fucking *baby* for Christ's sake. I really hate to be a story-topper on your special day, but..." She trails off with a grimace, slugs back a big sip of wine, and steadies her shoulders. "I gave a pretty sweet gift of my own, this year."

We all wait in suspense as she takes another sip.

"Divorce papers." Shelby smiles and, for the first time since I've met her, I see something like relief in the depths of her pretty brown eyes. "I served Paul divorce papers, with a big red bow right on top."

"Oh, honey," Chrissy whispers, wrapping an arm around her friend.

"Are you okay?" Gemma asks, crowding in on her other side.

"Should we kick his ass?" Phoebe asks. "And by *we* I obviously mean *Nate and his boys*."

Shelby laughs and waves away their concern. "Guys! Stop. This is a good thing. I mean it." She leans back on her barstool. "I never thought I'd get divorced. To be honest, it always felt a bit like admitting I was a quitter, or that I'd made a mistake. But I don't feel that way anymore. The bigger mistake would be continuing to shrink myself down to fit a relationship that I've outgrown. Frankly, I'm tired of making myself smaller so my husband doesn't feel insignificant or emasculated. It's not enough to have someone there to take care of your financial needs if they refuse to take care of the more important ones."

Lila's nose crinkles. "By *needs* you mean those of a sexual variety, correct?"

Shelby laughs. "I was thinking more about my emotional needs, but hell yes. I do yoga three times a week. I haven't eaten a carb in four years. I'm almost thirty years old, and I'm not going to waste another goddamned moment of my life fighting for someone who gave up on us a long time ago."

We're all quiet for a long moment.

"How did he take the news?" Phoebe asks after a minute.

Shelby's expression darkens. "Not well. Surprising, since I figured he'd be too busy boning his secretary to even notice I'd finally put my foot down."

There's a sad moment of silence where no one knows quite what to say.

What *can* you say to fix an unfixable situation?

"Oh, love." Gemma squeezes her tight. "Anything you need, we're here to help."

"I could bring over food," Phoebe offers. "Whatever vegan crap you want."

Chrissy's head tilts. "Or alcohol. Under the circumstances, I think tequila might be necessary."

"I'll help you change your locks," Lila contributes. "I've had to do that *several* times after ex-boyfriends got a little testy about me kicking them out."

Shelby smiles. "Thanks guys, but none of that is necessary."

I'm the only one who hasn't contributed anything, so I clear my throat. "I could hack into his computer and replace all his files with YouTube videos of goats screaming. Or, if you're really looking to inflict some emotional damage, I could put him on the government no-fly list so next time he's headed through security at the airport..." I smirk. "Full cavity check."

A startled laugh flies from Shelby's mouth. "Wait, that's awesome. Really?"

"I knew we liked her," Lila murmurs, grinning at me.

Phoebe slings an arm around my back. "Welcome to the club, Tink. Now that you're in, there's no going back."

"I would be lying if I said that didn't terrify me a little." I look around warily. "You're not going to have me killed by your crazy macho boyfriends if I decide I don't want to be friends with you anymore, right?"

They all laugh like I've said the funniest thing ever... but I notice not one of them contradicts me.

CHAPTER 19

THE KNOCKOUT

I'M SLIGHTLY TIPSY by the time Parker shows up to bring me to Luca's fight later that night.

"We'll see you there!" Phoebe calls from the doorway, swaying on her high heels. Her cheeks are red from the alcohol in her system. "Nate's coming with the big SUV in a few."

I wave and climb into the Porsche, smiling dopily at Parker as soon as the door shuts behind me.

"Hi."

"Someone's a little drunk." He laughs and leans over to kiss me softly. "What, did my sisters ply you with alcohol?"

I shrug. "Basically."

"I take it they shared the good news."

"You know!?" I gasp. "How?"

"Darling, Nate is my oldest friend. Who the hell do you think he asked for permission?"

My heart clenches. "That's pretty sweet. You're sweet."

"Wow. You're complimenting me?" His brow furrows. "Now I'm concerned. How many drinks did you have?"

"I'm fine!" I smack him on the arm. "What, I'm not allowed

to be nice? I seem to remember you demanding I do just that not too long ago."

"Yes, but the crux of our relationship is founded on the concept that I demand things and you flatly refuse me." His eyes crinkle in amusement. "You actually listening to me is unheard of, snookums."

Hearing the dreaded pet name, I cross my arms over my chest. "I take it back. You aren't sweet at all."

"Too late. You already admitted you think I'm sweet." His mouth hits my cheek. "I wonder what else I could get you to admit."

I feel a blush working its way up my neck. "We're going to miss the fight."

"You sure you're up for it?" His voice is soft. "I don't want you drunk in a crowd. These things get rowdy under normal circumstances — on New Year's Eve it's going to be a madhouse in there. I don't want you getting swallowed up."

"I'm not five."

"Zoe, darling, I don't care if you're five, twenty-five, or a hundred and five," he rumbles. "You're my girl. I'm always going to worry about you. Always."

"You're being sweet again," I say, feeling my eyes prickle suspiciously. "Stop it."

He laughs. "Okay, I'll say something terrible."

"Good. Do that."

His stubble scrapes my ear. "You look beautiful." He plays with a blonde tendril that's escaped my clip. "I like your hair like this."

I whip my head around to glare at him. "That's the *opposite* of terrible."

"Fine." He thinks about it long and hard. "Nope. Can't come up with a damn thing."

I sigh. "I see I'm going to have to lead by example."

"Ah, yes, because you've never insulted me before. This will be a fresh experience for me. Uncharted waters."

I giggle. "Shh. I'm thinking of insults."

"Very serious business." He forces his face into a somber mask. "I'm ready. Hit me with your worst."

"Okay..." I narrow my eyes. "You snore."

"Ah!" He throws a hand over his heart, as though gravely injured. "I'll never recover from that one!"

"And!" I point a finger at him, in case he thought he was getting off easy. "You have bad breath in the morning."

"No! Not bad breath!" He gasps. "You mean to tell me *I have bad breath before brushing my teeth?* That is just shocking information. Truly revolutionary."

I stifle a laugh. "Fine. You want me to play rough?" I make a show of cracking my knuckles, like I'm going into battle. "You once used the word *aggravate* wrong in a sentence. Technically it means *to intensify* not *to annoy*. Just for the record."

"Did you just correct my grammar?" he whispers lowly.

"...Maybe."

"Shit just got *real*." His eyes narrow. "There's no going back, now."

I bite my lip so I won't laugh. "Bring it."

"Oh, I will. This is war."

"I'm hearing a lot of empty talk, playboy."

"Fine." He drops his voice to a dramatic whisper. "I hope every time you charge your phone at night, the cord doesn't go all the way in and you wake up with a dead battery!"

I gasp. "Well... I hope the next chocolate chip cookie you bite into is actually oatmeal raisin."

"I hope you pick the slowest line at the checkout *every* time you go grocery shopping."

"I hope every prime parking space you find actually has a motorcycle in it when you start to pull in!"

"Wow. That's just... evil." He shakes his head. "I had no idea I was falling for such a sociopath."

"This is the worst fight ever," I say, laughing. "You're terrible at this."

"At fighting with you?" His eyes get warm. "Maybe that's because I'd rather be doing other things with you."

"Don't look at me like that."

"Like what?" he asks innocently.

"Like you know what I look like naked."

"But I *do* know—"

"Parker."

"Fine, fine." He reaches for the key and turns over the ignition. "Let's get this damn fight over with. There are several creative methods I had in mind for ringing in the New Year with you. Shockingly, none of them involved watching two sweaty, bare-chested dudes wrestle."

I roll my eyes. "Just drive the car, drama queen."

He sighs as we jolt away from the curb, one hand gripping the wheel tightly as we merge into traffic. His other hand is twined tightly with mine on the console between us, which only adds to the warm glow spreading inside me.

Lancaster is in custody.

Christmas was actually kind of amazing.

Five kickass women befriended me against my will.

And it's all because of this amazing man, holding my hand and simultaneously holding my whole world together.

I don't know if it's sheer force of will or pure stubbornness driving him to try to save me from everything — even myself. Frankly, I don't care.

So long as he keeps being here, holding my hand and leading me through this mess called life, I think I'll be okay.

Does that scare the shit out of me?

Of course. I've never been one to willingly depend on another person.

Does that mean I'm going to run?

No fucking way.

THERE'S a line around the corner outside the gym when we arrive. It takes an eternity to find parking nearby and by the time we make it down the narrow side street to Scythe Gym, there must be a hundred people waiting to get in.

More than a few boos and grumbles emanate from the crowd as I lead Parker to the front of the line where Colton is standing with several large bouncers, collecting cash cover charges and shamelessly ogling the girls at the front of the line who are wearing a shockingly small amount of clothing, given the fact that it's about twenty degrees outside.

"Colt!"

"Babe!" Colton reaches out a beefy arm and grabs me in a bear hug. He spins me around in a circle before setting me back on my feet. "Happy New Year."

"Put me down, you oaf." I elbow him and glance at Parker, who's glaring at the buff fighter with a look I've only ever seen him use around Luca.

I swallow. "Colt, meet Parker. Parker, meet Colton."

Parker gives a stiff nod to Colt.

Colt returns the nod with narrowed eyes.

Idiots.

"Oh-*kay*. Now that we've gotten those warm introductions out of the way, maybe we can go inside? It's fucking freezing out here." I glare at Colt and gesture at the doors.

"Go ahead." He sweeps an arm toward the entrance. "I'll see you in there."

"Okay. And don't forget, I have a group of friends coming, too. You'll get them in, right?"

"Depends." Colt looks contemplative. "Are they cute?"

"Well, one's married with kids, one's knocked up, one's freshly engaged, one's soon to be divorced, and the other is already half-in-love with Luca." I tilt my head. "So..."

"Babe." Colton shakes his head. "Never tell me the odds."

I laugh. "You're insufferable."

"Hey, what's a guy to do? I spent ten years pining over you, and you never even blinked at me. Had to move on eventually." He ruffles my hair until my clip falls to the pavement. His voice drops to a whisper. "Still secretly holding out hope though."

"Oh, shut up, you big buffoon." I roll my eyes. "You'll get them in?"

A dimple pops in his cheek. "For you? 'Course I will, babe."

"Thanks, Colt." I sigh and reach for Parker's hand. "Come on, playboy. Let's head in."

The men exchange another set of frosty nods, which makes me sigh deeply. Parker's fingers engulf mine as we walk into the gym, leaving a grinning Colton on the street. I shake my head disapprovingly at him before we disappear inside.

"What is it with you boys and your macho posturing?" I ask, staring up at Parker as soon as the doors shut behind us. It's pretty crowded inside — not full to capacity yet, but certainly getting there. The crowd pulses like a living organism as money and alcohol are passed around, charging the air with adrenaline.

"Another one," Parker mutters.

"What?" I yell over the roar of the crowd.

He looks down at me. "Another guy, in love with you."

"Colt was kidding."

"No, Zoe." Parker's eyes are serious. "He wasn't kidding at all."

"That was just his sense of humor. He likes his girls tall, busty, and brainless. Basically the *opposite* of everything I am. He'd never be interested in someone like me."

"Zoe." His voice is incredulous. "You seriously think *any* guy wouldn't trade his left nut for a chance with a girl like you, over some bimbo? You're fucking crazy, darling." He pulls me toward the wall, where it's a bit quieter, and cups his hands around my cheeks. "You're the kind of girl men spend a lifetime looking for. And you're mine. So forgive me if I'm not super fond of watching some random dude who admits to being in love with you run his hands all over your body."

"Don't be jealous." I wrinkle my nose at him. "There's no foundation for it."

"I'm not jealous, babe. I don't do jealous." He leans down and kisses me. "I've told you before — I don't want to make your decisions for you. I have no interest in controlling you." His voice goes soft. "You don't fall in love with a bird and stick her in a cage. You let her fly free and hope like hell she comes back to you."

"You know what?" I ask, kissing him back.

"What?" he murmurs.

"Tinkerbell and Peter Pan *both* knew how to fly."

He grins as he deepens the kiss.

"Gross!" I hear a familiar female voice yell, interrupting us. "Get a room, you two!"

We break apart to find Phoebe and Gemma glaring at us. Chase and Nate are standing behind them, arms crossed over their chests, looking amused.

"Get over it," Parker tells his sisters.

"When's this shindig starting?" Lila yells, appearing on the fringes of the group with two beers in hand, one of which she passes to me. Shelby and Chrissy both trail in her wake with drinks of their own, waving hello when they join the group.

"Should be any minute now," I call back. "I doubt they can fit another body in here."

"Come on!" Phoebe's eyes are sparkling. "Let's get closer to the stage!"

"It's not a ballet recital, little bird. It's called the octagon." Nate's voice is warm.

She waves away her fiancé's words. "Whatever."

I grin and sip my beer as we push our way through the crowd, Parker's heat at my back.

"Who is Blaze fighting, tonight?" Lila leans close so I can hear her.

"Jack Forrester. Really giant dude from Maine. Built like an oak tree. They call him Lumberjack. He has a killer knock-out punch."

Lila swallows. "Doesn't that worry you?"

"Every damn time," I admit. "I pray for the girl who ever falls for Luca. With what he does... you'd never get a good night's sleep so long as he's fighting. And I don't see him stopping anytime soon. There are UFC scouts here, tonight. If he wins..." I glance at her and see thoughts turning over in her eyes. "He's going all the way."

She nods slowly and sips her beer, but says nothing else.

Lila is a conundrum.

On the one hand, she's blunt and bold and funny as hell. On the other... she's a total mystery. Even her closest friends aren't exactly sure what she does for a living or how she spends her free time. I have a feeling there's a lot more lurking behind those glossy brown eyes than she lets on.

When we reach the ring, the girls engage in a heated discussion about which octagon girl has the best outfit as we watch them parade around, hyping up the crowd. (The one in the black leather lace-up bikini is winning by a landslide.) The men adopt carefully blank expressions and refrain from commenting on our debate.

Apparently, they're smarter than I gave them credit for.

Chase, Nate, Parker, Owen, and Theo form a towering wall at our backs, keeping the crowd from pushing in on us as the overhead lights start to flash, a telltale sign that things are about to begin. I'm laughing at something Parker's whispered in my ear when a young guy in a Scythe Gym t-shirt appears in front of me along the inner railing.

"You Zoe?" he asks, his brown eyes nervous.

I feel Parker and Nate both shift into high-alert mode.

"Yeah," I say, eyebrows lifting.

"Blaze wants to see you."

My face screws up in a confused mask. "But he never wants to see me before his matches. He's in his zen mode."

"Apparently he changed his mind tonight." The guy's expression is anxious — it's clear he doesn't want to let down the hulking, two hundred pound wall of pure muscle who sent him out here to get me. "He said he needs to talk to you before he fights. Alone."

Shit.

If Luca wants to see me, he must be more worried about this fight than I thought. I suddenly feel like the worst friend on earth — I didn't even check in with him today.

"I have to go," I say immediately, looking up at Parker. "I'll be right back."

"You're not going anywhere alone." His voice is totally serious.

Nate shakes his head, seconding Parker's statement. "Agreed."

"Guys! I'm not leaving the building. I'll be fifty feet away. Luca never asks to see me before a fight — if he's asking, it must be important."

"I don't like it," Parker growls. "This crowd is ready to combust."

"I'll stay with her," the gym guy assures him. "Bring her right there and straight back. I swear."

"Honey." I reach up and brush my lips against Parker's. "Remember that conversation we just had, about not putting me in a cage?"

His eyes flare with frustration and a muscle jumps in his jaw. "You come straight back. You're not here in my arms in five minutes, I'm coming in after you. I don't care what ginger boy has to say about it."

"Ginger boy?" I snort. "I'm totally telling Luca you said that."

"I don't give a shit what you tell him." His mouth crushes mine in a kiss. "Five minutes."

I nod and pass Lila my beer. "Here. I'm not going to finish this."

She shrugs and takes a sip. "More for me."

Parker doesn't look happy about it, but he lifts me up over the railing with a nod to the bouncers. I wave goodbye to my friends as the attendant leads me around the ring toward the doors where the fighters are waiting in their separate locker rooms, getting geared up. Just before the crowd swallows us, I look back... straight into Parker's eyes.

I see the worry there, in their depths. But also trust. And maybe, if I look a little deeper, I see love, too.

He loves me.

I hang onto that feeling as I hurry after the Scythe guy, cutting a path up the fenced-off walkway toward the back rooms and trying to ignore the screaming crowd. We leave behind the mass of fans and step into a secluded hallway, the heavy doors swinging shut behind us with a bang, blocking out the roar.

"Damn, that was loud," I mutter, ears still ringing. I shake my head to clear them as I follow the man down the hallway. "How do you stand working here, on fight nights? Aren't you worried you'll go deaf?" I joke.

The man doesn't answer; he just keeps walking down the deserted hall.

I'm starting to feel uneasy about this.

"...Or maybe you're already deaf," I murmur, eyeing the space around me. There are no locker rooms back here. I stop walking.

"Where's Luca?" I ask, my pulse picking up speed.

The man turns to me, and I see the remorse on his face a second before I see his fist swinging out to clip me across my temple.

"I'm sorry," he tells me, a second before his blow makes contact and everything goes black. "I didn't have a choice. He's got my family."

WHEN I WAKE UP, my wrists are bound with a zip-tie and my head feels like someone used it as the ball in a game of ping pong. There's also the fact that I'm being carried like a sack of flour over the shoulder of the guy who bashed my brains in.

I'm not sure if it's the blow to the head or the fact that he's holding me upside down, but I think I might vomit down his back. Which, seriously, would serve him right. I try to struggle, but none of my limbs are cooperating. The most I can manage is a weak kick against his shins as he hauls me from the backseat of his car across a parking lot. I see cracked asphalt passing beneath his feet and wonder vaguely if there's a chance this man kidnapped me by accident.

Maybe he was looking for another Zoe.

I've never even seen this guy before. Who would possibly arrange for me to be accosted and abducted?

Lancaster.

The thought creeps into the back of my mind and lodges there, until it's unshakably entrenched.

But he's in jail, a voice of reason reminds me. *There's no way he's behind this.*

My foggy theories don't matter, because we're suddenly moving up a set of dilapidated stairs and into what looks like an old office building, judging by the stained beige carpet. My head jostles roughly as he carries me through the space, and nausea stirs to life in my gut again.

I'm definitely going to puke.

Unfortunately, before I manage to vomit on him, my captor bends forward and deposits me on a stainless steel table, the kind you find bolted to the floor in a crappy doctor's clinic. Grunting in pain as he drops me, I fall to my side on the cold table, unable to keep myself upright with my head spinning.

He hit me really fucking hard, the bastard.

"Why are you doing this?" I moan as the man stares at me, both hands fisted in his hair. He looks more distressed than I feel, which is really saying something.

"I didn't have a choice." The man swallows nervously. "I'm just a part-time worker at Scythe. I don't even usually work on fight nights. But this guy... he showed up in my fucking house last night." He swallows again, Adam's apple bobbing nervously. "I have a wife. I have a three-year-old son. He said if I didn't help him..."

I try to breathe. "Who? Who are you talking about?"

"I don't know his name, okay? All I know is, he said I had to go to the fight, somehow get you away from the crowd, and bring you here." He leans back against the opposite wall. "And if I did that, he'd let my family go."

"Call the police," I hiss, struggling into an upright position.

"I'm not putting my family in danger." He runs his hands through his hair, breathing heavily. The whites of his eyes flash as he looks around the run-down doctor's office. It's clear he's spiraling quickly into panic. The guilt and the worry are eating away at him. He's probably not a bad guy, under normal circumstances.

Considering nothing about this circumstance is normal, it's safe to say he's not exactly my favorite human on earth, right now.

"What's your name?" I ask.

He glances at me, wild-eyed. "Steve."

"Untie me, Steve," I beg. "You've got the wrong girl. I don't know who the hell would want you to bring me here. I don't have anything to do with this... this... whatever this is."

He freezes. "You're Zoe Bloom, right? He said you'd be near the front, surrounded by those big guys. Blonde. Petite. You fit the description perfectly."

My forehead wrinkles. I lean back against the wall, feeling dizzy again. "This doesn't make sense," I whisper, more to myself than to him. "I didn't do anything."

"Oh, but you did." The man's voice slithers in from the doorway like a snake, dripping venom.

I go still as my eyes move to take him in... and gasp when I realize exactly who brought me here.

Doctor Charles Birkin.

CHAPTER 20

THE JUNKIE

HE'S MORE DISHEVELED than his picture in the Lancaster Consolidated staff directory — gone is his tie, his crisp white physician's coat. His hair looks dirty and overgrown. His clothes are stained and ill-fitting, as though he's lost weight too rapidly to replace them.

It's clear even before he enters the room that he's on drugs. Junkies have a particular look — flushed, fidgety, covered in a faint sheen of sweat. Their eyes are always a little too wide, their moments a little too jagged.

"Zoe Bloom!" Birkin claps his hands as he steps toward me. "Let's have a round of applause, shall we?" He looks at Steve. "Why aren't you clapping?"

Steve's hands curl into fists and he swallows. "I did what you said. Brought her here. Tell me where my family is."

"Oh, Steve." Birkin shakes his head and walks toward him, hands in his pockets. "Of course. You did a great job."

Steve flinches as the doctor comes closer. "Just tell me."

"Sure, sure." Birkin stops less than a foot from the man, who's practically shaking he's so overwhelmed. "They're..."

The doctor's voice lowers; Steve leans in slightly to catch his words, his neck extending like a turtle poking out of its shell. Before he can move, Birkin whips his hand out of his right pocket and jabs a needle straight into Steve's jugular.

I swallow a scream as I watch his eyes roll back in his head and his legs give out beneath him. Birkin laughs crazily as the big man crumples like a paper doll in the rain.

"Thanks for your help, Steve." He shakes his head and turns back to me, grinning widely. "What a great guy."

My heart is pounding; my eyes are locked on the empty hypodermic needle in Birkin's hand. "Is... is he..." I swallow. "Is he dead?"

Birkin laughs again. "Of course not! What, do you think I'm some kind of monster?"

I don't answer. Because *obviously* I think he's a fucking monster, but I'm really not keen on having a needle shoved in my carotid anytime soon.

He takes a jerky step toward me. "Just a sedative; he should wake up in a few hours. I don't kill innocent people."

That's good news.

"Then, please, let me go," I whisper.

"But, Zoe..." He makes a *tsk* noise. "You aren't innocent." I watch his hands pull back on the end of the needle a bit, so the tube fills with air. "Do you know what happens to the human body when you push an air bubble into a vein?"

Shit, fuck, damn.

My heart pounds harder.

"The medical term for it is an *air embolism*. Fancy name for a bubble, in my opinion. Then again, given that such a little bubble can do such amazing things... like travel to your heart or your brain, block the blood flow until you slowly lose consciousness and die... I suppose it deserves some elaborate terminology. Don't you agree?"

He takes a step closer, rolling the needle between his fingers.

"Please," I whisper, trying not to panic. "Please, you've got the wrong person. I didn't do anything to you."

"Well, now, that's just patently untrue, Zoe." He frowns at me. "I got a very interesting phone call from Robert Lancaster's Head of Security a few days ago! Mr. Linus – I believe you've met him. Not the friendliest man I've ever encountered, I'll say that much." His eyes narrow. "Want to take a guess where he was calling me from? I'll give you a hint: it wasn't his beach house in Palm Springs."

I drag in a shaky breath.

"Seems some people at the FBI had some questions for him. Questions about *me*. And the health of our employees." He leans closer and I try not to show how much fear his proximity inspires. It takes all my self control not to squeeze my eyes shut.

"You can imagine, he wasn't very happy." Birkin's pupils are constricted to pinpricks; a surefire sign he's high out of his mind. "He told me all about you, and your little investigation. And then he told me it was *my* fault for keeping those medical records saved to the company network. He told me to *fix* it."

I swallow, still watching the needle in his hand.

"So, Zoe, here I am." He comes closer; I can feel his rancid breath on my face when he speaks again. "You and I are going to have a little chat about what you gave the FBI. And then you're going to do what you do best."

My heart is pounding so hard I'm worried it'll give out. "What? What do you want me to do?"

He makes a disappointed face. "And here I thought you were supposed to be clever." He shakes his head. "You're going to hack their servers and erase all the evidence you gave them.

No evidence means no trial. No trial means no jail time for me or Lancaster or Linus."

He's nuts. Certifiably insane. Unfortunately, I don't think pointing that out at this moment is going to do me any favors.

"And, if you do it all perfectly..." Birkin's hand reaches out to stroke my face; I feel the side of the plastic needle pressing against my skin and tears of horror fill my eyes despite my best efforts. "...Then maybe I'll let you go."

I don't dare to breathe with the tip of his needle so close to my eye socket.

"Oh, don't cry, Zoe!" Laughing, he stumbles backward a few steps. "We're going to fix everything." He tilts his head. "Well... *you're* going to fix everything." His grin is manic. "Because, if you don't, I'm going to kill you."

I swallow hard.

Fuck.

BIRKIN TOWS me by my bound hands like a dog on a leash, leading me through the abandoned offices using his cellphone as a flashlight. The power was cut in this building a long, long time ago. We step over piles of trash and medical waste, around discarded particle-board furniture and past broken light fixtures.

"This used to be a nice place, you know," he says conversationally. "I had a successful practice. A loving family. A good life."

"What happened?" I ask quietly.

He goes silent.

"Drugs," I guess.

He jolts to a stop and looks back at me with his unfocused

eyes. His fist tightens on the needle in his hand. "You don't know. You don't know anything about it."

I press my lips together. "You're right. I'm sorry."

He nods and continues pulling me down the hallway. Eventually, we reach an office. There's a crappy laptop sitting on the dust-covered desk. Birkin pushes me toward it with an angry shove.

"Fix it, little hacker girl."

I stare from him to the laptop.

I couldn't hack a Girl Scout Troop blog with that piece of crap.

Am I going to tell him that?

Hell to the no.

If I can get online, maybe I can somehow call for help.

"Can you unbind my hands?" I lift my chafed wrists, bloody from the zip-tie's sharp edges. "I won't be able to type like this."

He stares at me flatly. "You'll manage."

Thinking it's probably best not to argue with the crazy, needle-wielding drug addict, I nod and walk toward the chair, trying not to sway. My head still feels foggy from Steve's punch; I wonder if I might have a concussion as I settle onto a creaky, springless chair.

"This is going to take a while," I warn, trying to buy myself some time.

He leans back against the wall and glares at me. "You have an hour."

It takes all my energy to keep my face from reacting. Even with a super-computer, I couldn't hack the FBI in under an hour. His demands just show how out of touch with reality he's become, addled by morphine and god only knows what else.

That actually works in my favor.

"Okay," I say in what I hope is an agreeable tone. "I'll do my best."

He nods. "Don't try anything stupid. I'm watching every keystroke. You try to call for help, I'll kill you before they ever get here." The look in his eyes tells me he means every word.

I take a deep breath.

So...

All I have to do is figure out a way to call for help while making it look like I'm hacking into a government agency on a computer so crappy, I'm surprised it's able to piggyback off the weak WiFi signal Birkin's iPhone is broadcasting, without alerting the drug-addled madman watching my every move.

Simple.

Right?

Mind reeling, I turn to the computer, prop my bleeding wrists against the edge of the dirty desk, and get to work.

"THIS IS TAKING TOO LONG," Birkin says for the tenth time.

He's getting twitchier by the minute; either he's coming down from his high, or he's starting to get suspicious that I am not, in fact, halfway through my hack into the FBI's secure servers, as I assured him five minutes ago.

"Almost done," I say, fingers typing nonsense into the terminal window. I figure so long as it at least *looks* like something out of the movies — green code on a black background, lots of complex number sequences — he won't know the difference. But if he's coming down from his high...

He might start paying better attention.

He might realize I'm lying through my teeth.

He might jab that air-filled needle into my neck.

I blink back tears as my fingers move, trying to push the thoughts away. If I can just stall a little while longer, until they get here...

"How much longer?" Birkin appears at my side, looking sweaty and feverish. His pupils are slightly more dilated.

"I'm almost inside their network," I assure him. "Should only be a few more minutes."

Where the hell are they? Come on, come on, come on.

A feeling of dread stirs inside my stomach.

What if they didn't get my message? What if they couldn't figure it out? What if I made a huge mistake, not just calling the police?

I fight back a shiver of panic. My fingers tremble against the keys as blood drips onto the desk, my raw wrists weeping steadily until the wood surface is slippery and red in the low light of the office. Only the glow of the laptop illuminates the space.

Birkin is unstable. That much is clear. If a team of policemen pull up outside with flashing lights and sirens, I'll be dead before they make it to the front door.

No way in hell am I taking that chance.

Plus, it's not exactly like I can call 911 and ask for assistance without him noticing.

I can, however, access his iPhone.

With the laptop piggybacking on his satellite signal for WiFi coverage, I'm already connected. Once I realized that, I knew I could send a text right from the computer. I could reach out to Parker and Nate. The only question was... what the hell kind of message does one send, in this scenario?

Writing something obvious like, "Help! Birkin has me tied up at his old office and is holding me hostage with a freakishly large needle, come save me ASAP!" basically guarantees my demise if Birkin so much as glances at his phone messages in the time it takes help to get here. He'd instantly know I hacked his phone.

Hello, needle to the neck.

Sending a cryptic message seems even less ideal; sure, in his drug-addled state there's a chance Birkin wouldn't realize I was the one sending texts from his phone if they aren't an overt call for help... but there's an equal chance that Parker and Nate would have no idea what I was trying to tell them.

Hello, slow and painful death.

In the end, the decision comes down to trust.

Trust that the universe isn't always out to get me.

Trust that, sometimes, you can count on people.

And, ultimately, trust that Phoebe's unfailing addiction to all things fashionable will finally serve a purpose other than making her look fabulous.

The message I sent has no words — only an image.

I have to hope it's enough to lead them to me.

As time ticks by, I feel my blood pressure slowly rising. I can't stop wondering if I made the right decision.

Of course you didn't, idiot, a nasty, doubtful voice whispers. *When Parker gets a text message from a random number with nothing but a picture of a Hermès handbag, he's going to think it's a butt-dial and ignore it.*

Another voice chimes in. *Don't worry. That guy you love? He's pretty smart. He'll know it's from you. He'll figure it out.*

"This is taking too fucking long!" Birkin is getting more belligerent with each passing minute. "Why is it taking so long?"

"I'm doing my best." I try to keep my voice steady as I watch him come closer. "They have a strong firewall. Maybe if you undid my hands I could type faster."

"Shut up!" He waves the needle closer. "For the last time, I'm not untying your fucking hands, you little bitch."

I type out a few more strings of nonsense code.

How long has it been since I sent that text?

At least a half hour, maybe more.

Assuming they understood what I was trying to say, it'll still take time for them to track down possible locations. His house. His old practice. I was unconscious on the ride here, thanks to motherfucking Steve, so I have no idea how long it will take them to find me...

Too long.

Birkin is itching at his skin like it's crawling with invisible bugs. He can't seem to stand still — he's pacing tight circles behind me, muttering to himself.

"Hurry up, hurry up, hurry up."

I type faster.

"I don't think you understand the severity of this situation, Zoe," he says, putting his face right up next to mine so his breath puffs against my skin. "Lancaster — he owes me money. I need that money to—"

Buy drugs.

"—to get out of here," he says, eyes flashing. "To get out of this damn city. I can't stay here anymore. My reputation — Lancaster said he'd give me so much money it wouldn't matter. But now..." He leans in closer. "You fucking ruined everything. Everything!"

I flinch back as his hands slam against the desk.

"What time is it?" he hisses, reaching into his pocket.

No, no, no, no. Don't look at your phone.

"Wait!" I yell, voice cracking. "I think— I think I'm about to crack the firewall!"

Birkin is strangely silent.

My fingers stop moving — they hover over the keys, shaking with the effort not to turn and look at him. My legs tense up, poised to run if no other option presents itself. With my hands bound and my head spinning, there's pretty much no way I'll outrun him. But I'm sure as shit going to try.

"What the fuck is this...." I hear him mutter.

I don't wait another second.

Pushing back with all my might, I roll the desk chair toward him as I leap to my feet.

"You little bitch!" he screams as the chair collides with his legs. I see him stumble sideways to avoid it but nothing more, because I'm too busy running for my fucking life.

I burst through the office doors and sprint down the hallway, trying to find my way out through the maze of hallways and broken furniture. It's dark — so dark I can barely see my hand in front of my face — and my progress is painfully slow as I lurch forward, almost falling several times.

I can't afford to fall. With my hands bound, it'll take me forever to get back up.

For a few mind-numbing moments, all I can hear is the sound of my own panting and the thundering of my pulse between my ears as I stumble forward. But eventually, another sound creeps in.

Footsteps.

Slow, steady footsteps, trailing me through the darkness like a spider in a web.

He's coming.

Pure terror cripples my system as my teeth sink into my lips in a desperate attempt to stifle my panicked breaths. I feel blood fill my mouth as I break the skin.

There's no choice but to keep going. I feel my way along the walls with my bound hands, trying to keep calm, telling myself I must be nearing the doors.

"Zoe," Birkin calls in a sing-song voice through the dark, sounding uncomfortably close. "We both know how this ends."

I bite my lip harder and keep moving.

"If you'd just cooperated with me, this could've ended differently." His tone switches from playful to pissed so fast it's hard to digest. "But you had to be a little fucking bitch. Tell me, who did you send that text to? Your friends at the FBI?" He laughs. "Trust me, they won't find you. Or... they will. Eventually. But, probably not in the condition they're hoping for."

I push on.

"I was willing to play nice. But you broke the rules."

I see the illumination of his cellphone creeping closer at my back. I hunch down into a crouch and try to move faster. The faint flashlight glow is a blessing and a curse. It means I can actually see where the hell I'm going... but it also means he's getting dangerously close to me.

Squinting, I can see I've left the maze of exam rooms and offices behind. From what I can tell, I'm in the waiting room.

There must be an exit somewhere.

My eyes move along the walls until I spot the faint outline of a door on the opposite wall. I know it's now or never. He'll catch up to me in a matter of seconds if I keep hiding in the dark. If I run for it, he'll know where I am... but at least I have a shot at escape.

I take a deep breath, steady my shoulders, and bolt straight across the open space to the exit. I can just barely make out shapes in the dark. Leaping over a broken chair, I nearly trip over my feet, but manage to right myself at the last moment.

Almost there.

I slam into the doors with a bang, my bound hands scrambling for the knob. For a second, I believe I'm actually going to escape. That I'm going to make it out of this horror show alive before he catches me. That I'll be able to count down the minutes until midnight with my boyfriend and my best friends, as I'd planned to before everything went to shit.

That is... until I feel the wood beams crisscrossing the door, nailed on so firmly I have no chance of pulling them off without a crowbar. No matter how I tug at the knob, the frame refuses to budge.

Fuck.

I whirl, eyes desperately seeking another means of escape, feet already in motion...

And smack straight into Birkin.

His hands close around my shoulders and I see his grin in the dark.

"Poor Zoe." He throws me against the wall with so much force, I feel a rib snap on impact. The world starts to fade in front of my eyes, which is strange because his flashlight is burning brighter than ever as he crouches down on the dirty floor in front of me. I try to breathe, but I only manage a wheeze of pain.

"Hurts, does it?" he asks, shaking his head as he reaches into his pocket and pulls out the needle. "Don't worry. In a few moments, you won't feel anything at all."

CHAPTER 21

THE FAMILY

I REMEMBER everything about the day my parents were murdered so clearly. Maybe *too* clearly. It's like watching a movie in high-definition. And it's not just the horror or its aftermath; I remember it all. The walk to my recital, the way my mom laced up my ballet slippers and styled my hair, how my dad fumbled with the video camera, making sure there was fresh tape inside so they could immortalize my performance forever in an embarrassing home movie.

I was nervous when I saw the size of the crowd gathered in the auditorium. So nervous, in fact, about five minutes before I was set to take the stage, I informed my dance instructor Miss Sally in no uncertain terms that there was no fucking way I was going out there. I knew, down to my five-year-old bones, that if I went onstage in front of two hundred strangers, I'd forget all my steps and make a fool of myself. Nothing she said could convince me otherwise.

So, naturally, she called my mother into the wings as backup.

Mom found me, curled in on myself like a wilted flower in my taffeta costume, and pulled me to my feet.

"Zoe, baby, what's wrong?"

I told her I was scared.

"Scared of what?"

Everything, was my answer.

At five, I didn't have words for my fears. In truth, I was scared to fail.

Scared to embarrass myself.

Scared to put myself out there.

But my mother said something to me, in that moment, that cut straight through the fear and wrapped itself around my heart.

"Honey. We're all scared. That's life. But the thing about having a family is, you don't have to be scared alone. You've got me and your dad right out there in the front row, cheering you on. We can all hold hands and be scared together."

She pressed a kiss to my forehead and looked into my eyes.

"If you live your life afraid of all the bad things that might happen, you'll miss out on all the good ones that definitely will."

I danced that night.

I nailed every step.

And when the music fell silent, I looked down into the front row and saw my parents there, beaming up at me with tears in their eyes, and knew, no matter what, I'd never be alone so long as I had them.

Thirty minutes later, they were dead.

I never recovered from that loss. For a long time, I carried my mother's words around with me like a curse.

The thing about having a family is, you don't have to be scared alone.

I didn't have a family. I'd never have a family again.

Which meant I was cursed to always be alone.

Until, slowly, so slowly I almost didn't notice it... I stared to build a new one.

We don't share any blood. We don't even have all that much in common. And yet... they're my family.

Luca.

Colton.

Phoebe.

Nate.

Chrissy.

Shelby.

Chase.

Gemma.

Parker.

So many faces. So many memories. So much love.

Lying there, dying on a dirty floor at the hands of a psycho, I realize my mother's words were never meant to be a curse. She wouldn't have wanted me to live my life alone. She didn't want me to spend my days just surviving, plugging along, going through the motions for lack of anything else to do.

My parents wanted me to *live*.

To *dance*.

To grab life by both hands and take it for a ride.

I never really understood how to do that, until I met Parker. I was so afraid to get close to anyone again, I didn't realize how dead I was inside.

Until he made me laugh, I didn't realize I'd nearly forgotten how.

Until he pushed my limits, I didn't realize how guarded I'd become.

Until he showed me love, I didn't realize how desperately I needed it.

Until he taught me to fly, I didn't realize how deep beneath the earth I'd buried my hopes and dreams.

And it really fucking sucks that I'm going to die without ever thanking him for that. Without telling him that he's my family. Without admitting how much I need him.

How much I love him.

I try to hold onto that thought as I drift into the darkness.

I always thought needing anyone else meant I was weak. In reality, it's the opposite. Asking for help doesn't make you spineless; it makes you *strong*. Leaning on people isn't cowardly; it's courageous.

It's a shame it took dying for me to figure that out.

WHEN THE DARKNESS starts to clear, I hear a familiar voice reciting a familiar story, his words occasionally catching on particular quotes as if it's a struggle to get them out without being overcome by emotion.

"Never say goodbye," he whispers, his voice shaky as he reads from the book in his lap. "Because goodbye means going away, and going away means forgetting."

My eyes sliver open and I see Parker's bronze head bowed over a thin green book, one hand gripping the pages and the other resting on my leg.

"Are you reading me *Peter Pan?*" I whisper, my voice cracking pathetically.

The book falls to the floor as he jumps to his feet, eyes flying to mine. There are deep shadows beneath them, as though he hasn't slept in ages, and I read worry and fear clearly in their hazel depths.

"Zoe," he breathes, his arms sliding around me as he hauls

me to his chest. His mouth hits my hair as he whispers my name like a mantra. "Zoe, Zoe, Zoe."

"Honey, I'm okay." I reach a hand up to twine with his. "What happened?"

He pulls back to look down into my face, his big hands cupping my cheeks as he presses a flurry of kisses on my forehead, my nose, my lips.

"How do you feel?" he asks, totally ignoring my question. "What hurts? Should I call the doctor in?"

"Parker, I'm fine. Sore as hell, but fine." I narrow my eyes at him. "What the hell happened to me?"

"You don't remember?"

"I remember being lost in the dark with Birkin. I remember him catching me. I think he threw me against a wall and I felt something break."

"Two ribs." Parker grimaces.

"Ah. So that's why it's so tough to breathe."

"The tube they put down your throat probably didn't help matters," he says softly. "They took it out yesterday, when you started breathing on your own."

I blink, startled by this information. "How long have I been here?"

He hesitates.

"Parker."

"Three days."

"What?" I exclaim, sitting upright — and instantly regretting it, as pain slices through my broken ribs. "Ow."

"Shhh. Don't move." He looks worried. "Maybe I should call the doctor."

"Please, don't." I sigh. "I'll behave. I promise."

He shoots me a doubtful look. "You don't know how to behave."

I smile. "Yeah, but that's what you like about me."

His eyes soften. "I like everything about you."

"You're corny."

"Yeah, but that's what *you* like about *me*."

A weak laugh escapes my lips. "Tell me what happened."

His expression gets somber. "You had a concussion and a brain bleed. They didn't have to do surgery, thank god, but they weren't sure how severe the damage was. Judging by your ability to insult me, I'm going to assume you'll be making a full recovery."

I roll my eyes.

He kisses my forehead. "But I really do need to call the doctors now, so they can make sure."

"But..." I take a shallow breath.

"What, darling?"

"You'll stay, right?" I ask in a small voice. "You won't leave?"

"Zoe." His hands cup my face again. "I'm never leaving you. Ever."

"Good." I press my eyes closed as relief floods my system. "I guess you can call the doctors, now."

AFTER A FULL EXAMINATION by a team of doctors who, according to Parker, have been watching me like a hawk for the past few days, I'm lying in my bed eating a chocolate pudding cup, listening to his version of what happened that night.

"We knew something was wrong almost immediately after you left. You'd barely been gone a minute when the match started — as soon as Luca walked down into the arena, we knew. Nate, Chase, and I headed for the exits, trying to find you. You were just... gone. Vanished into thin air. Eventually, we got surveillance video from the gym. Saw that douchebag hit you." His jaw clenches.

"Steve," I murmur.

"Yeah, *Steve*. He's a dead man."

"Birkin threatened his family. He felt like he had no choice." I shrug lightly. "I get it. I don't like it, obviously, but I get it."

Parker glowers. "Yeah, well, *I* don't fucking get it. I don't care what the stakes are. You don't sacrifice the life of an innocent woman. You find another way."

"It was a shitty situation. That's all I'm saying."

"Understatement." Parker runs a hand through his hair. "We knew Steve had you, but we didn't know where. We didn't know why. We figured it might have something to do with the case, but Lancaster and Linus were both already in federal custody. We contacted Agent Gallagher anyway, asked him to check the logs to see if either of them had made any calls, arranged for someone to attack you."

"And you realized it was Birkin," I murmur.

"Not at first. We suspected, but we weren't sure. He was the one piece of the LC puzzle unaccounted for. We assumed he'd fled the country with a shit-ton of money. Didn't foresee that his drug problem had made him desperate for more."

"He wanted me to hack into the FBI network in under an hour, using only an ancient MacBook and the weak WiFi hotspot from his iPhone." I shake my head. "The man was not thinking logically."

Parker sighs. "Clearly. But, anyway, we thought he might have you. We knew for sure when that text came through, though." His hand squeezes mine. "That was brilliant."

"I wasn't sure you'd understand it."

"My sister is Phoebe West. She owns four Birkin bags." He

grins ruefully. "There was no chance I would misunderstand that text."

I smile.

"Anyway, once we had his phone number, the boys at Knox Investigations were able to track its signal to Birkin's old offices. Luckily, Nate and I were already on our way there. As soon as we suspected he might have you, we started making our way down the list of his known addresses."

"Smart."

"Not smart enough," he says, guilt swimming in his eyes. "If we'd gotten there two minutes sooner, we could've stopped him before he laid a hand on you."

"It's not your fault, honey."

"Yeah, well, when we got inside and saw you lying there, that fucking scumbag standing over you..." Parker's expression darkens dangerously. "I would've killed him. I almost *did* kill him."

My eyes widen as they drop to his bloody, bruised knuckles. "Parker..."

"Don't worry. Nate stopped me." He sighs. "Barely."

I squeeze his hand gently. "I'm glad you didn't kill him. You know what I—" I almost say *love* but I chicken out at the last second. "—like about you?"

His eyebrows lift. "I wasn't aware you liked anything about me."

I elbow him and he laughs.

"You walk through life with this lightness inside you. It shines like a beacon. Your laugh, your sense of humor, the way you see the world... You remind me that there's still goodness and kindness out there. Even though you have your own slew of reasons to be bitter or negative... you always see the light." My voice gets thick with emotion. "And when you share that light with me, it makes me feel like... maybe I don't have to live in the shadows anymore."

He leans forward and kisses me until there are tears rolling down my cheeks.

"Okay," he breathes against my lips. "I'm calling the doctor back in here. Clearly, there was much more intense brain damage than they originally thought. I'm going to suggest brain surgery. Perhaps a pre-frontal lobotomy will restore you back to your former misanthropic self."

I smack him on the shoulder. "You're a jerk."

"I'm *your* jerk."

I roll my eyes. "Uh huh."

"How tired are you?" he asks.

I'm instantly suspicious. "Why?"

"There are some people who've been sitting in the waiting room for the past three days," he says carefully. "If you're up for it, I think they'd very much like to see you."

My eyes widen. "There are people here? Who?"

He shrugs. "Everyone."

"But... why?"

"Isn't it obvious?" He kisses me. "Because they love you." His eyes soften. "*We* love you."

My eyes fill with tears and I find I can't say anything. Not one single word.

Parker doesn't seem to mind. He just leans forward, brushes his lips against mine, and wipes away my tears with the pads of his thumbs.

"I'll go get them."

I nod.

THEY COME in groups of two — I guess they think it'll be less overwhelming, that way. Parker supervises from the corner, glaring at anyone who gets too close to my injuries like some kind of demonic guardian angel.

Phoebe and Nate are up first.

"Tink!" Phoebe throws herself onto my hospital bed, knocking the wind out of me. I wrap an awkward arm around her back and try not to wheeze as she crushes my sore ribs.

"Hi, Phoebe."

"You're hurting her," Parker points out in a gruff voice.

"Sorry! Sorry." Phoebe grimaces. "I'm just so relieved to see you sitting up, talking. You scared the crap out of us!"

"I didn't mean to," I say, laughing lightly. "Swear it."

"You're okay, though?" Phoebe's voice is concerned. "Because, I hate to break this to you, but you're kind of obligated to be a bridesmaid at my wedding. Mostly because I already ordered a dress for you."

My eyes widen. "You just got engaged, like, last week."

"It is never too early to start contemplating fashion choices," she informs me very seriously. "So, what do you say?"

My eyebrows lift.

"Will you be my bridesmaid or not?"

"Oh," I murmur, my heart squeezing. "Yeah. I suppose I could do that. But, I might not be any good at it. I've never been anyone's bridesmaid, before."

"Oh." Phoebe waves my words away. "Me neither. I'm pretty sure we just use it as an excuse to eat too many wedding cake samples and drink wine."

"Well, in that case, I'm in." I smile.

She grabs my hand and squeezes. "I'm glad."

Nate steps up to the bed. "Zoe."

My eyes snap to his expression, which is even more serious than usual.

"I want to apologize." His dark eyes hold mine captive. "I made a miscalculation when it came to Birkin. Thought he wasn't a threat. That's on me."

"Nate, it's not your fault," I assure him. "I don't blame you at all. No one blames you. Trust me."

His eyes slide to Parker and, for the first time, I sense the frosty air between the two men.

I feel my eyes widen. "Oh, please don't tell me you two are fighting over this."

"Damn right we're fighting," Parker growls. "You never should've been at risk."

"I apologized and acknowledged that fact," Nate snaps back.

"Boys!" I hiss. "Stop. You're both being ridiculous."

"Seriously," Phoebe chimes in. "Zoe is fine. Lancaster is in jail, and so is the bastard who hurt her. They'll be financially responsible for every LC employee's healthcare costs for the rest of their lives, while rotting in prison." She shrugs. "In my book, that's as close to a fairy tale ending as you can get."

I smile at my friend. "Thanks for coming."

"You kidding?" She leans down and kisses my cheek. "I'll be here until you're ready to go home. And when you're home, I'll visit you there, too, and cook you whatever you want." She grins. "I'm a fabulous cook. Anything you want, just name it and I'll make it for you."

"Chocolate cupcakes with peanut butter frosting," I say immediately.

"Consider it done."

After Nate and Phoebe leave, Chase and Gemma come in. Followed by Chrissy and Shelby. Followed by Lila and Colton. And, finally, by Luca, who needs no entourage.

I see his big frame fill the doorway and feel my eyes start to tingle. To my great surprise, I see Luca and Parker exchange nods and even shake hands before Parker slips out the door to give me some privacy with my best friend.

Luca's eyes are red when he stops beside my bed.

"Babe."

"Hey, Luke."

"Not gonna lie: you've looked better."

"Thanks, buddy."

He smirks. "You keep winding up in danger, I'm gonna have to put some kind of tracking device on you."

"Creep."

"I mean it." His light blue eyes hold mine. "Then again, I suppose I'm not the one who has to look out for you, now. Time to pass the torch, I suppose."

My eyes water. "I'll always need you to look out for me, Luca. You're my brother."

He looks swiftly toward the wall and I know it's because he's holding his emotions tightly in check. When he speaks, his voice is gruffer than usual.

"Could've done worse."

"What?" I ask.

He looks back at me with red eyes. "Parker. You could've done worse." He shrugs. "He's not a bad guy."

Wow. That's the closest thing to an endorsement I've ever heard Luca give.

"Thanks, Luke."

He scowls. "Don't get me wrong, it's not like I'm gonna be braiding friendship bracelets with the guy any time soon. But for the past few days, he's never left your side. And that night, when you went missing — I've never seen anyone like that. He was like..."

"Like what?"

"A man possessed." Something flashes in his light blue eyes. "He loves you, you know."

"I know," I whisper softly.

"You love him, too?"

I nod miserably. "I do."

He pulls in a breath. "Then tell him. Nothing I want more than to see you happy, babe. You deserve it. You deserve it so much."

He hugs me, then, and I let my tears flow. He'll never admit it, but I'm not the only one with wet eyes when we pull away.

In some ways, it's an ending.

For so long, it's just been Luca and me. Us against the world.

Now, things are changing. We've opened the doors to a whole new family of people, and that's going to take some getting used to — for both of us. But, like Luca told me not too long ago...

Change is scary. But you're not required to be the same person you were ten years ago, ten weeks ago, ten days ago. Hell, you don't even have to be the person you were ten minutes ago. You're free to be whoever the hell you want.

This life — full of friends and laughter and love — is a change I'm ready for.

My last visitor of the day is an unexpected one.

When Agent Conor Gallagher walks into my hospital room later that night, I'm pretty positive I'm hallucinating. I sit up straighter against my pillows and try to clear my parched throat. Parker's conveniently absent – he disappeared a few minutes ago with a flimsy excuse about getting me ice water. Apparently, he thought I'd need space for whatever conversation I'm about to have with the FBI.

"Miss Bloom." Conor's voice is gruff but his icy blue eyes have thawed a bit. "Feeling better, I hope?"

"Much."

"Glad to hear it. "

"Why are you here, Agent Gallagher?"

"People who help me take down bad guys get to call me Conor."

My lips twitch. "Why are you here, Conor?"

"Two reasons." He takes a step closer to the bed. "First, to officially thank you for your help on behalf of the Federal Bureau of Investigations. Robert Lancaster is behind bars because of you. Thousands of his former employees will get compensation for a slew of illnesses because of you. That's fine work, Bloom."

My eyes are stinging again.

Damn it. When did I become such a cry baby?

I nod because I don't trust myself to speak.

"The second reason I came will probably be more interesting to you," he adds, his voice careful.

My eyebrows lift. "Oh?"

"A few days ago, when things were touch-and-go with your health, I got a call from your boyfriend. Actually, I got about *ten* calls, until I finally realized he wasn't about to give up and called him back." His mouth twists into a grin. "Persistent bastard, isn't he?"

I laugh. "Yes. He is."

"Anyway, he told me about your parents."

I go still.

Conor's eyes narrow. "Guess that explains why you were so intent on hacking FBI files."

"I..." I swallow hard. "I..."

"I didn't come here to call you out." Conor shrugs. "I came here because I looked into it." He reaches into his jacket pocket and pulls out a blank envelope. "I'm not supposed to give you this – it's technically classified. But I've never been overly fond of bullshit protocols."

My eyes are locked on the envelope as he passes it to me. For a moment, I just stare at it, afraid to reach out and take it.

"You want to read this, Zoe," Conor says in a voice so unlike his typical gruff tones it makes my throat start to close. "Trust me."

Without another second of hesitation, I reach out and grab the answers I've been searching for since I was five years old. My fingers shake as I slide the single sheet of paper from the folder – the un-redacted version of the file I've been trying to decode for ages. As I read, my eyes fill with tears.

"Your father witnessed a murder, on his way home from work one night. It was a mob hit." Conor's voice is steady as he narrates the words swimming in front of my eyes. I'm crying too hard to read them. "He came to the FBI. Offered to testify, to put one of the highest boys in the MacDonough mob behind bars. It would've been a huge win for the Bureau, at the time."

"So... MacDonough had him killed." My voice breaks. "Before he could testify."

Conor nods. "Your father was a good man, Zoe. He was trying to do the right thing, trying to put away a criminal. A mob boss. Most people wouldn't have the guts to do that. I guess that brave streak running in your veins is genetic, Bloom." His eyes are steady on mine. "In a way... It's almost poetic justice that you were part of the efforts to put MacDonough away last spring, when you helped your friend Phoebe escape from him. Even if you didn't know it at the time, you were taking down the man who ordered your parents' murder. You got your revenge – he's behind bars. He'll never breathe free air again, if that's any consolation."

I take a shuddering breath. "Doesn't really change anything, though, does it?"

Conor shifts from foot to foot, looking uncomfortable as he

watches the tears stream down my face. "I just... thought you'd want to know."

My wet eyes lock on his serious blue ones. "I did. Thank you," I whisper hoarsely. "This... finally knowing... finally having answers... it means everything to me."

He nods.

"Can I keep this?" I ask, clutching the document in my hands.

"Of course." With a final nod, he turns and heads for the door. "And, Zoe?"

My eyes fly from the paper to the gruff, scruffy agent in the doorway. "Yeah?"

"I meant it. About the job offer." His eyes are intent. "You ever change your mind about working with the Bureau, you call me. I think you could do a lot of good for your country. I think you could make your parents proud."

He doesn't wait for an answer; he just walks out of the room, leaving me alone. I read the paper in my hands over and over, hugging it to my chest when the words start to blur before my leaking eyes. I don't try to fight the tears. I surrender to the hollow, aching awareness slowly filling my chest cavity.

I thought having the answers would give me closure. That, when the truth was finally unearthed, it would be a sweeping victory borne of bloodshed and triumph. A grand plot of revenge and restitution, doled out on those who stole my parents from me.

In reality, having the answers doesn't change anything – not really. The bad guy is already rotting in jail. Knowing how they died won't bring my parents back to me.

But maybe I don't need to bring them back.

Maybe, the whole point is, they never really left. They're inside me – in my heart, my soul, my memories.

And as long as I hold them close... I'll never be alone.

CHAPTER 22

THE HAPPY ENDING

A WEEK LATER, I'm standing on the dock with my hands on my hips, glaring at my grinning boyfriend.

"You're not serious."

"As a heart attack, darling."

I stride across the narrow gangway onto the boat, brush past him, and clamor down into the cabin. When my eyes land on the navigational station, I feel them go wide.

"You like it?" Parker's voice is warm and close. I turn to find him standing directly behind me, still smiling wide.

"You shouldn't have." My voice is dark. "This equipment costs a fortune! Parker..."

He shrugs and winds his arms around me. "You're leaving everything behind to go on a crazy adventure with me. The least I can do is provide a computer to keep you busy and let you stay in touch with everyone here at home."

I feel my throat starting to close. "How inconsiderate and terrible of you."

He laughs and pulls me closer. "Just the reaction I was expecting."

"Really. I hate it."

"Excellent. Then you'll be relieved to hear it's got satellite coverage and will perform at high speeds even in the middle of the ocean or on the most remote of tropical islands."

My eyebrows lift. "Which islands would those be, exactly?"

"Darling, the whole point of an adventure is to enjoy the ride. The destination doesn't matter."

"But—"

"No buts." He kisses my forehead. "I want to show you the world, Zoe Bloom. You plan on letting me? Or you want to ask a zillion questions so there's no surprise when we get there?"

I press my lips closed. "I suppose I can let it be a surprise."

He grins. "There's my girl. Now, come on. We have to say goodbye."

My brows lift. "To...?"

"You didn't think Phoebe and Gemma would let us sail off into the sunset without a grand farewell, did you?" He laughs. "Oh, my naïve little snookums."

I glare at him. "Call me that again and I will tie an anchor to your feet and throw you overboard as soon as we're in shark-infested waters. Just try me."

"Aw, darling!" He ruffles my hair, then releases me to climb up on deck.

I roll my eyes and follow him. As soon we enter the cockpit and the dock comes into view, the breath catches in my throat.

Everyone's there, waving and grinning at us.

Nate and Phoebe, holding a huge *BON VOYAGE* sign.

Chrissy and Mark, each carrying a kid.

Gemma and Chase, toting large bottles of champagne.

Lila and Shelby, already drinking glasses of said champagne.

Colton and Luca, towering like giants on the edges of the group.

"Come on," Parker whispers, tugging me toward the gang-way. "I want to show you something."

I walk onto the dock, grinning at everyone as I make my way down the line. Phoebe kisses my cheek, Gemma hugs me close, Lila passes me a paper cup brimming with champagne, Shelby slaps my ass, and Chrissy waves while bouncing a baby on her hip. The boys nod and smile, Nate reiterating his offer of a job while Chase assures Parker for the hundredth time that WestTech will be safe under his management. They both press polite kisses to my cheeks and wish us well on our trip.

Luca shows less restraint.

He wraps both arms around me, lifts me clear off my feet, and gives me the biggest bear hug imaginable.

"Gonna miss you, babe."

"You too, Luke."

"Check in, you hear me? I want to know you're safe."

"I will," I whisper, feeling my throat get tight. "And you – fight smart. Fight fast. Don't let them pin you."

"Hey, coaching is my job." Colton's voice cuts in. "Don't worry, Zoe – I'll look out for our boy."

"Don't let them break his nose again," I say, suppressing a laugh. "He'll never find a girl to love him if you get him too banged up."

"Who says I want a girl?" Luca grumbles, setting me gently back on my feet.

I peer up into his face. "You want a girl, Luke. And you'll find her. I know it."

"Don't get sappy, babe. Not your style."

I punch him on the arm. "We'll Skype after every match. I want all the details."

"And I want to hear about your adventures." His eyes soften. "Don't forget about me."

"Never," I whisper.

He looks down at his feet so I can't see how red his eyes are getting. But, as Parker's hand twines with mine and he leads me down the dock, I *do* see a certain curvaceous strawberry blonde sidling closer to Luca.

He'll be fine.

More than fine, if Lila has anything to do with it.

"Where are you taking me, playboy?" I ask as he pulls me along, the whole group following behind us.

Parker drops my hand only to circle behind me and cover my eyes with his massive palms. "No peeking."

"Hey!" I protest as he pushes me along blindly.

"Shh. Almost there." We take a few more shuffling steps and then I feel him pivot my body so I'm facing the other direction. "Okay." His hands drop away. "Now you can look."

My eyes fly open... and immediately fill with tears.

I'm staring at the stern of the boat, which used to say the word *Folly* in blocky letters. Instead, the name-plate now reads *Neverland* in beautiful black script.

"You renamed her?" I choke out.

He nods.

"For me?"

Parker's lips hit my cheek. "For us."

I hear the pop of a cork as Chase opens the second bottle of champagne and suddenly, everyone's there beside us – laughing, drinking, hugging, smiling. I look around at all these beautiful people who've come to mean so much to me and feel unbelievably lucky. My heart is so full I worry it might burst.

Turning, I lean into Parker's chest and tilt my chin so he can hear my whispered words above the revelry happening on all sides.

"I love you, Peter Pan."

His voice is rough when he replies, "I love you more, Tinkerbell."

I stretch up onto my tiptoes and kiss him until I'm breathless. When his lips pull away, he looks down at me with shining eyes. "You about ready to fly off into the stars with me?"

I'm not sure where we're headed.

I'm not sure when we're coming back.

But I know, with Parker by my side, life will always be an adventure – full of love and trust and more laughter than I can handle. And that's the only reason I need to justify the answer I give him.

"*Absolutely.*"

THE END

NEED MORE BOSTON?

Not ready to leave Boston behind? Don't worry... there's plenty more love & laughter ahead!

Go back to the very beginning with Chase & Gemma's story in **NOT YOU IT'S ME.** After that, don't miss Phoebe & Nate's story in **CROSS THE LINE.** Then, prepare to fall for Luca & Lila in **TAKE YOUR TIME.** Last but not least, get ready to swoon over Shelby & Conor in **SO WRONG IT'S RIGHT.**

All books are now available in e-book, paperback, and audio! They can be read in any order.

THE BOSTON LOVE STORIES:
NOT YOU IT'S ME
CROSS THE LINE
ONE GOOD REASON
TAKE YOUR TIME
SO WRONG IT'S RIGHT

Never miss a new release! Make sure you've subscribed to Julie's newsletter: http://eepurl.com/bnWtHH

ACKNOWLEDGMENTS

I never planned to write a rom-com series. I sat down at my computer in the dreary months of early 2015, fully intending to pen another angsty, suspenseful standalone novel.

Instead, a quirky brunette started speaking to me... and she refused to shut up until I'd written 100,000 words. A few months later, NOT YOU IT'S ME came out. And the rest, as they say, is history.

Three books later, the BOSTON LOVE STORIES are international bestsellers. That genuinely blows my mind *every time I think about it.*

It's not lost on me, even for a single moment, that I have *you* to thank for the success of this series. *You* are the reason I get to spend my days with this crazy cast of characters. *You* are the reason my life is full of so much laughter and love.

Thank you. Thank you. Thank you.

I could say it a million times; it wouldn't be enough. It brings me such joy to receive your messages, your videos, your picture collages. It means everything to know you share my enthusiasm for these characters, this city, this series.

Chase, Gemma, Nate, Phoebe, Parker, Zoe.

Each of them holds such a special place in my heart. I hope you've enjoyed reading their stories as much as I've enjoyed writing them.

Huge hugs to the fantastic ladies in my reader group, the *Johnson Junkies*. Your support and positivity is beyond lovely!

Big thanks to my family and friends for sticking with me — even during the crazy weeks when I retreat into my writing cave.

And, lastly... thanks to all the boys out there who (intentionally or not) provided inspiration for the love between these pages. If you weren't such idiots, my fictional men wouldn't be half as appealing.

JUST KIDDING.

(Not.)

PLAYLIST

- **Lost Boy** - Ruth B
- **Trouble** - Halsey
- **Please** - Sawyer Fredericks
- **Dance So Good** - Wakey!Wakey!
- **Coming Down** - Halsey
- **Make It To Me** - Sam Smith
- **Coffee and Cigarettes** - Michelle Featherstone
- **Little Do You Know** - Alex & Sierra
- **Unsteady** - X Ambassadors
- **Let It Go** - James Bay
- **Hold You In My Arms** - Ray LaMontagne
- **Boston** - Augustana

ABOUT THE AUTHOR

JULIE JOHNSON is a twenty-something Boston native suffering from an extreme case of Peter Pan Syndrome. When she's not writing, Julie can most often be found adding stamps to her passport, drinking too much coffee, striving  to conquer her Netflix queue, and Instagramming pictures of her dog. (Follow her: @author_julie)

She published her debut novel LIKE GRAVITY in August 2013, just before her senior year of college, and she's never looked back. Since, she has published more than a dozen other novels, including the bestselling BOSTON LOVE STORY series, THE GIRL DUET, and THE FADED DUET. Her books have appeared on Kindle and iTunes Bestseller lists around the world, as well as in AdWeek, Publishers Weekly, and USA Today.

You can find Julie on Facebook or contact her on her website www.juliejohnsonbooks.com. Sometimes, when she can figure out how Twitter works, she tweets from @AuthorJulie. For major book news and updates, subscribe to Julie's newsletter: http://eepurl.com/bnWtHH

Connect with Julie:
www.juliejohnsonbooks.com
juliejohnsonbooks@gmail.com

ALSO BY JULIE JOHNSON

STANDALONE NOVELS:

LIKE GRAVITY

SAY THE WORD

FAITHLESS

THE BOSTON LOVE STORIES:

NOT YOU IT'S ME

CROSS THE LINE

ONE GOOD REASON

TAKE YOUR TIME

SO WRONG IT'S RIGHT

THE GIRL DUET:

THE MONDAY GIRL

THE SOMEDAY GIRL

THE FADED DUET:

FADED

UNFADED

THE UNCHARTED DUET:

UNCHARTED

UNFINISHED

THE FORBIDDEN ROYALS TRILOGY:

DIRTY HALO

TORRID THRONE

SORDID EMPIRE

THE DON'T DUET:

WE DON'T TALK ANYMORE

WE DON'T LIE ANYMORE